ANGEL OF FIRE

More William King from Black Library

• THE MACHARIAN CRUSADE •

Book 1: ANGEL OF FIRE
Book 2: FIST OF DEMETRIUS
Book 3: FALL OF MACHARIUS (2014)

• TYRION & TECLIS •

Book 1: BLOOD OF AENARION
Book 2: SWORD OF CALEDOR
Book 3: BANE OF MALEKITH (December 2013)

• SPACE WOLF •

SPACE WOLF: THE FIRST OMNIBUS
Contains books 1-3 in the series: *Space Wolf,
Ragnar's Claw* and *Grey Hunter*

SPACE WOLF: THE SECOND OMNIBUS
With Lee Lightner
Contains books 4-6 in the series: *Wolfblade,
Sons of Fenris* and *Wolf's Honour*

• GOTREK & FELIX •

GOTREK & FELIX: THE FIRST OMNIBUS
Contains books 1-3 in the series: *Trollslayer,
Skavenslayer* and *Daemonslayer*

GOTREK & FELIX: THE SECOND OMNIBUS
Contains books 4-6 in the series: *Dragonslayer,
Beastslayer* and *Vampireslayer*

GOTREK & FELIX: THE THIRD OMNIBUS
With Nathan Long
Contains books 7-9 in the series: *Giantslayer,
Orcslayer* and *Manslayer*

A WARHAMMER 40,000 NOVEL

THE MACHARIAN CRUSADE

ANGEL OF FIRE

WILLIAM KING

BLACK LIBRARY

To my Sons, Daniel and William.

A Black Library Publication

First published in Great Britain in 2012.
Paperback edition published in 2013 by
Black Library,
Games Workshop Ltd.,
Willow Road,
Nottingham, NG7 2WS, UK.

10 9 8 7 6 5 4 3 2 1

Cover illustration by Raymond Swanland.
Map by Adrian Wood.

A CIP record for this book is available from the British Library.

UK ISBN 13: 978 1 84970 399 4
US ISBN 13: 978 1 84970 400 7

See Black Library on the internet at

www.blacklibrary.com

Find out more about Games Workshop
and the world of Warhammer 40,000 at

www.games-workshop.com

Printed and bound by CPI Group (UK) Ltd, Croydon, CR0 4YY

It is the 41st millennium. For more than a hundred centuries
the Emperor has sat immobile on the Golden Throne of Earth.
He is the master of mankind by the will of the gods, and master
of a million worlds by the might of his inexhaustible armies. He
is a rotting carcass writhing invisibly with power from the Dark
Age of Technology. He is the Carrion Lord of the Imperium for
whom a thousand souls are sacrificed every day, so that he may
never truly die.

Yet even in his deathless state, the Emperor continues his
eternal vigilance. Mighty battlefleets cross the daemon-infested
miasma of the warp, the only route between distant stars, their
way lit by the Astronomican, the psychic manifestation of the
Emperor's will. Vast armies give battle in His name on uncounted
worlds. Greatest amongst his soldiers are the Adeptus Astartes,
the Space Marines, bio-engineered super-warriors. Their comrades
in arms are legion: the Imperial Guard and countless Planetary
Defence Forces, the ever-vigilant Inquisition and the tech-priests of
the Adeptus Mechanicus to name only a few. But for all their
multitudes, they are barely enough to hold off the ever-present
threat from aliens, heretics, mutants - and worse.

To be a man in such times is to be one amongst untold
billions. It is to live in the cruellest and most bloody
regime imaginable. These are the tales of those times.
Forget the power of technology and science, for so much has
been forgotten, never to be re-learned. Forget the promise of
progress and understanding, for in the grim dark future
there is only war. There is no peace amongst the stars,
only an eternity of carnage and slaughter, and the
laughter of thirsting gods.

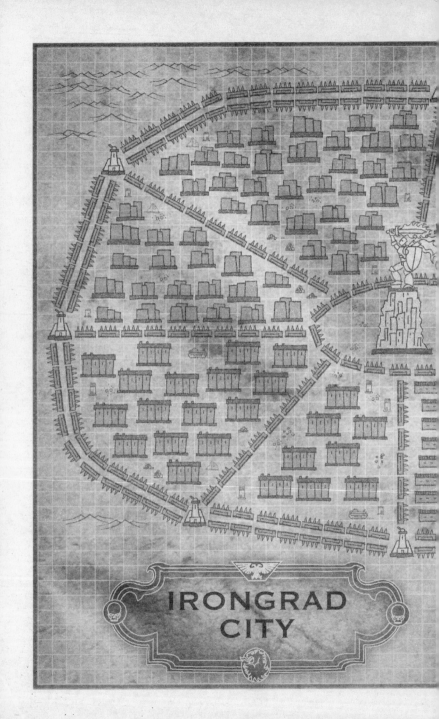

IRONGRAD
CITY

IRONGRAD CITY MAP KEY

Bastion

The Hospice
of St Oberon

Barracks

Factory

Governor's Palace

Defences

Hab-Block

Crematorium

Angel of Fire

Exhibit 107D-5H. Transcription from a speech imprint found in the rubble of Bunker 207, Hamel's Tower, Kaladon, containing information pertaining to the proposed Canonisation of Lord High Commander Solar Macharius and to the investigation of former High Inquisitor Hyronimus Drake for heresy and treason against the Imperium.

Walk in the Emperor's Light.

When the ork kicked in the door I knew I was dead.

Half again as tall as a man, with a huge chainsword gripped in one massive gnarled fist, the greenskin surveyed the barracks room with eyes the colour of blood. It threw back its ugly head, opened its tusked mouth wide and emitted a bellow of rage loud enough to wake the dead. It grunted something in its brutish language as if it expected us to obey. We would not have, of course, even if we understood it. We were Imperial Guard, soldiers of the Emperor, and orks have always been numbered among His enemies.

The greenskin should not have been so far inside the bunker. That fact alone told me at least a company of men were already dead. Hell, our whole army out there in the Hamel's Tower trench system might be dead for all I knew. We had not heard anything from command in days.

Before I could give any orders, the xenos sprang into the room.

Its chainsword flickered, taking off Bohuslav's arm at the shoulder then removing the top of Alaine's head, sending brain and blood and bone splattering across the chamber. Behind me I heard seats clattering to the ground and tables being overturned and the confused grunts of grey-uniformed men rising from their metal bunks to confront this sudden horror, the last thing they would expect to meet so deep within the fortified complex.

The ork took two more steps that almost put it within cutting distance of me. I brought up the shotgun and I pulled the trigger. It didn't fail me. It never has in thirty years of service. The few brains the ork possessed sprayed against the wall. The headless body toppled over, limbs still twitching, the chainsword still roaring and starting to slither across the bloody floor till it came to a stop, the teeth grinding against the metal leg of a bunk.

More orks raced down the plascrete stairs into this chamber, chanting their bestial battle cries. Some of them shot their guns into the air with wild enthusiasm. Others waved outsized, crudely serrated blades and axes, roaring with obscene joy in the knowledge they would get to use them soon.

I pulled the trigger of the shotgun again and sent the leading ork toppling backwards into its brethren. That slowed them down enough for me to ready a grenade and lob it into their midst. I dived, putting myself behind an overturned mess table as the wave of concussion rippled through the chamber. I looked at the rest of my squad. They were mostly just raw recruits, little older than I had been when I joined the Imperial Guard. This was what the proud legions that had followed Macharius across the galaxy had been reduced to. It was a sad thought.

I shouted at them to get ready. It was pointless telling them to fix bayonets – there was no way this sorry lot would survive any sort of close combat encounter with orks. The ones with any gumption were already doing so anyway. The rest were fumbling with their guns. One or two were struggling to put on their helmets and rebreathers. Andropov was trying to put his boots back on.

'Get those bloody lasguns ready!' I shouted as I stood up. I made sure my shotgun was pointing in their direction. 'At least die on your feet like men. Hell! Shoot well enough, you might not even die today at all!'

Most of the Guardsmen raised their weapons as if they at least knew what they were supposed to do with them. One or two of them looked completely stunned. It was probably the first time they'd ever got this close to an ork, which is not something calculated to reassure even the bravest. If they did not start doing something soon it would almost certainly be the last.

'You're supposed to be soldiers of the Emperor,' I bellowed. There might even have been some foam flecking the corners of my lips. They were starting to look scared of me now, which was good; better of me than the orks. 'Shoot the bastards!'

One of the greenskins was still alive even though one of its arms was only holding on by a thin thread of flesh – bloody hard things to kill, orks. It reared up onto its legs and roared something in a language that none of us would ever understand. I aimed the shotgun at it again and pulled the trigger. The blast hit it full in the chest and toppled it backwards. I stepped forwards and brought my size twelve Imperial Guard issue hob-nailed boot down on the fingers of its good hand, snapping them, then I hit its skull with the butt of the shotgun. You'd think I'd have known better by now. It bounced off the thick bony ridges. Hell, it barely broke the leathery green skin.

I stepped back and put another shot into it point-blank. I could hear more orks chanting on the stairs and I knew that the second wave would be arriving soon. I glanced back at the youngsters who looked to me for leadership and shouted at them again. It was an odd place to make a last stand, a grey-walled plascrete dormitory, bunks lining two walls, lockers lining others, a few metal tables and chairs scattered in the centre. Propaganda posters glaring down from any free space.

'They're coming! Get bloody ready!' I strode back over to them, putting myself out of the line of fire. I did not want to get cut down by a hail of lasgun bolts. It looked like we were about to make a heroic last stand down here in the guts of this half-finished bunker in a half-complete fortress on a backwater planet. I had come a bloody long way to die.

The orks raced in through the door. It was a choke point where they died in a hail of las-bolts, flesh sizzling and blackening as they fell. It did not stop the ones behind. It never does. They forced their way through, pushing wounded aside, trampling on the fallen, desperate to get to grips with us.

'Keep firing,' I roared, loud as any ork. If the greenskins got to grips with these lads it would be all over for us. 'You stop and I'll stick this shotgun up your arse and pull the trigger myself!'

They kept shooting but the orks kept coming, covering the distance faster than you would believe of creatures so big and awkward-looking. I found myself ducking the power axe of a monster almost the size of an ogryn, backing away as fast as I could. It took another swipe at me. I felt a wall against my spine and knew I could retreat no further. The axe passed so close I could feel the vibration its blades left in the air. I ducked down beneath the arc of the swing and brought the shotgun butt forwards, aiming for the knee. More by luck than judgement I hit. The ork grunted and fell, kneecap shattered. It still held on to the axe though and tried to hit me with it. I stepped away and shot again. The force of the blast took the creature to the ground.

I glanced around. It was not going well. The orks had got to grips with my lads, and were tearing through them like a chainsword through a gangrenous leg. I pumped the shotgun and put down another ork but that just got the attention of the remainder.

The distraction seemed to do something though. One or two of the boys with fitted bayonets tore into the orks with the desperate fury of men who know they are going to die anyway and want to drag something down into the grave with them.

One ork got stabbed five or six times before it realised what was happening. It bellowed in rage and fury before it fell to be stamped and trampled on. A few more orks poured into the room, slithering and tripping on the corpses and entrails of their kin. I noticed, and not for the first time, that ork blood was greenish and smelled like mushroom steaks back on Belial. I lobbed another grenade into the doorway, just to keep them busy. It took down another group of them.

The room seethed with violence. It was complete chaos with no way to tell what was going on. Smoke filled the air, and the smell of chemical explosive and ripped flesh. Las-bolts winked in the gloom. The air seemed to vibrate with the bull-bellow of orks and the roar of their chain-bladed axes. A head rolled along the floor towards me trailing droplets of blood. Andropov would not be struggling with his boots any more.

I strode forwards, shouting, 'Rally to me, men of the Seventh!' An ork stood in front of me. I smashed it in the mouth with the butt of the shotgun. It spat teeth and made to bring its weapon to bear. Two men leapt on it, clubbing and stabbing. It went down, a huge hand clutching one man's neck and snapping it. It thrashed around and I noticed the combat knife sticking out of its neck. It kept moving, wrestling with another of my men. I moved around it, unable to shoot without hitting Rostoky. Suddenly it reared up, throwing him to one side as casually as I might have thrown a rucksack. It gave me a clean shot. The shotgun roared. It went down again.

Suddenly, in one of those strange turnarounds you get in battle, I realised there were only a few orks left standing. No more of the greenskins were flooding into the room. There had not been so many of them as fear had made it seem. I knew then that we might actually be able to beat the bastards, if we were quick and held our nerve. Of course, no one had told the orks that. They fought on as if determined to kill and eat the lot of us, and as if we had no say in the matter.

'Stand your ground, you dozy bastards!' I yelled. 'There's only three of them.'

In point of fact there were five but why make the odds any bigger than I needed to. 'You're killing them.'

It gave the lads heart. Las-bolts flickered all around and took down another ork. A group of Guardsmen dog-piled onto one of the remaining greenskins and practically carved it to pieces. Suddenly there really were only three. I reduced the number to two with a quick blast from the shotgun.

The orks stood their ground though, roaring and lashing out with their blades. One of them took out some sort of autogun and snapped off a shot in my direction. I only avoided it by throwing myself flat. When I looked up again, I saw it had taken a bayonet through the neck. I launched myself at it, smashing it in the stomach with the barrel of the shotgun and then bringing the butt into contact with the hinge of its jaw, breaking it. A few heartbeats later it was dragged to the ground and finished by our boys. In another few seconds the fight was over and much to my surprise we had won.

'Well done, lads,' I said. 'That's how orks die!'

Afterwards we counted the cost. It seemed of the original twenty men who had been with me, more than half were dead and several of those who were left were dying. We patched the wounds of those that we could and the rest we covered with whatever sheets or sacking were available. Most of the time it was with blankets taken from the packs of the dead men themselves. The worst of it was sitting with those who were so badly hurt that they were almost gone.

'Is it true that you were once with Macharius?' Davis asked. His voice was weak and his brow was feverish. His skin had the unnatural greyish pallor of a man who has lost too much blood. 'Is it true, sergeant?'

He was from Dannerheim, one of the worlds that joined Macharius late in his great Reconquest. I suppose you could say that we conquered it although actually what we really did was bring it back into the Light of the Emperor of Mankind.

I was just sitting with him waiting for him to go, a duty I have performed many times and on many worlds with many soldiers, some of whom were my friends. I could see that he was looking up at the campaign badges on my tunic. They were all there – Teradon and Karsk IV and Lucifer and all those other places that we had followed the Lord High Commander through. I had a badge for all of them. I wish sometimes that I had back the blood and flesh I'd left on their surfaces. He reached out and grabbed my hand. He pressed it so tight that I thought perhaps he was gone but he looked up at me with feverish eyes and said, 'Is it true?'

I don't know why it was so important to him. Perhaps he just wanted to know that he was dying for something, that he was play-ing some part in the epic of Imperial history. Maybe at that moment in time he saw me as a link to that Great Crusade across the stars that Macharius had led. Maybe he was just in pain and wanted something to distract him through those last few seconds before everything went dark and he walked into the Light of the Emperor or whatever waits for us beyond death.

'Yes, son, it's true,' I said. 'I was with him on Karsk IV and I was with him on Demetrius and I was with him in a dozen different places.'

'Was he what they said he was? Was he a saint? Was he the cho-sen of the Light?'

I laughed. It was either that or cry. He looked up at me with such pain in his eyes that I stopped.

'Why did you laugh?' There was an intense edge to his voice now and I could tell that he was close to passing.

'No,' I said. 'He was not a saint. He was a man – a very great man and in some ways a very wicked one.'

His face twisted. I could tell that this was not what he wanted to hear. But what else was I going to say? It was the truth, and one of those things that Macharius always demanded was that we speak the truth to him and of him. Of course, like every other man, he often did not want to hear that truth when it was spoken but one of the things that made him what he was was the fact that he asked that it be done at all.

The boy looked disappointed and I cannot really blame him for that, because I was denying him his last wish, an affirmation of his belief in saints. Once they may have walked the world, once they may have stood by the side of the Emperor, perhaps out there in the darkness between the stars some of them still exist. The universe is vast and contains many strange things and I have not seen everything.

All I know is that Macharius was not a saint. He was perhaps the greatest general since the time of the Emperor. He was capable of great kindness and great wickedness but what man is not, given the opportunity? And opportunity was a thing that Macharius had a lot of.

I looked down at the boy, but his eyes were wide open and he was staring at the ceiling with that unblinking look that told me that he would not be closing them again himself. I reached out with my left hand and shut his eyes for him. I looked around at that chamber, full of the dead and dying, and I thought about Macharius, and about all of the others who had followed him and his great strange crusade to the edge of the known universe.

I thought about the Lord High Commander and I thought about Ivan and Anton and Anna. I thought about people I have not seen alive in three decades – I thought about Tiny and the lieutenant and the Undertaker. I thought about the fact that I had almost died today and that sometime soon I was certainly going to, and I decided that I needed to get it all down. I needed to leave what I knew so that someday it might be remembered: the truth about Macharius and Drake and their holy war to reclaim the galaxy, the truth about what they were like and how they died.

So here I am with this data-slate, making this recording. At least, it's something to fill the time until the orks come again.

For me it all started on Karsk IV. This is how it was...

From the top of Flamestrike Ridge I could see all the way into hell.

On the horizon, chemical flames erupted from newly born volcanoes. The molten rock of the lava lakes churned around islands of accumulated ash. Big, leather-winged predators drifted on thermals above the infernal pools. They might have been birds or bats or some mutant harpy out of ancient legend. It was too far to make out the full, ominous details.

Even at a distance of several Gothic leagues I could smell the brimstone on the wind. It made me cough and left a sulphurous taste on my tongue, adding its own special tang to the already acrid air of Karsk IV.

Off to the south, along the ridge-line, a battery of Basilisks pointed their pitted gun-metal snouts at the sky. Their crews had set them up according to the proper rituals and were traversing their weapons through ninety-degree arcs. I half expected them to start lobbing shells at the bubbling tar pits to test their accuracy.

'I don't think we'll be going that way,' said Anton, squinting in the direction of the flames. He leaned against a massive orange boulder at the same angle he had propped his lasgun. He had lost weight and looked taller and skinnier than ever. His grey uniform hung loose on his body. Huge sweat circles stained his plain dress tunic under the armpits. His rebreather dangled around his neck. His helmet was tipped back, showing the scar he had picked up on Charybdis. It had been sutured badly and the remnants of the scabbing puckered the flesh in small ridges so that it looked like a centipede crawling across his forehead just beneath the skin. Anton had acquired many interesting scars in his career as a soldier of the Emperor, some of them in his mind.

'Really,' I said.

I wiped the sweat from my brow as I watched an enormous geyser of lava spurt skywards. Huge gobbets of burning brimstone dropped back to splatter the ground. It was a sight at once awesome and extremely discouraging if you knew this was an obstacle between you and your objective. Soon we were going to have to find our way through that mass of flame and magma. 'What makes you think that?'

'The tanks will sink in the boiling rock and we will all drown.'

'We'd burn to death before we drowned,' said Ivan. His

prosthetic jaw and the mass of plasteel covering half his ruined face distorted his voice into something not quite human. It was a legacy of an ork cannon shell on Jurasik. He raised the magnoculars he had taken from the dead Schismatic colonel and squinted in the direction of the flames. He still had the broad build of the boxer he had been during our time in the guild factorum on Belial. Amid the sweltering heat he was the only one of us not soaked in sweat. I envied him that. 'The molten rock is called lava and we will be going that way. There are paths through it. You would know that if you paid any attention during His Lordship's briefings.'

Anton grinned his idiot grin. He had the rotten yellow teeth so common among the hive workers of Belial. 'Why would I do that when I got you to do it for me?'

'Because I may not always be here to haul your skinny arse out of harm's way.' Ivan rubbed at the bare patch on his upper arm where his stripes had been. He had suffered one of the drunken demotions that were as regular as his promotions. It took a lot of alcohol to kill the pain and smite the recurring infections the reconstructive tech-surgery on his face had left him with.

I could tell from the expression in his cold blue eyes that death was on his mind. It had been on all of our minds since Henrik's name came up in the lasgun lottery. I still looked around half-expecting to see old Henrik standing there, cracking jokes and offering up his hip flask. We had buried him in a mudhole on Charybdis six standard months ago.

Death was something you always thought about at the start of a campaign and this one was likely to be the biggest and most dangerous any of us would ever see, a full-scale Imperial Crusade, the first in a score of generations. Even Anton looked thoughtful. He pulled at his lower lip with a greasy finger. His frown made the centipede scar wriggle on his brow.

'You're very quiet, Leo,' Ivan said, looking over at me. 'Thinking too much again?'

'I have to think for two when Anton is around,' I said.

'Ha bloody ha!' Anton said.

'For you that was a rejoinder of unusual wit,' I said.

'You swallow a lexicon?' Anton asked. 'You always have to use big words to prove you are not stupid. Or are you just trying to sound like the lieutenant and his toadies? You spend enough time around them up in the cockpit.'

'I am not the man who joined the Imperial Guard because he thought he could get promoted to Space Marine,' I said. Ivan snorted.

'You thought so too,' Anton said. He had stopped tugging his lip and was probing the insides of his ear with the same finger. 'You just deny it now.' His tone was that of the aggrieved child part of him was always going to be.

Maybe he was right. Maybe we had believed that back on Belial, when all we knew of soldiering was what we read in propaganda novels written at the behest of the planetary government.

Was it possible we had been so naive? Well, whatever naivety had been in us had been burned out by ten years of constant warfare on a dozen worlds.

'I think I can see one of the paths the lieutenant was talking about,' Ivan said. When he turned his head, I could see the flames reflected in the lenses of his field glasses and the metal of his cheek. It gave him a daemonic look, like a premonition of dark things to come. 'I think we might be able to pass through and take the heretics in the flank.'

'It would have made more sense to drop in on top of them,' Anton said.

'Yeah, nothing like dropping on top of the planetary defence batteries for keeping casualties low,' I said. 'It's a good job General Sejanus is in charge and not you…'

'Space Marines make drops like that,' Anton said. He sounded wistful. 'Just once I would like to do the same. Or at least bloody well get to see one.'

Ivan laughed. 'We're just the poor, bloody Guard. We get to do most of the fighting and watch others show up late and take the credit.'

'If we're lucky,' I said. The words came out more bitter than I intended but we all knew I was speaking true. If we were lucky we would be alive to watch others take the credit. Plenty would not be. Henrik's death had left me thinking all three of us had lived longer than we had any reasonable right to expect. It was only a matter of time before our names were bellowed out at the Last Roll Call. The odds against us got longer every day we kept breathing.

Such were the joys of being one of the Emperor's soldiers in the bright new dawn of the 41st millennium. It was probably ever so.

We walked back down the hill to a camp seething with activity. Tens of thousands of grey-tunicked soldiers swarmed over the dry rock of Karsk IV. Hundreds of enginseer crews crawled over our Baneblades and Shadowswords and Leman Russ, scoping the armour plate, repairing the track mechanisms, testing the rotation of the turrets, elevating their guns, intoning battle hymns to placate the angry spirits of the great war machines. The roar of engines, the hum of servo-mechanisms and the chant of technical plainsong filled the air. The smell of drive exhaust rivalled the tang of the planetary atmosphere. The air vibrated from the engine-thunder of the enormous vehicles. Until you've witnessed it, you can never really appreciate exactly how much work and how much noise goes into getting an Imperial Guard army ready to move.

Over everything loomed the monstrous bulk of the landing ships on which we had dropped from the eternal dark of space. They were larger than ork gargants and down their belly ramps rumbled Leman Russ after Leman Russ. Company after company of soldiers exited through the external hatches. The Imperial Guard had arrived in force at this tiny outpost in the desert of Karsk IV. It was all part of some great plan which, as usual, no one had bothered to explain to us. An adjutant might just have stuck the pin in the wrong part of the map again for all we knew.

There was that air of subdued excitement and suppressed fear that you always get at the start of campaigns. It was combined with the simple pleasure of having real planetary dirt beneath our feet and real gravity tugging at our bodies. When you've been cooped up on an Imperial troopship for months, you cannot wait to see a sky again even if it belongs to a foreign world where you may well die.

We passed along a row of Chimeras. Their crews lay

around on their packs and blankets checking their lasguns and their filter masks. Ivan exchanged nods with the men he knew. There were far fewer familiar faces now than there had been when we set out from Belial all those years ago.

I thought about how different my surroundings were from that industrial world half a sector away. Belial was a cold place, much colder than this one and much more densely populated. There had been vast wastelands between the hive cities there too, of course. On Belial they had been slag heaps and ash deserts, the products of thousands of years of industrial production in the service of the Imperium.

Here, the wastelands were the result of shifting tectonic plates and the action of enormous volcanoes. This produced pyrite, the source of the planet's wealth and the real reason why Battlegroup Sejanus of the Second Macharian Army was on-planet. This world would provide us with the shells that would feed our tanks, guns across the surface of hundreds of worlds as the crusade of Macharius got into gear. We needed to control this planet if the holy war was to proceed.

Apparently, Karsk IV's rebel governor had different ideas. In the long years of schism that preceded the start of the 41st millennium his family had become a power unto itself. They controlled all the industrial worlds of this multiplanet system. The governor no longer saw himself as the Emperor's representative. He believed himself to be absolute ruler of everything he surveyed. He claimed he was descended from the Emperor himself and blessed by the Angel of Fire who stood guard at the Emperor's right hand. It was up to us to convince him otherwise. He needed to learn that the Imperium had returned in all its glory. The bad old days were over. The stability of the Emperor's rule was being extended into this sector once more.

We were the spearhead of an army of millions dispatched to reclaim thousands of worlds long lost to the light of the Emperor's presence. Under the Lord High Commander Macharius we had crossed the infinite depths of space to bring the Emperor's word to the lost and the forsaken.

We walked along a long line of Leman Russ stuck with their engines revving and going nowhere. Crewmen thrust their heads out of turrets and looked around. A few shouted to the troop carriers ahead of them asking what the hold-up was. If they had really wanted to know, they would have used the comm-net. The three of us were making better time on our own booted feet than the whole armoured column.

We soon saw the cause of the problem. One of the tanks was bogged down in a dust pool, holding up the whole line. A team of enginseers and their massive mechanical drones were laying a metal plate in front of the Russ, hoping that its tracks would get traction on it. Another team were attaching chains to the tow hook extruded by the tank in front so that it could help pull the trapped vehicle clear. We quickened our pace so we wouldn't get roped into the work crew. Ahead of us was a huge flat plain covered in thousands of blister tents. In the cleared areas between the sleeping zones, companies marched and drilled and dug latrines. The Imperial Guard likes to keep its soldiers busy.

'Look at them,' Anton said, taking in a company of new recruits with one bold sweep of his thin right arm. 'They should still be in schola.'

Their officer glared at Anton as he went by but said nothing, probably because in his heart of hearts he agreed. Maybe he noticed the campaign badges on our chests. We had more than he did.

There were a lot of new faces in the crowd, replacements right out of the training battalions for the casualties we had taken on Charybdis. They had the fresh-faced look that I knew only too well. I had worn it myself not all that long ago in the great scheme of things.

Ivan made the low whistling sound he sometimes used to signify amusement. The prosthetics made it hard for him to laugh. 'Are you going to teach them?'

It was not just the youngsters' faces that seemed clear and clean-scrubbed. Their uniforms had a newness to them that was dazzling. Their lasguns gleamed with the oil-gel coating they had when the Temple factorums shipped them. The newcomers were sharp-edged, bright and clear and not quite real yet. Some of them would not live to get that way. I already knew that. I had seen all of that before.

'It would hardly be worth my while,' Anton said. 'Let's wait a few months and see who survives and then we'll decide who gets taught.'

It was a cruel thing to say but we nodded agreement. We would help these newcomers where we could and do our best to keep them alive because doing that would help keep us alive, but we would not get close to them until we saw who lived and who died.

That was always difficult to tell. The confident assured ones, the ones you would have sworn to the Emperor knew what they were doing were often the first to catch a las-bolt.

The idiots, the incompetents, the sloppy ones sometimes surprised you and turned out to be good soldiers.

I mean who would have guessed looking at Anton back in the day that he was ever going to live through ten years of hellish violence. I suppose you could have said the same about me. Remembering what we had been like back then, Ivan was the only one I would put money on and look what had happened to him.

We walked all the way back to the *Indomitable*. Fondly I looked at the incept number ten inscribed on its side beneath the Imperial Gothic lettering of its name. For a good deal of my career as an Imperial soldier this ancient tank had been my guardian and my weapon. It loomed over us like a mountain of ceramite and plasteel. The Bane-blade cast a long cold shadow, even on the warm surface of Karsk IV. Its fierce presence welcomed us back to the only real home we had known in nearly a decade.

'Morning, ladies! Have a nice stroll?' Corporal Hesse's booming voice called down from the dorsal turret. He was stripped to the waist and the cog-wheel tattoos were visible on his straining gut.

'Piss off,' Anton replied.

'I think you meant to say piss off *corporal*, Private Antoniev,' Hesse replied cheerfully. He muttered something to somebody below him in the fuselage of the tank. Whoever it was handed a power-spanner up to him and he began tightening nuts on the hatch-cover hinge. The effort made his chubby face red. Sweat dripped from his cheeks onto the metal as he spoke the proper invocations. Hesse could always find something that needed work on round the vehicle. It was his pride and joy. Anything not so technical it needed to be handled by an enginseer was his particular pleasure to tinker with.

'Yeah, piss off corporal, Private Antoniev,' Anton said.

Hesse chuckled. 'Only you could tell yourself to piss off when trying to come up with a witty retort, Antoniev. Anyway, break time is over. Get your tools out and put them to some use. And I don't mean take a piss…'

'Ha bloody ha,' said Anton.

'You've used that one already today,' said Ivan. 'You'll wear it out.'

'Ha bloody ha.' Anton's scarecrow figure was already halfway up the metal ladder in the Baneblade's side. He reached the dorsal turret and threw himself flat beside Hesse, inspecting the servos of the rotator mechanism. Soon they were cheerfully discussing the lack of pressure in the hydraulics. Say what you like about Anton, when it came to machines he knew his stuff. It had been the same back in the factorum on Belial. Of course, if any real work needed done they would need to summon the tech-priests. The priests of that mechanical brotherhood were as jealous of their prerogatives as the Mechanics of the Factorum Guild back on Belial.

I climbed up a metal cliff and dropped into the Baneblade's innards. It smelled of oil and plasteel and recycled air. But at least it was cooler than outside. I fell into a tanker's stoop and scuttled along the corridor heading for the cockpit. I was surprised to find a stranger there checking the controls. He had the well-scrubbed appearance of the new intake. He fidgeted nervously, fingers drumming on the control altar. He looked like he was contemplating a particularly difficult mathematical problem. There was an abstracted, scholarly air to him.

'That's my chair,' I said. He looked up, startled.

'Sorry,' he said, rising up so fast he banged his head on the ceiling where it sloped above the driver's chair. I winced with sympathy. I've been known to do the same thing myself. He was a tall kid, a little taller than me. His hair was curly and dirty-blond. His eyes were a pale, pale blue. He smiled nervously, showing surprisingly good teeth.

I slumped down into my bucket seat and inspected the controls. It did not look like he had made any invocations, but it's always a good idea to check. One of our Russ went off a cliff once because a new boy had set the drives into reverse and the driver was too drunk on coolant fluid to check. Or so the story goes.

The boy stuck out a clean hand, with well-manicured nails. 'Matosek,' he said. 'Adrian Adrianovitch Matosek.'

I looked at his hand till it withdrew. 'Sit down, New Boy,' I said. 'And don't touch anything until I say you can.'

I muttered the first driver's prayer, pulled the periscope down into position and locked it. I twisted my driver's cap sideways so the brim would not hit the eyepiece. Looking through it I got a clear view of the tortured sky above us, and another look at the lava sea on the horizon. I adjusted the view angle until I saw the slope around us and all the other tanks and artillery lined up there, getting ready to move.

I closed my eyes, asked the blessing of the machine-spirits and sent my hands dancing across the control altar in the ritual gestures of invocation and control. The spirit of the great war engine was still quiescent.

I watched the needles on the volt gauges rise and fall in response to my devotions. I touched the engine pedals with my feet and heard the big drives roar. I checked the lock toggles on the control sticks to make sure they were still in place then invoked the Baneblade's tutelary spirit to watch over them.

'I never touched anything,' New Boy said. 'I know the rituals.'

'Don't say anything till I finish either,' I said. He fell into a silence, half-sullen and half-scared. I suppressed a smile. I knew what it was like to sit in that particular chair. Old Grigor had done exactly the same thing to me when I first saw the inside of a Baneblade. Well, he would learn by watching and doing, the same as I had to, the basic apprenticeship of the Imperial tank man.

I kept talking, 'There's been some shonky repairs done on Number Ten's port-side armour towards the rear. You need to cover for that where you can. Set her down with the starboard towards the enemy where you can and the gunners will traverse the turrets to compensate. Be that way till we can get proper repairs done. The requisition chit is in – has been since Charybdis. Any decade now we will get the parts.'

He nodded again and kept his mouth shut. He was doing all right so far. 'The number two drive has a tendency to over-rev at low speeds. You need to placate the spirit when it happens. It can be temperamental. Remember that.'

'Sure.'

'That's that then. Let's see if you can perform the basic rituals then.'

He shrugged. He looked at his control board. It was more or less a duplicate of mine. Hardly surprising really. Redundant controls systems are a feature of the Mark V Baneblade originated on Callan's Forge. They say that it's different on the Martian-sourced models but I would not know. I have never been inside one.

Nothing happened when he moved the switches. Nothing would unless the cut-outs on my controls kicked in which would most likely mean I was dead or so wounded I did not care. Or I toggled the switch and asked the machine to hand over control. I watched him. He was a good kid, careful. Everything went back into neutral when he had finished with it. Even though he was not directly communing with the spirit of the vessel he was taking no chances.

'What happened to him?'

'Who?' I asked although I already knew who he meant. Vehicles like this you were usually sitting in some dead man's chair.

'The one who sat here before me.'

'He died,' I said. 'It's an occupational hazard.'

'I see you two have met,' said a voice behind us. It had the relaxed, born-to-command tone of the Upper Hives. I turned to look at the lieutenant. He was a big man with a bleak-looking face and a shadow of stubble on his massive jaw he could never quite get rid of. His uniform was covered in braid. His eagle epaulettes were enormously ornate. Campaign medals festooned his broad chest. I have always suspected our officers' elaborate uniforms were designed as a deliberate contrast to the plain tunics of the common soldier in our regiment. It emphasises the class difference and our rulers on Belial have always liked to do that.

Behind the lieutenant was the Understudy, a moon orbiting the lieutenant's planetary presence, hoping to reflect some of his authority. His uniform braiding was scarcely less elaborate than the lieutenant's. The Understudy did not look much older than the New Boy. He was trying to appear relaxed the way the lieutenant did. Maybe in another twenty years he would have mastered the trick but somehow I doubted it. The lieutenant had been born the way he was. Or perhaps decanted from a glass jar, the way some of the Schismatics had been.

'Yes, sir,' I said. I did not quite get the words out of my mouth as fast as New Boy. He still had the discipline and the eagerness to please of the training camps on him.

'Very good,' the lieutenant said. 'Private Lemuel, I expect you to look out for Private Matosek. Show him the ropes, make sure he doesn't reverse us into a lava field, that sort of thing.'

'He's already started, sir,' said New Boy, not realising that it was unnecessary. It was just the sort of thing the lieutenant felt called on to say for the good of morale, mostly his own.

'I would have expected nothing less,' said the lieutenant in his most inspirational manner. In spite of myself, I was pleased.

The lieutenant lounged back in his commander's chair and invoked the controls. The command consoles emerged from the floor of the hull and locked into place around him as the spirit of the ancient tank responded to his prayers. The Understudy moved to a position two paces behind the throne and studied the screens as if his life depended on it. Maybe one day it would. The lieutenant studied the holo-images.

'I don't like the pressurisation on turret two,' the lieutenant said in the quiet murmur the upper classes always use to let you know that you should not be listening but even if you are, it does not really matter any way.

'You're right, sir,' said the Understudy. His private school had most likely provided him with a certificate in obsequiousness and daily lessons in toadying. 'Shall I have words with the repair crews, sir?'

'Hesse is already looking at it with Antoniev,' the lieutenant said. From his expression, you would have thought the Understudy imagined the lieutenant had uncovered this by some supernatural means instead of having issued orders for it this morning. 'If anything needs to be done I will petition it through the proper channels and with the proper offerings.'

'Very good, sir,' the Understudy said.

'Still, all things considered, I think we're set right to carry the Emperor's word to the heretics.' The lieutenant sounded sincere when he said that. It was a gift of his. 'What do you think, Private Lemuel?'

'I think they'll be sorry they ever saw us, sir,' I said with the right amount of stupid enthusiasm and bloodthirsty malice. It was what the lieutenant expected from us Lower Hivers and who was I to disappoint him?

'We'll know soon enough,' he said, taking his pipe from his pocket, stuffing it with lho weed and lighting it. I knew something big was coming. He puffed away for a few moments, like a Baneblade's exhausts on a frosty morning on Belial. He looked unspeakably cheerful, the way he always did when he was about to break very good or very bad news. 'We'd better put on a good show tomorrow.'

'Why is that, sir?' I asked. The Understudy glared at me. He had wanted to ask that question himself even though he had most likely already known the answer.

'Because we are under the eyes of the Lord High Commander Macharius himself.'

'He's here on Karsk IV, sir?' I was as impressed as the lieutenant intended me to be. Macharius was the most successful general the Imperium had produced in a millennium, although you've got to remember this was before the campaigns that really made his name.

'He soon will be,' the lieutenant said. 'His ship is in orbit.'

It seemed that Karsk IV was even more important than I had thought if Lord High Commander Macharius himself had come to supervise the opening of the campaign.

'It's possible there will be a surprise inspection tomorrow. Not a word of this to anybody,' the lieutenant said, tapping the side of his nose. He might as well have winked. If he had not wanted me to spread the word among the crew he would never have said anything.

'So Macharius is really here?' Anton said, studying his cards with the sort of concentration he normally reserved for his prop-nov. He sounded impressed. Everyone around the little counter in the Baneblade's galley looked that way, even the engine-room boys who normally didn't give a toss about anything.

I considered my hand. It was the usual rubbish that Anton always dealt me. It was such a regular event that if I had not known better I would have suspected him of being a card sharp.

'Apparently so,' I said.

'It's not the sort of thing the lieutenant is usually wrong about,' Ivan said, raising a finger to indicate that Anton should deal him a new card. A low whistle emerged from the corner of his mouth. I wondered, as I always did, whether he knew he was doing that. He looked at it for a moment and discarded the Four of Cogs. He drummed his metal cheeks with his fingers. There was the faintest of echoes.

'True.' Oily rubbed his grease-stained fingers on the chest of his uniform. It was how he had got his nickname. He raised two fingers and Anton handed him two cards. A frown flickered across his face. 'How do you do it, Anton? How do you always manage to give me exactly what I don't need?'

He discarded the two cards. One was the Black Commissar; the other was the Tech-Priest. I winced. Those two cards might have given me a winning hand in spite of Anton's skill at dealing trash.

'Why do you think he's here?' Anton asked. 'Macharius, I mean?'

'The lieutenant told me he wanted to check up on you,' I said. 'He heard you would make a good Space Marine.'

'Piss off,' Anton said.

Ivan gestured for another card and slotted it into his hand. He held all of his cards close to his chest. He looked at them for a moment, put them face down on the table and poured himself another glass of Oily's specially distilled coolant fluid, then unwrapped a ration bar and stuffed the whole thing into his mouth. He crunched it with his metal teeth as he frowned down at his cards.

New Boy entered the galley and looked at us. 'Playing Shonk?' he asked.

'No,' Anton replied. 'We're not.'

Oily looked up at him. 'Yes we are. Don't believe Anton. He lies.' There was nothing friendly in his tone. He was just annoying Anton.

'Can I play if a seat comes free?' New Boy asked.

'They never come free,' Anton said.

'It's another dead man's chair, is it?' New Boy asked. Silence settled on the game like a shroud. It was exactly the wrong thing to say and you could tell that Matosek suddenly appreciated that. He had spoken out of irritation and triggered more than he bargained for. Nobody looked at him. It was as if he wasn't there.

The game went on. Fingers were raised to indicate the number of cards people wanted. Glasses were filled from the coolant flask. Hands were tossed in as players folded. Eventually New Boy got the message and left. The air thawed perceptibly when he was gone.

'That boy has a lot to learn,' Oily said.

'He's all right,' I said. 'He's just nervous.'

'Let's hope he's not nervous when we meet the heretics,' Anton said. 'That could get us all killed.'

'You won't have to worry about that,' Ivan said. 'Macharius will have made you a Space Marine by then.'

'Ha bloody ha.'

Drums sounded. Bugles blared. We lined up outside our tanks, dressed in our parade best. The heat made us sweat but we stood still as statues. We'd been standing that way for hours. We'd keep standing that way for as long as it took. It was a general inspection, and Lord High Commander Macharius himself was conducting it.

I swallowed. The ash in the air was making the back of my throat dry and tickly. I kept my mind deliberately blank for as long as I could and when I could not do that any more

I let my thoughts wander where they would to memories of Belial and Charybdis and Excalibur and Patrocles. The back of my right arm itched but I could not scratch it. The combat shotgun it was my special privilege as a driver to carry felt heavy against my shoulder. I fought down the urge to fidget. That just made things worse.

Suddenly he was there, Macharius, flanked by his bodyguards and the colonel, the ranking commissar and the other high muckety-mucks and an orderly who carried his personal lion's head banner. He walked slowly along the line, looking the men in the eye, stopping for a word or two with some veteran, usually one decorated for valour or service. Within a couple of minutes he was close enough for me to see clearly.

Macharius was exactly what you expected an Imperial hero to look like. He was a big man, broad-shouldered, leonine. His hair was golden, his eyes were golden, his skin was golden. He moved with an easy grace. His uniform fitted him perfectly. Even then he was past what would have been middle age for a normal citizen but the juvenat treatments had taken perfectly. He looked no older than me. Hell, he looked younger and a lot fitter. He looked like you imagine the Emperor did when he walked amongst men; more than human.

When he spoke, he sounded the part as well. His voice was deep and perfectly modulated. There was an edge to it. It was the sort of voice you would expect a great predatory cat to have. His gaze settled on me as he passed. At first it was chilling. There was something cold about those golden eyes, something inhuman, but when he smiled, his face lit up and he seemed pleasant enough.

Beside him were others almost as intimidating, regimental officers, members of the High Command and others including Old Walrus Face, the colonel of the Seventh. One man in particular stood out. He radiated an air of cold authority noticeable even in the shadow of Macharius's dominating presence. He was a tall man with the long, pale, ascetic face of a priest. He wore heavy robes and a long cloak with the cowl down. This was Drake, as I was later to learn and wish I had not. Even then I sensed he was not a man whose eye you wanted to catch. My instincts about such things have always been good.

Surrounding the party were others: half-man, half-machine, members of the Adeptus Mechanicus. They circled around constantly. One or two of them carried huge devices that might have been weapons. They had long copper-covered barrels and strange lenses glittered at their extremities. Similar things were mounted on huge tracked vehicles on the edge of the parade area. They swivelled everywhere, tracking Macharius and his group. Like every Guardsman there, I wondered what they were for.

Macharius seemed well pleased. I imagine it flattered his ego to be the centre of attention for tens of thousands of soldiers. I did not, at the time, know the half of it.

Macharius swept past us and at first it seemed the inspection was over, but no signal to disperse was given. Instead, he went over and stood in the shadow of one of the Baneblades, Number Ten if the truth be told. He paused for a moment and then with the lithe agility of a great cat he scrambled up the *Indomitable*'s side. He stood poised above the track-guards studying the assembled army, one hand shading his eyes. Beneath him the tech-priests focused their strange weapons on him, like assassins getting their target in their sights. Macharius just stood, unworried. He clearly knew what was happening. As ever, his certainty communicated itself to the watching troops.

Beneath him, the chief of the tech-priests made a symbolic gesture. The smell of ozone and technical incense filled the air and suddenly, in the air above us was the face and form of Macharius, magnified a dozen times, looking down on us like that of the Emperor himself as you have seen him on many a painted ikon. The huge handsome visage considered us all for a moment and then Macharius spoke, his voice rippling out over the assembled army like that of a primarch during the Great Crusade. I did not know it then but his speech was being relayed out across the system even as he spoke, to every orbiting ship, to every soldier in the vast army sweeping through the skies of the worlds of the Karsk system, to every soldier in the force descending onto the soil of Karsk IV, and every word was being recorded for posterity.

'Soldiers of the Emperor,' he said. His thunderous amplified voice was rasping and calm and filled with a quiet authority that commanded attention and belief. There was a trace of the accent of the backwater world that had birthed him, a rough metallic burr that marked his speech and which only vanished when he was talking to the very highest notables. 'We stand on the brink of a mighty war.

'Soon you will face the first battle of many against those who would defy the Emperor's will and keep these human worlds buried in the foetid darkness of heresy and unbelief.

'For their own selfish reasons they seek to withhold from their fellow man the Blessings of the Emperor's Word and the goodness of His holy rule. We are here to save our fellows from this wickedness and restore order and light to these long-abandoned worlds.'

He paused for a moment as if overwhelmed by the scale of the evil he was contemplating. Not coincidentally, the pause gave his audience a moment to reflect on what he had said.

It was not the words themselves that convinced you. It was the tone in which he said them. When you heard Macharius speak you knew that he believed utterly in what he was saying, and that you should too. There was something about his blazing conviction that forced you to push aside any doubts and reassess your own thoughts on the matter.

The man had an immense presence, an enormous authority, an aura that enveloped him and everything he touched and transformed if not the words themselves then your perception of those words. All around me, hardened soldiers strained to hear what he had to say, listened as if their hope of salvation depended on it. More than any priest, more than any commissar, Macharius made you believe, in him if nothing else.

'Today we take the first step towards our greater goal. It is an important step. If we falter here, we will fail. If we do not harden our resolve, foreswear false mercy and carry ourselves with the firmness of purpose this great task deserves, we will condemn billions of our fellow humans to lives of squalid darkness and eternities of torment in the toils of the daemons who feast on the souls of the damned. Do not let your finger rest on the trigger of your weapon. Sparing our enemies merely extends their lives for a pitiful eye-blink in the Emperor's sight and condemns their souls for all eternity. Show mercy to the heretic and you do the work of daemons yourself.'

We've all heard similar sermons preached before battles and on High Holy Days and I am damned if I can tell you what it was about Macharius that made his words different. Perhaps his lack of doubt communicated itself, but that could not be all. Many commissars I have known were every bit his equal in faith. No – it was something about the man. When Macharius spoke you could have been listening to the Emperor speaking to you from the depth of his Sacred Throne. I know it sounds like heresy, but that is what it felt like. Something had touched Macharius; maybe the light of the Emperor, maybe something else.

And then, in a moment, the whole mood of the thing changed. Macharius went from being a priest preaching a sermon to an officer talking to his men, telling them the plan, letting them know what they needed to know.

'The way forwards is harsh. It carries us through lava seas and across great chasms where the jaws of the earth could swallow a Titan whole. It passes through sandstorms so powerful they can strip a man to the bloody bone in seconds. It takes us through clouds of poison so deadly that one breath is fatal.'

It should have sounded off-putting but he made it sound as if these were the sort of challenges that true men should expect to face and which it was their glory to overcome. His slight grim smile told you that he knew you, you personally, could overcome them. And he was letting us know that we were all in this together.

'This is all to the good.' He paused and smiled and as he had expected the whole army laughed at the joke, feeble as it was. Then his expression was grim again. 'I am serious. It is all to the good. While we are doing this, the second part of our force will be assaulting Hive Irongrad from the south, along the easy route, the way they expect us to come. They will not expect a massive armoured assault from the northwest, and we shall hit them where we know the defences are weakest. We will have the pyrite refineries and the weapon factorums. We shall bring millions of lost souls into the Emperor's Light.'

He paused again, to give what he had said time to sink in. We knew now where we were going, a hive city. He had even told us why.

If you have never had any experience of being a soldier in the Imperial Guard, you will probably not realise how unusual it was for a ranking general like Macharius to say things like this to an assembled army. He was telling us the plan – personally. He was letting us know that there was one and that it was a good one, that he and his officers knew what they were doing, and that he personally was taking the time to communicate the details to you so that you understood your place in it, and you shared his faith in its efficacy.

He had the trick of pitching his voice and casting his eye over the crowd in such a way that you felt he was talking directly to you. You felt as though you mattered. As if you had a central role to play in this great scheme. Everyone present was as important as Macharius himself.

He spoke on, outlining the plan in broad strokes and making it clear where each major battlegroup was to move and strike. By the end of it, every man present must have felt as if they had as clear an idea of what was going to happen as Macharius himself and all of them shared his certainty of success.

When he vaulted down from the side of the Baneblade, you could probably have heard the cheers in Irongrad, hundreds of leagues away.

That was my first exposure to the legendary charisma of Macharius. It was not to be my last.

That evening we sat around the table in the galley again. We did not play cards.

'So that was Macharius,' Ivan said. A trickle of drool puddled in the rusty corner of his metal jaw. He took a swig of the coolant fluid. 'Impressive.'

'Yes, he was,' said Anton. For once he looked thoughtful, and he sounded impressed.

'I am surprised he never mentioned making you a Space Marine,' said Ivan.

'Don't be a dick,' Anton said. There was something in his voice that stopped the smart reply short in all our mouths. We had never seen him this way before. He was like a zealot whose faith has been called into question. It took a moment for it to sink in, exactly how impressed Anton was with the Lord High Commander. He looked like one of the newly converted in the Holy Temple meetings the preachers used to give back on Belial.

Anton grinned, showing his missing teeth, and the moment passed. 'You should not make jokes about the man. He is going to lead us to the greatest victory in Imperial history.'

Normally we would have fell to mocking him but not this time. Everyone in the galley had listened to Macharius. Everyone knew he was something special. He would have to be, to make someone like Anton speak with the conviction and vision of a prophet.

'Let's play cards,' Ivan said. None of us were in the mood. All of us were filled with visions of victory, of what we were going to achieve. I believe if anyone had suggested prayer, we would have gone down on our knees on the spot.

'I hear the speech was recorded on vision crystal and is being sent out to every unit in the army,' Oily said. 'That's what all that Holy Mechanical Paraphernalia was for. Those words will be on record somewhere for as long as the Imperium endures.'

'Aye, but we were there,' Anton said. 'We saw it for real.'

It was the first time I ever heard a veteran of Macharius's armies speak in that tone you would hear afterwards, ever and anon, across the stars, in that mixture of pride and awe. We were there. We stood in his shadow. We were part of his legend.

It's the truth too.

Exhibit 107D-21H Abstract of Report VII – XII – MIVI

To: High Inquisitor Jeremiah Toll, Sanctum Ultimus, Dalton's Spire.

Source: Drake, Hyronimus, High Inquisitor attached to the Grand Army of Reconquest.

Document under seal. Evidence of duplicity on the part of former High Inquisitor Drake. Cross-reference to decrypted personal journals. See Exhibit 107D-45G.

Walk in the Emperor's Light.

I watched Macharius speak to the troops yesterday, his words recorded for posterity and to be broadcast to every soldier in this great army. To describe the man as impressive is an understatement. He is utterly certain in his faith and utterly convincing in his manner and he communicated all that he sought as vividly and clearly as my old preceptors in the training school on Telos communicated basic theology.

I am convinced that the Council has made the correct decision placing this man in command of our Great Crusade. He seems worthy of the trust placed in him and I say this as one trained to judge all men with the greatest of scepticism and the most extreme wariness. It is possible, but only possible, that he is the prophesied one, whom we have so long awaited. There are many milestones to pass on that particular road before the truth will make itself known.

My agents within the Grand Army assure me that morale is at the highest it has ever been and that the troops are full of righteous zeal to perform the Emperor's Will. Even discounting the natural tendency of such agents to exaggerate when reporting to a high inquisitor, the tone of their reports is very encouraging.

Macharius seems to have decided to trust me, at least in so far as he treats me amiably and explains his plans with the same forthrightness as he would explain them to any of his troops. I am allowed to attend all the staff meetings and there are no signs that anything is concealed. After so many decades of back-corridor intrigues I find this refreshing. It seems that Macharius is sincere in his attempt to forge a new army here and bury old rivalries among his commanders. It looks like this really is something new under the sun.

I digress. The plan for the reclamation of the Karsk system is under way. The army is ready to drive towards Irongrad arrayed in tight formation. Every company of troops has its own vehicles. All of them are in the highest state of maintenance and readiness. Progress will be swift. The main bulk of the battlegroup assaults Irongrad from the south. This force will sweep in out of the north towards the more lightly guarded parts of the great fortress city. All is to be done in accordance with Macharius's doctrine of attacking with the greatest of speed and the maximum of force at the enemy's weakest point. There are feints within feints.

Victory will be ours. It is what we will find once it is achieved that causes me disquiet. I have studied preliminary reports from our advance agents and negotiators and there is much here to recommend the attention of the Inquisition. What I have heard about the Cult of the Angel of Fire causes me some concern. It follows a pattern all too familiar to me from my early career. There are reports of human sacrifice of a most horrific sort. Such things often go hand in claw with the worship of terrible things.

Still we shall deal with such horrors when and if we encounter them. Sufficient unto tomorrow the problems of tomorrow.

The Blessings of the Emperor upon you.

Looking out of the scope I saw endless rows of armoured vehicles glittering in the early morning light. Greyish exhaust fumes made the air shimmer. Horns sounded. Engines roared. In my ear bead I could hear the constant chatter of comm-net communications. I was only supposed to be able to hear the lieutenant but there was some bleed through his monitor and very faintly in the background I heard signals coming down from the higher command echelons.

Out there, the army stirred like a great beast. Company after company of armoured vehicles made off, rolling downslope, crushing friable stone beneath their huge treads, raising enormous plumes of dust and ash as they gathered momentum.

I relaxed in the bucket seat and offered up some more technical prayers. I knew it would be several hours before we had to move. Our place was quite far back in the column. I looked down at the crystal of the console and watched the dots that represented units shimmer and shift, bees of greenish light swarming against a blood-red background.

I looked over at the New Boy. He had tilted his cap to one side in emulation of my manner. He caught me looking at him and grinned, a little nervously. It was understandable. We were not yet in any danger but this was the start of his first campaign and we would soon be moving into the eye of the storm of violence the Imperial Guard had brought to this world. He swallowed and made an aquila over his heart with his fingers and then closed his eyes. His lips twisted slightly and I knew he was praying.

Over the Baneblade's internal comm-net the lieutenant's calm voice sounded, chanting out the First Battle Catechism and getting the expected answers first from Corporal Hesse then from the remainder of the crew stations, then the gunners. From deeper within the *Indomitable* came the sound of turrets rotating and guns elevating. The machine shuddered a little as barrels reached maximum elevation and locked.

One by one the great tanks of our company rolled out; I watched their massive forms disappear downslope into the great cloud of dust like enormous mastodons moving through the dawn of time.

'Lemuel, move us out,' said the lieutenant. I invoked the spirit and our engines roared to full life. Somewhere in the depths of the vehicle I heard cheers and prayers as the crew reacted to the movement each in their own way.

The great armoured monster that was the *Indomitable* rumbled to life beneath my hands. In that moment, I wondered if this was how Macharius felt when he gave orders to an army. The mighty vehicle responded to my commands like some great beast responding to its rider. I felt all of those hundreds of tons of weight move at my will. An armoured behemoth capable of crushing men to jelly beneath its treads, of crashing through buildings and destroying lesser vehicles by mass alone, responded to my hands on its ancient controls.

At that moment, I felt alive, as if I was doing what I was put in this world to do.

Ahead of us a wall of flames stretched to the horizon, as if the entire planet had caught fire and the world itself was burning. The sands of the desert were the red of blood. Even through the filters, the air had taken on a curious metallic tang. The column slowed almost to a halt and began to move forwards cautiously as the leading scouting vehicles reached the edge of the lava seas.

'You'll want to be careful here, Lemuel,' the lieutenant said. 'This is not the place to make a mistake. We're approaching the causeways and if we fall off we'll never see Belial again or anywhere else for that matter.'

The New Boy gulped. I suspected that if I could have seen his expression I would have discovered that he was glad that he was not the one driving right now. I did not look. I was too busy concentrating on the paths ahead.

You could have marched an army over them company by company, but a Baneblade is not a company of soldiers. It can't narrow its frontage or move along in single file if it has to.

I could not see much ahead except for the clouds of dust raised by the tanks that had gone this way before, and the marks of their tracks in the reddish sand, and the ever-narrowing roadway as it pushed out into the lava sea.

Sea is misleading, it suggests waves and tides and regular movement. The lava was not like that. It glowed in different colours, from almost incandescent white to cherry red. It bubbled and it spurted. It was like a living thing. It was all too easy to imagine daemons living below its surface and emerging to devour the souls of men.

It was easy too to understand how the inhabitants of Karsk IV believed that the Angel of Fire stood at the right hand of the Emperor. Flame was the most powerful thing in this world. Its potency was a self-evident truth. Even the mighty frame of the *Indomitable* seemed a pitifully small thing compared to the endless, encroaching lava.

Not that I gave it too much attention. I was too busy keeping an eye on the path and making adjustments with the control sticks to keep us as close to the centre of it as possible. It was not easy. The way was neither regular nor smooth. Sometimes we would run up small slopes and I would feel the *Indomitable* tilt and for a horrible moment wonder if we were going to start sliding.

Ahead of us another Baneblade loomed out of the dust fog. The rock beneath its left tread had started to crumble. The weight of so many massive vehicles moving over the thin crust of this burning land was taking its toll. The driver struggled to keep the tank moving straight. As I watched it swerved dangerously close to the edge.

I wondered what was going on: guidance servo

malfunction, driver drunkenness, misheard command over the comm-net. I slowed down to avoid a possible collision. It was easy to imagine getting knocked into the boiling lava by a misjudgement on the part of the lead driver. I hoped the drivers behind us were paying the same attention as I was.

I let out a long breath I did not know I had been holding as the tank in front got back on course. I heard a gentle curse from the New Boy.

It was going to be a long day.

We emerged from the lava paths into the ash deserts beyond. I felt as if a weight had lifted from my shoulders. All around huge Imperial tanks ploughed ahead at full speed, raising bow-sprays of sand and dust. There was a sense of swiftness and motion that had been sorely missed in the cramped volcanic paths through the lava.

The sun glared down, a gigantic cyclopean eye. I studied a horizon that looked like a sea suddenly petrified by the magic of daemons, waves turned red as blood, layered with cobalt blue. Everything had a tainted chemical look to it. Huge, chitinous things scurried out of the way of the tanks. A few were crushed to a bloody purple gel by the tracks.

Over the comm-net relieved chatter filled the lower-level links. Anton and Ivan must have been as worried as I; they could see what was happening from their gun-position and could not do anything about it. At least I had some say in what happened.

Vulture gunships skimmed overhead, engines thundering, exhaust contrails scarring the desert sky white, like claw-marks made by the talons of some huge invisible beast, their twin-tailed shadows gliding over the sand beneath them.

The tac-map showed the position of an oasis ahead. The holo-spheres representing our forces were already surrounding it. In the distance a few brief high explosive shots rang out as some pueblo village rejoined the dust from which it emerged before our position could be reported.

Anton grumbled over the comm-net to Ivan. 'The vanguard get all the fun.'

'We'll be in battle soon enough,' Ivan replied. 'You'll have your chance to blow something up then.'

'Can't come soon enough for me,' said Anton.

'Stow the chatter, lads,' said the lieutenant, patching himself in to the lower level. 'Keep your eyes peeled for heretics. They will be out there somewhere.'

'Right you are, sir,' said Ivan. He sounded almost cheerful but then he always did when there was a fight in the offing. There was a darkness in Ivan that responded to incipient violence. I've seen a lot of soldiers get that way. Combat is a drug for them.

We thundered across the wastelands, engines roaring, officers barking out calm commands. I felt part of a vast invincible war machine, certain of victory, assured of triumph. I tried to enjoy the feeling while I could.

I knew it wouldn't last.

The night was quiet. We stood beside the tank and looked at the stars. They glittered cold and clear in the blackness of the firmament. All around us lay the rubble of a pueblo.

There was no sign it had ever been a military outpost, no sign that it had been anything much. The buildings were in ruins. If it had not been for the fires that still burned in some, they might have been that way for tens of thousands of years.

One by one we clambered up the side of the *Indomitable* and looked out of the crater we had set ourselves hull-down in. As far as the eye could see were the silhouettes of armoured vehicles. Men swarmed over and around them, doing what we were doing, escaping from the cramped inner quarters, stretching their legs looking at the night sky. Somewhere in the distance someone was playing a harmonica. It was an old tune from Belial, *My Girl Has Eyes of Blue*.

To the south, the sky turned white then black then white again in eerie flickers. A sound like thunder raced across the desert in its wake. If I had not known there was a battle being fought below the horizon, I would have suspected it was the mother of all storms, racing towards us through the night.

I sat with my back to the main turret of the machine with my legs dangling over the side. Anton had draped himself over the barrel of a gun and hung there like a spider-lemur we had once paid to see in the zoo in Jansen Hive. Ivan took a swig of coolant fluid from his flask, wiped the mouth of it and passed it to me. I took a swig and handed it up to Anton.

'It was awesome today, passing through the lava sea,' he said eventually.

Ivan belched loudly then whistled.

'You didn't have to do the driving,' I said.

'I suppose you want us to thank you for getting us through alive,' Anton said.

'It's my job,' I said.

'What you think they were like?' Ivan asked.

'Who?' I said.

'The folks who lived here.'

'Like us I suppose. This is a human world.'

'You think they woke up this morning expecting to be dead?' Ivan asked. The booze was making him melancholy, as it usually did.

'A world like this, yes, most likely.' Anton replied. 'It does not seem the most pleasant of places.'

'Why would you build a place out here in the desert?'

'Could be a relay station,' I said. 'Could be a rich man's ranch. Could be an energy farm. Who knows? Who cares?'

The coolant fluid came back my way. I took another swig. It tasted like medicine but kicked like a drill sergeant. Lasgun fire flickered down below us. I reached for my combat shotgun but Ivan shook his head. 'It's just Oily and the boys tormenting one of those big scorpions.'

I squinted into the darkness. By the light of las-burst I recognised the mechanic's squat form. He and a bunch of others were flash-frying one of the beasts, probably wanted to know what it tasted like.

'You know it's strange,' Ivan said, not in the least distracted from the job of depressing the rest of us. 'There's a whole army down there. This is probably the most people who have ever stood in this spot. Will most likely be until the end of time, till the stars burn out and the Emperor walks again.'

'And your point is?' I asked. Ivan shook his head and laughed bitterly. I heard the metal of the flask clink against the metal of his jaw.

'We'll never come back this way. We'll never see this place again. We blasted it to bits in the name of the Emperor and tomorrow we will be gone and all that will be left will be wasteland.'

'By the Emperor's Throne, you are a miserable bastard, Ivan,' Anton said. 'I came out here happy to see the stars. Another five minutes of listening to you and I'll be ready to eat a grenade.'

'You'll never get to be a Space Marine if you do that,' Ivan said. His mood was contagious though. Even Anton seemed thoughtful now.

'You think they'll have big guns over there?' he asked.

'It's a hive city – what do you think?' I said.

'Big enough to blow a hole in a Baneblade the way we blew this place up?'

'Big enough,' I said.

'I can see what this miserable bastard is so depressed about then,' said Anton.

'It's the way the world is,' said Ivan. 'Always somebody with a bigger gun. One day you're doing the blowing up, next day you're being exploded yourself.'

'Not if we're lucky,' I said. 'It'll be some other poor bastard's turn.'

I was fighting hard to keep up my spirits. The mood of total belief in victory that Macharius had given us had vanished into the night air. At least so it seemed for just a moment.

'How can we lose?' said Anton. 'We've got Macharius with us.'

'You're probably right,' said Ivan. 'He does not seem like a man in the habit of losing.'

And as quickly as it had come, the mood of pessimism vanished, seemingly dispelled by the magic of the general's name. In the distance thunder rumbled. The ancient daemon gods of war beat their drums. Man-made lightning flickered. Somebody somewhere was dying.

Soon it would be time for us to join in.

A monstrous storm blew in from the north. The hot desert winds brought clouds of abrasive dust. It ground along the side of the *Indomitable*, stripping the paintwork in places. The filters kept most of it out, but the air had a strange taste and my mouth felt gritty. My eyes watered so much I was forced to pull down my visor. Everybody else in the cockpit did the same thing.

The winds were strong enough to send small pebbles pinging like bullets off our hull. The external comm-net crackled. Only occasional fragments of vox were audible. There was something about the weather on this planet potent enough to disrupt even our comm-grids. That was disturbing to say the least.

I kept the Baneblade rumbling forwards, knowing that the dust would work its way into the mechanisms of the treads and eventually break them down. It would be unfortunate if it happened. There was no way anyone could go outside and perform field repairs. If we dropped behind the main battlegroup there would be no help available either.

We would be stuck out in the desert until the recycling systems overloaded and we died of hunger, thirst or bad air. It seemed unlikely that anyone would come looking for us while a war was being fought.

Even as these thoughts flitted through my mind, I concentrated on the way forwards. The New Boy was driving as my relief but I watched him like a hawk in case he made a mistake. I was ready to override the controls if any enemy appeared.

The lieutenant obviously felt the tension in the air. He spoke reassuringly into our local net, as if to make up for the lack of external chatter. 'I'm glad I am inside on a day like today,' he said. 'Now is not the time for going for a little walk in the fresh air.'

There were some chuckles at that, and the truth of it was that he was right. There was something oddly reassuring and even perhaps a little enjoyable about being inside a monstrous armoured vehicle and immune to the ravages of the deadly storm outside.

'Even the weather is on Macharius's side,' he said. 'If this storm does not cover our approach nothing will.'

That was certainly an optimistic interpretation of events but who was I to disagree? It was possible he was right. The lieutenant knew more about these things than I did.

'How long you think this will go on for, sir?' the New Boy asked.

'Our tac briefing says these storms can last for days. Sometimes the air outside can get so hot it's like stepping into a furnace. The heat would kill you if the dust did not strip you to the bone first.'

A pebble ricocheted off the hull as if to emphasise his point. It sounded as if someone was firing a boltgun at us.

'It's why every part of this force is mechanised. There's no other way of fighting on this planet until we're close enough to the hives to find some cover. Now keep your eyes peeled. We're getting close to the outer perimeter defences. There are bunkers full of big guns and lascannons. If this storm keeps up we'll bypass them and cut them off from supply. If it dies down all of a sudden, we need to be ready to fight.'

As if some daemon of the storm had heard him, the sound of the wind began to die away. The grinding noise lessened. Chatter on the external comm-net became audible again.

The great billowing clouds of dust started to settle, except where the passing of the tanks set it swirling.

'Oh shit,' I heard someone say. A glance into the periscope told me why.

Ahead of us lay an enormous armoured bunker. It was the size of a small hill, reinforced with plascrete and sheets of durasteel. The maws of several very large guns pointed in our direction. A huge turret traversed towards us. I hit the override and took the controls from the New Boy. He tugged at the sticks for a few moments not realising what was happening. It was hard to blame him. The same thing had happened to me the first time I went into battle.

I glanced around at the terrain. Dunes undulated all around us, some of them large enough to provide us with some cover. I picked the most likely looking of them and sent us in that direction a fraction of a second before the lieutenant gave the order to take us hull-down.

Of course, the dune would not provide the slightest smidgeon of protection against the blast from one of those lascannons. That was not the point. The point was not even to hide us from view. It was to make us less visible than all the other tanks around us. If we were less of a target, the enemy would seek somebody else. I would not have wished death on anybody on our side, but our first task was to see that we stayed alive. Dead men win no battles and they certainly do not tell tales about them afterwards.

The lieutenant barked orders into the comm-net. I heard Ivan and Anton and the others respond. The whole Baneblade vibrated as all of our batteries went off at once, thundering at one of those distant guns.

Lines of las-fire stabbed out at us from the smaller emplacements in the bunker. It was stupid. Hitting a Baneblade with a light weapon was like menacing an elephant with a sulphur match. Those weapons would have cut infantrymen down like chaff but were useless against us.

Our fire blasted into one of the larger emplacements, sending shards of broken metal flying. That was one gun silenced. As I watched, smaller Chimera units surged forwards across the dunes. Heavy bolters blazed from the small-looking turrets on top of their hulls. Blasts from the pillbox tore a few of them apart but many more got close, then huge explosions from below sent them hurtling broken skywards.

'Minefield,' I heard the lieutenant mutter. 'Lemuel, take us in, we are going to clear a path.'

There was no point arguing. The commander's chair was behind mine. He could put a bullet through my brain if he even suspected mutiny, which in truth was not something I had in mind.

As I urged the *Indomitable* forwards I was thinking more of the possibility that the mines might be powerful enough to breach our hull and that we would be sitting targets for those batteries in the great fortress.

The lieutenant just kept talking into the comm-net. Ahead of us the Chimeras began to reverse, moving out of our paths like a swarm of crypt rats passing round a mastodon. I saw one or two broken bodies in the minefield, one or two men still moving. I did my best to ignore them and the thought that in a few minutes that could be me.

I nudged the Baneblade forwards. Something exploded beneath us. For a moment, I felt as if my heart was going to stop. I heard the New Boy groan and when I looked over his face was white. The hull vibrated like a great drum but held.

'Keep us moving forwards, Lemuel. Those mines are not strong enough to stop us.' I wished I was as sure of that as the lieutenant was. He calmly commanded the turrets to keep up a stream of fire into the gun emplacements even as one of those mighty lascannons started to rotate towards us. I knew that if we were directly in its sights then we were dead for sure. Such a powerful, fixed position gun had power enough to take out even a tank like the *Indomitable*. Another mine went off. For a moment, the Baneblade shuddered and threatened to stop. It felt as if even the massive weight of the ancient tank was not enough to keep it on the ground. For a heartbeat I feared that one of the drive-trains had given way and that we were immobilised. The old monster kept crawling forwards. Our guns raked the nearest positions. Brown-clad infantrymen rose up out of concrete foxholes and scurried away. What might have been a commissar rose to shoot them. A hail of fire from our anti-personnel weapons killed soldier and leader both. The lascannon kept traversing towards us. It would only be a matter of moments now before it had us in its sights.

'Keep moving, Lemuel,' the lieutenant said. 'Just a few more metres.'

Suddenly I understood what he was doing. I fed the engines as much power as they would take and we surged forwards passing under the line of fire of the great lascannon. Its beam scorched the earth behind us but we were safe. The barrel of it could not be depressed any lower. We were under its arc of fire.

Along the path we had cleared through the minefield Chimeras raced forwards, guided by the mark of our tracks. The other Bane-blades were doing the same now. Within minutes the minefield was breached and our infantry swarmed over the sides of the pillbox, clearing bunkers and foxholes, breaking through the armoured security doors and swarming into the interior. We sat outside in the sun and provided them with covering fire.

'That's our first objective taken,' said the lieutenant with some satisfaction.

'Yes, sir,' said the Understudy. 'Everything is going according to plan.'

I wondered about that. I really did. Would it really have gone so well if the lieutenant had not been there, and seen the weakness in the minefields. And what if he had been wrong, what if the mines had been able to destroy the Bane-blade. You can drive yourself mad thinking about such things. It's best to stick to the things that actually happen and not what might have been. That's a good rule when thinking about life in general, as about the wars you have fought in.

By noon the sun, at its highest point, gazed down on our triumph. Prisoners were rounded up and disarmed or shot. We had won a small victory but it was a victory and that is always a good way to open a campaign, as I am sure Macharius and the lieutenant at least understood.

We climbed down from the Baneblade to stretch our legs. We had been given a break and who knew how long it would be before we managed to get out of the tank's claustrophobic interior.

The air smelled different. We lost the tang of incense and filtered air and cooped up sweaty bodies we had inside. I could smell the desert and explosives and burning and something else disturbing.

Atop a nearby ridge I noticed something. It was a cage, made of metal, resting on a metal platform on a high spot above us. It was an odd shape – not square like most of cages I had seen but curved towards the top. Inside it were a number of x-shaped structures made from metal. I was too far away to make out what exactly these cages contained although I could see that they were blackened and scorched and covered in what appeared to be soot. Curious, I set off up the hill, shouldering my shotgun just in case. Anton and Ivan followed me.

I began to notice something else about the cages. Beneath them was some sort of residue. The bottoms seemed more scorched than the tops as if fires had been lit beneath them and heated the metal framework. As I got closer, I saw that this was exactly the case and I saw something else. There were fire-blackened human skeletons attached to the x-frames within the cages. They had been chained there.

'What in the name of the Emperor?' Ivan said and whistled. Anton just let out a high-pitched nervous giggle as if not quite able to come to terms with what he was seeing. I walked closer, thinking there must be some mistake.

There was no mistake. Somebody had chained up a number of men within the cages. They had set them alight. In places the flesh was scorched black, in other places pink meat and charred bone was visible where the flesh had sloughed away. Long metal tentacles descended from the top of the cage. They contacted the scorched skulls. At first I thought they were more chains designed to lift the victims' heads at an unnatural angle but then I saw they were fire-proof tubes connected to metal rebreather filters over the victims' mouths.

I stared, not quite able to get to grips with what I was seeing. It was mechanically-minded Anton who figured it out.

'The tubes kept those poor bastards breathing,' he said.

'What?' Ivan said.

'The smoke from the flames might have suffocated them. The tubes fed air into their lungs, kept them breathing while the flames burned them alive.'

He paused for a moment and thought for a moment. 'No. It was worse. They were not just burned alive. There are heating elements in the metal. The bars, the chains, those cross-bars would all be white hot. They would be branded as they burned.'

'Why?' I asked, for once not astonished by the fact I was asking Anton the reason for something.

'Dunno,' he said. 'Discipline maybe?'

'You mean like a flogging?'

'More like an execution.'

'They are a cruel bunch on this world,' said Ivan. We had lived under Imperial Guard discipline for a decade so you had to plumb impressive depths for Ivan to think you were cruel.

We walked around the cages, looking at them from all angles, trying to make sense of what was going on here. I've fought orks and they can be vicious but this was something else. It was calculated and strange and nasty beyond words. Someone had wanted whoever was imprisoned in these cages to suffer in the most profound way, to drag out every second of their blazing agony as their red-hot surroundings consumed their lives.

I stopped and stared at it for a long time.

'What are you thinking, Leo?' Anton asked.

'I am thinking it would be a bad idea to be taken prisoner by whoever did this.'

'You'll get no arguments from me,' said Ivan.

'If I find the bastards who do this stuff, I'll show them the sort of burning a lasgun can do,' said Anton. He meant it to sound mean. It came out frightened.

I turned away from the cage and looked down at the aftermath of the battle. There were tens of thousands of Imperial Guardsmen down there, swarming over the position like ants, and I was suddenly very glad of that.

I could see the *Indomitable* and Corporal Hesse on top of it, waving up at us.

'You reckon we ought to report this?'

I glanced around. From up here I could see there were other cages and other groups of soldiers and officers clustered around them, gawping.

'I don't think we'll need to,' I said. 'Other people have already noticed.'

The columns of our mechanised force roared southwards, moving as fast as they could. Valkyries and Vultures filled the sky overhead. All around us the landscape began to change. Great pipelines ran to the horizon. Signs of human occupation became more visible: empty irrigation canals and the huge crystalline geodesics of hydroponic farms. There were small pueblos and larger hab-zones.

Sometimes in the distance I caught sight of dust plumes as if refugees were fleeing before us. Sometimes, very far in the distance the clouds seemed to glow, although I had no idea why.

So far, we had not met any real opposition, which was worrying. Karsk was an industrial world – it should have had a mighty army defending it. We had overcome all resistance a little too easily.

I found it suspicious.

I could tell from the chat that I heard on the comm-net that the others were uneasy too. Ivan was making a few slurred jokes about how soft the heretics were. We were all wondering when the real war would begin.

Here and there about the landscape were more of the cages for burning folks alive. Some of them were large enough to hold hundreds. They seemed to become more common as we approached the city.

The ground beneath us was firmer now. We were out of the great ash deserts and on to what was either more solid rock or a foundation of plascrete set there for purposes of construction. The buildings started huddling together to form small towns. We swept by them, heading for our goal. It was swiftly becoming visible on the horizon.

A huge excrescence emerged out from the planet itself, a dense jumble of towers, each thrusting into a polluted sky. The clouds hung so low over the city that they obscured the top of the towers, as if the world was ashamed of Irongrad and sought to hide it beneath a blanket of fog. It took some time for me to realise that the clouds and fog were a product of the city itself, so strong was this initial impression. At the very tip of the hive where it vanished into the clouds, the sky was lighter and flickered as if something was aflame within the toxic fog.

Around the city were what looked to be the cones of small volcanoes. Some of them were. Others were the terminus of pipes for industrial waste. It bubbled up and formed slagheaps and polluted ash fields.

The city had an odd organic look. Effluent from the factorum towers had flowed down like lava from a volcano. It had been caught in prepared frameworks and allowed to harden, forming layers between the buildings, roofs on which other structures had been built. Some of the layers looked like hardened candle wax. Others had been sculpted by builders. The imprint of intelligence was all too clear. Huge greenhouses glittered on the slopes.

Irongrad was as large a hive city as any I have ever seen and Belial was not a world short of giant metropolises. Each of those towers was a small fortress in and of itself. Each was like the bulkhead in a ship – it could be sealed off and defended even if its neighbours were taken or destroyed. And that would only be the beginning. Most of the city was hidden from view. Hives have endless layers, one on top of the other, descending into the very bowels of the planet.

The possibility of fighting street to street and block to block in that vast apparition was not a reassuring one. Of course, we had enough firepower to level the place if the need should arise. I told myself that was an idiotic thought – the whole purpose of the invasion was to take Irongrad and its pyrite processing plants. We needed what they could produce in order to keep the Crusade moving across the stars.

Another thought occurred to me – if they really wanted to cripple us, the inhabitants could simply destroy the city and thus remove all strategic reason for us attacking them. Of course, that would mean sacrificing their homes and seeking refuge in the empty, deadly desert. It would mean the rulers of that great hive city forswearing all of their wealth and possessions and reducing themselves to paupers simply in order to thwart our will and the will of the Imperium.

In my experience few nobles would do such a thing unless they felt they had absolutely no option. At the very least, as a last resort, they could use the destruction of the processing plants as a negotiating tool when and if they surrendered.

Of course, Macharius's plan had taken this into account – one reason for this attack from the north was to seize the parts of the city in which the processing plants were concentrated while all of the defenders were in the southern zones of the city. On paper it was a very clever plan but it has been my experience that plans often encounter practical difficulties in the execution.

Looking at that huge city as it came inexorably closer it was hard not to feel dwarfed by it. Our force, which just a few hours before had seemed so irresistibly mighty, now seemed barely adequate for its purpose. Perhaps Macharius had misjudged things. He would not be the first Imperial General to do such a thing, and surely he would not be the last.

How many people were in that hive, I wondered. Millions? Tens of millions? It did not seem possible that we could subdue them all.

Set amid the outskirts of the city, scattered among the slag heaps and volcanic maws were a number of fortresses, joined by thick walls along whose tops ran communicating roads allowing for the quick movement of reinforcements. Massive batteries of guns spiked out of them, covering the approaches. Tens of thousands of troops were moving into position even though most of the defenders had been drawn off to the south, leaving only a greatly reduced number of guardians on Irongrad's northern side.

It all looked formidable enough, with enormous turret-topped, armoured towers rising redly out of the desert. From them, guns spoke in voices of thunder. Towering plumes of ash rose all around us. Columns of dust erupted hundreds of metres high, springing into being at the summons of the distant muzzle flashes. The earth shook as if a gang of angry giants stomped a ritual war dance upon it. The beams of giant lascannon fused desert sand to crystalline slag. I prayed that one of them would not come to bear on us. I had the feeling that even a Baneblade might be reduced to fused metal in the blink of an eye by one of those awful weapons.

Our own forces were not slow to respond. Valkyries surged forwards through a hail of anti-aircraft fire and dropped their cargoes of storm troopers on the walls of the forts and the towers of the gates. As I watched dozens of them were hit and spiralled to the earth, belching black smoke. The rest kept coming, a swarm of angry mechanical insects attacking an enemy hive.

At the lieutenant's command I put us hull-down behind a dune. Our guns began to pound away at the heretics. I could see Chimeras, Manticores and Leman Russes hull-down along the tops of walls, blasting for all they were worth.

I had a view of the clear killing ground around the walls. For brief moments, it was empty of all life, with only buildings and craters and columns of dust rising in front of me. Then our force moved forwards, an inexorable tide staining the desert as it went. Thousands upon thousands of armoured vehicles belched fire at the distant walls behind which the hive towers rose like man-made mountains. The scream of rockets and roar of guns was dimly audible even through the hull of the Baneblade.

Our attacks clawed at the sides of the enemy fortifications pitting and scoring them. A titanic explosion split the side of one massive pillbox. Somehow, by one of those chances that sometimes occur in battle, a magazine had been hit and its contents had exploded in a chain reaction that tore the structure apart.

It was as if the sword of the Emperor had descended from the sky and split the world asunder. There was a flash so bright it was dazzling and the photo-mirrors of the periscope went temporarily black as the spirits reacted to protect our sight. When they became clear again, I could see a gigantic crater where the fortress had been.

'Bad structural design,' said the lieutenant, as if that explained everything. Suddenly I had a sense of something badly wrong. Glancing around I could see one of those massive guns was pointing directly at us. I felt the urge to slam the treads of the *Indomitable* into reverse. It was too late. Time seemed to slow as it sometimes does in moments of maximum danger.

I swear I saw the distant muzzle of that enormous gun flash and something huge blur towards us. A moment later the Baneblade rocked under a massive impact. Somebody somewhere in the cockpit screamed.

It was a natural and understandable fear but the old monster had been built to withstand worse and its front armour was the strongest part of the tank. The lieutenant rapped out orders, calling for damage reports. The all-clear came in from every part of the *Indomitable*. At the end, the lieutenant said, 'The Adeptus Mechanicus builds tanks better than the locals build fortresses.' Everyone laughed in relief and the tension melted away. Our turrets blasted away at their targets. Our ears were still ringing from the hammer blow of the impact.

'Move us back a couple of hundred metres, Lemuel,' the

lieutenant ordered. 'Straight back, front facing the enemy at all times.'

As if he had to tell me that. It seemed that even the lieutenant preferred not to have a repeat of another direct hit. A few seconds later another shell landed where we had been. It blasted a crater a hundred metres wide in the earth but we were not there to enjoy it.

As we retreated other Baneblades hove into view on either side of us. I studied the rear monitor, making sure we did not run into anything or back off a precipice. Men have been killed and tanks destroyed by stupider things in the heat of battle.

As we moved the gunner got the distance once again. Another mighty blow smashed into us. Such was its force that the front of the *Indomitable* rose into the air a metre or so and then fell back to earth.

I felt the crash through the padding of my seat. Ikons swung on their chains above me. I heard the New Boy groan as if he had banged his head on something. When I looked over he was bleeding from where his head had hit the 'scope.

Our turrets kept blasting. The lieutenant kept issuing clipped orders and I kept us moving out of the arc of enemy fire. We were lucky – after the initial burst none of the really big guns targeted us and the smaller enemy weapons simply were not powerful enough to harm Number Ten. I saw one of our brother Baneblades brewed up, oily black smoke pouring from its broken chassis. The dead bodies of some of the crew sprawled out of emergency hatches while the rest of its crew stood forlornly in the sand beside their former home.

Shadowswords erupted through one of the city gates, moving with great speed. They looked surprisingly long and lean for such large vehicles. As mighty as our own mightiest vehicles, their long guns could take out even a Baneblade or a Titan; they were mobile and deadly, great predators of the battlefield capable of destroying anything that they encountered. Supported by the heavy batteries within the city they might just turn the fight against us, if there were enough of them. I counted five emerging through the monster gate.

I have no idea where they came from. Perhaps they were a reserve unit swiftly rushed to the north of the city, perhaps they had simply been in the area. Their volcano cannons smashed into our smaller tanks and destroyed them with one shot.

A couple of them blew the treads of another Baneblade, immobilising it. I studied them through the periscope feeling the first surge of apprehension as opposed to fear. Those mighty tanks in their brown and red paint jobs and their low sleek silhouettes represented really worthy foes.

They raced right out at us, determined to find targets. The sheer boldness of it gave them a brief advantage. They destroyed a dozen or so of our Leman Russ before anyone responded. Those volcano cannons were capable of wreaking terrible havoc on even the heaviest chassis. Tension twisted in my gut as I saw the harm they were causing.

Someone on our side realised what was happening. I heard the background buzz of orders on the lieutenant's channel and then he rapped out commands. Our heavy turrets spoke. I saw one of our shells land next to the leading heretic heavy tank. It chewed up the tread, sending it snapping off, leaving the Shadowsword rotating on the spot, going round and round on one tread until its driver cut the power, leaving it a sitting duck.

A curtain of heavy weapons fire descended on it, obscuring it from sight. When the dust cleared the red Shadowsword was burning from end to end, its rear quarters mangled, its long barrelled killing gun twisted and useless.

The lieutenant calmly called out some more coordinates. I looked in the direction he indicated and another company of Shadowswords swept into view, coming over the dunes from the south-west. The lieutenant told me to turn and I brought the Baneblade round to face the new foes. Other heavy vehicles on our side joined us.

We got off the first shots and once again immobilised the leading Shadowsword, forcing the others to come round. I did not like this one little bit. If more and more heretic tanks arrived on our flanks they might be able to roll along our line and do terrible damage. Caught between the anvil of the incoming heavy tanks and the hammer of those heavy batteries we would be smashed to bits. I felt a moment of stark fear. I had no idea what we were facing, how many more enemies might descend on our flanks, whether I would be dead in the next few minutes. My mouth felt dry. My heartbeat raced. All it would take was one shot from one of those long-barrelled tank-destroyers and we would be gone.

More and more tanks hove into view till I gave up counting them. I had no idea how many more of the heretics were still to come. On the front line it really does not matter how much bigger your force is if the enemy has local superiority.

Our tanks were hitting their targets. The enemy as often as not would miss. Their formations were sloppy. They did not go hull-down until it was too late.

The difference between veterans of half a dozen campaigns and untested troops from the planetary defence levies was starting to show. I noticed too that green blobs on the holoscreen were circling round to the north of us. It would not be long before the flanking force of the enemy would find itself outflanked. All we had to do was hold our ground. Their vehicles did not seem as strong as they ought to be either. Obviously they had been constructed in-system and most likely from corrupted templates.

Shots clanged off our hull. Every time I heard that horrific clamour I thought for a second that I was going to die. I held my breath, as if by doing so I could somehow postpone the moment when I took my last lungful of air. I prayed the *Indomitable* would not catch fire. It is every tankman's worst nightmare, to be trapped within a burning vehicle.

At last our own flanking force was in position. I could not see what was happening but the heretics in front of us began to reverse, moving away from us. The lieutenant ordered us forwards in pursuit. We passed the burned out shells of those red-and-brown tanks. Our anti-personnel gunners mowed down their fleeing crews. I crushed one screaming man beneath our treads. Soon we were on the reverse side of another slope.

Our own forces were hammering in from the north-west.

The retreating heretics had been caught in the flank, hit where their armour was weakest. A few had turned to face these new attackers and were now presenting sides and rear to us. The lieutenant was not slow to take advantage of this, nor were the Baneblades of our formation. Soon what had looked like a threatening force had been reduced to smoking slag. We looked down on a graveyard of broken tanks and fleeing crew who swiftly fell victim to our heavy bolters.

Looking east, I could see the same thing as the lieutenant saw. One of the gates in the city wall was open. Obviously the attacking force had come through it. It was not yet shut. I wondered whether something had gone wrong with the closing mechanism. It was either a huge opportunity or a deadly trap. I heard the lieutenant make a swift call up the open command channel. I was very surprised by what I heard next.

'This is General Sejanus! Advance and capture the gate. Hold it for as long as you can. Reinforcements are on their way.'

I thought it was all very well for the general to give those orders. He was not the one heading straight to his death if it should prove to be a trap. Nonetheless the lieutenant did not hesitate.

'You heard the general, Lemuel! Make for the gate.' He sounded as if he was on a training manoeuvre.

'As you wish, sir,' I said, trying to keep my voice from quaking. The walls of the city came ever closer. I kept my eyes focused on the gate, not certain whether to hope or be afraid that it was going to slide shut in front of us. I half expected us to be targeted by the city defence but most of the defenders' attention seemed to be focused on the battle raging on the far side of the ridge. Was it really possible that no one had noticed us?

A shot from something massive answered my question for me. The Baneblade shook, a rivet dropped from the ceiling above me. I heard what sounded like shrieks of fear echoing along the corridor.

'Hull breach,' I heard the lieutenant say. What in the name of the Emperor could have done that, I wondered? Maybe one of the Shadowswords had caught us unawares.

'Keep us moving forwards, Lemuel,' the lieutenant said. 'Hard right five degrees.' That correction would put us off-course for the gate. But a second later another blast impacted the ground where we had been. The earth shook as if a daemon-god were stamping his foot. It seemed whatever was shooting at us had got the range.

'Hard left eight degrees, emergency speed,' said the lieutenant. I did as I was told. The Baneblade picked up speed and shuddered as the same titanic impact split the ground behind us. I felt sick to my stomach, thinking about the sort of weapon that could hole a Baneblade and the fact that we were being targeted by it. The lieutenant gave no sign of nerves.

'Steady all,' he said into the internal comm-net. 'We'll soon be below the angle of fire.' That could not happen a moment too soon, I thought.

Through the periscope I could see tiny figures in the gateway. They looked like tech-priests and they were working frantically on some exposed mechanism. The lieutenant spoke. Our guns roared. Anton and Ivan placed shells right in the opening, tearing those distant tiny figures to bloody pulp.

Maybe this was not a trap. Maybe this was a chance to be the first into the city, to cover ourselves in glory. As the lieutenant spoke, I was already revving the drives to the max, sending us ploughing across the wastelands towards the gateway, huge dust columns sloughing skywards in our wake. Figures on the wall had noticed us now. Tiny people gesticulated frantically in our direction. Another maintenance team rushed into the gateway and died just as quickly as their predecessors.

We were almost within the arch now. We were going to be the first into the city. I was excited in spite of myself, as were the others. They cheered and whooped over the comm-net. It was idiotic. For all we knew we were about to be blown to the Throne of the Emperor by heretic heavy weapons, but we could not help ourselves.

On the wall, soldiers opened fire, blazing away pitifully with lasguns and heavy bolters. A few of them threw frag grenades at us. They might as well have used the airguns we had for toys during our childhood back on Belial.

Our return fire swept them from the wall. Some were cut in half. Others had their heads blown apart. The lucky few managed to duck down behind the plascrete and get out of sight.

I heard the lieutenant report that we were in. More vehicles were moving into position behind us and more Chimera-mounted troops were being diverted our way to take advantage of this sudden gap in the defences.

Following the lieutenant's orders I drove a few hundred

metres down the street and brought us to a halt at an inter-section where we could block the way and keep the heretics from retaking the gate. I felt as if it was only a matter of time before someone realised what was going on and began to make the effort.

'That was fortunate,' I heard the lieutenant say. There was a certain understandable satisfaction in his voice. It had been lucky but there still needed to be someone who understood the opportunity and took advantage of it on the spot and he had been the man. There would be decorations in it for him and most likely a promotion. I did not grudge him it. He was a better commander and a better man by far than many officers in the regiment.

The Understudy could hardly disagree. 'You are correct, sir.'

'Now all we have to do is make sure the enemy don't retake the gate and try not to get killed while we are doing so,' said the lieutenant. 'What do you think, Private Lemuel?'

His voice was calm but I could tell he was in a good mood from the fact he had chosen to talk to me at such a crucial moment.

'I think that's a good idea, sir,' I said. 'If we can hold on for an hour or so, we'll take the city for sure.'

'We were always going to take the city, private,' he said. 'This has just made it a little quicker, that's all.'

I nodded so he could see the back of my head going up and down. Speaking again would be leaving a hostage to fortune. Looking at the tactical map I could see our forces were rushing ever closer.

* * *

Darkness was starting to fall as we rumbled through the outskirts of Irongrad, crushing parked groundcars beneath our treads. Our way was lit by the glow of giant flames of industrial gases vented from the sides of the factorum towers. In the distance, something even brighter illuminated the underbelly of the clouds in the sky over the central hive.

Resistance was very light. Macharius's plan had succeeded. Ahead of us was an entire factorum zone filled with the pyrite production facilities that we needed. In a matter of hours we had seized all of them and taken up defensive positions to prevent the troops of Irongrad from retaking them.

The lieutenant ordered me to put the Baneblade hull-down behind a factorum wall so that our guns would still be able to rake the approaches. I did as I was told and the great armoured beast came to rest. We sat there at our controls studying the empty streets and the mighty towers surrounding us and waited for the enemy to approach. It had been many hours since we had had any sleep. I munched on a stimm tab and protein bar combination washed down by a swig of brackish water from my canteen.

I glanced out through the periscope, studying the long shadows. I was not unduly troubled. I would be able to see anything that approached and mechanised infantry were starting to deploy on foot around us, taking up positions on top of the walls, setting up heavy bolters to rake the streets. One or two of them were already snatching some sleep where they lay. It was nice to know we had some veterans with us. The two-tailed airframe of a Valkyrie hovered above some huts while storm troopers swarmed down a fibre-rope ladder descending into the clouds of trash and dust raised by the aircraft's drives. They deployed by squad; their heavy carapace armour made them look bulkier than a normal man, and their outsize lasguns did nothing to make them look less formidable.

A line of fire darted out from its nose-mounted cannon. I wondered whether the gunner was firing at hidden heretics or just practising on some of the local giant rats. Such things have been known to happen.

I glanced around the command cabin. The lieutenant was cat-napping while the Understudy watched the tactical grids. Our commander still had his headpiece in and I knew from long experience that any incoming signal would wake him. Looking at him with his head slumped on his chest I felt something like affection. Once again, he had brought us through the firestorm of battle. At the end of the day we were still alive and in the Imperial Guard that is all you can reasonably ask.

I offered up a prayer of thanks to the spirit of old Number Ten. The *Indomitable*, as much as the lieutenant, had brought us through the battle. No drives had failed at a critical moment, no guns had misfired. The armour had held. We still enjoyed the great beast's blessing. At the time, foolishly, I can recall thinking that maybe Macharius's presence on the Baneblade's side had blessed us too. Perhaps some of his luck, or the Blessing of the Emperor or whatever it was he had enjoyed had rubbed off on us too.

I wondered how much longer it could last.

* * *

It seemed I had barely closed my eyes when the lieutenant was barking orders at me. I glanced at the chronometer. A couple of hours had passed since I last looked. Even the stimm tabs had not been able to keep me awake. I glanced into the periscope. It was still night out. The infernal flames of the factorum towers still illuminated the area.

I looked down the long street and saw a number of small vehicles moving closer. Our guns spoke, tearing a huge crater out of the plascrete of the roadway as they destroyed the first of the oncoming Leman Russ. The others swerved around it and kept coming, fire blazing from their main turrets, belly mounted lascannon and side-sponson bolters. They were on killing ground. Our battle cannon swiftly reduced them to burned-out shells. Bailing out of their metal carapaces, their crews had no chance of survival in the wave of fire that descended on them.

While this was going on, heretic infantry had taken up position in the nearby buildings. They had set up their heavy weapons on balconies and along the external piping of the buildings where it was broad enough for scores of men to stand.

Among the troops, giving orders as if they were officers, were a number of robed and cowled figures. The thing that made them so visible was that someone seemed to have set fire to them. Around their heads flames rose, so bright and intense that they should have spread and burned but they did not. Instead they merely outlined their bearers like halos seen in religious pictures.

'Sir, have you seen this, the burning men?' I said, just in case the lieutenant had not noticed.

'They are priests of the Angel of Fire cult, Lemuel,' the lieutenant said. There was an undercurrent of disquiet in his voice and I wondered if he, like me, was thinking about the cages we had seen with all those burned bodies within them.

'Is it some sort of heretical trick, with the burning?' the New Boy asked. It was a reasonable guess. Many times in my career fighting heretics I had seen very strange things that turned out to be products of some ancient dark technology

Before the lieutenant could reply one of the priests raised his hands. The aura of flame spread from his head to surround his entire body. It blazed up around his hands as if he was carrying a flamer. He made a gesture at the walls and waves of flame surrounded a squad of our troops, setting their uniforms alight and then consuming their flesh.

It was not the burning that was so horrific. I had seen many men burn to death before. It was the suggestion of something otherworldly about it, as if it were not just their bodies that were being consumed but their souls too. Some of our lads were shooting back, but their las-bolts simply disappeared when they hit the priest. The flaming shield surrounding him grew brighter as if it fed on their energy.

I think the horror of it left us paralysed for a moment. I was very glad I was within the ancient, warded hull of the *Indomitable* at that moment. The prospect of being outside and facing those burning zealots held no appeal whatsoever.

The priest spread his arms wider and his aura blazed ever brighter, twin columns of flame erupting from his back until it seemed as if he had wings of fire, as if he was becoming the living embodiment of the supernatural being he worshipped. He was a living flame, vibrant with a terrible power. The blaze of energy around him should have consumed those with him but it did not. It left the heretics untouched even as the fires he had invoked consumed our soldiers.

'Enough,' said the lieutenant savagely. 'Antoniev, Saranin. Kill the bastard.'

Anton and Ivan did not need to be told twice. Our main guns sent an enormous shell into the heretic position. It was overkill. Whatever protected the zealot from small arms fire, it was not enough to stop an explosion that could shatter a main battle tank. The whole vast web of piping the heretics perched on exploded, sending blazing, smashed bodies tumbling through the air to land on the ground below.

'Keep firing till you have cleared the streets,' said the lieutenant.

They did.

On the second day, curtains of heavy artillery fire descended upon us, smashing into our position, killing anyone who was not dug in deep. The soldiers brewing *chai* in the shadow of our tracks were reduced to a bloody smear on the stone. The outskirts of the factorum went from being an ordered, organised grid of plascrete walls to a smashed, desolate landscape as bleak and jumbled as the surface of some meteor-bombarded moon.

The Baneblade rocked on its treads as high-explosive shells rained down upon us. The noise was deafening and the sheer sound of the chaotic blasts would have driven you crazy. It was like being at the centre of an inferno of noise. A legion of devils beat on the armour with a thousand mighty hammers. Monsters roared outside the safe zone that the hull of the *Indomitable* represented.

A wall tipped on us, burying us beneath tons of shattered plascrete. It felt as if we were being trodden on by a giant. I put the drives into full reverse and the Baneblade shook off broken stone like a dog shakes off water as it emerges from a stream.

One by one, the towers surrounding us crumbled.

The first time it seemed impossible. One moment, there was a huge starscraper standing there. The next moment the earth shook and a cloud of dust erupted skywards. The whole huge structure slid into the ground – that's the only way I can describe it. One moment the building was there and the next it had retracted into the plascrete leaving only a column of dust and a pile of rubble the size of a small hill.

The heretics were destroying the buildings with demolition charges, clearing the ground for a massive counter-attack on the factorum zone. They had infiltrated them with combat engineers from the hive below. It showed how desperate and fanatical some of them were that they would consider doing such a thing. Those towers had been the homes of tens of thousands of people and had contained shops and schola and medicae and all the other things that people need to live. All were flattened at the whim of some commander somewhere who had decided that they represented an obstacle to his great plan being accomplished.

Where before we had looked out upon rows and rows of skyscraper towers, now we gazed upon great dunes of rubble across which we knew our enemies would soon attack.

The lieutenant had one hand on his earbead and glanced down at his tac-grid. I was looking into the periscope.

Over the huge mounds of rubble created by the collapsing towers an enemy army approached. In the lead were Shadowswords, the greatest tank killers on the battlefield of the newborn 41st millennium, an enemy vehicle that filled me with dread. Around the Shadowswords were hundreds of Leman Russes and thousands of Chimeras, and around them were hordes and hordes of infantry. They were packed very closely. It was like watching a bloody-red tide come in. Their crimson uniforms made the oncoming heretics seem like a lake of blood puddling out from the corpse of a giant.

'Lieutenant! Lieutenant!' I said. 'We're under attack.'

He looked up from the tac-grid and spoke rapidly to whoever was on the other end of the comm-channel. After a few seconds he began to give orders to the gunners and he told me to hold myself ready.

I don't think I've ever seen a larger force coming at me. I certainly had not up till that day. I had put the Baneblade hull-down behind what was left of the factorum wall. There was only a small stretch still intact. The rest had been reduced to rubble by the constant bombardments. It was not much but it was much more than many of our comrades had. Most of the other tanks stood alone in the rubble around the factorum, providing such cover as there was for many of our infantry. The smarter soldiers had already taken up position among the collapsed walls and buildings.

'Steady! Steady!' the lieutenant said. His voice was unnaturally calm. I could tell he was thinking exactly what I was; that there was no way that we were going to survive this. We were outnumbered and outgunned by those oncoming Shadowswords and all their support. The enemy general who had planned this attack had known what he was doing. This was probably the weakest part of our defensive perimeter, the softest spot in our defensive line. He had aimed a hammer blow at the most vulnerable point. It was unfortunate for us that we just happened to be there.

The Shadowswords opened fire. One of the tanks next to us was hit by storm of super-heavy las-fire. Its turrets were crippled immediately. A beam penetrated the side armour. I don't know what happened next. Possibly there was an internal fire or one of the drive cores overloaded. There was an enormous explosion and the main turret lifted right out of its mounting before tumbling to one side.

I have never seen a Baneblade quite so comprehensively destroyed. The fusillade of fire was overpowering even for one of these ancient monstrous tanks. All I could do was offer up thanks to the Emperor that we were partially concealed by the tumbled-down wall. I knew that we were next in line. Our own guns opened fire. The shells fell among the enemy. The destruction was enormous in that closely packed formation. Unfortunately, it did not touch the Shadowswords but no Leman Russ could withstand the impact of our main batteries, not when they were fired by gunners as accurate as Ivan and Anton and the others.

The poor infantrymen surrounding the tanks had no chance whatsoever – they were simply reduced to bloody jam smeared on the plascrete.

The enemy did not stop coming. The Shadowswords kept firing.

I kept my hands on the control sticks. I offered up prayers to the spirit of our great tank. I felt useless and helpless.

There was nothing I could do. Instinct urged me to unlimber my combat shotgun, for I felt certain that if I survived the next few minutes, I was going to have some use for it.

The New Boy groaned. The Understudy was probably wetting himself. I kept my eyes focused on the enemy, willing them to die. If terror and hatred could form a lethal beam, I would have killed a few hundred just with my gaze. The enemy were not impressed by my attempt to use psychic powers. The lesser tanks were firing now and even a few of the infantry. Las-bolts flickered in our direction.

Some of our own soldiers had started to respond in kind. I could see one of their commissars rushing around, dust covering his normally immaculate uniform, bellowing orders and gesticulating frantically as he sought to get them to hold their fire. An explosion bloomed on the spot where he stood and he went to greet the Emperor in the company of the men he had been trying to lead.

It let me know in no uncertain terms that the Emperor was not with us that day.

The enemy horde raced on, the tanks leaving the infantry behind now except where the footsloggers had scrambled up onto the hulls of the armoured vehicles. They had about them that certainty of victory that keeps men coming even in the face of near inevitable destruction.

Every one of those soldiers over there was convinced that somehow death would pass him by. It might tap the shoulder of his comrades but it would leave him alone. That and rotgut alcohol are the only two things I know that can be relied on to keep men walking forwards in the face of the sort of fire we laid down – those and maybe a stern-faced commissar standing behind them with a bolt pistol and a chainsword in his hand.

I could tell from the panicked chatter over the comm-net that our own forces did not possess such conviction. All of us knew that we were doomed. There simply was no place to run in the face of that oncoming wave of killer tanks and bloodthirsty soldiers. Our gunners fired like madmen, blowing huge holes in the enemy line. There was no way they could miss. There were just too many targets.

Tens of thousands of las-bolts hailed down on our position. Of course, they could do nothing to the *Indomitable* but it was like trying to peer into an incoming blizzard through the visor of a helmet. The *Indomitable* shuddered under near impact from incoming shells.

Another of our tanks brewed up. More men I had fought alongside for a decade died in the burning inferno it became. I waited and I waited. I offered up more prayers. I hoped that the lieutenant would say something, anything. I hoped that he had a plan as he so often had in the past. All I can remember is that calm voice saying, 'Steady lads. Steady!' The smell of stale sweat and fear filled the cabin. My hands felt clammy on the sticks.

The Shadowswords started to target us with everything they had. At first the beams ploughed through the rubble around us, adding to the chaos of broken brick and plascrete.

Every time they missed I breathed a little easier, but I could tell that the shots were coming closer. They were starting to bracket us, and then it was only a matter of time before they got the range. Their gunners were not as good as ours but they would get there in the end.

I took a deep breath and fought down the urge to throw the Baneblade into reverse and try and get us out of there. Doing so would just get me a bullet in the back of the head.

Anton and Ivan kept firing. They hit one of the Shadowswords and immobilised it. A moment later something else hit it and sent its crew to hell. I heard cheering over the internal comm-net. It was a small victory but our gun crews felt the need to celebrate it.

The next moment the *Indomitable* shook. We had been hit although I had no idea how badly. I heard the lieutenant bark some questions. He wanted reports from every part of the tank. Most of them came in but there was nothing from the drive rooms.

That was bad. If we lost all of our drives we would have no power. We would be unable to move. In the worst-case scenario, the servomotors on the guns would stop working and crews would need to crank everything by hand.

In quick succession we were hit three more times. It was as if we were inside an anvil and a giant was pounding on us. It was only afterwards, when I had time to think, that I realised that was the case. The shots were so close together and so powerful and the effect was so devastating that I did not have time while it was happening. One of the shots must have hit the tracks because afterwards I saw that they were torn to shreds. I know another hit one of our turrets and killed its entire crew. I was much more concerned by the effects of the third shot. I felt those personally.

The entire command chamber erupted in a blaze of light. The air was filled with the smell of ozone and melting fuse wire. My display went mad for a moment and then dead.

Instinctively I tugged at the sticks but nothing happened so I looked over at the lieutenant, hoping for instructions.

It was then that I saw the great gaping hole in the internal bulkhead where something had torn through it.

I saw also that the lieutenant was not going to be giving me any orders ever again. Whatever had smashed through durasteel had not been slowed down in the slightest by his mere flesh.

All that was left of the lieutenant was a torn corpse, a mess of entrails strewn across his commander's chair. His head lay where it had rolled on the far side of the cabin. Some quirk of fate had spared the Understudy. He stood there, horror-stricken, blood splattered on his beautiful uniform and on his face. His eyes were wide. His mouth was open. He seemed to be screaming and groaning at the same time.

I don't suppose he had expected to take over command of the Baneblade under quite these circumstances.

I listened on the comm-net but it was dead. I looked around to see if anybody was capable of giving orders. In my heart of hearts, I knew there wasn't but, such was the ingrained habit of looking to command for instructions, that I could not stop myself.

I unstrapped myself from my chair and tried to stand up but my legs would not respond to my brain's instructions. I looked down, half-fearing to see that they had been blown off but they were still there. They just refused to move.

I looked over at the New Boy. He was shaking his head as if he did not quite understand what had happened. He was feeling at the back of his skull, touching the dark stain there.

At first I thought that he had been hit, that his head had been broken open and something was leaking out. It took me a moment to realise that he was okay. It was simply that a chunk of meat had been thrown across the room as the lieutenant's body had been torn apart and had landed on him. It was mixed with blood and hair but he had not taken a scratch. I think he came to that conclusion at roughly the same time as I did.

I put my hands on the dashboard and pushed, raising myself up out of my seat. My legs decided to work again and I managed to stand upright, swaying dizzily. I staggered over to the Understudy and began to shake him. There was an odd madness in his eyes and he was still making that strange sound.

I don't think he was entirely there. I think his spirit had gone somewhere else for the duration. I slapped him on the cheek. It did not bring him out of it. I would have thought if anything could have, that would. The upper classes on Belial were not used to being struck by their social inferiors.

He just kept staring at me and staring at me. I looked over at New Boy. He seemed to be waiting for instructions and it came to me that right at this moment in time, I was in charge.

Warning lights strobed redly through the inside of the tank. Alarm horns sounded. I unslung my shotgun and strode over to the breach in the hull. I looked out and saw that we were surrounded by the enemy. They just seemed to be there, as if somehow they had crossed the distance between us and where they had been instantly.

I realised then that some time had passed since we were hit and I simply had not grasped that fact. Such things often happen in the chaos of combat. You never get used to them.

I smelled burning and I saw black smoke rising above the hull of the Baneblade. I noticed that the escape hatches near number one turret were open and Anton and Ivan had clambered out along with one of their loaders. I could not tell who in the gloom.

Such is the size of a Baneblade that I was actually a long way above the ground with a clear view of the enemy soldiers below us and the enemy Shadowswords passing close by.

They were just as huge and much more menacing. Perhaps for the first time in my life I truly realised exactly how terrifying a main battle tank can be as it passes. You feel completely insignificant compared to that vast monstrosity and you just know that with the slightest sweep of its smallest weapon it could extinguish your life like an officer treading on the stub of a lho stick.

Even as I watched, a small anti-personnel turret on the side of the Shadowsword began to rotate. I shouted a warning to Ivan and Anton and pulled my head back inside the gaping hole in the *Indomitable*'s side. Bolter shells bounced off the iron walls outside. Some of them passed through the gaping hole in the hull. Something ricocheted around the interior of the command chamber and I dived for cover instinctively.

When I heard voices outside speaking the guttural accent of Irongrad I knew the enemy soldiers had started clambering up the hull of our Baneblade. The anti-personnel fire had stopped. More time had passed without me realising it. I think I was in shock.

I could hear the enemy coming closer and closer. I turned

and saw that New Boy was standing beside the Understudy, trying to get him to say something, but nothing was happening. I turned and shouted at them, 'Get into cover! Now! Get out of here!'

He looked at me as if he did not quite understand what I was saying. I brought my combat shotgun around and he flinched as anyone will when a weapon is pointed at them by someone of whose intentions he is not sure. 'Go!'

At that moment, a soldier in brownish-red uniform clambered through the hole in the metal wall. He saw me at once and began to swing his lasgun towards me. I turned and fired. The shotgun spoke in a voice of thunder. The kick of the weapon almost dislocated my shoulder.

The heretic screamed and fell backwards, tumbling to the ground far below, carried back out through the hull-breach by the force of the shotgun blast. His blood stained the floor. More heads poked through the gap. I pumped the shotgun and fired again then I dived behind what was left of the command throne, almost slipping on the lieutenant's slimy remains.

The knees of my trousers were sticky. My hands were red too. I did not really have time to consider the implications of this. The New Boy had taken the Understudy and disappeared through the internal hatch.

Smoke billowed along the corridor and through it and for the first time I wondered if I had done the right thing ordering him to run. In the depths of the Baneblade fires were raging and smoke can be as deadly as poison gas under the wrong circumstances. I told myself that he had his rebreather and that he knew how to use it but I was not entirely certain that under the circumstances he would remember to do so.

Even as that thought occurred to me, I realised that I had not adjusted my own mask. I pulled the rebreather into position and immediately it flattened out the stink of torn-apart bodies and burned control systems.

I adjusted my goggles and squinted at the door again, half-wishing and half-dreading that the heretics would appear again. A kind of madness descended upon me, filling me with bloodlust. It's not that I lost all fear – it was more that I knew that death would put an end to the terror clawing at my gut and so I feared it less.

I waited and I waited and no one came.

I heard footsteps clattering in the corridor behind me and I turned, half-expecting to see the New Boy again but it was Ivan and Anton. They were dragging the loader along with them. He was pale and had lost a lot of blood and it seemed obvious that he had been hit by a bolter shell. With both hands he was holding his stomach and I could see the pink squirming thing that was one of his intestines trying to escape from between his fingers. Even as I watched, he coughed and what seemed like a river of blood gushed from his mouth. He slumped to the floor, clearly dead.

Ivan and Anton held their lasguns at the ready. They looked just as prepared to shoot me as I was prepared to shoot them at the moment.

'It's Leo,' Ivan said, 'don't shoot!'

'That would be nice,' I said idiotically. 'If you don't shoot me, I won't shoot you.'

'Excellent plan,' said Ivan.

'I do my best,' I said.

'Is that the...' asked Anton. I nodded.

'It's the lieutenant.'

'He deserved better,' said Ivan.

'We all do,' I said. 'But I doubt we'll get it.'

'I thought I saw some of the heretics climbing the side of the tank,' Ivan said.

'You did,' I said. I patted the barrel of my shotgun. 'My friend here discouraged them from entering uninvited.'

'It's good to have a friend like that,' said Ivan.

'Cover me,' I said. 'I'm going to take a look around.'

I took a couple of steps and threw myself flat where there was less blood and then I wriggled forwards on my belly towards the hole in the hull wall. When I got there I looked out and surveyed the battlefield. The man I had shot lay on the ground below me. Another had been run over by a tank. You could tell by the tread marks on his belly. What was left of our Baneblade was a metal island rising out of a sea of heretics.

We were on our own, I realised, surrounded by our enemies. I did not see any way we were going to get out of this.

All around us I could see the heretics. There were hundreds of tanks and tens of thousands of soldiers surging past. Most of them paid not the slightest attention to the broken-down Baneblade in their midst. They were too busy concentrating on the factorum zones ahead. They had their eyes on the objective they had been sent to retake.

I felt utterly insignificant. It did not seem as if I was even worth killing.

I noticed in the ranks of the enemy there were many priests with halos of flame. They seemed to take the same position in the heretic's army as commissars held in our own. I saw them exhorting the soldiers and threatening them and when one of them looked up at me I got back out of sight certain that the worst thing I could do would be to attract the attention of such a fanatic.

Anton and Ivan threw themselves down next to me and peeked out over the edge of the breach in the hull.

'Bloody hell,' said Anton. 'It's like there's an army down there.'

He grinned a cheesy grin and unclipped a grenade and dropped it over the side of the tank. It fell amid the heretics and exploded, killing a dozen of them. The unbelievers looked around, unable to understand what had happened. Perhaps they thought they were under artillery fire. Perhaps they thought that some distant tank was shooting at them. I could cheerfully have just lain there and let the heretics pass by but the two madmen I was with were not prepared to do that.

Ivan grunted and threw a grenade of his own. He tossed it further and it landed beside a Leman Russ. The explosion ricocheted off the side of the tank, leaving it unscathed, but killing more heretics. Ivan laughed and Anton giggled and I cursed the pair of them for being idiots.

They did not care. I think they had already decided that they were dead and they were just going to take as many of the heretics with them as they could. It had all become a big childish game to them. I did not know whether to laugh or cry.

At that moment, all I really wanted to do was keep living for another few heartbeats. I looked up at the sky. For once there was a hole in the clouds above us and I could see a patch of pure reddish-blue. The sun was shining through it and briefly I saw the contrail of some aircraft passing at high altitude. It was an incongruously peaceful sight in the midst of that vast assault.

Anton threw another grenade. Then Ivan did the same. They kept doing it and they kept laughing and there was something contagious about their mad mirth in the middle of all that death so I joined in.

Of course, it was only a matter of time before the heretics realised what was happening. Someone in the turret of a passing Leman Russ tank noticed us and turned the heavy bolter on us. We barely had time to duck back out of sight. Sparks flashed off the edge of the hull. Then I heard shouts below us and I knew that the enemy were starting to clamber up the side of the Baneblade again.

'Now you've done it,' I said. I sounded just like my father at that moment. The pair of idiots had known my old man and they flinched at my tone. My father had been a famously violent man in his day and some of that came out in me sometimes.

We scuttled away across the command chamber, jumping over the loader's corpse, trying to find some cover from the attack that we knew was incoming. There was no place to hide in the corridor and the smell of burning was becoming more intense. We scuttled back along the way Anton and Ivan had come and clambered up the metal ladder, making our way to the top of the Baneblade.

I'm not exactly sure why we did it. There was no escape. The heretics would eventually catch us. Perhaps it was pure instinct, trying to keep ourselves alive for just that little bit longer. Or perhaps it was simply part of the childish game that Ivan and Anton were playing, sort of like hide and seek, forcing the enemy to come and find us, wasting their time as much as possible. It was probably some mixture of the two.

Eventually we clambered up through the topside hatch and emerged on the roof of the Baneblade. We were a long way above ground, out of the arc of fire of the heretics. There was plenty of cover along the top of the tank.

'We can drop grenades on them when they try and climb up,' said Anton. He smiled again and there was madness in his smile. He was like a child being too clever. On the other hand, I could not think of anything else to do.

'And then what?' I asked. Anton shrugged.

'And then we die,' Ivan said.

'At least we'll take a few of them with us,' Anton said. 'And that's all a soldier of the Emperor can ask for!'

He had read too many prop-novs. Still, I could not fault his logic. I heard voices below us. I smelled smoke. Looking out from the top of the tank, all I could see was enemies as far as the horizon.

It was like standing on top of a huge durasteel cliff looking down on a sea of hostile flesh. I took a deep breath, offered up another prayer to the Emperor, checked my shotgun and, for a mad moment, considered throwing myself off the edge of the tank with a live grenade in each hand. After all, what did it matter whether I did that now or got fried by lasgun fire in a few minutes? The desire to live for those few extra minutes stopped me but it was touch and go.

Ivan looked at us both. He scanned from face to face. There was no expression on his ruined metal features but I thought there was a certain sadness in his glance. 'Well then, I guess this is it. You're a pair of sad bastards but I'm glad to have known you.'

Anton gave him a salute and then looked up and squinted at something in the sky. 'What the hell is that?' He asked.

I followed Anton's gaze. Hundreds of objects dropped out of the sky. I was not exactly sure what they were. They did not seem connected in any way to what was going on round about us. I noticed something else. In the distance, behind us, absolutely monstrous figures were striding out from behind the skyscraper towers that our forces still held.

'What in the name of the Emperor?' Ivan said. There was awe in his voice.

'Are those what I think they are?' Anton asked.

'I'm pretty sure they are,' I said. They were like animated statues, perhaps a hundred times the height of a man, made of dura-steel and ancient alloys. They moved with a massive, lumbering grace. They were ancient god-machines produced by the Adeptus Titanicus, perhaps the most powerful war engines ever built and I wondered where they had come from. It was only then that the size and power of the force that Macharius had assembled really began to sink in. And that was not all; the things dropping out of the sky began to hit the ground all around us and what was in them broke out in a whirlwind of violence.

They were drop-pods and within them were Space Marines of the Death Spectres Chapter of the Adeptus Astartes. They were massive, armoured men, moving almost too fast for the eye to see. They smashed their way through the oncoming heretics and it did not matter that they were facing tanks and were outnumbered perhaps ten thousand to one. Where they struck, their enemies died. Bolters coughed in their hands and blasted holes in heretics. Chainswords decapitated enemies two or three at a time.

We did not have long to watch the violence. Our own enemies were coming closer from below.

'It was all a trap,' I said, thinking out loud. Ivan saw it at once. Anton, as ever was a bit slower.

'They left this part of the line weak,' Ivan said. 'They knew the heretics would attack here in force.'

It was easy enough to understand and even quite admirable if you did not happen to be the bait in the trap. A massive enemy force had been drawn into the counter-attack. It overextended itself as it came on, certain of victory. It punched a salient out of our line and then once it was entrapped, it was encircled on both flanks by our armour and the Space Marines dropped on it from above. I worked it all out as I stood there. It was typical of Macharius or those who had studied his methods like Sejanus. There were feints within feints, traps within traps. We had walked into what looked like a trap ourselves only to draw our enemies into a bigger one. Maybe Macharius had not been quite so open with us as I had thought back when he was giving his speech from the side of the *Indomitable*.

Suddenly Anton shouted, 'Look out!'

A grenade arced up through the open hatch and we dived for cover. I scrambled into place behind an anti-personnel turret and heard shrapnel ping off the metal. When I looked up I could see heretics scrambling out of the hatch. One was already up. Another had just popped his head out. I blasted with the shotgun. I took the top heretic's leg off at the knee and put multiple holes in his friend's head. Ivan and Anton's lasgun made sure of them.

'Shit,' I heard Anton say and looking up I saw why. While we had been busy at this hatch more of the enemy had emerged from the other topside hatches. We shared the roof of the Baneblade with at least a dozen heretics, and more and more were emerging all the time. Our situation had gone from bad to worse.

I hunkered down behind my cover and pumped the shotgun. Anton lay flat behind a small raised seam of metal. Ivan raced across the duralloy, las-bolts burning at his heels, and dropped into place beside me.

'They've fallen into our trap,' he said. His voice was flat because of his metal jaw-work and his metal-plated face had no expression but there was a grim humour in the set of his eyes.

'Yeah, we've got them where we want them now.'

A grenade dropped into place between his feet. Without the slightest hesitation, he picked it up and lobbed it back. It must have been at the end of its timer because it burst while it was still in the air.

Heretics screamed.

I popped up and blasted with the shotgun. The enemy were closer than I had expected. At that range it was impossible for me to miss. The leader went down, his chest a bloody ruin.

A grenade landed among them. Half a dozen of them were caught in the blast. The nearest ones fell clutching ruined faces and chests. One or two had been shielded by their comrades' bodies. They kept coming. In one glance I took in the sheer number of heretics. There were just too many of them to be overcome.

And then it happened.

Something big landed on the hull of the Baneblade. It was huge and not unlike an egg and it crushed half a dozen heretics beneath its weight. Even as it began to slide off the hull, its sides burst open like one of those magical mechanical toys shops used to sell when I was a child. Massive armoured men erupted out of it. They moved much too fast for me to follow them. Bolters fired, weapons far larger than any mortal man ought to be able to carry. Where the shells hit, and they always hit, the target seemed simply to explode in a welter of blood and bone and flesh. Chainswords swung. The great egg fell off the Baneblade but I know for a fact that none of the men who had ridden it down from orbit were still in it. They were all with us on the Baneblade.

The remaining heretics looked just as astonished as we were for a few seconds. Those seconds were all they had left of life. The armoured figures smashed into them. One of them was lifted by the throat one-handed by one of the armoured giants and simply tossed away, dropping from the side of the Baneblade legs flailing. When he hit the ground below, he exploded, skull shattering, body reduced to shambles. Somehow, without me seeing it, the new-comer had slammed a grenade into his mouth before he fell. It was an action guaranteed to inspire terror in the heretics witnessing it and that was the intention.

When I looked back, the whole area around the new-comers was clear. Bodies were piled at their feet, limbless, headless, broken-backed and broken-boned. One man howled wordlessly as he flopped, his spine shattered. One of those massive armoured boots descended on his head, turning it to jelly.

Anton just stood there with his mouth open as if he was trying to catch flies in it. Ivan tilted his head to one side and studied them. I did the same, not exactly sure that what I was seeing was real.

They were big men, bigger than me by a long way, and their ceramite armour made them look bigger still. It was painted glossy black. White skull patterns were painted on their helmets. A similar pattern was emblazoned in white warpaint on the black face of the giant warrior facing us. I flinched for a moment as he raised his boltgun and fired. The shot passed between my legs and I heard a groan. I turned and looked and saw the heretic who had been sneaking up on me. How the Space Marine had known he was there in the chaos and having just sprung out of the drop-pod I will never know. How they had avoided killing us in the opening few seconds of the carnage I will never know either. If it had been me, I would just have shot everything in sight, but somehow in the heartbeat between evacuating the damaged drop-pod and entering the fire-fight, they had managed to tell friend from foe and killed every enemy, and spared our lives.

'Thanks,' I said stupidly.

The Death Spectre grunted what might have been an acknowledgment and then leapt off the side of the Bane-blade, plunging into the heretics below. If I had tried that I would have broken both legs. He landed, weapons firing, and blazed a bloody path towards the priest with the burning head. When I looked back, all of those other massive armoured figures were gone, the only evidence they had been there being the piles of the dead.

'It's a bloody miracle,' I muttered.

'Space Marines,' Anton said.

'Macharius must have sent them to get you, Anton,' said Ivan. Somehow, in the face of the awful reality, the joke fell flat.

The Death Spectres fanned out from their drop point, killing the psykers it turned out were concentrated all around us. Tanks did not slow the Space Marines down. They clambered up on to them, ripped off durasteel hatches as if they were made of paper and dropped grenades into the interior.

Sometimes they dropped in afterwards themselves and there would be sounds of awful violence and moments later a Death Spectre would emerge covered in gore. It was terrifying to watch. I have made war alongside hardened veterans, done more than my share of killing. I have fought orks and daemon-worshippers and monstrous xenos things and I would rather face any ten of those again than one soldier of the Adeptus Astartes.

They moved with a terrible combination of efficiency and ferocity that was oddly graceful. I saw a heretic sniper taking a bead on one of them from the top of a burned-out tank. He was too far away for my shotgun to hit. I shouted a warning but I was certain it could not be heard through the roar of battle. Just as it seemed he was about to be shot, the Space Marine raised his gun in a casual motion and blew the top of the heretic's head away. From the position in which he was standing you would have sworn he could not have seen his target take aim and he did not even seem to look in his direction, merely pointed his bolter and fired then returned to killing the heretics closer to him. The shot was uncannily accurate for the range.

An enormous shadow fell on our position. The gigantic humanoid shape of a Warlord Titan loomed over us. I looked up, an insect confronting an angry god. The Warlord's monstrous head scanned from side to side like a predator looking for prey. I sensed the ancient, terrible spirit within it. This was not some inanimate unthinking engine. It was a living thing, bred to war, intended to kill, and full of dreadful fury. Just the sight of it made me want to throw myself back into the wreckage and hide.

Massive pistons hissed in the Titan's limbs as it moved. The god-machine's huge Volcano Cannon swung around. The rush of the air it displaced ruffled my hair. The vibrations of the metal giant's stride passed from the earth through the shattered hull and echoed through my body. My skin tingled from the halo effect of its void shields.

The Titan fired.

The smell of ozone and alchemicals filled the air. The high-pitched whine of the weapon's capacitors hurt my ears. I ground my teeth in pain. A heretic Shadowsword went up in flames. There is ancient hatred between the god-machines and those tanks. It is said that the Shadowswords were built to kill Titans and the Titans return the favour any chance they get.

Ivan braced himself on a maintenance node in the shattered fuselage, pulled out his magnoculars and studied the destroyed vehicle, a thin line of drool dribbling down the rusted metal of his prosthetic jaw.

'See anything interesting?' Anton asked.

'There's an idiot standing beside me,' Ivan said.

'It's not nice to talk about Leo that way,' Anton said. 'Best be quiet or he'll hear you and he has a shotgun.'

That's the way I like to remember them, chattering like loons while all around us what felt like the end of the world raged.

The battle stalked away from us. The Titans, our reinforcements and the Death Spectres tore through the heretics like a sandstorm stripping an unprotected man to the bone. We watched them killing as they went. They took no prisoners. They did not have the time. That was left to the Imperial Guard regiments who followed up. It's not glamorous but it beats getting your head shot off.

We were left alone on top of the tank, looking at the piles of broken bodies and heaps of destroyed armour around us. Anton produced a flask of coolant fluid and we shared swigs.

'Bloody hell, Space Marines,' Anton said. 'We saw Space Marines. They saved us.'

From the tone of his voice it might just as well have been the Emperor himself descended from the Golden Throne to save our lives. I understood that. Very few men in all the worlds of the Imperium can say they have stood in a Space Marine's shadow or even talked to one, however briefly.

You hear about them. You hear their praises sung. You never expect to meet one. Somehow all of the stories had not prepared us for the reality.

Ivan took another swig and gazed into the distance. He was thinking about the experience, I could tell, but like me he was still trying to digest it among all the other events of the day.

Anton cackled and said, 'We saw Space Marines today. They saved us.'

'I noticed,' I said.

'You think they noticed us?' he asked. His eyes narrowed and his brow furrowed. The scar tightened on his forehead. I was surprised that he sounded so serious.

'Well, they did not shoot us,' I said.

'I mean did they even see us as people? Will they remember us and think, yeah, we saved those Guardsmen on Karsk?'

I thought about the fierce, savage face of the Death Spectre. I remembered the controlled, killing fury in those cold, black eyes. I remembered the way he had grunted when I spoke to him. 'The Emperor's Angels' I have heard the Space Marine Chapters called. There seemed very little angelic about them to me. I thought Death Spectres an entirely appropriate name. They certainly looked like manifest death to me, and they had proved themselves to be to all those they encountered on the field of battle. Among all those bodies down there, among all the thousands of casualties, I had not seen one encased in ceramite armour.

'I doubt it.'

Ivan nodded and scratched his metal cheek. It made a nerve-jangling grinding sound. 'Like mortal gods,' he said. 'Like something out of Scripture come to life.'

He sounded uneasy and that too was understandable. It is all very well hearing legends and heroic tales. It is another thing to find one of those legends standing in front of you, wielding a bolter and filled with righteous fury. The uncomfortable thought sidled into my mind: what if the Death Spectre had decided I was one of the Emperor's enemies? He would have killed me on the spot and there was absolutely nothing I could have done to stop him. Space Marines have a way of making you feel your mortal insignificance. I was glad they were on our side but I was not sure I wanted to be that close to one ever again.

Anton, as ever, chose to give voice to his own reveries. 'You know I don't think they are like us at all.'

'They are certainly not like you,' Ivan said.

'I mean it. I think they have no more in common with us than orks do.'

'That's not true. They were men once, if the tales are true.'

'Once, Leo. Not any more. I looked into one's eyes. It was not like looking into a man's eyes at all. And I don't think he looked back at me and saw someone who was the same species as him. They say they live forever, you know.'

'They don't. Just longer than us, if they are not shot.'

'Yes, but they have a gene-seed in them that is passed on from one to another. That lives forever. Some of them must be carrying seeds that date back to when the Emperor walked among men.'

'I don't think I have ever seen you this thoughtful,' I said. It was true too. Of all the strange and wonderful things I saw that day, a thoughtful Anton was not the least strange.

'And… and those Titans, they were old too, old as the Imperium maybe. Some of them must have walked when the Emperor did and that Space Marine's gene-seed was new. We live in a strange and terrible universe, Leo,' he said.

'It's taken you all this time to work that out?' I said.

He just stared at me bleakly, as if he was about to cry. There was a lost look about him, like a child separated from his parents in a hive-world crowd who does not know his way home. It was odd seeing those eyes looking out of that tall gangling body.

A strange gloom started to settle on us. I looked down at the armoured hull of the *Indomitable*. I knew at once we were all thinking the same thing.

I was the first to say it. 'It's dead.'

They understood what I meant. There was no sense of presence in the *Indomitable*. Whatever spirit had been in it was gone. Anton nodded. Ivan shook his head. They reflected the confusion of the moment.

There was the sound of gunfire and all the thunder of battle in the distance but it was as if we sat in our own small pool of quiet. We were all thinking about the Baneblade. Old Number Ten had carried us across half a dozen worlds. We had looked after it and it had looked after us. It had been in a very real sense the only home we had known in the past decade.

'What are we going to do?' Anton asked. They were both

looking at me, in that hangdog way that they'd always done even back in the guild factorum on Belial.

'We need to find an officer to report to,' I said. None of us moved. A dying heretic started to scream for water. He lay in the shadow of a smashed Leman Russ across from us. Anton turned, raised his lasgun and put him out of his misery. We returned to contemplating our own problems.

'There's always the Understudy,' I said. 'He might still be alive. I suppose we should look.'

It was something we had been putting off and I hated to bring it up but someone had to. We had to go back into the shattered remains of the Baneblade and start looking for bodies. I doubted that anyone had survived but it was always possible and we would need to account for the casualties anyway at some point if we were the only survivors. The Imperial Guard always has a great curiosity about such things. We would need to reclaim the logs as well. As surviving crew it was our sacred duty.

Anton gulped. He acted tough and he was, most of the time, but there are some things nobody likes to do and this was one of them. It was also the first time any of us had been called on to do such a thing. The old tank had seemed indestructible. I don't think it was quite real to any of us just yet.

And there was something else, a certain inertia. While we were sitting here we were out of things. Nothing was quite real. We were alone in a world of ruins and dust and corpses, committed to nothing except watching the universe pass us by. Once we started doing something we were back in the world of following orders, performing duties, a world in which we could be killed and in which, at very least, we would have to work. For all our depression, there was still an odd holiday mood in the air. It came from still being alive and having no supervision and, for the first time in years, having no real idea of what to do.

Ivan grunted as he started to get up. 'I suppose we have to,' he said.

You could always rely on Ivan to bring you down.

'Come on you two,' he said. 'We've got work to do.'

We clambered back down into the body of the *Indomitable*. We moved very cautiously, much more cautiously than when we had made our escape. There was something ominous about going back down there. It was as if we were rummaging about inside a huge corpse.

We were in the burned-out shell of something that had once been living but was now dead. I think all of us felt that way. They let me take the lead, quite wisely, because nobody really wants to stand in front of a man with a shotgun. Not if they have the slightest smidgen of a sense of self-preservation anyway.

I found that I was holding my breath again and walking on the balls of my feet. I was ready for anything – it was always possible that the Space Marines might have missed someone and that there might be enemies still left alive down here.

We entered the command cabin again. None of us could look at the lieutenant. I paused there and looked at my old seat. How many hours had I spent sitting there? How many leagues had I driven that ancient tank over? One thing was for sure, I would not be doing that again in a hurry. It seemed like a different place now and I felt like a different person from the driver who had sat there taking orders from the lieutenant.

'Nothing,' said Anton, shaking his head. 'No one here except the dead.' No one made any jokes. Even for us some things were not a subject for humour.

'I suppose we're going to have to go below,' said Ivan. Even he did not sound very keen on the idea. None of us were.

'I suppose we are,' I said. There were dead bodies in the corridor leading towards the engine room. They were heretics. They had that strange look, as if their chests or their heads had exploded from within, that is so characteristic of the corpses of those who have been shot with a bolter. There is nothing, with the possible exception of grenades, that leaves quite such a mess and I say this as a man who is quite proficient with a shotgun.

Our boots made a strange sucking sound as we walked. It was impossible to tread through the narrow corridor without stepping in blood and entrails. Something bad had happened in the drive room. It must have taken the first hit and it had been a nasty one. The engine had exploded and taken out the engineers. Oily had been beheaded by a slice of metal half the size of the door that had been blown off in the explosion. The rest of his team had been so badly chopped up that we could not really work out which body parts belonged to which person.

'It looks like we were lucky,' said Anton. 'I'm not sure anybody else made it out of here alive.'

Of course at that point we heard a groan from down the corridor. We pushed down to the head and banged on the door and the groaning stopped. 'Who's in there?'

'Yeah, let us in, I need to use the head,' said Anton.

'Is that you, Leo?' I heard the New Boy ask.

'No! It's Lord High Commander Macharius, come to offer you a promotion,' I said. 'What the hell do you think?'

The door swung open. Crammed into the tiny space of the toilet were the New Boy and the Understudy. They both looked pale and ill. They blinked at us like some nocturnal thing caught in the beam of a torch. The New Boy looked at us and then was violently sick. I stepped back just in time to avoid having vomit added to all the other gunk on my boots.

'What happened?' New Boy asked. 'I heard shooting – some sort of gun I have not heard before – and then nothing.'

'You missed the Space Marines,' Anton said. 'They saved us.'

'Space Marines,' said the New Boy.

'Yes,' said Anton. 'Those were bolters you heard.' He sounded as satisfied as if he had been firing them himself.

'That's all very well but we need orders,' I said. I looked pointedly at the Understudy. He just stared at me. I suppose having your superior's brains blasted over your face will do that to you. That said, the New Boy had had the same experience and he seemed to be handling it. It seemed to me at the time the Understudy really had not been a product of the same school as the lieutenant. Just goes to show how wrong a man can be.

'Are any of the others alive?' the New Boy asked. It was a sensible question but Anton turned and spat on the floor.

'That's what we are trying to find out,' he said. He looked in disgust at the Understudy. The man just stared at him blankly.

Ivan said, 'Best get him out of here. I doubt the air down here is helping him recover.'

His words were almost kindly. There was that thing about Ivan. Just when you thought with a fair degree of certainty that he was a brute, he surprised you with his sensitivity. He had been the same as a boy back on Belial but his ruined face and metal-plated skull made me forget that sometimes.

I nodded. 'We'll all go,' I said. 'Just in case there are a few heretics left over.'

We stepped out into the fresh air, if that was the right word for it. It had some of the tang of the desert in it but it was also the air of a hive city, full of trace chemicals and the stink of heavy industry. Added to that was the taint of the dust of fallen buildings and the smell of explosive and burned flesh and burned-out machinery. Not even the filters of rebreathers could extract every trace of all of that.

I looked around. There were bodies everywhere, like in some of those religious paintings showing the Day of Judgement when the Emperor returns to pass sentence on the Guilty. Some of the bodies were still moving, with the faint pathetic shifts of posture that men slowly dying of thirst, air poison and terminal wounds make. Most of them were in the uniforms of heretics. I told myself I had no sympathy with them, that they had been trying to kill me only a few hours before, but, of course, it is never that simple.

There was one young boy lying there. There did not seem to be anything wrong with him except for the red stain spreading across the chest of his tunic. His face was very pale and he licked his lips when he saw me. He was frightened and he wanted to ask for something at the same time. I tried to ignore him and walk past.

'Wait,' he said. He was speaking Low Gothic. The local accent distorted the word but it was recognisable. Something made me turn to face him. 'Drink. Please.'

I looked him in the eye. He was very young, even younger than the New Boy, younger than I had been when me, Ivan and Anton had run away to join the Guard. He held my gaze evenly. Who knew what he was really seeing? He had that visionary look that some of the dying get. I've seen it a thousand times. A man gets past a certain point and he just lets go. Indifference and a certain sympathy battled in my mind. I stuck out my hand. It surprised me to see there was a canteen in it.

'Thank. You.' He took a swig and lay back. He was dead before his head hit the ground. I wondered whether the act of drinking had killed him.

'You going soft, Leo?' Anton asked. He still looked thoughtful but the hint of his usual maniacal grin turned the corner of his lip up.

'One day that might be me,' I said. 'Or you.'

'Nah,' he said. 'I am planning on living forever.'

'The Guard might have something to say about that.'

'I know. They have their stupid plan to get us killed at every chance they can, but we are too smart for them.'

'Anton, you could not outsmart that rock.'

'I am still smarter than the Imperial Guard.'

'You may be on to something there.'

'You know it.' He bent over and closed the young boy's eyes.

'They are not so different,' he said. Somehow I could tell he was still thinking about the Space Marine. I think what he had realised that day had really shocked him. All his life he had idolised Space Marines. There had been a day when he thought he could become one.

'You still want to be a Space Marine?' I asked. He stared off at the rising dust clouds in the distance for a long time before he turned and grinned at me.

'Hell, yeah,' he said. 'Put in a good word for me with Lord High Commander Macharius.'

'I will when I see him,' I said. At the time, I thought it was a joke.

We squatted beside the burned-out shell of the Baneblade, listening to the Understudy mumble to himself and keeping our weapons close at hand just in case. It was quiet where we were but the thunder of battle muttered on in the distance. Sometimes the earth shook and I wondered what had happened. The New Boy rummaged about inside the tank for a while, then I heard his voice.

'Hey, Leo?' He peeked out from beneath the belly of the Bane-blade. He gestured for me to come follow him. I considered shouting at him but the fun was fast fading from that so I crawled underneath the corpse of the old monster and saw what he wanted me to see.

Corporal Hesse was there. At first I thought he was a goner but I saw his chest was rising and falling and it took me a moment to realise he was asleep. I moved closer and noticed the open maintenance hatch above him. He must have crawled through it and just waited out the fire-fight raging above and around him.

Asleep though he was, he had a lasgun near at hand so I gestured for New Boy to come away. You can have some truly terrible accidents when you wake an armed man suddenly.

'What you find under there?' Ivan asked as I crawled back out.

'Corporal Hesse – the fat bastard is snoring away under the maintenance hatch.'

'Good for him,' Ivan said. He whistled as he did to show when he was pleased. Anton smiled as well. I think he was just happy that there would be another familiar face about. I was happy that my brief period as a figure of authority was over.

Even as that thought occurred to me, I felt the earth shake and heard the rumble and clank of a massive machine coming closer. Turning, I saw it was a huge multi-sectioned transporter. A horde of smaller vehicles followed in its wake, mostly Atlas recovery tanks with the crane attachment. Some of them had bulldozer blades attached to their modified Leman Russ chassis. Loping around them were Sentinel power lifters, little bi-pedal hounds snapping at the heels of their tracked masters. They pulled up next to our position. It took about a minute for the cloud of dust to settle.

I caught the whiff of technical incense and sanctified grease. I heard the plainsong chants that the tech-adepts repeat to themselves even when they are not performing their rituals. They had come to see which tanks could be repaired and which they would need to perform the last rites on.

'Red cowls,' said Ivan. The Adeptus Mechanicus and their devotion to their ancient mysteries always made him nervous, had done ever since he had the mechanical parts added to his face. I think maybe he thought the devotees of the Omnissiah might want to salvage them some day. He was probably right but they would likely wait until he was dead. On second thoughts, I can see why he found their presence disturbing.

A few of the adepts clambered down from their vehicles. In their power armour, with their cowls and face masks they looked more like Space Marines than members of the Imperial Guard. At least, they did until they moved in that lumbering way of theirs. They had none of the deadly grace of the Adeptus Astartes. They moved more like the clockwork wind-up toys my mother had bought me before the sickness took her when I was a kid.

They stepped up to the wrecked Baneblade, looked at it and shook their heads. Their leader stared at me as if the destruction of the ancient tank was somehow my fault.

'Who is ranking here?' their chieftain asked. I indicated the Understudy with a jerk of my thumb. The enginseer made that weird clicking noise they use to indicate disapproval.

'He is malfunctioning,' he said. 'Where is the fallback control?'

'That would be Corporal Hesse,' I said.

'And where would I find this unit?'

'Carrying out an inspection under the main chassis,' I said. 'Such is not his prerogative.'

'That is a matter you should take up with him.'

'I will.' One of the adepts produced a small tracked trolley from within the Atlas. He placed it on the ground and the chief lay down on it. At a command in technical dialect it carried him flat on his back to where Hesse was. A few moments later he and the corporal were in heated discussion.

The rest of the tech-adepts moved around the wreckage. They paid as much attention to the heretic vehicles as they did to our own, which felt subtly wrong, until I realised they were looking for salvage and what they could strip down for parts. They walked around wrecks, banged them with massive, ceremonial spanners, chanting diagnostic catechisms and consulting with their portable divinatory altars.

Once the basic rituals had been performed, they marked some of the less damaged vehicles with reclamation sigils. The rest they began to strip. Soon I saw sparks flying from welding cutters. It reminded me of the guild factorum back on Belial.

Corporal Hesse emerged from beneath the Baneblade. He looked as if he was almost in tears. I would not have believed it myself if I had not seen it.

He indicated the chief with a nod of his head. 'They are going to perform the last rites on Number Ten,' he said, 'then they are going to drag him away for reclamation.'

It did not surprise me. It meant the tech-adepts thought the martial spirit had definitely fled from the old tank. It would be sent back to one of the Temple factorums and be imbued with a new one if that was possible, broken up for parts if it was not.

'He wants me to surrender the logbooks,' Hesse said. He made it sound as if they were asking him to give up his first-born child.

'I suppose we'd better go and get them then,' I said. It was not something I was looking forward to. Of course, I had known I was going to have to at some point but it meant going back into the control cabin of the Baneblade once again.

Corporal Hesse nodded. He was going to go and get them himself but he looked as if he would be grateful for the company. I climbed up into the *Indomitable* with him. The control cabin did not smell any better. I wondered whether they were going to remove the bodies themselves or whether they expected us to do so. I guessed it would be the latter – if there's a dirty job needs doing it's always the poor bloody Guard that needs to do it. It's a universal law.

Hesse looked at the lieutenant – it was the first time he had seen the body. He made an aquila over his heart and turned and looked away and if I had not known better, I would have sworn there was a tear in his eye. I did not look any closer than I had to. I walked over to the lieutenant's body and I rummaged around until I found his keys. I will spare you the details of exactly what was needed to extricate them from the decomposing mess that was his corpse.

I walked over to the locker and opened it and removed the large leather-bound books I found in it. I raised them reverently, knowing that these were the last in a long line of volumes dating back to when the first commander took charge of this vehicle after it emerged from the Temple factorum.

Curiosity forced me to open one.

I started with the pages towards the back and noticed that they were all in the lieutenant's fine handwriting. There was nothing particularly thrilling about the text. Mostly it seemed to be descriptions of maintenance routines, notes about how far we had travelled and similar such stuff. Even so, just looking at some of it made me nostalgic. I saw one passage noting the death of Henrik on Jurasik. I noticed the names of several old battles we had fought in. Just the words made me think about them. I found that I had a lump in my throat and I swiftly leafed through the book towards the beginning. The handwriting changed many times and the dates stretched back over decades then centuries.

I felt a tap on my shoulder and I turned around to see Corporal Hesse standing there with his hands held out. I handed the book over to him and he took it reverently and he muttered some words over it as if he was a tech-priest performing some sacerdotal ritual.

Of course, it was just gibberish he had picked up back on Belial the same as the rest of us. He was no more a tech-priest than I. And yet, at that moment, for all the difference it made, he might as well have been a member of one of the sacred orders. He spoke with just as much devotion. There was something touching about it and I did feel as if I was in the presence of something holy just for a moment.

The moment passed and we clambered back down out of the Baneblade and, reluctantly, Corporal Hesse handed the logbooks over to the chief. He accepted them formally with all the ceremony of someone performing a high religious duty. He turned and he handed them to one of his minions and then he requested that we remove the bodies for burning so that he could, in turn, purify the Baneblade for its long journey back to its eternal home.

There was not a lot left of the lieutenant and many of the others were heavily mutilated. We piled their corpses together with those of the heretics, bodies mixed with anything inflammable that we could find. We threw technical oil over the whole damned mess and lit it with a lho stick igniter.

It seemed somehow appropriate that the worshippers of the Angel of Fire should be consumed by flame. Even as that thought struck me, I felt vaguely disturbed by it. The flames ate their flesh hungrily and sometimes I thought I saw small, snarling faces looking out of the fire. Corporal Hesse spoke the words of the funeral ritual, commending their souls to the Emperor's Light. We stood staring into the fire for ages afterwards, despite the stink of burning meat. We were thinking about the dead we had known and remembering them. I even remembered the boy I had given a drink of water.

Where did they go, I wondered? What really happens when the life goes out of us? The Texts tell us that our souls walk into the Emperor's Light, but do they? I have been on many worlds and seen and heard many things and I do not know if I believe that any more. Perhaps I never truly did.

One or two of the tech-adepts joined in the ritual, more from curiosity it seemed than for any reason of sentiment or belief. Perhaps I do them wrong. Or perhaps they were simply being diplomatic. While we saw to the empty shells of our fallen comrades, they did the same for the vehicles. Sometimes out of the corner of my eye I saw them performing their rituals with the same care that we did.

For a brief moment, the oddness of it struck me. I felt as lost and alone as I sometimes did as a child. I was standing amid the rubble of a burned-out hive city breathing the strange air of a world unimaginably far from the planet where I had been born. All around me men were performing rituals that had been old when my home-world was first colonised.

Near at hand were the corpses of those whose souls were about to take a journey beyond all comprehension. By the light of burning bodies, amid the shadows of ancient war machines, I saw the rapt faces of Ivan and Anton and the New Boy and Hesse and I felt something, a closeness that I cannot find the words to describe even now.

Amid the ancient darkness and gloom, I felt the comradeship the living have in the face of the immeasurable dead. We were all tiny sparks of light, like those rising from the flames of that pyre and disappearing into the unknowable darkness.

Sometime after the funeral ceremony, the Understudy stopped gibbering. The light of intelligence returned to his eyes.

'Water,' he said. His voice was strange and rasping as if all those hours of making that inhuman sound had damaged his vocal cords. His face was grim. I am not sure what had happened to him. It was as if during the long madness of that day his spirit had left his body and something new and darker had crept in. When he looked at me, there was a feral insanity in his eyes, well-concealed but present.

I handed him the canteen and he drank from it without wiping the mouth, which is not something he would have done in the past.

'Report,' he said in that croaking voice.

Corporal Hesse brought him up to date on the situation. His burning glance moved from face to face. If he was embarrassed by what he had been told of his performance he gave no sign. He accepted all of the information with a brusque nod of his head. He got up and he walked around what was left of the pyre. He stirred the ashes with the toe of his boot and then he returned to where we sat.

'We need to report to Company HQ for reassignment,' he said.

'We need to find it first, sir,' said Hesse. I could tell he was as disturbed by this apparition as we all were.

'I don't think that should prove beyond our wit, corporal,' said the Understudy. 'Those adepts have access to the comm-net. We can use their machinery to contact Company.'

Hesse looked confused for a moment then he smiled and said, 'Yes, sir.'

All of us nodded. We were accustomed to following orders and it was reassuring to have someone who could tell us what to do again. 'I'll see to it at once, sir,' Hesse said.

'We need to set sentries for this evening,' he said. 'This sloppiness stops now.'

He kept barking out commands until we responded like

a well-drilled infantry company and only once everything was organised to his satisfaction did he settle down by what was left of our fire. He just sat there staring into the flames, unmoving as a puppet whose strings had been cut. He was still doing it as those of us not on watch drifted off to sleep.

He was in the same position when Anton woke me at dawn to relieve him on watch. I wondered what he was seeing in the ashes.

The next morning one of the techs came over and spoke to the Understudy.

'Some of our units are going to Central Command. If you wish you may accompany them in our vehicles.'

The Understudy nodded. 'Get ready to move out,' he said to us. He turned to the adept and said, 'We're ready to go whenever you are.'

'Our units will be in ready state for departure in five minutes and thirty-one seconds,' the adept said. 'You may ride in vehicle number two. Be warned – tamper with nothing on pain of extinction.'

The Understudy looked at the tech. 'You do not have the authority to execute me or my men.'

'You misunderstand me – tampering with our equipment without the requisite ritual may cause extinction without intervention on the part of any.'

The Understudy nodded. It was as clear to him as it was to me what the tech meant. He looked at Corporal Hesse. 'You heard that! Make sure every man in the unit knows the same.'

Hesse nodded and turned to me and said, 'You heard the second lieutenant. Make sure everyone knows not to touch any of the stuff. Explain to them that if the techs or the gear do not kill any would-be tinkerer then I will. And I particularly mean you, Anton!'

'When have you ever known me not to do something stupid, corporal?' Anton said with one of his most maddening grins.

'When you are asleep,' Hesse replied. 'And even then I don't doubt your dreams are full of idiocy.'

We loaded as much gear as we could carry into our backpacks. Mostly it was ammunition and food with one or two keepsakes from our fallen comrades. I stood at the back of the Atlas, unwilling to get into the recovery vehicle as the others filed past me. I glanced back at our old Baneblade, now covered in strange white technical symbols, determined to get a last look at it.

I did not move until Corporal Hesse pulled me in and then slammed the heavy metal door shut behind me. The last I saw of the ancient war machine was its gigantic shattered hull that reminded me of bones peeking through the flesh of a corpse. I can still see it now, if I close my eyes and let the memories come.

It was distinctly cold in the interior of the Atlas. We found places wherever we could. The techs had not done anything to make us more comfortable. Heavy metal packing boxes were stacked everywhere. Salvaged parts were thrown among them and we found spaces wherever we could to sit down or lie down. It was quite dark and no one had thought to put the lights on. I suppose the techs relied on their night vision goggles. Anton banged on the bulkhead and someone upfront must have understood what he meant for a glowglobe flickered on and illuminated the scene dimly.

The Understudy sat on top of one of the packing cases and stared off into the distance even though there was nothing to see. He seemed lost in thought. It was almost as if he was a machine himself and had just shut himself down while he waited. The rest of us studied the packing cases curiously. All others were wondering what was in them and I know that Anton and Hesse in particular must have been feeling a bad case of itchy fingers. However, the warnings of the techs took effect and nobody made any move to try and open one of them.

I felt confined inside the Atlas in a way that I never had in the much more restricted interior of the Baneblade's command cabin. I stood there, swaying with every lurch of the recovery vehicle, holding on to some pipework on the wall and wondering why that should be. Perhaps it was because there was nothing for me to do except stand there and because I had no control over anything that happened. I will say one thing for being the driver of a Baneblade – it gives you a tremendous sense of power having those mighty engines respond to your command.

I began to feel claustrophobic. I envied the Understudy his ability to ignore his surroundings. Sometimes, over the roar of the engines, I thought I could hear the distant sound of heavy artillery. Of course, that just made me worry about being hit by some stray shell or lascannon shot. Every time the Atlas hit an obstruction or lurched around because of uneven ground, my stomach clenched. I began to sweat. My mouth felt dry. I was more scared than I had been in the battle around the Baneblade.

I told myself I was being foolish but it did not help. Perhaps it was some sort of delayed reaction to the events of the day before. Perhaps it was simply that death was on my mind, but I began to think that I was going to die inside that small, cramped chamber, that I would never see the light of day again, that the inside of the Atlas would be my coffin.

I noticed that Anton and Ivan were looking at me strangely.

'What are you looking at?' I asked.

'I don't know but it's looking back,' Anton said. It was an old challenge from our childhoods. He smiled as he said it.

'You're looking a bit green around the gills,' Ivan said. 'Got something on your mind?'

He said it quietly so that neither the corporal nor the Understudy could hear him.

'No,' I replied. 'I'm just thinking.'

'I'm not surprised that you look sick then,' Anton said. 'You don't want to put too much strain on that tiny brain of yours.'

'At least he has a brain,' Ivan said. 'When I look in your ear I can see clean out the other side.'

We kept bickering and chatting quietly as the Atlas moved on across the ruins of the city towards the distant sound of battle.

Eventually, the Atlas came to a halt. The back doors were

thrown open and a red-cowled adept stood there. 'You must exit here,' he said. 'This is as far as we can take you.'

We were all grateful to pile out. I looked around and saw that in the direction we had come there was nothing but rubble for leagues and leagues. Around us now though were some more starscrapers. I heard the thunder of heavy weapons fire very close and the roar of vehicle engines and the monstrous tread of Titans as they walked.

The Understudy was the last out of the Atlas and he consulted his wrist chronometer. Like all officers' watches in the Seventh it had a navigator built into it. Having checked the coordinates of our present position he turned and walked towards where he knew headquarters must be. He did not say thank you or goodbye to the techs but they did not seem to notice. I waved to them as we departed and none of them waved back or said farewell.

We marched through streets blocked with the rubble. When you are on the side of a hive, you lose all awareness of the fact. It is like being on the side of a volcano. We had a view of endless starscrapers retreating into the distance, each higher than the next, like a range of mountains that might cover half the world. The towers we had seen as we approached the city were little more than tiny replicas of these enormous structures. It seemed foolish of us to have attacked this place. We were like an army of ants trying to invade a human city. The vast height of the hive was lost in clouds. In the distance was a peculiar glow, illuminating the sky, a blurred patch of light at once ominous and mystical. I wondered what it was. I had seen it before but I was no nearer to understanding.

As we got closer to the sound of battle, we were suddenly enclosed by a tide of men and armoured vehicles storming towards a distant goal. It was strange because we were the only part of that mass that did not have orders. Soldiers moved all around us, running into place, taking up position, at first hundreds and hundreds of them and then thousands and thousands.

It did not seem like we even had a goal but I had underestimated the Understudy's newfound determination and resourcefulness. We kept going until we entered the rubble-strewn ruins of a city square. There were tents here and signs pointing towards cellars and, when he asked, the Understudy was given directions to our new HQ.

Much to my surprise we were hustled through the place and into the august presence of the colonel. I don't think I had been so close to old Walrus-face as I was then. I could have reached out and plucked a bristle from the great moustache that drooped down long past his narrow chin. I could have reached out and pulled one of the scores of medals and ribbons from the chest plate of his enormously elaborate uniform.

The inside of the bunker was full of the officers of his entourage, studying maps, listening to the comm-net but mostly trying to toady to our regimental commander while they had the chance. Lho stick fug filled the air. The subdued hum of reports coming in and being responded to was audible all around.

'Ryker, good to see you,' he said, using the Understudy's real name. 'Thought we had lost you when the *Indomitable* brewed up.'

The old Understudy would have fawned at his notice, would probably have offered to lick his boots clean. The new Understudy just stared at him as if trying to decipher meaning from the words of a xenos.

If the colonel was discomfited by this, he gave no sign. I suppose he had enough lackeys grovelling around him. Or maybe he had more experience of talking to young officers just emerged from the hell of battle than I give him credit for.

'Well, it's a jolly good show that you survived. Lord High Commander Macharius himself was asking after you and Lieutenant Doblinsky and your crew. You are all to be decorated by him personally for being first through the gate.'

'Lieutenant Doblinsky is dead, sir,' said the Understudy in his rasping monotone.

'Then we'll be needing someone to take his place, won't we, Lieutenant Ryker?' He beamed as he field-promoted the Understudy on the spot. 'Of course, we will have to put in the appropriate paperwork but don't worry, it will be confirmed within a decade or so.'

Everyone laughed at his little joke except the Understudy. I think he had passed into a world without humour as well as without sanity. 'Thank you, sir,' was all he said. 'Will we be reassigned to a Baneblade?'

The colonel slapped his side as if the Understudy had made a good joke. 'Of course, as soon as the replacements are delivered. That should be right about the time the paperwork for your brevet comes back from Headquarters.'

'I see, sir,' said the Understudy, obviously baffled.

'Anyway, we'll need to keep you and your boys close at

hand until you can all be presented to Lord High Commander Macharius. It would not do to lose any more of you, would it, Lieutenant Ryker?'

I could see the strangeness of the Understudy was starting to get through even to the colonel. He was obviously not used to such a cold reaction to his bluff good humour. The officers of the colonel's entourage were beginning to stare at the Understudy a little disapprovingly. I had the feeling it would become a whole avalanche of disapproval if the colonel gave the sign. If the Understudy was aware of any of this, his mask-like features gave not the slightest sign.

'No Baneblade, sir?' was all he said.

'Keen to get back in the saddle, eh?' said the colonel. 'Can't say as I blame you! Want to take another swipe at the damned heretic, eh?'

The colonel was obviously keen to put the best possible interpretation on the Understudy's behaviour. The expressions of the faces of the entourage warmed as they realised this. Suddenly they all admired the Understudy's martial spirit.

'Yes, sir,' was all the Understudy said. I was glad for his sake that he at least had the sense to say that.

'Don't worry, you'll be spilling heretic blood soon enough. For the moment, I want you and these keen lads close by. You can guard Central until the Lord High Commander gets here.'

'He is coming here, sir?' For all the interest in the Understudy's voice, we might have been discussing the possibility of canned synthi-protein for dinner again.

'He's in the city, reviewing the troops. I am sure as soon

as he hears that the crew of the *Indomitable* survived he will want to meet them personally. He was impressed by the way you took the Gate.'

I had the sense that this had better prove to be the case or we might all find ourselves in trouble. At the moment, it looked like we were the colonel's pets. That could all so easily change.

A glance at the faces of the rest of the crew showed me they were excited. We would meet Macharius personally. We would be decorated. There would be bonuses and privileges and all manner of seven-day wonders. All we had to do was live long enough to see the day.

How difficult could that be, I asked myself? After all, we were being set to guard Central HQ.

We left the colonel's bunker and were assigned quarters in the basement of a nearby starscraper. It seemed that the colonel was serious about keeping us alive to meet Macharius because we were not given any duties at the time. In fact, we were given a pass that enabled us to wander around headquarters as we wished until summoned. I had never seen such a thing before but I was profoundly grateful for it because I had a lot on my mind.

The rest of the survivors of the *Indomitable* dumped their gear in the room and went out to explore but I lay in the chambers – a small cell really, but it had beds and some blankets and it felt like luxury after many nights sleeping inside a Baneblade or on the ground – and stared at the ceiling and thought about all the people I had known over the past ten years. An alarming number of them had died, which was only to be expected I suppose since I was a soldier of the Imperial Guard. I was in no mood to do anything but think and sleep and since the latter was preferable to the former, I soon closed my eyes and drifted off into strange and claustrophobic dreams.

I was woken by what felt like an earthquake and I thought the building was being shelled and that there was a chance that I would be buried alive. It turned out it was only Anton. He was sweating and there was a wild keenness in his eyes and he kept shaking me and saying, 'Come and see this, Leo! Come and see this!'

'You will be seeing my fist in your face,' I said, 'if you don't stop shaking me.'

'I'm serious! Come and see this! You've got to see it while it's still visible!' Something of his mad enthusiasm communicated itself to me and I rose from the bed and pulled on my boots and picked up my shotgun. 'If this is not worth it,' I said, 'you'd better start running really quickly.'

I pumped the shotgun to make my point.

'Oh – it's worth it! You'll believe it when you see it.' He led me to an elevator tube. Ivan and the New Boy were waiting in it and both of them were grinning too.

'When did you all get so friendly?' I said.

'Pay no attention to Leo,' Anton instructed the New Boy. 'He always gets depressed as soon as the battle is over.'

I might as well have been talking to myself. They just ignored me. The elevator took us all the way to the roof. I complained all the way up, and six hundred floors is a long way.

I emerged from the elevator and saw at once what had

them so excited. A strong wind had blown in from the north-west. It had cleared the sky above the hive city and from the enormous height of the skyscraper I had a clear view all the way to the horizon. Ahead of me lay the sides of the hive, endless lava-strewn slopes rising gigantically into the distance. Here and there more giant towers protruded from the sides. Enormous fortified roads snaked across the surface. Huge gates disappeared into the interior of the hive. It was an awesome sight, like looking at the sides of a man-made mountain. It was not that that had got their attention though. Tremendous as it was, the city seemed irrelevant compared to the sight of the Angel of Fire.

It drew your eye as if by magic. You could not help but stare at it. It looked like an enormously tall androgyne, possibly five hundred times the size of a normal man. It stood atop the spire of a gigantic building. It was armoured and it held a glowing sword in its hands but that was not what held your attention either. Spreading out from its shoulders were two enormous fiery wings, each bigger than the statue itself. This was the source of the glow that had been visible on the horizon for so long.

It was monstrous and awe-inspiring and it made you feel completely and utterly insignificant. I later learned that those wings of fire were created by venting industrial gas through the metal core of the statue. There was something about the atmospheric conditions or possibly the way the gas was emitted that made the flames spread in that way. I did not know that then and I did not care. I was astonished by the mere sight of the thing. Suddenly it became clear to me why the locals all thought that the Angel of Fire stood at the right hand of the Emperor. You would have too if you spent all of your life under the burning gaze of that enormous metal angel.

'Was it worth it?' Anton asked. I forgot even to pump the shotgun. I simply nodded and did not say anything. Ivan was studying the Angel through his magnoculars. The expression on his ruined face was impossible to read but you could see from the rapt tension of his stance that he was entranced, and could not tear his gaze away. There was a compulsion about the statue and I began to suspect that more than engineering and architecture was involved in this.

We had returned to the foot of the tower when sirens started to blow all around us. The racket was deafening. The horns blew three blasts and then stopped. We all looked at each other not quite understanding what was going on. We heard the sound of cheering all around us so I figured it could not be all bad. Maybe Macharius had arrived and was being greeted with suitable enthusiasm by the troops.

As we entered our chambers I saw the Understudy had returned. 'What is going on, sir?' I asked.

He looked at me with those strange eyes of his and said, 'The heretics have surrendered. General Sejanus just announced it over the comm-net.'

We all looked at each other incredulously. 'It looks like this war is over,' said the New Boy with the overconfidence of the young.

'We'll see about that,' I muttered but no one seemed to share my misgivings. They were all too busy laughing and slapping each other on the back. All except the Understudy, that is. He glanced around with empty eyes, as if he did not quite understand what was going on.

Corrobrative Evidence Cross-Reference 42K9-Cross-Reference J6. Under seal.

Extract from Record of Deaths Battle Group Sejanus Karsk IV
Campaign 05.07.40012
Quota Record Form 6a
  Approved: Varisov L, Colonel 7th Belial
  Compiled: Parzival K, Captain 7th Belial
Forwarded to Battlegroup HQ, Karsk V Orbital

Section 124: Record of Deaths in Combat
  Site: Irongrad.

Doblinsky M, Lt Commanding Imperial Baneblade
Indomitable.
  Cause of Death: Enemy Action.
  Notes: Recommended for Order of Merit, Gates of Irongrad,
Approved.

Bazilkov, O, Private, Engineer, Imperial Baneblade
Indomitable.
  Cause of Death: Enemy Action.
  Notes: Recommended for Order of Merit, Gates of Irongrad,
Approved Pending Investigation.

Korzakov, P, Private, Engineer, Imperial Baneblade
Indomitable.
  Cause of Death: Enemy Action.
  Notes: Recommended for Order of Merit, Gates of Irongrad,
Approved.

Krakov, V, Private, Engineer, Imperial Baneblade
Indomitable.
  Cause of Death: Enemy Action.
  Notes: Recommended for Order of Merit, Gates of Irongrad,
Pending.

Manzurian, K, Private, Gunner, Imperial Baneblade
Indomitable.
  Cause of Death: Enemy Action.
  Notes: Recommended for Order of Merit, Gates of Irongrad,
Pending.

Manzurian L, Private, Gunner, Imperial Baneblade
Indomitable.
  Cause of Death: Unknown. MIA.
  Notes: Recommended for Order of Merit, Gates of Irongrad,
Pending.

Zenikov, I, Private, Gunner, Imperial Baneblade *Indomitable*.
  Cause of Death: Enemy Action.
  Notes: Recommended for Order of Merit, Gates of Irongrad,
Denied.

**Document under seal. Extract From the Decrypted
Personal Files of Inquisitor Hyronimus Drake.**

  **Possible evidence of duplicity on the part of former
High Inquisitor Drake.**

  **Cross-reference to Exhibit 107D-21H
(Report to High Inquisitor Toll).**

Walk in the Emperor's Light.

I have personally put several of the heretic commanders to the
question. Under extreme duress and in the presence of sanctioned
psykers they have revealed much. As always with heretics, it is difficult to sift through their deluded rantings and extract the core of
truth, if any truth there ever be. The heretics of Karsk System have
fallen into many of the Ten Great Errors. They believe themselves
to be the sole possessors of cosmic truth and the true bearers of the
Emperor's Word. They believe us to be deluded invaders even in the
face of their demonstrable error. They are prepared to die in the
service of the false beliefs they hold.

Most of their commanders seem sincerely to believe, as is always
the case, and refused to recant even under instructive surgery. The

capacity to hold to such faith is admirable and I believe will prove most worthy once this world is re-educated into the Faith.

We have so far failed to take one of the so-called Sons of the Sacred Flame alive. When on the verge of capture they spontaneously combust, often taking those sent to bring them to the question with them into death. They have demonstrated psychic powers of alarming strength. I am reminded of many other heretics I have encountered who were proven to have drawn their power from daemonic sources. So far there is no proof that the Sons of the Sacred Flame draw energy from the Enemies of Mankind but I fear it will only be a matter of time before this is shown to be the case.

In the meantime, I have placed a request at the highest level that sufficient resources be allocated to the capture of a ranking member of this cult so that we may get to the truth of the matter. I am also ensuring that agents of the highest degree of competence and discretion are being infiltrated into position in the locality.

En masse we marched in triumph through a great arched gateway, flanked by two fire-winged angels fifty times as tall as a man, and passed into the depths of Hive Irongrad. Behind me stretched out long lines of grey-uniformed soldiers. Up ahead massive tanks roared like victorious beasts. In our hundreds of thousands we strode beneath banners that showed our regiment, our unit and our triumphs on a thousand different worlds. The High Command wanted no one to be in any doubt that the legions of the Emperor had returned to reclaim this world in His name.

I felt odd, marching along behind the tanks instead of driving the *Indomitable*. It had been a long time since I walked in parade file down the ramp-streets of a hive. Ahead of me a long line of machines receded into the distance. Overhead the lights of the level roof glittered like low-hanging stars.

Beside me were Hesse and Anton and Ivan and the others, their weapons slung over their shoulders, their boots polished and a swagger in their stride.

For the first time since we set foot on this benighted world I began to feel at home. The air had the recycled taste of a hive interior. It was different from that of Belial Masterforge but it had something of the same tang, of having been breathed a billion, billion times. There was the faint chemical undercurrent of the purification filters and the slightly rotten under-taste that I came to associate with Irongrad. It was warmer in this hive than it was in Belial Masterforge and the people were not so over-dressed. If the life-support systems broke down their problem was not going to be freezing and clearly they all knew this.

The hive was different in many other ways. The hab-towers were massive columns which supported the roofs that were the floors of the levels above. All of them were covered in titanic copper pipes through which ran gas and hot water and sewage and effluent. The sides of each tower vented flames as if they were engaged in some vast industrial process that was also a sacred rite. Each of the vents was moulded to resemble the Angel of Fire. It looked like a legion of rebel angels were poised for fire-winged flight across the city.

Between the hab-towers were expansive plazas and in every plaza was a fountain of fire. Emerging from their flames was a metal replica of the great statue of the Angel of Fire. Near every fountain was one of those sinister cages. Some were massive enough to hold hundreds of chained victims, some so small they seemed designed to hold children or dwarfs.

Time and again as we made our way down into the belly of the hive I saw those ornate cages we had first seen in the desert with their x-frames and those devilish face-masks. No matter how crowded the streets were, there was always a clear space around them. It did not take a lot of imagination to work out why. Some of them were held on winches over the streets while below them flames vented from the pipes in the building sides.

Massive crowds watched us as we progressed downwards. The streets were full of folk looking down at us from every window and balcony. The people did not cheer but they did not seem hostile either. They were not sullen. They were curious. We were their world's new masters. I suspected we could not have been much worse than their previous ones if we had been cannibal orks. The population had been so beaten down, so accustomed to the lash that they expected it from us and they did not even resent it.

The Irongradders seemed like typical hive dwellers: pasty-faced, undernourished, weary-looking from long, long hours of work. They could have been dropped here right from my old home-world. It made me feel oddly nostalgic and I could tell the others felt the same way.

Overhead glow-globes hovered. We passed flickering signs that exhorted us to worship the Angel and believe in his might. Our tech-priests had not got round to their ritual re-invocation yet. I found the images of the flame-winged angel and his burning-headed priesthood disturbing to say the least. I thought of the strange powers they had displayed and it seemed unlikely to me that there was anything holy about them. The Angel inspired awe and fear in me in about equal parts. The priests simply inspired fear and a desire to do murder if I got the chance. There must be many of them still out there and I very much doubted that they would give up the fight, whatever the planetary governor and the nobles of his court said.

Eventually, the long march ended, deep within the hive. We were confronted with our new home, billeted in factorum hab-units requisitioned by our Commissariat. The rooms within the massive buildings were huge and high-ceilinged and did not seem full even with a company of soldiers camped out in them. There were sinister fire-winged angels everywhere, astride the cornice of every building, worked in the frescoes of every ceiling. It was the sort of artwork, mass-produced and replicated in industrial scale, that only hive worlds can manage. In every alcove, on every desk, glaring down from every wall there were representations of the focus of the local religion. Someone had even used a small metal statue to prop open the door to the chamber in which we were to sleep.

'Could be worse,' Anton said as we entered and surveyed the huge hall with its hundreds of beds each with a locker beside it. I knew what he was thinking. It reminded him of the guild dormitories back on Belial. Hundreds of men swarmed around the place, lying on beds, stowing their gear, making a claim to some space. I recognised none of them. They were all like us, survivors of broken units, waiting to be reassigned or reformed into new companies. They might even be our new company for all I knew.

How many times had I done this, I wondered?

How many times had I dumped my gear in a new room

or new tent or new barracks' locker, looked around at Ivan and Anton and told them that if they touched my gear they were dead? How many times had I watched Anton grin his idiot grin and Ivan make that chirruping whistle that shows he thinks I am talking nonsense again? Too many times to count or remember, I suspect.

It's part of a soldier's life – to make camp constantly and move on again, to leave rooms and buildings and cities and worlds in their wake. To leave behind buried friends and lost loves as well. To be a soldier in the 41st millennium is to be a small atom of life, constantly in motion, never truly at rest anywhere until they burn your body or put you in the ground.

'They say the locals call this place the City of the Angel,' Anton said. He had tossed his pack on the floor and was busy scouring through it for his prop-nov. The rest of his gear joined a growing untidy pile on the floor. Tunic lay on shirt. His hip flask clinked when he tossed it beside his boots and badges.

'I wonder why that is?' I said sourly.

Ivan whistled a few descending notes. 'Could that be because there is a huge bloody iron angel looming over the whole place and a statue of it on every street corner?' He had stowed his gear under his bed and just sat there, taking a slug from his hip-flask. I wondered how much there was left in it. Not much at the rate he went through it and we would not be getting any more cooling fluid that would convert to rot-gut alcohol any time soon.

Anton held up a map and unfolded it, as if he might find his prop-nov within. I recognised it, soiled as it was. It was an old Imperial Survey map of Zone Three on Jurasik Prime. We had left a trail of dead heretics strewn across that place. Some of the stains on the map came from their blood. A sudden vivid image of green jungles and tropical islands came back to me. I remembered a pillbox built into cliffs and the *Indomitable* racing through waves all guns blazing.

'I didn't lend you my book, did I, Leo?' Anton asked.

'Why the hell would I want your bloody prop-nov?' I said. 'I've read it almost as many times as you.'

That strictly speaking was not true. Anton must have read that piece of Imperial propaganda a thousand times or more, almost as many times as he had read *The Imperial Infantryman's Uplifting Primer*. He had been reading it at least once a week since we had started work in the factorum in Belial when we were twelve. I always remember him, hunched over it, tracing the line with his finger, his lips moving as he spelled out the words even though anyone else would have known them by heart.

'Ivan?' he asked.

'You know I hate the bloody thing!'

'All the more reason for you to take it and destroy it,' said Anton.

'Now you are putting ideas in my head.'

'Don't even think about it.'

'You try the external pocket in your pack?' I asked.

'Of course I did. You think I am an idiot or something?'

'You already know the answer to that.' I reached down and lifted the pack up out of the growing pile of unwashed clothing and the gee-gaws Anton had acquired over the years of campaigning. I flicked open the seal on the right tab pocket where Anton always kept the book, reached in and pulled it out.

'You just put it there,' he said petulantly.

'Yeah – I used my psyker powers to do that. Maybe I'll use them to combust the book now.'

'Don't you dare!' He stuck out a long bony hand. Behind him Ivan nodded his head. I tossed the book over Anton's head to him.

'Give me that, you bastard,' Anton shouted, turning to try and grab it out of Ivan's hand. Ivan tossed it to the New Boy.

'You'll hand that over right now, if you know what's good for you, New Boy,' Anton said. The New Boy looked abashed and hung his head down. He humbly held the book out and then when Anton reached for it, he tossed it to me.

Anton howled and dived at me. I just had time to toss the book away before he grappled me, his hand going for my throat. I noticed the others had gone oddly quiet and when I looked over Anton's shoulder I could see why. The Understudy was standing there. He had caught the book as he entered the chamber without knocking.

Anton turned to see what I was looking at and his face went white. We saluted, ludicrous as that must have looked from our current position.

The Understudy said, 'You are to report to the parade ground at nine hundred Imperial. You will be presented to Lord High Commander Macharius for decoration.'

He turned the book over in his hand as if inspecting some xenos relic then he put it down on the bed and said, 'Carry on.'

Then he left. After that, no one was in the mood for brawling.

I stood before the assembled regiments in the great square outside our new barracks. They were illuminated by the dancing flames of the central fire fountain, drawn up in massed ranks before their vehicles, dressed in their best uniforms, all scrubbed and polished for the occasion. All it would have taken was one well-placed artillery shell and a whole regiment could have been wiped out, leaving their tanks for the enemy to take.

Our own regiment stood to the fore. The Seventh Belial had been first into Irongrad and had held the factorum zone in the teeth of a massive rebel counter-attack. We had been the spearhead of the crusade and had been tested and not broken. Of course, there were a damn sight fewer of us than there used to be but what did that matter to Command. We could always be replaced. There is no resource more common in the universe than the flesh of human soldiers.

All of us were waiting for Macharius. It seemed like the whole galaxy was back then. There was an air of anticipation about the ceremony that I had never experienced before. I stood to the left of the podium raised between the chassis of two Baneblades and I sensed it. It was as if every soldier awaited the arrival of a prophet, of someone who would transform their lives with his words. Only the Understudy did not seem touched by the atmosphere. Not even the revivalist feel of that great crowd could get through to the surface of whatever desolate world it was in which he walked.

A huge roar announced Macharius's arrival. The gleaming oval of an aircar appeared in the sky overhead. It was the governor's own vehicle, not military but a gorgeous gold and gem-encrusted aerial carbuncle. Under other circumstances, it would have seemed impossibly gaudy compared to the grim durasteel tanks lined up below it, but the idea that Macharius was within it transformed all that. The aircar seemed entirely appropriate for a conqueror of worlds. Just the sight of it brought cheers from the assembled troops.

The golden vehicle descended until it hovered over the platform. A door in its side opened and a long stairway extruded itself. Moments later Macharius strode regally down it, surrounded by his entourage. From my place beside the platform I got a clear view of him in profile. As ever, he looked like a mortal god. There was a radiance about him that had nothing to do with the personal body-shield he was wearing. He simply eclipsed all of those around him, even formidable men like Inquisitor Drake and squat, muscular General Sejanus. Tech-priests followed his every move with their monitoring devices. Technical cherubim hovered observantly over them. As ever the occasion was to be recorded and broadcast to the armies.

Macharius spread his arms wide in majestic greeting and then his imperial progress took him out of my sight. He spoke to the crowd briefly, his voice amplified by ancient technological artifice, his words relayed to our forces across the face of the planet and all the worlds of the system by the arcane science of the Adeptus Mechanicus.

I have seen the recordings of it since, the way he took the acclamation of the army as nothing more than his due and yet managed to make you feel as if it was deserved and not mere arrogance. There was something about Macharius then that made you think you were in the presence of something more than mortal. He had that quality that Space Marines have, of making you feel insignificant, but unlike them, there was no apartness. He was human, and he regarded you as human and being in his presence raised you up to the same exalted plane on which he lived.

Eventually the time came for us to be ushered into that imperial presence. He smiled as he saw us. You can see it in the recordings. He looks sincerely pleased and maybe he was. You can see all the surviving crew of the *Indomitable* as he pins the First-In medals on our chests. We all look much smaller than him and faintly embarrassed by the attention. All of us except the Understudy – he looks inhumanly distant.

Macharius praised us and pinned the decorations on our tunics. I remember standing close to him as he did so and thinking how tall he was and how young he looked. He radiated power and good health and a certain reserved good fellowship. When he looked at you, you felt the full power of his attention fall on you. When he spoke, he seemed genuinely interested in what you had to say, even if you only stuttered out your words as Anton did. He placed his hand on your shoulder in a comradely fashion and then moved on.

What I remember most about him is his sense of presence. Macharius was truly there. It was as if he was a solid thing and everything else around him was a shadow. Damn, I could spend the rest of my life trying to find the words to describe that but in the end all descriptions would be irrelevant. They could never give you the sense of the sheer primordial power of the man.

I know he talked to me and to this day I cannot remember what he said or what I said in return except in the vaguest of ways. I know he praised my bravery and I thanked him for it, and that he meant it and I meant it, which given how cynical I am, is a tribute to the man's charisma.

At the end of the ceremony we were cheered by the assembled troops while Macharius watched and applauded himself. He got back into the governor's air-chariot and flew away and I watched him go thinking that was the last time I would ever speak to him.

Of course, I was wrong.

I crouched behind the wreck of an autocar while a bunch of maniacal gangers took pot-shots at us with their home-made pistols. A slug ricocheted off the hood of the vehicle and bounced through a shop window, shattering the glass.

'Just like the old neighbourhood on a feast-day night,' Anton said, rising and snapping off a shot with his lasgun. Somebody screamed. Anton dropped back into place and grinned.

'Makes me nostalgic,' Ivan said and whistled through his iron teeth. I could tell he was thinking of taking a few shots himself or maybe even charging. He had always been fond of a brawl in the old days.

I stuck my head up and gazed around the street. There were still plenty of armed youngsters there, high on blaze and full of fight. They lurked behind overturned autocars and inside burned-out ground transporters. The battle to take Irongrad might have been over but it's always a war inside a hive. In this neighbourhood it had probably been war since the hab-blocks went up.

Many of the local gangers had taken the overthrow of the Sons of the Flame as a signal to indulge in an orgy of looting and rape and general score-settling. The Fire worshippers must have been feared indeed to have kept so tight a lid on the seething cauldron of violence that was Irongrad. We had been sent out into the street with the rest of our new company to restore some order.

Overhead iron angels looked down from the high spots that their wings of fire had carried them to. Ordinary citizens had dived for cover in doorways, behind trash cans, in the sumps that led down to the sewers. A ganger shouted abuse in his incomprehensible dialect and took another shot.

Once we had been decorated and the colonel had had his chance to strut in front of Macharius we were returned to duty. Our medals had not brought us any special privileges. We were assigned to a new scrub company made up of a motley assortment of soldiers – crews who had lost their vehicles, squads who were the only survivors of their companies, officers who had been wounded when the last big push came and had missed the chance to die in glorious battle when the heretics overran us. I could see some of the others huddled down in a doorway, getting ready to move up the street. One of them signalled that he wanted covering fire. I raised my hand in acknowledgement and got ready to give it to him.

'What in the name of the Emperor...' Anton said.

I followed his gaze and saw what had him so upset. The Understudy was walking up the street. He had his pistol held in his hand but it was by his side and he was not aiming at anything. Bullets ricocheted all around him, kicking up small clouds of dust in the street. He walked through them as if they were raindrops dropping from the sky on Jurasik. It was as if he did not believe he could be hit and somehow his faith created a force field around him that prevented that from happening. His face was pale. His eyes were focused on the distance. A bullet knocked off his cap and he bent down to pick it up and adjusted it on his head as if the wind had blown it off. I swear another bullet passed through the air where his face had just been.

It did provoke some action though. He stood up, pointed his pistol and snapped off a shot. I heard a scream from the direction he was firing in. He just kept walking forwards, firing as he went, and was occasionally rewarded with another scream. I looked at Ivan. Ivan looked at me. We were equally bemused. Anton grinned and said, 'What the hell!' He stood up and fired his lasgun. The bolt passed over the Understudy's shoulder and struck another ganger. Ivan and I sprang to our feet and raced forwards. The rest of the squad did the same. It seemed like the Understudy was getting all the attention anyway. They sent a hail of las-bolts pounding into the gangers and mowed a few down. Some of the others broke away and ran.

I had the shotgun in my hand but I couldn't use it because the Understudy was in front of me. That did not stop Ivan from shooting. I think he was doing it more to keep the gangers pinned down than because he expected to hit anything. All three of us, the Understudy, Ivan and me, reached the gangers at the same time. I pushed my combat shotgun forwards and pulled the trigger and the spray from the pellet cartridge took out another three of them. The Understudy shot one and Ivan simply pointed his lasgun and said, 'Surrender!'

The gangers dropped their guns. I don't know what they found more frightening: the look on the Understudy's face or the look of Ivan's metal jaws. To tell the truth, there was little to choose between the two in terms of their frightfulness.

The Understudy studied the gangers with no more animosity than if they had been squabbling children. I cannot say that Ivan and Anton and myself were particularly gentle with them. I've never really cared for people who shoot at me.

The gangers were hauled off for either execution or forced conscription and we returned to patrolling the streets and keeping our eyes open for devotees of the Angel of Fire.

It was another typical day on the streets of Irongrad. I remember it only because it was that night we met the girls.

We sat in the cellar of the Angel's Blessing. I studied the room from my seat in the corner. It was small, it was dark and it was full of fug from lho sticks and glittersmoke. Small gas-lights guarded by crystal bowls threw flickering light out into the gloom. Behind the bar, a shaven-headed local dispensed rotgut alcohol from bottles that inevitably displayed on the label some scene from the career of the

Angel of Fire or one of his many associated saints, and the name of the factorum that produced it.

I looked across the table at Anton and Ivan and the New Boy. They all had glasses in front of them. Ivan had an open bottle which he was reserving for his own exclusive use. The rest of us went the more conventional route and had a waitress bring us drinks.

'Well this is cosy,' said Anton. Locals were coming down the narrow stairs, taking in the clientele at a glance and mostly leaving. At least the men were. Some of the local girls stayed. It was the usual pattern. You see it on a thousand worlds.

There were plenty of men from our unit there. Some wore the local trinkets, little metal angel pins or chokers. Others had more sinister souvenirs, numbers made up of small skulls inked on arms and necks and foreheads with the name of Irongrad underneath them. The tattoos were an old regimental way of indicating how many people they had killed in that battle. Some of those were lies, some of them were boasts and some of them were understatements. I thought it was premature. I was not entirely certain that the battle for the city was really over. The gangs were still fighting in the streets. There was unrest in many of the habzones and no one really knew what had happened to the cultists who had caused so much trouble.

'Did you see the Understudy today?' the New Boy asked. 'He walked through the hail of fire as if he never even noticed it.'

'Maybe he didn't,' I said.

'I can't believe it's the same man I had to carry out of the cockpit of Number Ten.' How easily he called it Number

Ten, I thought. It was almost as if he had spent ten years in the tank the same as me, and not the few days he had. I felt like telling him you had to earn the right to use the nickname but what was the point.

'He's gone daft,' said Anton.

'You know it's pretty bad when Anton calls you daft,' said Ivan.

'I am serious,' said Anton. 'Come on, we've all seen it. Sometimes men snap. Something in their brain breaks and it changes them. Remember Yuri after we pulled him out of the bunker on Jurasik? Kept gibbering that the green men were all around and coming to get him.'

'Well, we had been fighting orks,' I said. 'So he was probably right.'

'We had killed them all. He was seeing bloody invisible orks.'

'You can't see invisible things,' Ivan pointed out. 'That's what being invisible is all about.'

'You know what I mean. He was mad, gibbering mad.'

'The Understudy is not like that,' I said.

'I know but it's a similar thing. Sometimes men see something and their minds break.'

'You're safe then,' said Ivan. 'You don't have a mind.'

'Ha bloody ha!'

The New Boy shuddered and took a swig of his greenish-coloured drink. 'I think there are things here that might do that to a man, if he stuck around long enough.'

He was starting to get round to it now, the thing that was really on his mind. 'What do you mean?' I asked, to give him a reason to go on talking.

'I mean what are all those cages about?'

'They are for putting people to death,' I said.

'Who the hell puts anyone to death that way?'

'Does it matter? People die whatever.'

'Yeah but...'

'We use firing squads,' I said. 'They use cages.'

'It's not the same,' the New Boy said.

He was right of course, but there was drink in my belly and I was feeling contrary. I usually do once I've had a few. 'Isn't it?'

'You know it's not, Leo,' said Ivan. 'One way is quick and clean, the other is slow and cruel.'

'And yeah, the Imperium is never slow or cruel,' I said.

'Not this way.'

'Ivan's right, Leo,' Anton said. 'There's something rotten about killing people that way, something strange. It's the work of those priests.'

'You may be right,' I said.

'You know I am. It has the stink of heresy to it.'

The debate might have taken a downright theological turn but we were interrupted.

Corporal Hesse came in. His uniform was clean. His boots were polished. His small moustache was well-trimmed. He had a girl under each arm. He did not look like much, did the corporal, but he was always a hit with the ladies. He looked kind and jolly and he was always generous to them so I suppose it was understandable. His presence dispelled the last of the gloom hanging over the table even though all he did was sweep past us, slap some of the local scrip on the table and say loudly, 'Have a farewell drink for old Number

Ten on me.' Then he was gone. It was like a personal ritual he had to perform and we all have some of those.

'Thanks, corporal,' I said to his departing back. 'I don't mind if I do.'

Anton nudged me in the ribs with an elbow. I glanced up to see what he was looking at. A group of three pretty young women had entered.

'Just what I need to take my mind off your gloomy chatter,' he said. He rose and went to introduce himself. He spoke for a while and returned to our table, leading a small blonde girl by the arm. 'This is Katrina,' he said.

He indicated a tall, dark girl. 'This is Lutzka and this is Yanis.' The third was a plump and pretty girl. 'They are nurses at the Hospice of Saint…?'

'Saint Oberon,' said Katrina. 'It's the best hospice in the hive. All of the nobles go there for treatment.' She seemed very proud of that.

'I'm sure they do,' said Anton smoothing his hair. 'And I'm sure you give them the treatment they deserve.'

Ivan dragged over some chairs for them with a courtliness you would not have believed possible and they sat down. Katrina was next to Anton. Lutzka was next to Ivan and Yanis was next to the New Boy. I was stranded in my corner, next to none of the girls. Not that I cared enough to move anyway. I was in a foul and contrary mood.

They settled down to chat and smooch and I settled down to drink. Maybe I should have chatted to one of the girls. If I had my life would have been much different. I would probably not have fallen in with Anna for one thing. I had a few more drinks and then I staggered back to the barracks. We had a patrol in the morning. The others did not seem to mind. Their attention was all on the women.

It was crowded in the Chimera. I didn't care. I was in the turret, watching the streets go by. On these, the deeper levels of the hive, it was always the same. The buildings towered over us, festooned with metal seraphim. A titanic angel glared down on us from gigantic murals set in the roof, details picked out by wandering spotlights on the hab-tops. Trash had piled up like snow drifts along the side of the buildings, where maintenance tubes had broken down and services were impaired. Rats the size of a man's head watched us with glittering, malign eyes and chittered to each other in the language of their kind.

There had been an ambush. One of our patrols had been set upon by hordes of the heretics. They had called in for help. We had been sent in response.

Ivan held the controls of the heavy bolter and studied the streets. If he was hungover you couldn't tell. He was looking for targets. All we could see were people garbed in the light robes so common among the workers here. We were getting closer to the ambush site though. You could tell from the smell of burning flesh.

The fight had come to a climax in one of those plazas that centred around a burning cage. Our boys had made a good show of it. They had left hundreds of dead behind them as they went. Corpses still littered the ground despite the hordes of collectors who had gathered to strip the bodies and drag them away to the gigantic crematorium. Bounties were still paid for that. It was one of the local laws that Macharius had let stand.

A few of the dead might have been innocent bystanders. I doubted it. In my experience, factorum workers are rarely so heavily armed.

We were not the first on the spot. A company had already deployed in the square. I saw officers gesturing and shouting orders. I saw a ratling sniper perched on top of a winged angel statue and surveying the crowd of corpse collectors through the scope of his high-powered rifle.

The Chimera crunched bodies under its treads until a commissar gave the signal to halt. We stopped. The squad deployed. I clambered out of the turret and dropped into place beside Anton, my shotgun at the ready. Ivan stayed in the turret, hands still on the gun. I felt reassured to have him there. If trouble broke out, he knew how to handle such a weapon.

The commissar strode up to us. He was one of the icy-faced types. 'Secure the perimeter, Lieutenant Ryker,' he said. His voice was beautiful and mellow like that of an avuncular priest. It was surprising that such a man had such a voice.

'Sir,' said the Understudy. He began to rasp out the orders and we responded, moving to the edge of the plaza, taking cover behind burned-out cars, plascrete walls and podiums of statues. Anyone could see that it was too late, that the fighting was over, but no one was taking any chances. If an angry torch-bearing mob came back this way they would find themselves cut down in a hail of las-fire.

I found myself sheltering behind a plascrete bench with

Corporal Hesse and the New Boy. Hesse did not look so jolly this morning. He was all business, just like the lasgun he held ready in his hand.

'You see what they did back there?' he asked, when he was sure that a horde of fanatics were not about to erupt from the side alleys and assault us at just this moment.

I had and I had been trying not to think about it. Around the fire fountain were half-burned bodies. More had been stuffed into a cage and set alight. I did not doubt for a moment they had been our boys and they had been alive at the time. It could not have been a nice way to go.

'I don't think I want to be taken alive by these heretics,' said the New Boy. He was not being flippant.

'Best way to do that is shoot them with a lasgun,' said Hesse. 'See how they like being burned.'

'I saw some of those priests back at the factorum,' said the New Boy. 'Las-fire did not even slow them down. It just made them stronger, like they fed on it.'

Hesse smiled grimly. 'Then don't shoot the priests, shoot the people with them. Leave the local holy men to Lemuel here. See if they like shotgun cartridges as much as they like las-bolts.'

I was not at all sure that I appreciated Hesse volunteering me for priest-killing duty but what he said made a certain amount of sense.

'Alternatively you could always try a grenade,' I said.

'I don't care if you piss on the bastards to put out their burning heads, you see one of those psykers, you put him down, however you have to.' The corporal sounded angry, which was understandable given the circumstances. I was not in the best of moods myself. We stared at the plaza as if we expected a horde of fire-worshipping heretics to manifest at any moment. They kept stubbornly away.

We waited and waited but the heretics did not return to do any more burning. Clearly odds of less than a hundred to one did not suit them. Eventually the officers and the commissar and the people who seemed to be consulting with them decided they had seen enough. We were ordered back to the vehicles and headed back to base.

The next day we stood on the walls and watched the army depart. Endless lines of massive battle-tanks roared off in advance of troop carriers. Valkyries swarmed in the air over them. Titans strode gigantically through the red murk of the dawn. The air vibrated with the passage of the army. Our words seemed to resonate inside our chests when we spoke.

'We should be going with them,' said Anton. 'We should be in Number Ten.'

I wasn't going to argue with him. If there was any justice in the galaxy we would have been out there in the *Indomitable*. The lieutenant would have been leading us and Oily and Henrik would have been with us. Instead we were with all the other troops of our hastily assembled company, standing guard on the walls of Irongrad, watching the army leave to go with Macharius to new conquests and victories. Somewhere in the distance were new hives, new heretic armies, new enemies. I told myself I should be glad that I was here, out of the way of danger, but I was not. I was disappointed.

'It'll be years before we get another Baneblade,' said Ivan gloomily. 'If ever we do.'

'I've dreamed of being a tank driver,' said the New Boy. 'Now I am with the bloody footsloggers.'

'Life's not fair,' I said. 'You'll get used to it.'

'Like you have?'

'Now you are just being disrespectful.'

'They'll get all the action,' Anton said. His gaze followed the huge dust plumes kicked up by the army wistfully.

'I am sure the locals will come up with something to keep us busy,' I said. I was thinking about the increasing levels of violence on the streets and the rumours we had heard about the priesthood of the Angel of Fire becoming more active.

I shielded my eyes and kept staring out over the red-and-orange wastes. There were still some burned-out tanks out there from the days of our assault. The tech-adepts had not managed to salvage everything. It was pointless trying to count all the armoured vehicles down there but that did not stop me trying. I reached several dozen, a small fraction of the total, when Anton distracted me with one of his idiot questions. 'Hey, Leo, what are the chances of us getting another Baneblade?'

'About the same as you learning to think,' I said.

'I am serious,' he said.

'So am I,' I said.

'No, seriously, what do you think?'

'I think we'll all be dead of old age by the time we get reassigned. You know how the Munitorum works. If we're lucky we won't be reassigned to Valkyries.'

'I quite fancy being a pilot,' said Anton.

'You have any training for it?' I asked.

'How difficult can it be?'

'If it wasn't too difficult for you, the Munitorum would never assign you to it,' said Ivan.

'Listen to the man, Anton,' I said. 'He understands military bureaucracy.'

'I could learn,' said Anton, never one to let the idiocy of a statement discourage him from making it. I watched Titans lope out now, the smaller Warhounds racing ahead as if to get to grips with the enemy all the sooner. The giant Reavers followed in their wake, cautious enough on the surface of a world that manufactured Shadowswords.

Despite myself I felt something like pride swell within me. It was an awesome force and it was only a small part of the army the Imperium was bringing to bear on this part of the universe. I felt like I was watching a metal tide that could cover an entire planet and crush all resistance and I was a small part of it. I looked at all the others and I think they felt the same.

'How far do you think they are going?' the New Boy asked.

'To the edge of the galaxy,' I said.

The words had the ring of prophecy.

'I am starting to hate this place,' Anton said, conversationally. He held his lasrifle casually, in the crook of his arm, but I could tell he was ready to use it at the slightest provocation. His helmet was tilted back. His rebreather was slung round his neck. He rubbed his scar with his long fingers as he looked out into the crowds. The people watched us as we swept the streets on patrol. They did not look hostile. They did not look friendly. They just looked. We kept moving, bringing up the rear of the foot patrol. We were just there to be seen.

'Why is that?' I asked. I was not really interested but sometimes Anton's inane chatter could provide distraction. I already thought I knew what he was going to say.

In the interval since the bulk of the army departed, things became ominously quiet in Irongrad. There was something odd going on beneath the surface though. Whenever I scanned the faces of that huge crowd I felt as if they were waiting for something, a sign perhaps, from us or from the Angel who had ruled their world for so long. I could not help but feel that concealed within those oceans of flesh were people who meant us ill.

Everywhere we went the gaze of the Angel looked down on us. Perched on the side of every hab-tower those metal-bodied seraphim stood ready to take flight on wings of fire. On every ceiling, murals showed its androgynous form. Every day we walked the streets of the hab-zones, just to show the fact that we were there, to remind the natives that a new order had come. Our grey uniforms looked drab and alien among the bright, ruddy colours favoured by the locals. In every square the fountains of fire still burned. Our tech teams had started to take away the sacrificial cages. Many a day I stood watch over them as the great machines demolished them and reclaimed the metal. I studied the faces in the crowd around me. I looked down the vast avenue of hab-blocks stretching to the horizon wall of the hive. Anton surprised me.

'It looks like home in some ways, but it's not.'

'It does not look like Belial,' I said. 'It looks nothing like Belial.'

'It's a hive,' he said.

'And that's it,' I said. I looked around and saw no similarity. Belial was grim and grey and all around had been the signs of the heaviest of heavy industry. Pollutant smog had filled the streets and snaked below the level bridges like rivers of mist. The air temperature had been lower and the humidity far greater.

Everything had carried the signs of the different guilds and factories. Here, there was an awful uniformity about everything. The Cult of the Angel of Fire had strangled everything else, like a weed choking the life out of normal plants in an overgrown garden. Everything bore its stamp. All of the people bore its symbol. Metal angels hung from chains around every neck. There were more of those bloody angels than there were of any other Imperial ikons, including our own.

'I hate those cages,' Anton said. 'Whoever thought of putting people to death that way was a madman.'

'If you are being put to death, what does it matter how you die?' I asked.

'If you were going to greet the Emperor which would you prefer – a bolter shell through the head, quick and clean, or being burned alive inside a brewed-up Leman Russ?'

'Neither,' I said. 'I plan on living till I am eighty and collecting a pension.'

'And I planned on becoming a Space Marine,' Anton said. 'Let's see how those things work out for both of us…'

'Hush, the pair of you,' said Ivan. 'Something's up.'

We had just entered a large square. All around were stalls where vendors sold hot food and cold metal religious trash, amulets and ikons of the Angel. A small group of people stared at us resentfully. They had been handing out pamphlets whose covers, inevitably, featured pictures of the Angel of Fire standing over the corpses of grey-uniformed off-world invaders.

Most people watched us blandly but some of the pamphleteers looked at us with a ferocious hate. Once a few of them picked up stones and bits of trash and pelted us with them. The Understudy stood there and watched and then strode forwards. A sense of menace, of strangeness, of quietness radiated out from him. I saw some of the stone-chuckers pause in mid-throw.

'Put those down and go home,' the Understudy said. His odd rasping voice carried even over the hubbub of the hive. 'Go home and you will live.'

Somebody pulled back his arm to throw. Suddenly there was a pistol in the Understudy's hand. He pulled the trigger. The shot went right through the hand. The heretic screamed and fell. He writhed on the ground in agony.

'Anybody else?' the Understudy asked. They just looked at him. 'All right then, go.'

The locals looked shame-faced and shuffled their feet but he just stood there, quiet, gun in hand, a single figure confronting scores of them, unafraid. I watched to see what would happen next. I had the shotgun in my hand in case things turned nasty.

Much to my surprise, the crowd backed away. The Understudy gestured for a couple of the lads to come forwards and take the wounded man away for interrogation then walked back to the ranks and watched as the demolition team continued its work.

'Understudy we used to call him,' Anton said. 'More like a bloody Undertaker these days.'

'You keep calling him that and the name will stick,' I said.

'We'll see about that.'

The Understudy had his hand to his ear, listening to something on the comm-net in the ear bead. He looked around and gestured for us to follow him. It seemed like something was up. We piled into the Chimera and roared through the streets.

By the time we arrived, the battle was over and our side had taken heavy casualties. I looked around to see if there was any sign of the attackers. All I could see was at least a dozen of our boys lying dead on the ground. All that was left of them was scorched bodies. Their flesh was black and cracked in places. Most of their uniforms looked as if they had been set on fire. Their weapons lay close at hand, buckled and melted as if someone had thrown them into very intense flame.

Anton studied the survivors. There were half a dozen of them and they all looked pale-faced and frightened. I clutched my shotgun very close and surveyed the streets. The battle had taken place in a narrow alleyway close to a main thoroughfare. Some of the mountains of trash piled up against the walls still burned. Thick, oily stinking smoke rose above them. The corpses of roasted rats lay nearby. Cockroaches the size of dinner-plates had exploded in the heat.

I looked up and I could see the towering tenements rising hundreds of storeys above me. I wondered if our boys had come under attack from ambush and whether someone was still lurking on the balconies of the tenements waiting to take shots at us.

One thing I could not see was any sign of the people who had attacked. I looked around very carefully for bodies. There were probably two score civilians but none of them had any weapons.

I surmised that the survivors had gathered up the guns and taken them for themselves because I could not see any sign of flamethrowers or the sort of heavy weapons that would have resulted in this sort of loss. Some of these soldiers looked as if they'd been hit by a lascannon. There were a number of people heavily wounded – they had suffered very bad burns. The last time I had seen people who look like that, they had been dragged from the cockpits of burning tanks. Most of them had not lived very long afterwards.

Anton walked over to one of the survivors of the company. 'How many of them attacked you?' He sounded as cocky and arrogant as usual but he was just trying to be friendly.

The soldier looked up at Anton as if he was an idiot, a thing that Anton must have been very used to by now. 'Just the one,' he said.

Anton shook his head and made a low tut-tutting sound. He walked over to another soldier; this one's face was all smudged with soot as if he had been standing next to a blazing building or perhaps had worked in one of the forges back on Belial. 'How many of them attacked you?' Anton asked again.

The soldier looked up at Anton and shook his head. 'You heard Boris,' he said. 'Are you deaf?'

Anton turned around and looked at us, his face blank. He made a circling motion with his little finger close to the side of his forehead. He quite clearly thought that the soldiers had been made just a little bit crazy by what they had just been through. We had all seen that before. He went over to third soldier and said, 'How many?'

'One, you moron,' said the soldier. Anton's eyes narrowed and I was not sure whether it was because of the insult or because of the information that the soldier had imparted. It was starting to look as if there was no mistake here.

I walked over to the first soldier that Anton had talked to and I squatted down beside him. I offered him a lho stick from one of my packs and he took it and stuffed it into his mouth gratefully. I produced my igniter and he squirmed away at the sight of the flame as if it brought back some terrible memory.

'Just one of them did all this?' I kept my voice flat and level and did not let any fraction of emotion show. He took a long puff on the lho stick and he nodded. A cloud of smoke emerged from his lips and he pulled it back in again with a long breath as if he somehow thought that he could cover the smell of burning flesh that surrounded him with the odour of tobacco.

'That's right,' he said. 'Just the one.'

'Was he in a Hellhound, complete with a flamethrower attached?' Anton asked. He was never the most sensitive of souls.

'He was a psyker, one of those priests,' the soldier said. The others nodded agreement. I saw Anton flinch. I did too. None of us liked the idea of having to face a psyker. Regimental rumour had it that an unbonded psyker could be possessed by daemons. It was one of the truths preached by the Imperial cult and none of us had any reason to doubt it. Ivan gave out a low whistle. It was the one he used to indicate that he was disturbed. The New Boy looked as pale as the soldiers who had been fighting against the psyker. I don't suppose I looked any better.

The first soldier continued to puff away at the lho stick. His eyes were focused on its burning. It looked as if he was seeing something strange there. Maybe he was. Who can tell?

'We got a call,' he said. 'We were told that there was a heretic preacher ranting in the street and that someone had better come and do something.'

'You did,' Anton said.

'We arrived in force,' the soldier said. 'We did not know what to expect but we thought we were prepared for the worst.'

He shook his head, considering how silly that statement sounded now. 'There was a preacher here – he was dressed in simple robes and he was telling the crowd how the Angel of Fire would return and scour the face of this world, cleansing it of unbelievers. The commissar ordered Honza and Johan to go forwards and arrest him. The rest of us were to watch in case of ambush. There was an ambush all right – it just did not come the way we expected it.'

'The preacher was a psyker?' The New Boy looked frightened as he spoke. The soldier nodded his head.

'As soon as Honza and Johan got close, he just laughed and called upon the Angel of Fire to smite the heretics. That's when it happened–'

'What?' Anton asked.

'Wings of fire erupted from his back and a halo of flame surrounded his head. He gestured with his hands and Honza and Johan were burned down on the spot. They just caught alight – one second they were there, the next second they were surrounded with just as much flame as the preacher. The only difference was that it burned them; it did not burn him.'

'You opened fire?' Anton said.

'Of course we did,' the soldier said. 'Some of us tried hard not to hit our boys but most of us just fired our lasguns. We might as well have been using flashlights for all the difference it made. The bolts from our lasguns just seemed to make the preacher stronger and he kept invoking the name of the Angel and telling us that we were all going to be destroyed. The sacred flame was going to cleanse this world and we should repent.'

'I take it you didn't,' Anton said. I stared at him hoping to forestall any more misguided attempts at humour.

'We kept firing and firing and firing,' the soldier said. His eyes were fixed in the middle distance now and it was obvious that he was not looking at us but at the scene that the words were pulling from his memory. 'It didn't make the slightest difference. It just made him stronger. The commissar told us to stop shooting and use grenades. It was the last order he ever gave. The heretic burned him down where he stood.'

Anton looked at me. His eyes were wide and he looked a little more frightened now. He had always assumed that commissars enjoyed a special protection from the Emperor in return for their faith.

'Of course, most of the boys just kept on firing. Some of us tried using grenades but there was something in the air around the heretic that sent them flying back towards us. The explosions killed even more of our lads.'

'But you got the bastard in the end,' Anton said. 'Otherwise you would not be sitting here talking to us now.'

The soldier shook his head. 'Those wings of fire on his back spread wide open and he leapt into the air. It was like something out of one of those old pictures from the time when the Emperor walked among men. He just hovered in the air and threw bolts of fire at us. All the time he was smiling and laughing and ranting. His voice got louder and when I looked I saw his eyes were glowing, like there was a fire inside his skull.'

My mouth felt dry and I wanted to mock but I could not. The soldier just kept talking. 'He looked happy, ecstatic, there was this glow within him now, getting brighter, as if there was a light inside of him so brilliant it could shine through flesh. He shouted that he was going to meet the Angel and the Angel would come and judge us all then he jumped among us, his body on fire. Everyone he touched just burned. They rolled on the ground, beating at themselves but nothing could put the flames out. The heretic kept on coming. His flesh was being consumed from within now. He was getting thinner and thinner, vanishing like a sugar cube in water. He had almost reached me when he was gone. The flames leapt up all of a sudden and I thought I was dead, but when I opened my eyes there was no one there, except our boys, all burning and dying.'

Anton looked on appalled. Ivan studied something in the middle distance. Corporal Hesse and the New Boy moved around, dispensing med-packs, applying sacred balm.

'You know the worst of it?' the soldier said.

'What?'

'I kept thinking, what if he was right? What if the Angel had blessed him and we were the heretics here and we were all going to be judged?'

'Just as well your commissar got burned,' Anton said. 'If he was alive now you and he would be having words.'

'You never know,' the soldier said. 'He might have agreed with me.'

Document under seal. Extract From the Decrypted Personal Files of Inquisitor Hyronimus Drake.

  Possible evidence of duplicity on the part of former High Inquisitor Drake.

  Cross-reference to Exhibit 107D-21H (Report to High Inquisitor Toll).

Walk in the Emperor's Light.

Things are worse in this system than even I feared. The roots of heresy run deep. My agents have interrogated many of the locals and they have a faith in the Angel of Fire that is stronger even than their faith in the Emperor.

My necessarily brief attempts to grasp the history of the local cults have revealed some very disturbing things. The true Imperial cult in this system was long ago subsumed and subverted by the Cult of the Angel of Fire. Its priesthood was diminished until it played a minor role in ritual and rule.

Once I had hopes that the cult might provide a link between our force and the local community, that its leaders could be encouraged to take on the role of advocates for our ways and spearhead the reclamation of this world. This may prove more difficult than I had imagined. No priest of the cult of the Emperor has more than a limited role, and they are not respected by the populace as the priests of the Angel are. Worse yet their ritual and liturgy have been contaminated by long subservience to the Angel Cult. It will be a very long time before this can be changed.

I have prayed and warded my soul and studied the texts of this cult that have fallen into my hands. They are written in High Gothic like the testaments of the True Faith that superficially they resemble.

Many disturbing things have emerged. The role of the Emperor and His holy works has been relegated to the background. He is still portrayed as the font of wisdom and legitimacy, but His role in the parables is that of a remote and distant figure. All of the emphasis in the texts is placed on the part of the Angel of Fire and its saints and prophets. They are portrayed as the intercessors between humanity and the Angel just as the Angel is portrayed as the messenger between them and the Emperor.

This is not the worst of it. It has become obvious that many members of the Cult of the Angel are unbonded psykers. They have caused many casualties among our troops and shown themselves to be beings of considerable power. It is as if the cult deliberately encouraged and cultivated the use of psychic powers and promoted their wielders within its ranks. This raises many dreadful possibilities, not the least being contact with the daemons of Chaos. It is becoming increasingly obvious that the cultists of the Angel have been channelling power from somewhere and I have my suspicions as to the nature of the power on which they are calling.

When I consider the nature of the terrible sacrifices that were made and the structure of the cult who oppose us, I am reminded of many other worlds that have fallen to the most awful of heresies.

Despite the fact that the believers of this world claim to be following a power of light, there is a growing darkness here that needs to be opposed. I pray for the strength to do so.

'You ready for when we meet the bastard?' Anton asked, glaring around the interior of the Chimera. A score of troops looked at him. It was cramped in the compartment and his voice seemed too loud. There was no question of who the bastard was. He could only mean one person: a preacher of the Angel of Fire. The armoured troop carrier raced through the street. There had been another sighting and we had been sent out to break it up and take prisoners if we could.

I pumped the shotgun. It was audible within the armoured hull even over the roar of the vehicle's engines. 'What do you think?'

I had listened to all the stories. There were few things that the survivors always agreed on. Las-fire did not slow the psykers. It made them stronger. Grenades might work. They might not. No one really knew. All we knew was that the psykers died eventually but they took a lot more of our boys with them.

'I think the best thing to do when we meet one is back right off,' said the New Boy. He was looking serious now, more serious than he had ever done since he first joined us. A few weeks of fighting in the streets and listening to horror stories about rebel psykers had put him in a nervous frame of mind. He was doing his best not to show it.

'You might well be right,' said Corporal Hesse. He had raised his voice so that everybody could hear him. 'If you see one of them, keep your distance. Don't fire lasguns at him. Use any physical projectile weapons you have and wait for the heavy weapons to come up. They'll take the bastard down.'

He sounded calm and confident but I knew him too well to be fooled. There was a shiftiness about his eyes and a refusal to meet my gaze that told me he knew that I knew as well.

'They are getting stronger,' the Understudy said. The words just came out in his odd rasping voice. They were toneless. He did not sound frightened but he did not sound particularly sane either.

'Sir?' said Corporal Hesse.

'The psykers are getting stronger. The reports keep coming in. It came down from Headquarters. Something is making them more and more powerful. They are feeding on something or something is feeding them.'

Hesse kept looking at him, waiting for some piece of reassurance. None came. The Understudy just rasped on.

'If we meet one, pin him down. Wait for heavy weapons, reinforcements or our own psykers. Split up. Don't stay in groups. It just makes it easier for them to burn us down with area effects. Don't take cover in the AFVs either. The last few of the Flame worshippers have been powerful enough to take out a Manticore.'

'Anything else, sir?' I asked. I had to admit I was curious in a morbid fashion.

'They'll most likely be accompanied. It seems they have acquired retinues now, guardians who are just as prepared to throw away their lives as the heretic preachers. Some of them will be carrying combustible pyrite. They'll throw themselves among us and the psyker will detonate the package.'

This was new. 'Not heard of that one before,' Anton muttered.

'That's because none of the units who have encountered them have survived. The intelligence was only put together afterwards by field investigation units.'

The Chimera lurched just like my stomach. This was not the sort of thing that I wanted to hear. None of us did. The Understudy just kept talking. 'It seems they have found a way to keep their psykers alive and still inflict enormous casualties on us.'

In one way it was good or it ought to have been. It should have made the preachers less frightening. It showed they had some regard for their own lives. It didn't though.

'There are other reports,' the Understudy added, almost as an afterthought. Every man present was silent. All of us stared at him. Anton licked his lips. 'These have not been confirmed but it seems that some of the pyrite carriers have been transformed.'

'Transformed, sir?' Hesse asked.

'They become monsters of living flame; avatars of the Angel of Fire, some of the reports call them.'

'He really doesn't want us here, does he, sir?' Anton said.

'Who, Antoniev?'

'The Angel of Fire, sir.'

'It does not matter what the Angel of Fire wants,' the Understudy said. 'It matters what the Emperor commands.'

I believed him. The way he said it, you had to. The Chimera ground to a halt. The metal blast doors were thrown open. We deployed into the street.

They were waiting for us to show up. Our Chimeras had rumbled up to the plaza where a heretic was preaching sedition. Around us massive hab-blocks loomed. Great sign-boards still showed images of the Angel of Fire, flickering animated scenes from its holy books, miracles performed by its saints, burning-headed fanatics exhorting belief.

Nearby a group of enforcers waited. Either the crowd was too large for them or, more likely, because they were locals the majority of them did not want to take action.

We took up position, covering them with our lasguns. The locals looked at us. I could see that the vast majority of them were edgy, stuck in that no-man's-land between fear and anger. A bunch of them were armed but they did not like the idea of facing units of fully trained soldiers with armoured back-up.

There was something else though, something in the air, a feeling of anticipation, of hunger maybe. Or maybe that is just my imagination looking back on the thing. It seemed to me that an ominous presence hovered over everything. The Understudy gestured for us to advance. We moved towards the crowd. For a moment, they stood their ground but then their nerve broke and they split apart. Small channels appeared in the midst of the mass of people. We moved forwards at a run, wary, wanting to seize the leaders and get this over with. As we did so the crowd began to scatter, all except the core of ringleaders who waited for us, smirking. I think we all knew what was coming. I was very glad I had a shotgun and not the standard issue las-weapon.

'Behold the Unbelievers,' said a tall man with the unmistakable aura of authority. 'They have come from beyond the stars to die here.'

'Oh shut it,' shouted Anton. 'I am sick of listening to your sort.'

It was not the smartest thing to do but Anton had never been the smartest man. The heretic glared at him and raised an arm and a halo of flames played around his head. 'You are doomed, stick man, and you are blessed. You will be purified by the sacred fires of the Angel. He will burn the sin from your soul.'

He gestured at Anton. I pulled the trigger of the shotgun. The shell broke up en route to its target, coming apart in a spray of molten metal. It never reached the heretic priest but burning hot pellets landed amid his followers. They grimaced but they did not shriek. They were prepared for martyrdom.

My shot distracted the priest. The bolt of fire he threw at

Anton went off target, creating a splashing puddle of flame at the skinny bastard's feet. Anton leapt back as if his boots were on fire. Despite orders, a bunch of the lads opened up. Many of the heretics went down. Our boys were not being entirely stupid. They were not shooting at the priest but his followers. A group of them went down. One of them exploded. He was obviously wearing a pyrite shirt. The wash of flame swept out over them. The priest laughed and shouted praises to the Angel.

About half of the heretics were down. The remainder were transformed. They became larger and far more terrifying. They burned like dry wood but they kept moving and shrieking and laughing like madmen. Halos of flame surrounded their charring bodies, making them seem much larger. You could see a moving man in the core of an infernal monster. They came closer. The sickly sweet smell of burning flesh filled the air along with the muted blast-furnace roar of the strange magic that animated them still.

'Disperse,' the Understudy shouted. 'Don't let them close! Don't let them grab you!'

The boys did not need to be told twice. They fanned out. The crowd was already in motion, trying to get as far away from the burning fanatics as possible. I took aim and fired at one of the blazing figures. The shell hit him in the chest. What was left of the human being within flew apart. It was as if I had shot at a statue made of ash. The flames surrounding him momentarily flickered but then pulled back together again. There was no martyr left now, only an elemental that burned ever brighter as if consuming the soul of the dead man for fuel.

Foolishly I shot at it again. It was exactly like putting a shell into a flame. It went straight through and out the other side. The priest was shrieking instructions to his surviving minions now. The monster I had fired upon rushed straight towards me, a roughly humanoid outline of roaring flame. From the retreating crowd guns opened up. The fanatics were not alone after all and we had walked right into an ambush.

There was not a lot I could do. I turned and ran, knowing that agonising death was at my heels. I seemed to hear the roar of its flames coming ever closer. I heard something else above that. The scream of aircraft engines. It seemed like support was coming our way although what it could achieve against the supernatural horror following me I was not at all sure.

I cursed the thing and turned at bay, wanting to at least face the thing that killed me. It wasn't there. Some idiot had opened fire on it with a lasgun and it was racing towards them, not in the least affected by the blindingly bright bolts. As I watched it enveloped the shooter and turned him into a human bonfire. Whoever it was died screaming.

Autogun bullets kicked up dust at my feet and reminded me that the elemental martyrs were not the only threat. A small group of local gangers were taking pot-shots at me, for all the world as if they were in some plaza tormenting pigeon-bats. I turned the shotgun on them. It discouraged them from their sport. Permanently.

Things in the plaza were chaotic. Our lads had dispersed. The elementals chased them down. In the centre of it all, the priest of the Angel of Fire chanted his strange litany. There was an evil exultation in his voice. An aura of flame played around his head. Wings of fire emerged from his back.

Hate twisted my guts, pure visceral loathing for the fanatic and what he was doing. Mad rage filled my mind. I strode towards him, fumbling at my belt for a grenade. I had a clear run at him. His pet fire daemons were busy slaughtering our lads. I was never going to get a better chance.

He saw me but it troubled him not a jot. I was beneath his notice now that he was filled with the spirit of his master. He had to control his pets while they slaughtered my comrades. One lowly Guardsman was not something that made him feel threatened. I lobbed the grenade at him. It exploded in the air near him, detonated by the aura around him. The force of the blast sent him staggering back. The elementals flickered like a dying blaze. I thought if I can only keep this up I have got him. Then I looked into his blazing eyes and I knew that I had run out of time.

At that point there was a sound like thunder. I flinched, convinced that the heretic had blasted me with his fiery power. I closed my eyes expecting a surge of agony to rip through my body. Instead, I saw the huge black-armoured figure of a Space Marine before me. He had charged the priest with a chainsword and lopped off a limb. Whatever power protected the heretic from our weapons, it was not enough to save him from the wrath of the Emperor's chosen. An enormous wave of psychic power smashed down from above. Looking up I saw another Space Marine standing in the doorway of a Thunderhawk gunship. This one's face was visible. Elaborate skull-mask paint concealed his features. A bolt of power emerged from a black spot on the Imperial psyker's forehead. It warred with the flaming shield around the heretic psyker, suppressing it, while his comrade chopped the heretic down.

With the death of the priest, the elementals dissipated. The Space Marines smashed into the crowd. There was only a score of them but they did more damage in a few seconds than our entire company had done in the entire battle. A few heartbeats after their arrival the remainder of the heretics were in flight or surrendered, demoralised by the onset of the Death Spectres.

I stood and watched, awed by the power and majesty of the Emperor's angels. One of them passed me and clapped me gently on the back. Maybe it was an accident. I like to think he had seen me standing my ground and was complimenting me on my bravery. Hopefully he did not notice that my eyes were closed as I faced death.

Looking at the scene of carnage, listening to the distant rumble of bolter fire, I realised this had been a trap for the heretics and we had been the bait. It was the battle of the factorum all over again albeit on a smaller scale. I could not find it in my heart to resent that fact. At least the High Command had given us a chance to survive which was more than the previous companies who had encountered the priesthood of The Angel of Fire had got. The Death Spectres had saved us.

I looked around to see if any of the others were still alive. I found them clustered around a Space Marine watching him with slack-jawed awe. They looked as if they expected him to perform a miracle before their very eyes. Personally I would not have been surprised if he had. There was something vastly reassuring about the presence of these massive, black-armoured figures. I felt safe in their shadow. While they were there nothing could harm us. No threat was too terrible to be faced. They radiated power and confidence. You felt something of the distant majesty of the Emperor himself. These were his chosen.

Guardsmen reached out to touch their armour as they passed. It was a thing they would tell their comrades in decades to come. Others bent their knees as they would before a priest. I doubt the Death Spectres noticed.

Even as I watched I heard the massive figure say something into the comm-net. I moved closer and I heard something about a hulk moving in-system.

The Death Spectre gestured to his comrades and they returned to their vehicles and departed. There was something urgent in their manner as if they had been summoned to some new and important duty. Within minutes they were gone and the only sign they had ever been there were the corpses they had left spread across the square.

The Guardsmen watched them go in silence. The locals did too, such as had been spared. Dozens of them were on their knees babbling and praying for mercy or forgiveness. It seemed they had for once witnessed a force as capable of filling them with awe as the minions of the Angels of Fire.

The body collectors had already scuttled out of hiding and were loading the dead onto their trolleys.

Rumours abounded in the Angel's Blessing that night. The city was on the verge of open rebellion. Macharius had been wounded at the new war front. Macharius had been killed. The Death Spectres had gone off-world to deal with an ork invasion fleet. Plague had erupted on Karsk V and would be coming our way soon. We sat in the dark and drank our rotgut and tried not to pay too much attention. We were looking for distraction.

That night the girls brought a friend. She was tall, dark, and strikingly pretty with dark hair cut very short. Her name was Anna. I studied her as she sat opposite me. She seemed quiet and self-possessed and calm. She had the competence that nurses always have but she was distant.

'She's as new around here as you are,' Yanis said, as if making a joke.

'What do you mean?' I asked.

Anna smiled a little coldly, I thought. 'She means I just transferred in to St Oberon's. I was working two levels down in the old Flat Tunnel Hospice.'

'Might as well have come from another planet,' said Yanis. There was some tension between the two. 'It's a different world down there.'

'It's poorer, if that's what you mean,' said Anna. 'But people still need healing.'

'I never said they didn't.'

'It is different down there,' Anna said. 'Darker, more dismal. The nobles who come to St Oberon's have no idea what it's like.' She let that hang in the air, with the implication it was not just the nobles.

'It's always the bloody same,' said Anton. 'The higher up the hive you go, the snottier people get.' That got him some nasty looks from the other nurses. Not that Anton cared. He never paid too much attention to what other people thought.

Katrina looked at the table and said, 'Do we need to talk about this? There are other more interesting things to talk about. I've never been out of the hive, let alone to a different planet, neither have you, Yanis or Anna. You boys have. What was it like?'

'Dangerous,' said Anton. 'The bloody places always seemed full of people who wanted to shoot us for some reason.'

Ivan gave him a dark look. 'It's understandable. I feel that way every time I look at you.'

'Ha bloody ha!'

Katrina's attempt to change the subject and the booze

worked though. We spoke of the campaigns we had fought in – Jurasik, Elijah, Lucifer and the others. We did not talk about anything we were doing at present but it would not have mattered very much – if they had been spies they could have learned a lot just from the stories we told of the old times and about the battles we had fought in. It did not seem very likely that they were spies although you can never tell. Little did I know…

'Tell me about the Angel of Fire,' the New Boy asked.

I frowned at the way he spoke. It seemed to me that he was more interested in the Angel of Fire than he ought to have been. He was a studious lad with a scholarly turn of mind and this was his first campaign and his first time off the leash on an alien world. He was curious about everything – I suppose if I had been in the same situation I would have been too. My friends were drunk and I knew what they were thinking anyway so I concentrated on the girls, wondering about their response.

It was interesting. Anna and Yanis wore the conventional pious look of the faithful. Lutzka looked blank and far more interested in her drink. Katrina looked angry and stared off into the distance, biting her lower lip and frowning. I wondered what she was thinking so I asked. She just shook her head and looked even more angry and then she got up and stalked away towards the ladies room. Anton looked at me annoyed as if I had done something wrong. 'What was that all about?' He asked of no one in particular. The other girls looked embarrassed and a little afraid.

'Her brother was burned by the Sons of the Flame,' Yanis said at last.

'He was not the only one, judging by the number of cages

I have seen recently,' said Anton with his usual mastery of the diplomatic arts.

'It's not that common,' Yanis said.

'It looks as if they burned thousands,' said Anton.

'And what are thousands or even tens of thousands in all the millions that a hive contains.'

'It matters to the thousands,' I said.

'It teaches the rest of us to respect the Angel,' said Anna. 'You need to be firm to keep a hive under control.' I thought I heard an implied criticism there; that we were not being firm enough with the locals. Maybe she felt things were starting to spin out of control.

'So what was Katrina's brother being taught to respect?' I asked.

'Ask her,' she said, not responding well to the aggression in my voice. Maybe I had had too much to drink. 'It's not my business to say. I am new here.'

'I'll tell you,' said Lutzka. 'They are burned for their own good.'

We all turned to look at her. She seemed to deflate a little then her jaw firmed and she said, 'Well, it's true.'

'Would you care to explain that?' I asked.

'You're not very nice,' Anna said.

'Because I want an explanation?'

'Because you have a nasty manner.'

'I would still like to know how you burn someone alive for their own good. Call me an apostate but I can't see how that works.'

'Their souls go to join the Angel,' said Lutzka. There was a dreamy look in her eye, the sort you sometimes see on the faces of the really devout when they are at prayer. 'The flames cleanse them of their sins and they join his choir purified and free of the bonds of flesh.'

'I doubt there is much flesh left on them at this stage,' I said.

'Scoff if you like but it's what it says in scripture.'

The New Boy rubbed his eye and said, 'They say that the psykers the Black Ships take join the Emperor. Might this not be the same?'

'I don't think you can compare the Emperor with the Angel of Fire,' said Anton. He sounded outraged. Maybe it was the drink.

'Why not? They say that the Angel of Fire stands at his right hand.' Lutzka said. I could see the girls nodding.

'Only on this world,' said Ivan. 'I think if it was true we would have heard of it on Belial and all the other worlds.'

'How do you know it's not?' Anna sounded annoyed now at the faith being called into question. 'Have you visited every world in the galaxy?'

It was a fair point. Silence fell. I wondered why she had pushed things so far. She could be arrested for trying to undermine morale. Strictly according to regulations we should be locking her up and taking her for trial. The girls looked at us. Most of them pushed their chairs back, as if trying to put some distance between them and Anna but at the same time there was approval in their faces. Anna had said something they had all thought, had voiced their resentments for them. Maybe all she was trying to do was fit in, a new girl in a new place trying to make new friends. She did not realise it could get her killed.

Anton and Ivan looked at me. They knew as well as I did that things could go very sour very quickly from here.

'No, we haven't, but in this we are right,' I said, staring at her very hard, hoping she would take the hint, realise what she was doing. 'I am sure that in your heart of hearts you feel the truth of that.'

She kept staring at me challengingly. Inwardly I cursed her. She was really so drunk and stubborn that she could not see what was happening here. I held her gaze and slowly her eyes sank and her face flushed.

'You are right,' she said eventually. Her hand played with the small ikon of the Angel of Fire that rested between her breasts.

The next morning I sat up and pulled on my tunic. Anna stirred in the bed beside me. Her hair was mussed. Her eyes were full of sleep. She looked very pretty. Her face was chilly for a moment then she smiled and it brightened wonderfully.

'What are you doing?' she asked.

'I've got to report for duty,' I said. I could not say any more.

'If you stick around we can have some breakfast,' she said. 'There is a stall in the corridor that does the best skewered drop-frog.'

'Sounds like a prime local delicacy,' I said. I checked her clock. I still had an hour before I had to report. My head felt thick and muzzy. My mouth felt dry. I remembered leaving the bar with her early in the morning and a long walk to this hab-block. I remembered endless corridors and endless alcoves all filled with statues of the Angel.

I looked at the room. There were the usual small personal belongings you find in a hab-cell. Some pictures of Anna as a girl with her family, some little trinkets – sacred prints, knick-knacks. You can see them in a billion, billion hab-cells anywhere in the galaxy.

She looked at the pictures on the tabletop as if some memory were coming back to her. I reached out a hand to help her up. She rose to her feet lightly, but as I tugged, just for a moment, before she got into motion, she felt heavier than she looked. I remembered getting the same impression last night when I had lifted her onto the bed. I put it down to drunkenness then but it was odd that it had returned now.

'You want to go get breakfast?'

'Sure,' I said.

There were people in the corridors outside the hab-cell. Just like on Belial, there is no real quiet time in a hab-block. People are always coming and going. One or two of them stared at my uniform but not for long when I stared back. A group of young gangers shouted abuse from a crossroads. They were armed. So was I. It made for a tense few moments. Anna looked a lot calmer than I would have expected but I supposed she was used to such sights. They were common enough on Belial where I grew up as well. Anna did not look at all troubled. At the time, I thought that perhaps she was just used to such things from her experience in the underhive. Or that maybe my presence reassured her.

Fortunately the gangers were not on blaze or any of the other synthetics. Otherwise there might have been trouble. They just wanted to let everybody know how tough they were.

We found the stall Anna mentioned. It was crowded with people. Mostly workers coming or going from their shifts. Again most of them looked at me. There were odd tensions written on people's faces, as if they knew something I did not. Uneasiness settled in my stomach. I told myself it was just my imagination.

I let Anna order for both of us and I paid. She was right. The food was good. We ate in silence for a while with that odd embarrassment that two people feel when they have gone to bed drunk with a stranger and then have to make conversation in the morning.

'How long do you think you will be in Irongrad?' she asked.

'I don't know.' I really didn't but I would not have told her anyway if I had. Regulations. 'When do you have to go to work?'

'It's an off half-day for me. That's why we were all in the bar last night. My shift doesn't start until noon.'

'Lucky you,' I said.

'Lucky me,' she agreed. 'You get any off-days?'

'A soldier of the Emperor is always on duty,' I said. It was the sort of thing the square-jawed hero always said in the prop-novs Anton read. She laughed.

'You don't take me seriously,' I said.

'I think you are a very serious man.'

I took another bite of some sort of flat-bread. It was tough and chewy but not unpleasant. There was some kind of protein baked in.

'Would you really report me to your commissar?' she asked quietly. I was glad she was so cautious. I remembered threatening to do some such thing during our argument the previous night. I thought it funny what could spark a night of passion. I remembered saying other things as well.

'It's what I am supposed to do,' I said. 'Otherwise I imperil my soul as well as yours.'

She considered that for a moment. I could see she was turning things over in her mind. At least I thought that then.

'What are they like, your commissars?'

'They are not gentle with unbelievers,' I said. 'Or with anybody else for that matter.'

'Why did you become a soldier? Were you conscripted?'

'I volunteered, believe it or not. It's most likely one of the reasons we are talking.'

'How so?'

'The Imperial Guard are the elite of the planetary levies. One of the things they look for is superior motivation. Volunteers have more of that than conscripts.'

'You volunteered out of a desire to fight then. You wanted to do your duty out of love of the Emperor.' There was a sarcastic tone to her voice that needled me a little. Maybe it was meant to.

I shook my head. 'Anton and Ivan and I were wanted by a gang boss. He would have killed us if we had stayed on in the hive and kept working at the guild factorum. The Guard was a way out.'

'You worked in a factorum?'

'Yes.'

'What did you make?'

'Gear sprockets for tanks.'

'I can't really picture you doing that.'

'I can easily picture you as a nurse,' I said. I could too. She had a coolness about her that told you she would behave well under pressure. And there was a detachment to her as well, I thought for a moment.

She laughed and it made her look younger and suddenly I liked her. You know how it is.

She looked at me sidelong as if a thought had just struck her.

'What is it?' I asked.

'It's strange. For so long we were isolated here. We only traded with the other worlds in the system. The Imperium was just a legend. Now, you are here, telling us we are part of it, that we never left it.'

I tried to imagine what it must be like for her. This world had only been contacted by rogue traders for millennia. Those contacts could easily have been centuries apart. The Imperium itself had only made contact a decade ago. The rulers of the world had pretended not to believe in the legitimacy of the contact. They had ruled too long to give up power without a fight.

I had a vision too of the strangeness of it all. The Angel of Fire Cult had grown up on this world in a time when there had been no contact with the true faith of the Imperium. It has its roots in the same theology but had grown wild and strange, mutated over all those long centuries of isolation. Who knew what had really happened here, how the Sons of the Flame had gained their powers. No one could challenge them with the Imperial truth and slowly and surely they had bent the faith of an entire system of worlds to their will and now plunged that system into an unwinnable war with the Imperium of Man.

'You are looking thoughtful,' Anna said.

'It's nothing,' I said, looking around, suddenly very aware that I was a long way from home and surrounded by strangers. I felt oddly vulnerable although there was no menace in any of the faces around me. Overhead though, the Angel of Fire's thousand metal incarnations stared down at me with their blind eyes. I sat in the shadow of its fiery wings.

'I have to go,' I said. Something in the back of mind told me I had better be getting back.

When I got to the barracks everything was in a frenzy of activity. I entered our room and saw that the others were already there.

'Where have you been?' Anton asked. He looked more than a little upset.

'I think you can guess if you cast your mind back to last night,' I said. 'There was a girl involved…'

'You haven't heard then?'

'Heard what?'

'There's been a massive heretic counter-attack, backed up by space-drops. Macharius has been shot. Some say he has been killed.'

I looked from face to face to see if they were kidding me. All of them looked equally serious just like all the others I had seen on my way in.

'That's not possible,' I said.

Their expressions told me that they thought differently.

Exhibit 107D-21G Abstract of Report VII – XII – MIVIII

  To: **High Inquisitor Jeremiah Toll, Sanctum Ultimus, Dalton's Spire.**

  Source: **Drake, Hyronimus, high inquisitor attached to the Grand Army of Reconquest.**

  Document under seal. Possible evidence of duplicity on the part of former High Inquisitor Drake. Cross-reference to decrypted personal journals. See Exhibit 107D-45G.

Walk in the Emperor's Light.

I know the question you are asking yourself, I have asked it myself – how could one mere system, a group of worlds orbiting a single sun, withstand the full might of the Imperial armies that Macharius has at his command?

The answer is that it takes a very long time to organise an Imperial crusade and it takes an even longer time for all of the elements of that crusade to be put into place. There are complications that are not immediately obvious as well. Interstellar travel is far from predictable. Whole fleets of transport ships have been lost as they journey through the under-space of the warp.

The Lord High Commander has done a superlative job of organisation, but I begin to suspect elements of the Munitorum and even the Administratum may be working against him. Imperial politics can lead to all manner of betrayals. There are those who dream of a return to the chaos of the Schism and the free hand they enjoyed during it.

In the case of Karsk there were five inhabited planets in a system of twenty-seven worlds. Each of those worlds helds at least five hive cities and in some cases as many as forty. Each of those hive cities contained enormous armaments factories and populations numbering in the tens of millions. All of those armies were defending their homelands and knew their way around. All of them started already concentrated and highly motivated. The wonder of it is not that the system managed to resist us but that we scored so many victories so early. I put that down entirely to the planning of Macharius. His entire army had not yet arrived and already we had seized three of the five hives on one of the major industrial worlds.

Initially, we had the benefit of the element of surprise and we descended upon Karsk IV like a sledgehammer dropping from space. We took Irongrad before our enemies had any chance to realise what was happening and the swiftness of our victory demoralised them. At least to begin with. However, the governor managed to get away to Karsk IV where his brother had already begun to organise relief armies and very soon the fightback had begun.

I have been told that the Imperial Navy ought to have been able to control the space between the worlds but something happened which gave the heretics a chance to break out of their worlds and begin relieving Karsk V. I still am not sure what. One rumour has it that the admiral took umbrage at some of Sejanus's remarks about his uniform and withdrew his fleets temporarily. It sounds so stupid I can almost believe it. The most likely reason is that they have come under attack by a hulk that has drifted in-system. The matter is pending investigation. The Death Spectres have taken it on themselves to investigate. This could not have happened at a worse time.

Even though we control the comm-net in the cities, word has managed to get out to the local population. They have gone from being sullen but neutral to being actively hostile. I suspect that the priesthood of the Angel of Fire is responsible. It appears they have their own methods of communicating between worlds and I have my suspicions as to how.

In a hive of millions it does not take an enormous percentage of the young, violent and disenfranchised to turn against us to provide our enemies the basis for recruiting a powerful army. Irongrad is a major producer of weapons. The cult of the Angel of Fire has a huge number of contacts in the Temple factorums. I suspect it is easy for our enemies to arm their new recruits. Of course, they were also a priesthood and have had a hold of the souls and imaginations of an enormous number of the local people. Generations of preaching had seen to that. The situation here is potentially explosive and becoming more so every day.

And our forces are coming under attack by the worshippers of the Angel of Fire, potent psykers who seem able to draw upon the darkest and most hellish powers. This too is a matter pending investigation. I have given orders that one of these priests must be taken alive. So far that has proven to be a problem.

'I don't believe it,' Anton said. He was sitting on his bed in the barracks, his prop-nov hanging loosely in his hand. 'Macharius cannot be dead.'

'I heard he had just lost a leg,' said Ivan. 'That's what Fat Mikal down in the kitchens says.'

Anton shook his head. 'He was a great man.'

'He's not dead yet,' I said. 'We've not heard any word of that.'

'Yeah, they'll come and tell you won't they?'

'There would be an announcement,' I said. 'A day of mourning, at least.'

'Not if they want to keep it from us.'

'Why would they want to do that?'

'You know as well as I do the effect that his death would have on morale.'

'It's good to see you are doing your bit to keep it up then. I am glad you are not one to give in to despair. Or help spread it.'

'Damn!' Anton said. He got up and kicked the bed. The metal of the frame rang. You could tell from his expression that he had hurt himself but was just too stubborn to admit it. 'Finally, we had a competent commander in charge. Finally we were getting somewhere. Now this. It's so bad even the Space Marines are deserting us.'

'I would not say that too loudly if I were you,' I said.

'Why not? It's true.'

He was right. The Death Spectres had departed. No one knew why or where. Or if they did they were not telling us. They had been summoned elsewhere or else were being dispatched.

'For one, if you say it too loud, they'll never adopt you into their Chapter. For another, a commissar might hear you and decide to put you on bullet-stopping duty.'

'I don't see one here,' said Anton. 'You planning on reporting me?'

'The only thing I will report is your stupidity. You seem to be scaling new heights of it at the moment.'

Ivan whistled ironically to show what he thought about our bickering. The New Boy rushed into the room and said, 'Macharius is here!'

'In the building?' Anton asked.

'In Irongrad. He was flown in from the battle front. He's at the Hospice of Saint Oberon.'

'How do you know?'

'Word just came in to Command. I heard one of the

company scribes talking as he was on his way to give the report to the captain.'

'You sure?' Anton asked.

'If you don't believe me, go ask him yourself. Where is the hospice anyway? Isn't that where the girls are?'

'Yeah, it's down by the cathedral, near the hive core-zone,' Anton said. He picked up his lasgun. 'I'm going down there.'

'Why?' I asked.

'In case any of those Angel worshippers show up and...' He looked embarrassed now.

'And?' I said, not willing to let him off the hook.

'And so I can pray for him.'

'You can do that just as well here,' I said.

'I'd feel better doing it there.'

Ivan stood up. 'I'll go with you.'

'Me too,' said the New Boy.

'What about you, Leo? You coming?' Anton asked. I considered it for a moment. After all, what difference would my presence down by the hospice make? I felt all three of them staring at me. There was something accusing in their gaze.

'All right,' I said. 'Let's go.'

Apparently we were not the only people with the idea. The square outside the Hospice of St Oberon was full of off-duty Guardsmen. There were thousands of them. We looked like an army about to lay siege to the place. Soldiers stood around and smoked and ate street food and talked in subdued voices. You would have thought we were all in the sick room of a dying relative from the expressions on everyone's faces.

The hospice itself was a massive building made from an orange local stone. It looked more like a fortress than a hospital. It was twenty storeys high, low compared to the surrounding hab-blocks but massive all the same. It felt enormously solid. It seemed to have been designed to resist a siege or withstand a direct hit from heavy artillery.

There were Leman Russ tanks drawn up all around it and I could make out ratling snipers on the balconies and in among the metal angels that clutched the thick walls. It seemed that no chances were being taken with security. Soldiers on guard checked everyone who went into the building. The girls had not been exaggerating. It was a famous place apparently, with the best chirurgeons on the planet.

For once there were more than the statues of the Angel of Fire to look at. The entrance was a massive arch. On one side was the inevitable flame-winged angel ten times the height of a man. On the other side was a massive muscular warrior who looked more like a master-sergeant than a saint. In one hand he held a bolt pistol, in the other he held a blazing torch. His foot was on the neck of an ork. Five ork heads hung from his belt. He gazed on the Angel with a face rapt in worshipful contemplation. I was guessing this was the Blessed Oberon of local legend.

Looking around I saw many of the soldiers came from the same regiments. They were all part of the old Guard who had followed Macharius right from the beginning. They wore green uniforms with gold trim and their helmets were an odd shape, an odd, ancient-looking shape more suited to a tribe from a feral world. They had nose and cheek guards but left the lower half of the face visible at the front while sweeping all the way down the neck at the back. Many of them wore the lion's head insignia of Macharius's family on their gear.

There were soldiers of the Grey Legions of Asterion all in silver and grey, with their metal collars on their neck symbolising servitude to the Emperor. There were short solid men from Trask in the red and black of the Ninth Hussars. Some of them had brought their horses. They had just come from crowd control duty in the Cathedral Square. There were ogryns and ratlings and one or two commissars. I don't know whether they were there out of respect for Macharius or to keep an eye on the rest of us. I am guessing it was the former but you never know.

There were moments when all conversation seemed to stop and everyone looked towards the great arched doorway. It was not silent. You could still hear the industrial noise of the hive city, the roar of the gas-jet flames, the wheezing bellow's breath of the air-circulation systems, the distant rumble of the elevated railroads. It was odd and awe-inspiring to see so many quiet men with rapt faces, lost in thought, and you've got to remember that many of these were not the sort of men given over to brainwork. I think we were all wondering about Macharius, and his fate in an odd way was a mirror image of our own.

It was not difficult for us to empathise with him. Every soldier in a Guard regiment dwells on wounds and death at some point. Many of us have taken a hit and all of us have known someone who has. All of us dread that wound that will cripple us, leave us limbless or blinded. All of us fear

it as much as death. Many of us have waited for comrades
to die of their wounds. In that moment I think everyone
present saw in Macharius a reflection of all the wounded
brothers, friends and comrades we had lost, and all of us
were waiting to see if we had lost another.

We waited for hours, but no word came. In the end we
departed, summoned back to duty, still not knowing how
things went with the Lord High Commander.

Our temporary captain of our temporary company summoned us into his august presence the next morning. All
of us wondered what was going on. We could not think of
anything we had done to earn his wrath but, as ever, the
fact that we could not conjure up anything did not mean
there were not reasons. It's a rule in the Guard that they can
always find a motive for punishment if they want.

The captain did not look annoyed when we entered his
chamber. It was a large room that had once been some sort
of scriptorium by the look of it. Dozens of desks lined the
walls and dozens of clerks made notes in great ledgers still.
This time they were probably totting up the ammunition
we had used rather than the number of cogwheels shipped.

The captain was sitting on a great padded leather chair
while his batman shaved his cheeks with a cut-throat razor.
The usual cabal of junior officers preened themselves around
him, admiring their reflections in the array of portable mir-
rors the batman had set up. Some of them had more gold
on their epaulettes than I would get if I looted a bank vault.

'Ah there you are, lads!' he murmured as if delighted to
see us. His voice was very quiet for an officer and you had

to strain to hear him. I suspect that was the effect he desired. It made him stand out in an army where those in charge could be reliably expected to boom, bellow and shout. We stood at attention and waited for him to clarify the situation. The batman towelled his face and the captain ran his hand over his tanned cheeks to check for any remaining stubble. A small tight smile told us he had not found any. He stroked his well-clipped moustache for a moment as if encouraging it to speak.

'I have a special duty for you all,' the moustache said. The captain's lips did not seem to move so it must have been the whiskers speaking. We kept our faces stony. Special duty covers a multitude of potentially lethal options. I wondered if I was about to be volunteered for a suicide mission.

The captain obviously understood what was going through our minds. He was not nearly as dim as he chose to appear. He laughed his fruity laugh and murmured, 'It's nothing dreadful, I can assure you. In fact it is a very great honour. '

We looked at him and kept our mouths closed. 'As you may know General Macharius was wounded while investigating the front lines at Pentegrad. He was inspecting our forward positions when a squad of heretic fanatics attacked. He managed to fight his way clear with some of his bodyguard.'

Macharius was famous for wanting to be where the action was, but I wondered that he had really gotten so close to the heretics that they had a chance to attack him personally.

'He is well then, sir?' Anton asked tentatively.

'As well as a man with several bits of shrapnel and numerous heretic bullets embedded in his body can be expected to be, Private Antoniev,' said the moustache.

'He is not well then, sir?' Anton said, not knowing when to leave well enough alone.

'I have been assured by the Master Surgeon that he will make a full recovery. It takes more than a few wounds to put down a campaigner like the Lord High Commander. He's had worse in the past and I dare say he will have worse in the future. I should know. I've taken a few such scratches myself in my time.'

'Why are you telling us this, sir?' I asked.

'Because the surviving crew of the *Indomitable* has been assigned to guard the Lord High Commander personally. You are to be quartered within the Hospice of St Oberon forthwith and report for guard duty on the Lord High Commander's ward immediately. Any further questions?' His manner told us there had better not be.

'Why us, sir?' Anton asked. The captain sighed in a long-suffering manner.

'The Lord High Commander personally decorated you. You are known to him. You have won great honour for the regiment and I *know* you will not let us down now.'

'It will be an honour to defend the general, sir,' said Anton. He sounded like he meant it.

'And one well-deserved,' said the captain. 'You distinguished yourself in the taking of this city, and I am sure you will distinguish yourself again, if you are called upon to protect the Lord High Commander.'

'We'll do our best,' said Anton. He actually looked pleased at the prospect of laying down his life to defend Macharius. I think in the back of his mind, he was already picturing a heroic last stand. For myself, I decided that it would not be a bad thing to be safe in the hospital away from pyromaniac priests and their suicidal disciples. The next time there might be no Death Spectres to save us.

'Very good,' said the captain. 'Very good indeed. Mind your manners and don't do anything to embarrass the regiment and you'll find me very grateful.'

For myself I had very little doubt that he would forget about us as soon as we were out of his sight. Still, it was going to be nice, safe cushy billet, I thought. Little did I know.

We went to collect our gear. At least we knew how to find our way to the hospice.

'There are worse places in this world,' murmured Anton as we walked through the corridors of the hospice. He was right too.

We were on the upper levels of the building, where the very rich and very noble of the city would normally have been treated. The entire level had been cleared and given over to Macharius. Medical adepts came and went. High-ranking officers waited around and discussed strategy. Couriers and orderlies raced along the sumptuously carpeted corridors, trying to be both quiet and quick at the same time. We had just been given time to move into small private rooms on the lower floor before being sent up to start our duties.

We took up a position at the entrance to the ward, relieving some of the troops from Macharius's own personal guard. They were easy to spot because of the lion-head pattern on their uniforms.

We checked the perimeter rooms of the ward ourselves

and found only chirurgeons and nursing staff, all of whom had been cleared to be there. We did not get close to the sealed chamber in which Macharius lay. Tall, silent warriors of his personal guard watched us with cold eyes. They held their weapons at the ready. They were taking no chances.

I began to understand why we had been sent for. It would not do for just Macharius's own regiment to be given the honour of guarding him. Every component of the army had to share in that honour. It would have been bad for morale otherwise.

The Understudy had given us a detailed briefing on our way over. Only authorised personnel were to be allowed past and they had to both show us their clearance documents and know the password which changed with every watch. If they did not we were to hold them. If they resisted we were to shoot them even if they had a general's epaulettes.

The duty itself was eight hours of pure tedium. We stood there, weapons at the ready, and we checked papers. Every half-hour the Understudy returned to check on us. He moved from guard post to guard post on a constant loop. He seemed neither bored nor overwhelmed with interest. He performed his duties like an automaton. He could have been a machine animated by the ancient technical magic of the Adeptus Mechanicus.

When the corridors were clear and no one was in sight we chatted, as soldiers will under such circumstances wherever they are in the galaxy. We talked about women, and the places we had been and the people we had known. We kept our voices pitched low and we kept scanning the corridors as if we expected a horde of heretics to arrive at any moment. I was wondering if we would run into Anna or any of her friends.

'Who would have thought we would end up here?' Anton asked. 'It's like being at the centre of the world.'

He was excited. We had challenged generals. So far they had all had the proper documents and spoken the proper passwords. We had not been given the chance to shoot any of them for resisting arrest. It was probably just as well since that would likely have ended badly for us.

It was strange. The corridor was hushed and the rooms around us were quiet. Quieter than any place I had ever been. You could not tell that beyond the walls was the thunderous din of a hive city. The sound-proofing was that good. I realised that quiet was a luxury that the rich enjoyed. It did not thrill me too much. I missed the reassuring beat of the hive's industrial heart. I wondered how the wounded Macharius felt about such things.

Our duties done, we returned to our rooms. The locals looked at us oddly as we made our way there. It felt as if everyone was simply waiting for something to happen. Everyone looked pale and tense as if they knew something we did not, were listening to some secret whispering voice that talked only to them and not to us. I told myself it was my imagination, that all I needed was some rest.

I stared out the armoured glass windows. The streets were unnaturally quiet. The crowds of waiting soldiers had gone now that it was certain that Macharius would live. They had other duties to perform than waiting in the plaza.

Something woke me. It seemed my head had barely hit the pillow and I had fallen into nightmares about flame-headed priests putting me in a cage. I looked at my chronometer. It was late in the night cycle for the hive. The external lights were dim. I pulled the curtains open. My shadow danced in the flickering illumination from the surrounding gas-lit buildings. There seemed to be a huge crowd gathered in the street below. I could see flickering lights down there too, as if naked flames were burning. I was still groggy from sleep when I noticed a banging on the door. Some instinct made me uneasy. I snatched up my shotgun before I opened the door. Anton stood there, his face was pale. Ivan was behind him, dressed and armed.

'What is it?' I said.

'The heretics are attacking.'

'What?' I repeated. 'Attacking? Where?'

'Everywhere. They are attacking Irongrad. A massive army dropped from orbit and relieved Pentegrad and it's moving north from there. It's smashed through Battlegroup Sejanus. More are dropping from space; they're coming in from Karsk III and the asteroid fortresses. The city has risen against us. Bloody traitors.'

'The whole city?'

'Enough. The priests have got them all whipped up against us. The local nobs have decided to side with their old masters. They think they can beat us.'

'Maybe they can,' I said.

'They'll never beat the Imperium,' Anton said.

'That won't matter to us if they kill us now.'

'Point taken,' Anton said.

'Where did you hear all this?'

'Couldn't sleep so I went to have a smoke. Heard the comm boys gabbling.'

Ivan reached for his bottle, took a swig then picked up his lasgun from where it leaned against the wall. 'It sounds like we're going to be busy.'

I dressed and grabbed my gear. I heard booted feet running in the corridors. Everybody except us seemed in a hurry to get somewhere. I knew that soon enough someone would come along and let us know what to do.

As if summoned by the thought, the Understudy poked his head round the door. Corporal Hesse was with him. 'Assemble, lads,' the Understudy said. His face looked pallid but that might just have been the light. His voice was the same rasping monotone as always. 'It looks like we've got some work to do. Looks like the priests have whipped up a mob and they are coming to get Macharius.'

He might have been telling us he had just gone for a short walk to buy a protein sandwich for all the emotion he showed. I took another look out the window and suddenly everything snapped into place. Massive crowds surged ever closer to the hospice. Priests with halos of flame clung to the sides of massive demolition vehicles and shouted encouragement to the vast surging crowd. It was like looking out at a sea of hate-filled flesh: of very foolish, hate-filled flesh.

The Exterminator variant Leman Russ and the Manticores stationed around the building opened fire. There was no way they could miss. Explosive shells tore into the crowd. Autocannon fire scythed through flesh. Thousands died in seconds. The rest screamed and tried to run but it did them no good. At first the people behind them had no idea what was happening and kept pushing forwards. You could see them knocking down those who tried to retreat and trampling over them, and then in turn come face to face with the reality of intensive weapons fire.

'This is mad,' the New Boy said.

I looked at the slaughter and thought about what was going on. It came to me what was happening. 'Not if you don't care how many civilians die.'

'You are a hateful man, Leo,' said the New Boy. He sounded almost as if he admired me for it.

'It's not me. It's the priests of the Angel of Fire.'

'I don't follow.' The rest of them were looking at me now except the Understudy. All of them looked interested in what I had to say.

'They want this massacre to happen. It will whip up the population against us. We fired on unarmed civilians. We massacred the locals.'

'It's them that's leading the locals on,' said Anton. He sounded outraged.

'I suspect they will forget to mention that.'

'It makes sense,' said Corporal Hesse. He was half-looking at me and half-looking at the crowd that were being mown down by our superior firepower.

'The priests don't care how many of the hivers we slaughter. We waste our ammunition. We make new enemies. We reveal how strong we are.'

'It's a distraction too,' said the New Boy as if he had suddenly seen the light. 'While these people tie us down their armies are getting closer.'

'It seems they've learned a lesson or two from Macharius.'

We looked at each other. Macharius was here. In the hospice. Surely the priests must know that. This could be a distraction of another sort. A massive frontal assault while inside...

The Understudy realised it at the same time as I did. 'Let's go,' he said. 'We've got to get to the Lord High Commander – fast!'

Our floor of the hospice looked normal. Medical adepts and Sisters Hospitaller and soldiers in the uniform of the Guard were everywhere. Temporary field hospitals had been set up and the wounded were being treated. The Understudy ordered a passing sergeant to take his report to whoever was in command. He did not slow down on his way to the elevator though. We clambered into the pneumatic tube and headed up. It stopped on the nineteenth floor as if some sort of command override had been given.

'All out,' the Understudy said. He was frowning. It might have been a simple malfunction. Such things were common enough but under the circumstances, it was suspicious. We raced along the corridor, heading for the emergency stairs. There were guards there but I did not recognise any of them. Some of them had spots on their uniform, as if they had been splattered with dark, red liquid.

'Password,' one of them demanded. He had a local accent. I raised my shotgun and pointed it at them. They went for their weapons at the same time. I pulled the trigger and then dived to one side moments before a las-bolt flickered over my shoulder. The rest of the squad opened fire and cut the sentries down.

'Why did you shoot them?' the New Boy asked.

'They were not our boys,' said Corporal Hesse. 'And look at the bloodstains on their uniforms.'

'Might have been from old actions. Or maybe Leo put it there with his shotgun.'

'No time to argue,' the Understudy said. 'Up the stairs. If you see anything suspicious shoot first and ask questions later.'

We nodded. There was something strange in the atmosphere. All of us could sense it now. Something had gone very badly wrong.

We rushed up the stairs as fast as we could. A short way up we found out what had happened to the sentries. A group of bodies lay there in their underwear. They had been stabbed.

One of them still had a scalpel in his chest. Someone must have put it there after they took away his clothes.

'Whoever did this was probably garbed as a medical adept,' Corporal Hesse said.

'Must have been damn good with a scalpel,' said Anton.

'Make sure you don't give them a chance to operate on you,' said Hesse.

'Do my best,' said Anton.

We hit the head of the stairs expecting the worst and we found it. Gunfire echoed down the corridors. It hit me that if this had happened a few hours later, it might have been Anton, Ivan or myself lying cold down there with a scalpel through the heart. The thought did not make me feel charitable towards whoever had done it.

Another idea sidled into my brain. This was a well-planned attack. We were a small group of men. We were most likely outnumbered and we might not be getting out of this alive. Even if we did, there was a city out there full of people who hated us and about to be invaded by an enemy army. I pushed the thought to one side.

'One problem at a time,' I muttered.

'Look sharp,' the Understudy said. 'Find Macharius. If they get him, this whole thing is over.'

There were more dead bodies strewn around the corridor. Most of them belonged to our boys. A few belonged to men who looked like medical adepts except for the fact that such people don't usually carry lasguns. Still, it looked like our boys had put up a bit of a fight. A number of the heretics had gone down. The burned meat smell of las-bolt wounds and the scorch-marks on their robes told the tale of how they had died.

'Bastards must have put a regiment in here disguised as medical adepts,' said Ivan said. His frozen metal features gave nothing away but his gaze flickered around the entrances. He was taking no chances.

'What fool ordered Macharius put here anyway?' Anton asked. It's always easy to be wise after the fact. It was about the only time Anton ever managed it.

'There's something odd here,' said the Understudy. I looked at the bodies and I saw that he was right. The dead heretics had all been shot in the back of the head with a very high-calibre slug gun of some sort. They lay sprawled on top of our soldiers.

'It wasn't our boys killed them,' I said. 'Looks more like the sort of thing a commissar would do if they were going to run.'

Ivan frowned. 'What sort of lunatic would pause to execute a half a dozen of his fellow conspirators over the bodies of the men they had just killed? And in the middle of an assassination attempt?'

He was right. It made no sense.

'Maybe somebody on our side took them by surprise,' I said. I had no idea who it could have been though. It certainly wasn't an Imperial Guardsman. Those weren't las-bolt burns. The corpses did not have the exploded-from-the-inside look of bolter victims either so that ruled out Space Marines.

'We don't have time to puzzle this out,' rasped the Understudy. 'We need to move.'

We reached the head of the stairs and moved out into the corridor. The Understudy indicated we should push on. We were close to the ward where Macharius was resting now.

The sounds of fighting got louder. The Understudy looked at me. I knew what he meant. Close order combat is what the shotgun was intended for. I stepped around the corridor, saw a group of men in hospital uniforms carrying guns. None of them looked friendly so I opened fire, pumping shot after shot into my targets. As soon as they heard the thunder of the shotgun in the constricted space, the others stepped up. Las-bolts flickered past me, eerily silent by contrast to my weapon, except when their bolts sizzled into flesh.

The attack might have been well planned but the execution was sloppy. There was no one guarding the rear or keeping look out. Or maybe whoever had killed those heretics had removed it for us.

It seemed the fanatics were keen to take Macharius's head. A few of them turned to shoot at us though and for a few moments it was touch and go. There was no cover in the corridor. I just had to stand there and trust to luck. I had the advantage of not being taken by surprise. A searing pain in my right bicep told me it was not enough. I walked forwards. It was crazy, I know, but it meant I was moving and more to the point, I think it scared a few of them, fanatics though they were. The sight of a bloodstained maniac with a combat shotgun coming towards you shooting is rarely a reassuring one.

The air stank of roasting flesh and entrails suddenly released from bodies. Piss and excrement gave their usual testimony to the effects of terror. Plants and statues caught fire. Smoke billowed and then as suddenly as it started, it was over. The enemy were all down. In the distance, along the corridor from a different part of the ward, I could hear the sounds of combat. Some sort of slug gun was being fired. After every shot there was a scream.

I looked down. There were more bodies and not just of heretics. They wore the uniforms of Macharius's personal guard, complete with lion's-head insignia. They looked like they had died hard, but they were still dead.

The Understudy walked by me, stiff-legged as an automaton. 'Lord High Commander Macharius,' he shouted. 'Are you in there?'

'Is that you, Ryker?' came back a familiar resonant voice. Somehow, Macharius had remembered the sound of the Understudy's voice. Obviously he was not one of those generals who needed an aide to remind him of the names of those he had met.

'Yes, sir. We've cleared the corridor. We need to get you out of here.'

'Come in with your hands up. Bring a few of the lads from your unit with you, if they are there.'

He was cautious, give him that. I don't know how he expected the heretics to impersonate the Understudy but he must have seen some odd things in his time. The Understudy nodded to me and we stepped through the door. For show I held my shotgun at arm's length above my head. I did not want any mistakes made as to my intentions.

Macharius was in there, crouched down behind the bed he had been using for cover, an antique bolt pistol in his hand. He looked pale and his upper torso and head were wrapped in bandages. More of his guard were sprawled on the ground near him. They had died to the last man to protect him. Macharius himself grinned at us. There was a glitter in his eyes that was close to madness. I realised then why it was the Lord High Commander led assaults and how he had collected his wounds. He enjoyed combat, loved it with a burning passion. Some men do. He was one of them. The bolt pistol he pointed at us never wavered. I sensed without needing to be told he would be happy to use it if given any provocation at all.

As ever the Understudy gave no sign of fear. I wondered what it was he had seen when he was splattered with brains back in the Baneblade. 'We need to get you away from here, sir. The heretics have taken the entire upper floor and they're on their way now. The hive may fall any time soon.' Macharius nodded, as unabashed by the situation as the Understudy.

'Right,' he said. 'Let's go.'

Just like that he took control of the situation. Newly risen from a hospital bed, drugged with painkillers, attacked by surprise in what was supposed to be a secure zone, he was ready to lead. It was strangely reassuring to have him there even though he was now the most wanted man on the planet.

The sound of shooting stopped. It was all eerily quiet as we walked out into the corridor ahead of Macharius. The door at the far end slid open and we turned to face whatever new threat it represented.

Much to my surprise, it was Anna. Her nurse's uniform was covered in blood. She was holding a very large gun in her hand and showing no signs of strain. Her face was cold and calm. The weapon pointed directly at us. She looked as if she knew how to use it. She was looking directly at me. I think the fact she recognised me was all that saved us. Looking back now, I am certain of it. She was quite capable of killing all of us before we could react. The Understudy was already blocking Macharius from exiting the room. 'The flesh of heroes is the bulwark of the Imperium,' she said.

'Don't shoot,' said Macharius. 'She's one of Drake's. She knows the passwords.'

She walked towards us. She gave no sign of recognising any of us. She did not look like anyone I knew. Her eyes were cold as the vacuum of the void.

'Bloody hell,' said Anton. 'Is that–'

'Yes.' I cut him off before he could say any more. I tried to remember what I had said when I was drunk. If she was an Imperial agent then I was in deep, deep trouble. I shrugged. I was one of a small handful of Imperial Guard survivors standing in a building being overrun by heretics. I was already in trouble. Being reported to the Imperial authorities seemed the least of my problems.

Macharius stopped for a moment to look out the stained armour-glass of the window. If he was daunted by the sight of the heretic hordes pouring into the plaza he gave no sign of it. He glanced at the emergency escape diagram on the walls beside the stairs. He seemed to memorise it in a glance then he turned to Anna and said, 'You know your way around this place.' It was not a question.

'Yes, sir,' she said.

'Get us out by the fastest and most secure route.'

Whatever Anna was, Macharius seemed in no doubt that she would obey him.

Anna took us down the nearest fire escape. There were heretic guards at the bottom. Their backs were to us. Ivan pulled out his knife. He wanted revenge for what their fellows had done to our boys with the scalpels. He needn't have bothered. Anna raised that long-barrelled gun of hers. There was a faint hissing sound, like a blow gun being used. Heads exploded in quick succession. A few of the heretics managed to turn, confused by the swift savage assault. All that got them was a bullet through the eye or forehead instead. The only accuracy I have ever seen to match it was from the Space Marines. Surely, I thought, she was not...

I let it slide. I had no idea what she was then and truth to tell I did not really want to know any more. All I knew was she was terrifying. It was as if something else had taken possession of the woman I thought I had known, if ever so briefly.

Macharius looked at the carnage.

'Scout ahead,' he said as she coldly inspected the corpses. 'We'll follow. Clear away any obstacles.'

Swiftly and silently she loped away as if walking into a hornet's nest of heretics was no more than a feast-day stroll.

Macharius looked at the bodies. He stripped a corpse and put the chirurgeon's gown over his jacket. 'Take some of the heretics' medical robes and put them on,' he said. 'No sense making your men targets,' he said.

The Understudy rasped, 'You heard the Lord High Commander, lads,' he said.

'No ranks, no insignia, no titles,' Macharius said. He did not need to tell us why. All of those would identify him and the Understudy as the officers and make them targets. I don't doubt that the enemy could have identified him anyway. He had the look of eagles, had Macharius.

Moments later, we were on our way, looking for an exit. Macharius bent over and picked up a comm-vocoder from one of the heretics. He listened to it for a moment to see if he could pick up any chatter and then we moved on as fast as our feet would carry us.

We dragged the bodies out of sight and moved down into the lower levels of the hospice. Ahead of us were more dead bodies all with the same head wounds. They just lay there, sprawled in death. There was no sign of Anna. I had stopped fearing that we would find her corpse among the enemy. The scale of the devastation she wrought seemed almost supernatural.

She waited for us at the foot of the stairs, looking relaxed and unafraid. There were no bodies but I knew from the way she held that odd-looking gun that there easily could be, if anyone came upon us unannounced. The building shook. The roar of the crowd was audible. I smelled burning flesh and molten metal.

'The heretics are overrunning our forces around the hospital, sir,' she said. 'There is no safety there.'

'How?' Surprise tore the words from Anton's mouth. 'There were tanks out there.'

'Psykers,' said Anna. 'And it looks like traitors from inside the hospice. If we join with them we will be overrun with them.'

Macharius took this with more calmness than I could. 'You know another way out? We need to escape from here and go to ground until we can regroup.'

Anna nodded and led us towards another exit. We emerged into an inferno of heat and noise and violence. The crowd surrounding the building had turned into a seething sea of flesh. I saw a Leman Russ with oily black smoke billowing from its turret and a flame-headed priest standing on its chassis, howling imprecations at the mob. Even though our regimental uniforms were covered by the heretics' robes, I felt as if the massed crowd of enemies was bound to spot us. I expected them to start shouting and pointing momentarily. I decided if that happened I would not be taken alive. I did not want to end up in one of those cages.

All around us heretics howled for blood. The plaza was packed with a chanting crowd. Priests with halos of fire led them. They screamed and shouted with the best of them. There was an atmosphere of mania; a sinister hysteria that I sensed the priests were feeding on. Everywhere I looked the Angel of Fire stared down. Its gaze was everywhere. It seemed to be watching us specifically.

I smelled burning and heard explosions. Looking up I saw the entire top floor of the hospice was on fire. The crowd groaned ecstatically as if this had some occult religious significance. I caught sight of the expression on Macharius's face. He seemed to be drinking it all in – the shouting crowds, the burning war machines, the fire-winged angels perched on the buildings all around. It was as if he wanted to memorise the entire tableau, as if he wanted to recall every face so he could seek personal vengeance on them all.

'We had best keep moving,' he said. 'This is not the safest place to be.'

We began to shoulder our way through the crowd, which remained blessedly unaware that the man for whose blood they were howling was making his way through their midst.

'What now, sir?' I asked once we had battled our way to the edge of the crowd.

'We need to find a place to hide until we can find out what is going on and make contact with our own people.'

'If there are any left,' said Anna. She did not sound too hopeful on that score.

'Any suggestions?' Macharius asked.

She nodded and glanced at her feet. 'The underhive,' she said. 'It's a lawless place but the priests don't hold too much sway down there. No one does.'

She sounded as if she had first-hand experience of that. She was right too. When you're in trouble in a hive city there is only one way to go – down. It is proverbial that everything rolls that way in a hive – poverty, excrement, crime.

'Lead on,' said Macharius. He looked drained but there was no strain in his voice.

We made for the nearest ramp and started our trip to the bottom. No one paid too much attention to us. The city was in an uproar. Sensible people were keeping off the streets. The heretics assumed we were with them. We avoided any sounds of fighting.

At first, we went through the prosperous areas with commercia and factorums and reasonably well-maintained hab-blocks. As we kept on with our downward progress, things started to look a little grimmer. The blocks were not so nicely built; the people were not so well-dressed. More and more trash was piled up against the walls until the heaps of rotting stuff looked like great buttresses. More and more locals stared at us and then walked on. We were wearing blood-stained robes with medical symbols on them. We were carrying weapons. It was no wonder that people stared at us and equally it was no wonder that they left us alone.

Groundcars swept by. On the upper levels they had been well-maintained, some of them had even been luxurious: the vehicles of administrators and well-off merchants and all the vast cloud of hangers-on that surround the nobles of the upper hive. The lower we went, the less luxurious the cars became, the more dented, the less well-maintained. The paintwork was chipped and rusty, the engines squeaked and roared. More and more transit trains passed overhead and gigantic, multi-trailered buses carried the hive dwellers home from their work. It was astonishing in its way. Above us, war had come to the upper levels. Down here life went on as it always did. People had to make a living. They kept their heads down.

I saw more priests than I had seen since we arrived in

Irongrad. One or two of those give us strange looks but no one approached us although one or two headed towards the public vox communications systems. Anton wanted to chase them but the Understudy said no. I understood his logic. It would only draw attention to us and we needed to keep moving.

Macharius looked tired and pale. For a man of his age, getting over major surgery, he was incredibly fit. It was a tribute to how well the juvenat treatments had taken but he was still recovering from his wounds. He was not at his full strength. He had come this far on willpower. It was a commodity he possessed in abundance but I wondered how long even his ferocious determination could keep driving his damaged body. He was reeling now and looked like he would have fallen over if the Understudy had not helped steady him.

We found a huge public elevator and we rode it down as far as it would go. One by one the crowd that surrounded us thinned out – leaving through the exits that would take them to whatever hovel they called home. Every time we looked out the scene got dimmer – there were fewer lights on and whatever roads led away from the elevator door looked emptier and emptier. Eventually, a red light flashed and a warning klaxon sounded and some sort of automated speaking system told us to vacate the elevator. We obeyed and strode out into a dimly lit public thoroughfare. I could almost feel the weight of the hive pressing down upon us. We must have come down several kilometres from where we had been through multiple layers of the hive city.

We were moving for the sake of moving, not because we

had any idea of where we wanted to go. I think it was an instinctive urge to find a lair and hole up. I began to study our surroundings ever more carefully. If you grew up in a hive city, like I did, they were the sort to make you wary. Great sparking cables of ripped out wire descended from the ceilings like vines dripping from jungle trees. Stacks of rubbish and rubble piled up against the walls, narrowing the streets into funnelled walkways. Fungus grew around stagnant pools of urine and leaked sewage. Huge rats scuttled from burrow to burrow, their semi-intelligent eyes gleaming as they chittered to each other. Groups of equally hungry and feral-looking youths armed with ill-maintained weapons eyed us warily. I understood why – they were wondering who we were, if our bloodstained medical robes were the insignia of some new gang. I thought it best if they kept wondering. It provided us with some local cover.

Trash fires burned in the gloom. For the first time the metal angels with their fiery wings showed signs of being defaced. What was all the more impressive was that sometimes their gaseous pinions were the only source of illumination in what were increasingly becoming mere tunnels.

And yet if you knew what you were looking for there were the signs of a culture of sorts and even an economy. Vendors sold skewered rat-meat roasted on braziers. Street sellers hawked ammunition and holy symbols. They had spread their wares out on rotting tapestries resting on fallen columns, broken plinths and what looked like looted pews from temples. Their makeshift shops were set up under the arches of overhead viaducts.

We came across a vast bazaar where second-hand clothes

were sold alongside all of the necessities of underhive life – synthetic proteins and carbofoods, ammunition, wargear, toys and amulets. Fortune tellers did a thriving business and hooded figures scuttled round the edges. Once I caught sight of a face so disfigured it was difficult to tell whether it had been marred by mutation, radiation burns or some exotic disease. Possibly it was all three.

The most reassuring thing, strange to say, was that there were no priests visible, and mad-eyed preachers ranted all manner of strange and unsettling sermons as the crowd passed by. We had local currency and we bought food and what the seller claimed was purified water. Our money went a lot further down here than it had closer to the surface and I realised how much we off-world invaders had been over-charged compared to the locals.

No one paid any attention to my accent when I spoke. No one seemed too curious as to where we had come from. I realised that if we wanted we could most likely begin new lives down here. Our life expectancy would most likely be greater than if we remained soldiers of the Emperor on the surface.

It's not as hard as you would think finding a place to stay in the underhive. There are plenty of holes in the wall and abandoned hovels that you can take over but there are also plenty of gangs who have an interest – they have territory to defend, tithes to extract and simple bullying fun to be had with their victims.

We found a burned-out shopfront that no one seemed interested in and we made camp there. To tell the truth, it was considerably better than some of the places I have slept while on campaign.

Macharius lay inside, his back against a wall, his weapons close at hand. He did not look well. It seemed as if the strain of fighting his way clear of the hospice and then finding the way down here had taken a greater toll on him than I at first realised.

Anna sat beside him applying chemicals from the medical pack. She did this with all the competence of a real nurse or a medical adept. She even had some sort of sensor-altar which she attached to him and invoked. Macharius lay there watching her. Sometimes he closed his eyes as if asleep. I wondered if he was ever going to open them again.

The Understudy watched her. Corporal Hesse stood by the door and smiled at passers-by in a menacing fashion. Anton and Ivan were with him. The New Boy stood in a darkened corner. Sensibly, he had a lasgun in his hands.

Naturally, the arrival of a group of well-armed men did not go unnoticed by the local youth. A deputation arrived to enquire as to our business and find out how much we were willing to pay for the privilege of their protection.

I stood back in the shadows with my shotgun in my hand and I observed the newcomers. They were typical under-hive scum of the sort that were all too familiar on Belial. Of course, here they were dressed differently. On Belial they might have worn long leather trenchcoats and goggle masks. Here they favoured flowing robes and rebreathers all in varying shades of red. Most of them had facial tattoos depicting flames. They had similar tattoos on their arms and shaven heads. Some of them had skeletons in burning cages as well. The basic message seemed to be, as it is on every world, that they were alienated outsiders who were not afraid to die. Which was good, I thought, because I was perfectly prepared to kill them.

'You must pay,' said the tall burly one who was obviously the leader. His shaven head was marked with a flaming skull. It made a nice target for me to point my shotgun at. 'You must pay and you must swear allegiance to the Khan of the Flames. If you do not, you will die.' He slapped the autogun holstered at his side for emphasis.

'That's all very well,' the Understudy said. 'Ask the Khan to come here and we will see if he is worthy of our fealty.'

'You're talking to him,' said the ganger. 'You want to swear or you want to die.'

The Understudy looked at the small troop of tattooed maniacs following the Khan. I could see the calculation he was doing in his head. They outnumbered us but not by much. They were well armed but not as well armed as we were.

'I propose an alternative,' said the Understudy.

'What is that? the Khan asked.

'You can swear allegiance to me and I won't kill you.' The Khan went for his gun. I stepped forwards and pulled the trigger. Where the Khan's head had been was only a bloody stump of neck. Anton and Ivan raised their lasguns and suddenly the Understudy was there with a pistol in one hand and a grenade in the other.

The gangers just looked at us as if not quite understanding what had happened. They were used to bullying tradespeople and other underhive feebs. I don't think they were used to people who were even more ruthless than they were. 'Go away and don't bother us,' the Understudy said. 'And don't come back unless there are more than a hundred of you. I'd like some target practice.'

It was terrifying the way he said it. There was no emotion in it. He was simply stating a fact. It made me shiver and I was not the one he was threatening. The gangers turned on their heels and ran and I can't say I blamed them.

'What to do now?' Corporal Hesse asked in a parody of the Khan's speech style. We stood in a small group by the entrance, watching the street. It was dark save for the light of angels' wings. Small groups of people lurked in the pools of shadow, watching us watching them.

Anton looked pointedly over at where the wounded Macharius lay. 'I think we wait for the man to tell us that.'

'What if he can't?' Hesse asked.

'Then he will,' Anton nodded at the Understudy.

'Chain of command,' said Ivan. 'I am surprised you need us to tell you that.'

'I was more thinking of foraging for food and keeping the priests off our back,' said Hesse. 'And maybe being ready in case some of the local gangers decide to pay us a return visit.'

'We're as ready as we are ever going to be,' I said.

'We need to find out what is going on,' Hesse said. 'How it is going with our lads on the surface. How the war is going.'

'Our lads are most likely being herded into cages and set alight,' said Anton.

'That's going to make things a bit difficult,' said Hesse.

He slumped down thoughtfully with his back to the wall and his lasgun in front of him. He looked at us and then the Understudy and Macharius then back at the street. 'It's a pretty small fighting force to take back a world but I suppose it can be done.'

'Your faith is touching,' said a cold voice from near the doorway. All of us went for our weapons. None of us were sure how such a large man could have snuck up on us without us noticing. The figure was tall and lean and his face was covered by a cowl and yet there was something familiar about his manner and those features we could see.

'Put the guns down,' he said. 'You are not going to shoot me.'

Anna had her weapon pointed directly at his head. He made some sort of gesture with his hand and she lowered it slowly. I told myself it was not some form of psychic control. It was merely an understood signal.

He said it with the same sort of utter certainty that Macharius might have done but there was none of Macharius's warmth in his voice. He pulled down the cowl so we could get a look at his face. All of us recognised his features. We had seen him accompanying Macharius on the very first day of campaign.

'I am High Inquisitor Drake,' he said. I shuddered; back then I had heard only the vaguest of rumours about the Inquisition, the sort of scuttlebutt you picked up from people who knew people who knew people who had heard something once on a campaign three systems away. The Inquisition was feared by men who feared almost nothing else. I was destined to understand why. At the time, I found

Drake frightening enough and I did not even know one tenth of the reasons I ought to be afraid.

The Understudy looked up at him. He had not lowered his gun but he did not look like he was planning on using it either.

'How did you find us?' he asked. Drake's fingers stabbed out at Macharius. 'I found the Lord High Commander. He has a most distinctive aura. You should be grateful that none of the Angel's more devout worshippers are as familiar with it as I am.'

'You are a psyker?' Anton asked. He gulped as he said it but the words came out anyway. I could tell the fact that Drake was a psyker scared him in a way that the fact that Drake was an inquisitor never would.

'I am overwhelmed by your powers of deduction,' Drake said. He walked over to where Macharius lay and looked down at him. He glanced at Anna and she nodded to him. Clearly there was some sort of understanding between the two of them. Drake passed a hand through the air over Macharius's recumbent form and nodded, as if satisfied by something that none of the rest of us understood. 'He will recover.'

He said it with utter certainty. It came to me then and there that I disliked the inquisitor and likely always would, even though we were on the same side. Let me rephrase that – my suspicion is that I was on the same side as him. He was on his own side, whatever that was.

'How did you escape?' I asked, just to show I was not afraid, although I was.

'The heretics attacked our quarters. I departed. They did

not see me.' He said it as if it was simple. Perhaps for him it was.

'You left all your people behind?' The words just came out of my mouth before I could stop them.

'You are judging me?' There was a dangerous edge to his voice now. He was not a man used to being questioned. He was a man to be feared. The fact that he had found his way here without aid told me that. I felt like I ought to say something but I could not. Resentment was at war with fear. The cold grey eyes bored into mine. They seemed to look right through me. Perhaps they did. A tiny smile quirked his thin lips as if something he was looking at amused him.

'I saved those I could,' he said.

'Where are they now?' Anton asked. 'We could use the reinforcements.'

'They are where they will be most useful. And if an ill fate befalls us they will be useful to those who come after. There are things on this world that the Imperium must be warned of.'

'And what would those be?' The Understudy's rasping delivery was calmer than mine would have been under the circumstances.

'This world is steeped in the darkest sort of heresy.' Anton shot me an I-told-you-so look. 'The priests of the Angel of Fire are worse than anything you have encountered before, Private Lemuel.'

I did not need to ask how he knew. Doubtless as an inquisitor he would have access to our campaign histories. He saw me staring at him and for once misinterpreted my thoughts.

'Yes, I know who you are. I looked into the backgrounds of all those assigned to guard Macharius. I know you are loyal and I know you are decorated for bravery.'

It was an alarming thought that we had come to the attention of this cold, vain and supremely powerful man. Having an inquisitor look closely at you was worse even than having a commissar do so. I wondered if he had been in touch with Anna before this. I did not doubt that they would know each other. They were of a kind. I wondered whether she was another inquisitor.

'You were saying about the priests of the Angel of Fire,' the Understudy said.

'I fear their cult is merely concealment for something older and much darker. Their use of unsanctioned psykers tends to confirm that but it is what those psykers are in touch with that troubles me.'

'And what would that be, my friend?' Macharius's rich, powerful voice carried easily through the chamber. How long had he been awake and listening? It was possible he had been so the whole time. Macharius was a man who liked to seize whatever advantage in whatever situation he found himself.

'Something daemonic,' Drake said, without missing a beat. His gaze focused on the Lord High Commander and there was respect there and a challenge, and something else. I am not sure what. He had that look you sometimes see on the faces of the wounded when they are about to experience a religious conversion. Why an inquisitor would look at Macharius that way I do not know. I heard Anton gasp but when I looked at him he seemed secretly pleased. He was caught up in the sort of high drama he had only ever read about. I wished him luck with that. It was the sort of drama I could live without ever seeing.

'You are certain?' Macharius asked. His tone was flat and fatal.

Drake nodded. 'I told you as much when the reports started coming in from my agents.'

'How bad is it?' Macharius was not going to give even a high inquisitor a chance to say I told you so.

'As bad as can be. There are strange currents in the air now and odd and terrible rituals are being performed. Every death those blasphemers have caused contributes to it. Something is feeding on it.'

'Why?'

'I think there is something preparing to break through into this plane of existence. I think our presence here has contributed to that.'

'You are saying that we are somehow the cause of all of this?'

Drake shook his head. 'I think this was going to happen anyway at some point, our presence merely hastened the event. The heretics need aid against us. They are using supernatural means to acquire it before the full force of the Imperium arrives.'

'There's more, isn't there?' Macharius said.

'Our presence has allowed them to move openly, to cloak their evil rites in the mantle of patriotism and resistance to the invaders. The people might have risen against them if they had simply gone about their ritual murders on such a huge scale. Now it is all part of the war effort.'

'You are saying that the locals are not all heretics then,' said Anton.

'They believe in false gods and false prophets but they are not the pawns of daemonic powers,' said Drake. 'At least, not yet.'

'And we are stuck here in the underhive,' said Macharius.

'For the moment,' said Drake.

'We must come up with a plan,' said Macharius. He slumped back in weariness and stared at the ceiling. He had the abstracted look of a man in deepest contemplation. His body might have been weak but his mind was racing.

'It will need to be a very good one,' said Drake. 'I fear the forces we had left in the hive are totally overrun.'

I thought about that for a long moment. If we were the only loyal Imperial troops left in the city, what chance did we have? And how long would it be before the heretics started looking for Macharius even down here?

'Tell me about Belial, Lemuel,' Macharius said. 'What is it like?'

I sat beside him. He had beckoned me over. I looked down at the Lord High Commander. He lay on his back. His eyes glittered. The surge of energy he had shown when speaking with Drake had faded. Or maybe he was just saving his strength. With Macharius it was always hard to tell. He had recovered from wounds that would have left me flat on my back for weeks and he seemed to be recovering very well. I wondered what it felt like to him at this moment, to have won so much and to have lost it, to have gone from a palace to this rancid, rotting shell of a store in the underhive. I did not ask him though. Macharius had a reputation for speaking to private soldiers, for wanting to know what his army was thinking, but I was not tempted to any familiarity and I suspected he would not brook it.

'What would you like to know, sir?' At the moment, Macharius seemed to want to talk. There was just the two of us in this part of the building. The Understudy was nearby. Drake was by the door working on a datacore slate. His eyes were closed and he appeared to be talking to himself but I suspect it was all a lot more complicated than that. The rest of them had gone out foraging for supplies. Anna sat near him, weapon on her knees, watching the entrance. I doubted anything short of a small army was going to get past her.

'What was it like? A forge world of some sort?'

'An industrial world, sir, allied to the Adeptus Mechanicus but not a forge world. We supplied components. I am not sure what for. The trade routes were disrupted during the Great Schism and trading ships were rare.'

'You worked in a factorum?'

'A guild factorum, sir. It was before I volunteered for the Guard, before we all did, sir. Anton and Ivan and me.'

'Why did you do that? Were you looking for adventure?'

This inquisition was making me uncomfortable. I did not want to tell him we joined up because we had no alternative. It was either that or be tortured to death by local gangers. I just nodded.

'I can understand that,' he said. I sensed that he could too. Sometimes you can tell more about a man by the questions he puts to you and the motives he ascribes to you than he can tell by your answers to his questions.

'Looking for adventure, sir?'

He nodded back. I suspected that he knew what I had been thinking. He was a very good reader of men was Macharius.

In his position, you had to be. 'That and other things, Lemuel. I want to serve the Emperor. I want to restore His peace and His Light to our sector of the universe.'

If anyone else had said that to me I would have mocked them. It seemed like a tall order for one man. With Macharius though, it was different. He took it seriously and somehow that made you do so too.

'A worthy goal, sir,' I said.

'The only worthy goal, Lemuel,' he replied. 'The Schism made humanity weak. It opened our territories to invasion by xenos and heretic. It left thousands of our worlds and billions of our people prey to cosmic evil. We can put an end to that. We can make a difference.'

'It seems like a big job, sir.' I said.

'Too big, you are thinking, but it is not, not for the Imperial Guard. It is too big for one man, or one million men, but with the resources of the Imperium to draw upon no task is too large.'

His words were those of the great politician he was but you could tell he believed them. That was what gave them such force. And he spoke with the same passion to an audience of one as to an audience of hundreds of thousands. 'If we don't stand together, we are doomed. I don't care what the Schismatics believe as long as it includes belief in the Emperor, Lemuel, strange as that may sound. What I care about is the way heresy fragments the realm of humanity and tears us apart. United under the rule of the Emperor we are invincible. Split into thousands of warring schismatic states we will fall. Someone needs to put it all back together.'

'And you think you are that someone, sir?' It was almost disrespectful of me to say it, but Macharius was in a strange mood. He seemed to be talking to himself as much as to me. Perhaps he had been more affected by his wounds and his overthrow than I thought.

'In the absence of anyone better, Lemuel, yes. I am that man.'

And there it was – the iron core of his self-belief, the secret of what made him what he was. Macharius was a believer. He believed in the Emperor, he believed in humanity, but most of all he believed in Macharius. All of his beliefs were in perfect alignment and all of them supported each other. If you opposed the Imperium, you opposed Macharius. If you were the enemy of Macharius, you were the enemy of the Imperium. I was to see evidence of just how ruthless that could make him, before the end.

'I believe you, sir,' I said. And I did. Just like everyone else who ever followed him, except maybe one.

'I have a question for you, sir, if I may ask,' I said. I nodded at Anna. 'That girl, what is she?'

Macharius laughed. 'Not who, what! An interesting question.'

I kept my face blank. I did not want Macharius to know exactly how much of a personal interest I had in Anna and what she might say. Macharius's eyes flickered in the direction of Drake as he considered his reply. 'She is an agent of the Imperium, Lemuel. I would go as far as to say she is a highly trained one, possibly even altered by ancient, arcane science. An assassin.'

'An assassin, sir?'

'The Imperium has other tools than armies, Lemuel, more subtle ones. Sometimes a stiletto is needed instead of a chainsword.'

'Why was she there, sir?'

'I can see you are disturbed by this. She was watching over me.' I thought of the circumstances in which I had met Anna. She was a newcomer at the hospice. She had arrived there a mere day before Macharius himself was flown in. It seemed a little too much to be a coincidence. Macharius watched me closely and for once came to the wrong conclusion. 'She is not someone you have to worry about, Lemuel. She is a loyal servant of the Imperium.'

I suppressed a shudder and wondered what would happen if she decided that I was not. I looked over at Drake and wondered what would happen if she passed on a suspicion of that to him. I made myself shrug, for one brief instant forgetting that Macharius was watching me. He laughed. 'That's the spirit, Lemuel.'

He closed his eyes and returned to sleep. I noticed that his gun was in his hand. It would not do to wake him suddenly I thought, so I moved quietly away.

I walked over to Anna. She stood in the shadows now, leaning against the wall with its peeling plasterwork, studying Macharius and the room and our surroundings without seeming to. She looked completely relaxed but I knew that any moment she could erupt into violent action. Approaching her was like approaching a great predatory beast.

She watched me without seeming to and as I approached, I knew she was as aware of my presence as I was of hers.

'Private Lemuel,' she said as I reached her. I was almost close enough to reach out and touch her. Her voice was pitched low. It might have been not to disturb Macharius. It might have been so she could not be overheard.

'Anna?' I said. I kept my voice just as soft. 'Is that your name?'

'It will do, for now,' she said. I looked at her with a mixture of fear, embarrassment and something I could not quite put my finger on. Attraction, maybe? She looked back at me as if I were a complete stranger.

'I must say I was surprised to see you,' I said. Idiotic, I know, but you try making conversation with a stone-cold covert killer that you just happen to have slept with and who knows enough to have you executed at whim.

'I wasn't surprised to see you. I knew you were on the detachment guarding Macharius. I approved it.'

'You approved it?' I was confused but a little reassured.

'I transferred into the hospice when it became obvious that Macharius was going to be sent there.'

I thought about that. The timing was certainly right. We had met the night before we had found out Macharius was wounded.

'If I had arrived sooner some of this unpleasantness could have been avoided. As it was, I was just in time to forestall the Lord High Commander's assassination. You and your comrades helped. You have my thanks.'

I wondered if she was joking. She did not seem to be. There was no trace of the girl I thought I knew in her face. She was gone, as if she had only been a mask of flesh and just as easily removed.

'You saved us as well.'

'It was incidental to saving the Lord High Commander but you're welcome.'

I smiled at her. She was letting me know exactly how little the rest of us meant to her in no uncertain terms.

'All of the other stuff, what happened between us, that was just part of your cover story wasn't it, part of fitting in with the girls and avoiding suspicion? That's why you defended the Angel so strongly.'

'Exactly so. You are a perceptive man, Private Lemuel.'

'I said some things…'

'Yes. You did.'

'Are they…'

I didn't know exactly what I was going to say but she finished the sentence for me. '…on your file?'

I looked around to make sure no one else was listening to us. Drake seemed wrapped up in his note-making. Macharius was asleep. I nodded.

'Not yet,' she said. 'They may never be.'

She left that hanging in the air. It seemed she had a lever to use on me if she wanted. I wondered why she would need one of those. I did not then understand the truly devious world in which she lived and operated. Perhaps I do not now.

'I see,' I said. I turned to stalk away, hoping I looked more disgusted than afraid.

'Leo?'

I turned and looked at her over my shoulder. She smiled and looked a little like I remembered her from before. 'It was fun.'

I shook my head and kept walking. I was wondering whether she meant the night we had spent together or what she had just done to me.

'We need to find out what is going on,' Macharius said. He looked more energetic now after a cycle of rest. We were all back in the shop-front, listening attentively. 'We need supplies and we need to make contact with our own people if there are any left alive.'

He looked at us. His leonine gaze moved from face to face as if seeking dissent. No one disagreed with him. No one had thought of deserting either. Where would we go?

In the few hours since he had returned to his senses he had taken charge completely. We were like small asteroids who had fallen into the gravity well of a gas giant and become temporary moons. Only the Understudy seemed completely unaffected but then he was not affected by anything much any more.

'If we head up, the heretics will most likely spot us. They will be looking for you in particular, if they realise they do not have your body.' Drake was the only one of us who felt capable of speaking out against Macharius. The rest of us would probably have followed him if he had ordered us to charge the Cathedral of the Angel of Fire single-handed. 'All we need to do is remain hidden until General Sejanus arrives and takes back the city. We can contact our forces then.'

'You have agents here,' Macharius shot back. 'You spent the first few weeks putting them in place and putting pressure on the locals.'

'Our own people will be reliable if they are not caught,' said Drake. 'I doubt the locals will be of any use. They were with us because they thought we were winning or because we could put pressure on them. We don't have a lot of leverage on them now.'

'You can contact your people by the usual means?' Macharius's tone let us all know he was talking about using psyker powers.

'It might not be wise. The heretics employ many of the unsanctioned. They might be able to detect me.'

'Might. Might. Might. It seems to me that you spend an awful lot of time telling me what cannot be done, high inquisitor, and not very much telling me what can be.' Drake shot him a cold glare. He was not used to being talked to in that tone. He was used to being feared. Macharius matched his stare easily. He might only be in charge of an army of less than a dozen but he was still every inch the Imperial field commander. It was perfectly possible that Drake had the power to kill us all without any effort but Macharius gave no hint that he took such a thing into consideration. In the battle of wills between general and inquisitor, it was the inquisitor that looked away first.

'I will do what I can,' he said.

'Good,' said Macharius and grinned. 'The rest of you gather supplies and get ammunition. We'll need all we can get. Try not to draw too much attention to yourselves while you are doing it.'

His manner was cheerful and in control. You would never have guessed that we were alone in a city full of potent enemies. He never doubted for a moment that he was going to find some way to turn the situation into a victory. At that moment, I began to suspect that Macharius was not quite sane as most of us measure sanity.

Sane or not though, he was a great man.

'We've been in worse situations,' Anton said. We sat in a bar in underhive Sector 13 and no one paid too much attention to us. We were just two more armed men in blood-stained coveralls. The medical robes had become progressively more grubby as we hauled stuff back to our new base. Our faces were smudged and we had a few days' growth of stubble. He took a sip of the distilled alcohol and winced. It must have been bad to make Anton do that. We were talking in Belial street dialect and that got no attention either. No one around here seemed too bothered by strangers' talk. In hive cities there are all manner of technical dialects spoken by various castes and guilds. Sometimes people raised a couple of kilometres from one and another cannot understand what the other is saying. 'Care to name some,' I said. I was feeling gloomy. There was a strange pressure in the air, a feeling of expectancy and something else. I think we all felt it and we had no idea what it was. It was something other than the despair of defeat though. It was as if an invisible psychic miasma was drifting down from the upper levels of the hive and polluting our souls.

Ivan let out a low whistle. The flickering gas-lights reflected in his metal cheeks. I wondered if anyone might have recognised him because of those. I doubted it. The city was too big and the people too many and anyway, what were we going to do about it?

'The idiot boy is right,' Ivan said. 'We've got money, food, ammo and most of the time no one is shooting at us. It could be worse.'

'Thanks,' Anton said, 'I think.'

I glanced around the bar. It was a small place with half a dozen seats, just some shelves propped up against the hive wall, a few planks set on top of some empty barrels and some old stools set in front of it. We had a clear view of the street. The barman was a huge, burly man with doughy skin and an interesting wart the size of my fist on the side of his neck. Such stigmata were not uncommon in the underhive.

'We could set up a gang down here,' said Anton, the alcohol warming him to the topic. 'We could rule these streets.'

'We've got Macharius with us and an inquisitor, you think they are going to be happy with us running some street corner extortion racket?'

Ivan said, 'It won't be long before Sejanus and the rest of the army get here. All we need to do is wait for that. You heard the inquisitor.'

I was not as sanguine about that as he was. I suspected Sejanus would find Irongrad a lot harder nut to crack this time. I was not exactly sure why yet, but I felt it was going to be so.

'So what's going on with your girl, Anna?' Anton asked. He had been dying to know but had not asked in her hearing. I don't think he was exactly afraid of her. Just understandably cautious.

'She's not my girl. She's an Imperial Assassin. She's protecting Macharius.'

'An Imperial what?'

'An Assassin, some sort of agent, specially trained and equipped.'

'She tell you that?'

'Macharius did. I asked him.'

'You what?'

'I asked him. I was going to ask him about making you a Space Marine but you all came back in and interrupted.' This was not something I really wanted to talk about. Ivan at least had sense enough to know that.

'She's no worse than the inquisitor,' Ivan added. 'He's doing some scary stuff. Never cared much for psykers.'

'You going to tell him that?' I asked.

Ivan shrugged. 'He already knows. Or at least he does if he bothered to read my mind.'

'Damn! Anton's the only one who's safe then.'

'Why is that?' Anton asked, obliging as ever.

'Because you don't have a mind to read.'

'Ha bloody ha.'

'We could just not go back,' I said. I was floating an idea that I knew had passed through all our minds.

'And do what?' Ivan asked. He looked at me sidelong. It's surprising how judgemental his immobile metal features can look in the right light.

'What Anton says, start up our own gang or join one of the locals.'

'Keep dreaming,' Anton said. 'Three men are not a gang and you think any of the locals will take strangers? Nah – I think I am going to stick with Macharius. I am curious as to what he will do next.'

'We took an oath,' said Ivan. 'When we joined the regiment.'

'I guess I'll stick with you then,' I said. 'Someone needs to keep you out of trouble.'

'Let us know when you find him then,' said Anton. He took another drink.

Drake did not look pleased when we returned. He looked tired and coldly angry.

He sat opposite Macharius and was in the midst of arguing about something when we walked in. They both looked up and fell silent.

Drake suddenly stiffened and stood up. He swayed. His brow went tight and his face went suddenly pale. He forced his eyes shut. Red teardrops dripped from them and ran down his cheeks before speckling the rockcrete floor beneath him. He ground his teeth and muttered and clutched at his forehead. I wondered if he was having a stroke. Anna walked over to stand beside him. She looked as if she was ready to catch him if he fell over.

Suddenly he slumped down onto the floor and glared around fiercely. His eyes were bloodshot. He raised his hand and touched his cheek and then inspected his blood-stained fingertips.

'What is it?' Macharius said.

'I have had a vision,' said Drake. 'The Emperor has granted me a gift of the sight.'

'Tell me,' Macharius said.

Drake's eyes narrowed. A small frown crinkled his lofty brow. He looked as if he wanted to be sick.

'Tell me,' Macharius repeated.

'They have started burning the prisoners. From among

our men. The ones they captured.' The words hung in the air like a bad smell. It was obvious that this was only part of it. Drake studied the ceiling for a few moments. I followed his gaze. There was some mould there but the pattern was not interesting enough to justify his concentration.

'They are burning them in cages,' he said. The words came out at a steady measured pace like a regiment of troops marching on parade. 'They are performing a ritual. They are spending lives to work great sorcery.'

'That does not sound good,' said Anton. Drake glared at him and then shook his head. Obviously he understood the sort of idiot he was dealing with. He continued talking as if he had not been interrupted.

'They are summoning something,' he said. 'A being of great power and cosmic evil.'

'The Angel of Fire,' Anton said.

'That is one name for it,' Drake said. 'It is the entity they have worshipped all these years.'

'Why now?' Macharius asked.

'There is a war on,' said Drake. 'They seek to use the power of this daemonic entity to strengthen themselves and smite our righteous armies. If they succeed before General Sejanus lays siege to the city then they will have the power to destroy him.'

I looked at Drake. He seemed deadly serious. I was wondering what could possibly have the power to destroy the sort of force that General Sejanus would bring to Irongrad. I had a suspicion I would not like the answer if I was given it. I glanced at Macharius. He was obviously taking the inquisitor's words very seriously.

'What will happen if this being manifests?' Macharius asked.

'It will be dreadful. It will bring with it things from the hellish space it inhabits, from the warp.' He seemed to be forcing the words out, as if he did not really want to speak them. I doubt he would have if Macharius had not been there. The force of the Lord High Commander's will was great enough to daunt even an inquisitor. 'It will have vast psychic powers at its command and legions of daemons. If it gains a foothold here nothing short of Exterminatus will remove it. General Sejanus's force will not be able to stand against it.'

'We need to stop the summoning then,' said Macharius. He said it as if it was the most obvious thing in the world. I suppose it was. I could foresee a few problems. The half a dozen or so people we had here had been barely enough to get him out of the hospice. How would we be able to stop the manifestation of some daemon-god? Such trifles did not seem to bother Macharius. I suppose the difference is what made him what he was and me a common soldier.

'Very good,' said Drake. 'Now all we need to do is work out how.'

'We need a plan,' said Macharius. We need several Chapters of Space Marines and a couple of Imperial armies, I thought, but I kept my mouth shut.

'I believe that is your department,' said Drake with an impressive amount of controlled sarcasm.

'Yes,' said Macharius. 'And I know what must be done. Can you find the locus of this summoning?'

'It is centred on the cathedral. If we get close enough I can pinpoint it more precisely. You cannot be thinking to go there…'

'We are the only ones who know and can do anything. If we don't, no one else will.'

'But breaking into the cathedral will be impossible.'

'Nothing is impossible,' said Macharius. 'Bold men can overcome any difficulty if the Emperor is with them and their faith is strong.'

Anna nodded. She quite clearly believed what the Lord High Commander was saying. So did Anton and Ivan and Hesse. The Understudy's face was blank.

Drake looked at him coolly as if not quite sure what to say. Macharius rattled off orders telling us how to prepare. None of us seemed to know what to say. What he was proposing was quite clearly madness but then so was waiting for a daemon-god to appear. And he was Macharius and our commander. We could not disobey him. I looked around the shabby, half-abandoned shopfront. It suddenly seemed quite home-like, now I knew we were leaving and where we were going.

We left within the hour.

On the upper levels of the hive, the cages were in use. All of those hideous metal artefacts were full and all of them were frying Imperial soldiers like a Belial beer-hall vendor making rat steaks on a feast-day night. Every plaza was full of people watching men burn. The air was full of the smell of charring human flesh and the screams of men dying in agony. A lot of people stared. You'd think they'd get tired of it but they never seemed to. There was a strange festival atmosphere about the whole thing. Over everything hung that ominous sense of presence, of something waiting and watching and feeding.

It had its advantages, of course. No one had paid the slightest attention to us as we moved back into the upper levels of the city. Everyone on the street there was taking part in a screaming, chanting, hysterical victory celebration.

The priests of the Angel of Fire were ringmasters of this carnival – shouting out paeans of praise to their master through amplification systems, demonstrating their power by igniting the gas jets of the sacrificial cages with a wave of their hands.

They shimmered with power. There was something terrifying and terrible in the air, a hideous, gloating presence that got fractionally stronger with every heartbeat. It felt as if a monster was coming forwards with a slow inevitable tread. Drake looked nauseous. He dabbed tears of blood from the corners of his eyes. He was far more sensitive to whatever it was than I was. Of us all, only Macharius and the Understudy did not look worried and one of them was quite mad. Even Anna looked troubled.

Once as we walked through the crowd we heard a scream and saw a burning figure reeling through the crowd towards us. I reached for my shotgun, wondering what was happening, but the blazing figure only ran by us screaming with an odd mixture of agony and ecstasy.

'A martyr to the Angel, a martyr to the Angel,' the crowd chanted.

Some of them reached out to touch him, burning their hands. I tried not to flinch away lest I look suspect. People were starting to spontaneously combust in the street, as if all the hysteria and faith was too much energy to be contained within their frail human forms and needed to be transformed into fire. A madness had taken over the city and sometimes, when I looked into the eyes of the people around me, I saw no more humanity there than in the blood-red orbs of an ork.

It got worse the closer we got to the cathedral. It was the focus of all the madness and badness going on. There were more priests in the open area surrounding it than in all the other sectors of the city put together and there were armed soldiers from the local militias come to gape in awe and show their faith. They stood at the base of the tower looking upwards at the sanctified sky where the Angel stood atop the cathedral. It was like standing at the foot of a burning mountain gazing at the blazing peak. The cathedral towered above us, awesome and gigantic, a massive structure guarded by an army of fire-winged metal angels. A web of piping clutched its sides like metal ivy.

No one paid us any attention. They did not feel threatened. They thought they had already won.

Macharius looked interested in everything around him. If the horror had touched him he gave no sign. If he knew the faintest flicker of fear at the prospect of entering the heart of all this evil and confronting its source it did not show. He looked, as always, at ease and utterly in control of himself and the situation. There was no sign of the wounds that had slowed him just a few days ago. His health seemed to have been miraculously restored. There are those who would take that as a sign he was blessed but a medical adept told me that some people simply take very well to the juvenat treatments and that the cellular stimulation helps them regenerate wounded tissue. He thought it most likely Macharius was one of those. Of course, who is to say it was not both? Why should Macharius out of all those millions treated have been so blessed? Sometimes miracles are subtle instead of overwhelming. Or so the Testaments tell us.

Drake looked physically ill, as if the manifestation of whatever evil was here was crushing his spirit and his internal organs. I could almost feel sorry for him. He, better than any of us, knew what was going on. Given his training and his background this place must have been anathema to him.

Anna looked calm but her face had a frozen look as if she was keeping the expression on her face by an effort of will. It made her features seem mask-like to me although that might just have been my imagination and what I knew of her.

Anton looked pale and scared. At long last he was on the sort of big adventure he had always dreamed of being part of. I don't think it had turned out to be quite what he had expected.

Ivan loomed large in the gloom. His metal features showed no emotion but his eyes were feverish and he fidgeted and whistled loudly, always a sign he was nervous.

Corporal Hesse was sweating and he had bags under his eyes. He smiled nervously and studied our surroundings closely but gave no other signs of fear.

The New Boy, oddly enough, looked fascinated. I suppose he had passed through that stage of being afraid to acceptance of the inevitable. Or maybe he was just a better actor than the rest of us.

The Understudy looked stone-faced as he had from the day the lieutenant was killed. He was not frightened. He was not looking too human either. I wondered what was going to happen to him if his humanity ever returned. There did not seem much prospect of him living long enough for that to happen but I was curious nonetheless. As it was, in his inhumanity, he did not look out of place amidst these revels. There were plenty of people around us who looked crazier than he did.

One thing Drake had made clear – we needed to make this attempt. If the Sons of the Flame succeeded in what they were doing not only were our lives forfeit but also our souls. This ritual was going to birth something dark and strange and terrible and it would devour this world and all the worlds around it, until the overwhelming might of the Imperium arrived to confront it. The chances of us being around to see that were infinitesimal.

Macharius gestured for us to proceed. We shouldered our way through the crowded ferrocrete plain around the cathedral, making for the entrance. Its shadow fell upon us as we neared the huge structure. It felt warm, perhaps from the heat of all those burning wings.

The entrance to the cathedral was an enormous arch twenty times the height of a man. It was flanked by two enormous stone saints carrying bolter and chainsword. Perched over it, as if about to take flight, was another representation of the Angel of Fire. The local sculptors never seemed to tire of those.

No one stopped us from going in. I was astonished. Either the heretics really were confident or there were other safeguards against intrusion. I would not have taken a bet against the latter. Over the years I have developed a healthy distrust of things that seem too easy.

There were armed men wearing the robes of priests inside but they merely blessed us as we passed. They made a strange gesture in the air with their fingers. Their finger-tips left a blazing trail in the air, an oddly shaped rune that seemed to leave its mark on your retina long after you had stopped looking at the original. Everyone ahead of us was dropping the bronze local coins into offering slots so we did the same.

Inside was the nave, a long corridor with a ceiling even higher than the entrance arch. Murals painted by an artist of genius covered it. The Angel of Fire led its cohorts against armies of daemons and orks and mutants, slaying them with its sword of flames. Its prophets watched armies of stony-visaged faithful with burning eyes.

From up ahead came a terrible smell of burning flesh mingled with incense. The sound of choirs singing an infernally beautiful hymn filled the air. We walked on. People greeted us and slapped us on the back, celebrating victory, drunk on the strange carnival atmosphere, assuming that we were like them.

For a moment, I felt my view of the world tip towards heresy. There were thousands of people here, and millions outside in the hive and billions scattered across the system, all of whom believed in the absolute truth of the Angel of Fire. I was one of a tiny band of unbelievers. Who was to say that they were wrong and I was right? Who was to judge the truth of the words I had been taught on Belial against the words that were spoken here?

The cathedral was gigantic and awesome, the sense of imminent presence all but overpowering. It was certainly stronger than anything I had ever encountered in the temples of the Imperium. It was as if some great mystic revelation was about to unfold and all I had to do was surrender to the truth of it and I would become part of something greater than myself.

Perhaps these people were right. Perhaps the Angel of Fire really did stand at the right hand of the Emperor. How was I to tell? I had never been to Blessed Terra or stood before the Emperor's Throne and yet I took the existence of those things for granted, because I had been taught to, because I believed what was written in a book. These people had books too and they told a different and perhaps greater truth...

I felt a pinching grip on my arm and turned to look at Drake. There was a warning glance in his eyes.

'Resist,' he said. Perhaps his words shocked me out of the trance state. Perhaps it was something else entirely. I felt the lure of temptation recede but I was aware of how attractive it was and how easy it would be to succumb. I saw something in Drake's eyes and for a moment I felt something like sympathy for him and I was convinced he felt something like sympathy for me. These were issues he spent his whole life dealing with. He was constantly confronted with challenges to his faith and had to defend it. Did he have his doubts? At that moment I felt certain that he did and that he had to work harder than I to maintain his faith.

I noticed up ahead of us that there was another great arched doorway but this one was barred by lines of armed men who refused all admittance. Instead, lines of people separated to the left and right of the great aisle, passing up stairs and out of sight. Macharius indicated we should go to the right and we joined the crowds going up that way. It seemed better than milling aimlessly in front of the arch-way until someone became suspicious.

We moved up the steps with the crowd. The stairwell snaked upwards and after what seemed like hours we found ourselves in a huge gallery that looked down into the heart of the cathedral. We gazed out into an immense space. The ceiling was so high above us that it seemed like clouds had formed below us. Perhaps that was only the incense and the smoke of burning flesh from the enormous caged altar. I realised now why the sound of the choir was so loud. It drowned out the sound of the screams of the men being burned alive below me.

People all around watched enthralled as the priests per-formed their rituals. In the centre of the cathedral was the most beautiful statue of the Angel of Fire I had yet seen. It was perfect and lifelike in every detail. It seemed as if a steel angel with wings of fire really had incarnated itself before us. It looked as if it was just about to open its blind-seeming eyes and gaze down upon us in judgement. Perhaps it was just the flickering of the flames from the altar but it seemed to tremble with life. As I watched a great crane arm lifted the cage full of smouldering corpses from the altar. A sec-ond one swung a new cage full of living men into position. Another cage was rolled into place. The people around me watched enthralled. Clearly a high point of the ritual had been reached.

For a moment, there was silence from the choir and the crowd. You could hear only the panicked screams of the men in the cage and the subdued roar of the flames below them. They were burning with a low intensity now, clearly not at their full ritual strength. On a high lectern a priest of the Sons of the Flame spread his arms wide and began to preach a sermon. He talked about heresy. He talked about atonement. He talked about punishing the invaders who had defiled the sacred soil of Karsk. Then he spoke a word and the choir began to sing again, ancient ritual words invoking the blessing of the Angel, asking mercy for the souls offered up and hope that their impure souls would achieve grace as they fed the Emperor's great servant, the Angel of Fire.

I saw it now in the ancient, beautiful Gothic words of the sacred song. It was an evil parody of the Imperial liturgy. It echoed the words but used them to put a shimmering gloss on this awful sacrifice.

Part of me, the doubting part, whispered that the true Imperial ritual did the same thing, asking men to give up their lives and souls for the Emperor. I quashed it. There is a difference between asking men to act heroically and truly of their own free will and feeding them into a fire in white-hot cages.

I knew looking at the beautiful statue with its beatific face that whatever it represented was nothing holy but something evil and clever which used a shroud of holiness to conceal a corrupt and rotten heart. Below me men burned as flames leapt higher. I thought it could be me down there and realised that we were doing the right thing by opposing the cult even if it cost us our lives. Then it occurred to me that it was most likely going to do just that.

We gaped in horror as more of our comrades were burned. The local people watched agog. I wondered what had made them come. Was it the spectacle? Were they particularly devout? Was this some form of entertainment for them? They did not look any different from the average citizen of Belial and yet here they were, watching people die as if it were entertainment.

I looked from face to face. Some of them wore expressions of awe. One or two of them licked their lips and sweated as if they were taking some sort of pleasure in the brutish spectacle. Most looked a little stunned. I would like to say it was all down to the unholy power of the ritual the Sons of the Flame were enacting but I am sure it was not.

Many of the people looked on, eyes narrowed, features concentrated. They were simply fascinated by the fact of death. For many of them, this was as close as they were ever going to come to it until the day they died. There was an awful mystery here, beyond even that of the rituals of the Angel. I think they were hoping to see something mystical, to get a glimpse of the reality that lies beyond reality, to be witnesses at the moment of transition from life to death, to see something spiritually meaningful.

In this, they were doomed to disappointment. All they saw were men dying. All they heard was a choir drowning out screams. All they smelled was incense and roasting flesh. If there was anything mystical in the air, it was a horror, a sense of something dreadful slowly approaching, a monster lured by the savour of the killing, drawn to the scent of burning meat and departing spirits.

As the ritual ended and the cranes swung the old cage out and a new cage into position, ushers moved us out of the gallery so the next set of spectators could enter and bear witness. It was all well organised, a great machine designed for no good purpose, human sacrifice on an industrial scale.

We shuffled through the exit and back down a set of stairs along with all the believers. I looked at Anton and saw he was as appalled as me. Ivan looked glassy-eyed. Hesse looked almost sick. Anna had the same air of restrained calm she always wore. I was not in a position to see how Drake or the Understudy or Macharius reacted. I wish I had been.

The trudge down the stairwell was long and there was no way of avoiding it and we found ourselves out in a courtyard where vendors sold souvenirs – small metal cages, and bits of burned bone that purported to be from victims already cleansed. Somehow this was the worst part of it all. People were buying trinkets and souvenirs as if this day was important to them and they wanted to carry away some small thing as a reminder.

It was all I could do to keep from shooting.

We huddled together in the corner of the courtyard. It was not unusual, there were other small groups of pilgrims gathered in a similar manner, praying or discussing what they had witnessed in low, awed voices. All of us looked to Macharius for guidance, even Drake. He looked back at the inquisitor.

'How long?' Macharius asked. 'How long before whatever they are summoning manifests?' His tone was low enough so that it would not carry far.

'I do not know, hours possibly, days at most. I have read about these things but it is the first time I have witnessed a ritual of such potency from so close at hand.'

'And what happens if they succeed?'

'The Angel will manifest, only it will be no Angel and its manifestation will be a dark and unholy thing.'

'How can we stop it?'

'Somewhere in there a psyker of vast power is drawing all the mystical energy from those deaths and weaving it into a lure for a daemon-god. If we could kill the psyker that would do it...' Something about his tone told us that it was not quite so simple as that, if you could call walking through a temple full of fanatics and assassinating a psyker powerful enough to summon a daemon prince simple.

'But...?' Macharius said.

'But if we succeed in slaying him then there will be no one to control all the energy, the ritual will run out of control. At very least it is likely that anyone in the vicinity will be killed. At worst, a hole will be torn in the fabric of reality and hell will crawl through.'

'Hell is crawling through anyway,' said Macharius. 'This way there is at least a chance of stopping it.'

Drake nodded. He was a brave man but something was clearly preying on his mind. 'Also, if we die in there, there is a good chance our souls will be sucked into the hells from which they are summoning the daemon. They will be devoured and we will be damned for all eternity.'

'We'll be damned anyway if we don't at least try.'

Macharius looked at us. His steely gaze flickered from face to face. 'We do not have any choice. We must stop this. If we do not our comrades will be destroyed and our armies on this planet overwhelmed. The souls of millions will be lost.'

His voice was quiet enough not be overheard at any distance and yet I heard every word distinctly. He was right, of course. Something had to be done. For a moment I wondered whether I was the man to do it. Briefly I considered the possibility of simply running but under the gaze of Macharius it was no possibility at all. There was nowhere I could flee to anyway. If the Angel of Fire manifested itself, this whole world would be doomed and my soul and most likely my life would be lost.

I saw reflections of my doubts in Anton and Ivan's eyes. We could wait. Sejanus would get here with the army soon. Surely, the might of that great force would be enough to overcome what was happening here.

'There is no time for anything else,' Drake said. He sounded resigned but ready. 'If it costs our lives, they will be well spent if we can stop the Angel of Fire.'

'If we die here, we will die as heroes of the Imperium,' said Macharius. 'And if we triumph, our names will be remembered for as long as it endures.'

I could see that swayed Anton and Ivan and the New Boy. They were nodding now. I guess they were thinking what I was thinking. Death and damnation lay on all sides. There was no escape from it no matter which way we leapt. Macharius was offering us the possibility of glory.

'Can you find this psyker?' Macharius asked Drake. He studied the nearby pilgrims, looking as relaxed as if this were some holiday outing.

'His presence is hard to ignore. I am surprised you cannot sense him yourself. The aura is that strong.' Drake pitched his voice low so that only we could hear it.

'You will need to lead us to him.'

'He will be guarded,' Drake said. The discussion was between him and Macharius. The rest of us waited on their words. Drake was the expert. Macharius was our leader.

'They are overconfident,' said Macharius. 'They expect no trouble here. We can use that to our advantage.'

'As you say,' Drake said. Clearly he was not confident. 'We do not have any allies here.'

'There are companies of Imperial soldiers down there,' said Macharius. He indicated somewhere below us. He was thinking about the men we had seen being sent to sacrifice. There were scores of them. He did not seem to have any doubts that we could somehow free them. We stood at the mouth of hell, half a dozen men in the midst of a world full of heretics, and when he told us that we were going to do the impossible, we nodded our heads and thought, yes we can do this.

'If we can find them,' said Drake.

'I know where they are,' said Anna. 'I have studied the plans of this place. I can find them and I can free them.'

She nodded to a doorway in the wall. It was marked as forbidden. 'That doorway leads to a maintenance section. It must lead also to the machinery of sacrifice. The prisoners will be kept there.' She obviously had a very clear idea of the topography of the cathedral in her head.

'Open it,' Macharius said. He did not seem to have any doubts she could. She began to walk over to the doorway as if it was the most natural thing in the world. We followed her. Her hands flickered over the lock and the door was open. She walked through and we followed before anyone had a chance to object. Up ahead I could hear the whine of heavy machinery and the creak of cages on heavy rollers. The air smelled of grease and incense and men cramped together with no latrines. We walked forwards and came out on a ledge in a tunnel. There were the cages full of prisoners. There were robed guards. We were in the secret heart of the cathedral now, where the mechanisms of sacrifice were visible. There were stairs leading up from here that pilgrims would never see. I wondered if Anna knew where they went too.

'How do we get them free?' Hesse asked.

'We'll need to be fast,' said Macharius. 'Overpower those guards. You will take the keys, Lemuel, and open the cages. Get the prisoners out. Tell them to grab what weapons they can and free the others.'

'Once they are freed, we need to go up,' Drake said. 'And keep going up till we find the heart of this evil.'

Macharius nodded and rattled off orders, clearly and calmly, telling every man exactly what to do, speaking exactly as if we had a chance of pulling off his mad scheme. He did not repeat anything. He spoke as if he had complete confidence in us. He knew we understood and would not let him down. He was right in that too.

We followed him down towards the lines of cages where the prisoners waited. We walked directly towards the guards as if we had every right to be there. One or two of them glanced at us, wondering what was going on, asking themselves if something was wrong, then pushing the thought aside and telling themselves someone else would deal with it. A priest walked over to us and said, 'You are in the wrong place, pilgrims, be gone or be burned!'

Macharius shot him. All hell broke loose.

I raced forwards, producing my shotgun from beneath my robe. I opened fire at the closest guard and took him down. A moment later I rammed the butt of the shotgun into the face of a second. Bone broke. Blood flowed. I bent down and picked the keys from the guard's belt. I handed them to the nearest prisoner. 'Free yourself!' I told him.

The man just looked at me stunned. Like the guards, he did not quite understand what had happened. 'Free yourself and free your brothers! Macharius is here!'

It was as if I had spoken a magic word. The hopelessness disappeared from the man's eyes. His shoulders squared, he began to work the key in the lock and free the others. As one man got free of the chains, I picked up the guard's weapon and handed it to him. 'Arm yourself. Arm the others. Take what you can! Kill!'

Along the line others were doing the same. I caught sight of Macharius. He was fighting with a group of guards. In action, he was utterly lethal, a whirlwind of movement, a blur of motion, too fast to be pinned down or targeted. More of our men were breaking free now, attacking the heretics with anything they could pick up: their chains, censers, weapons ripped from the hands of screaming guards. More and more of those to be sacrificed were joining them. A chain reaction rippled through the cathedral as our soldiers broke free, ready to make a desperate last stand. It was hopeless but it was better than being burned alive in those incandescent cages and having your soul devoured by daemons.

Macharius beckoned. I followed. Macharius had his

distraction. I was stunned by his ruthlessness. Having freed the men, he had left them to fight. He was sacrificing their lives so that we had a chance. The horrible thing was that he was right, and what was even more awful was the fact that the death he had granted them was better than the one the prisoners had been going to face.

We raced up the stairs, on our way to meet the psyker at the heart of this wickedness.

I made sure my shotgun was loaded. Below us I heard the sound of conflict.

Drake led us up through a maze of corridors, balconies and stairwells. There were no glow-globes, only gas-lamps carved in the shape of the fire-winged angel. The air was dry. It was warm enough to make you sweat and got warmer with every step we took. We came to a junction.

'Left,' Drake said. No one asked him how he knew. We just took his instructions.

We heard footfalls on the stairs ahead of us. A squad of guards rushed down to meet us. We opened fire. There were a score of them but they fell in the first burst. One tried to raise a weapon but Drake raised his hand and gestured and the guard suddenly froze, the weapon falling from his nerveless fingers. The veins in his forehead bulged. The tendons in his neck stood out like cables pulled taut. Fear and rage warred in his eyes. He fell clutching his heart and I did not need to be told he was dead.

'Put on those uniforms,' he said. We dug around amid the corpses, performing the unsavoury task of finding garments not too burned and blood-spattered. Eventually we looked like a small squad of Temple Guards who had been in the wars

Below us far away came the sounds of battle. The smell of burned flesh reached my nostrils yet again, a reminder of the fate awaiting us all.

Up and up we went following an intricate web of walkways, balconies and bridges woven around the central space of the cathedral. I realised that the whole core of the place was an empty space surrounding a great central chimney-pipe that rose all the way to its peak and the statue of the Angel.

We circled many times around the central space, crossed a web-work of bridges. Looking down made me dizzy we had climbed so high. Below us the fight rumbled on. At least I think it did. I heard the sound of shots and screams drifting up the central well. The Guard kept going though it seemed like we had been walking for leagues. My breathing got rough. Ten years as part of a tank's crew does not leave you at optimum fitness for climbing artificial mountains.

The sounds of fighting faded. I did not know whether it was because our comrades were overcome or simply a product of distance but I feared the worst. The air became hotter and the oppressive sense of presence became deeper. I felt like I was walking towards something hellish – that is the only word I can think of to describe it. It was like going into the maw of a great beast. Macharius marched steadily on. Drake went with him. I followed. I always followed.

We emerged onto a massive landing. There were many priests there and many guards. There was nothing else for it but to keep walking forwards as if we had every right to be there.

The heretics did not expect intruders – why should they? This was their most sacred temple. We wore the robes of their sect.

I sweated and my hands felt clammy. At any moment I expected us to be denounced and seized and thrown into one of those terrible cages. My flesh crawled at the thought. I had already decided I would turn my shotgun on myself if the worst came to the worst but only after taking down as many of these bastards as I could. We walked into another enclosed space and Drake came to a halt. Instantly we all formed up around him.

I looked about to see if anyone had noticed our small group huddled together. So far no one had. Maybe they thought we were wrapped in some evil prayer. Many of the heretics present seemed to be. Many were on their knees intoning dark hymns of praise.

Drake paused for a moment, grimaced then shrugged. He began to move confidently further into the complex of chambers. We followed him into a large chamber, lined with leather-bound codexes. Through a massive arched window I caught sight of the outside of the city, far below us. I had not realised we had come so far although I should have realised it from the ache in my legs. A priest looked at us and said, 'What are you doing here? What is your business?'

Macharius raised his pistol and shot him. 'My business is with your master,' he said.

Heretics poured into the room. They had the advantage of numbers but we had the advantage of confusion. They did not know what was happening; all they saw were people in their own robes fighting. They had no idea who was responsible for what. 'They have come to assassinate the master,' Macharius said in his commanding voice. 'Quickly, we must protect him.'

We strode forwards deeper into the sanctum. I knew then that my life was all but over. No matter what happened, there was no way out of this place. We were surrounded by our enemies and at some point suspicion would fall on us or someone would work out what was going on. So far, speed and confusion had carried us through but our luck was bound to run out sooner or later.

I noticed every little thing, the faint shimmering halo of light that played around Drake as he used his powers, the smooth interplay of muscles as Macharius moved ahead of me, the strange blankness in the eyes of the Understudy, the way the light gleamed on Ivan's metal cheekbones. Anna's eerie, trance-like calm as she fired shot after unerring shot and never missed. Once a heretic got close to her. She killed him with a blow to the windpipe with the side of her hand that was almost too fast for me to see.

I noticed the almost drugged stares of the heretics. They looked like men on the edge of an ecstatic religious trance, who were expecting some great revelation, who might at any moment be transported into the heavens to meet their gods.

Little did they know, I thought. Now I suspect that perhaps they did. There is more than one kind of revelation and certain souls are as drawn to the darkness as to the light.

The sense of power around us was great. The air shimmered with it. It was like in one of those old religious paintings where the primarchs stand by the body of the fallen Emperor. There was the same sense of imminence of the immaterial, of the onrush of the transcendent.

There were bodyguards within the chamber. They knew at once that there was something wrong. I could see just from the way their postures changed that they were immediately on guard. I opened fire with the shotgun. Fast as I was, Macharius was a long way faster. He shot the nearest, clubbed down a second with the butt of his pistol and blasted a third. With a motion almost too fast to follow he picked up one of the fallen heretic's chainswords and slashed it through the knee of another. He was among them now, moving too fast for the eye to follow, killing everything within reach, almost as deadly as a Space Marine. The rest of us followed in his wake.

We charged deeper and deeper into the sanctum of evil. It was a titanic chamber whose vaulted ceiling rose far above us. Enormous banners fluttered. Gigantic tapestries depicting yet more scenes of angelic triumph dripped from the walls. In the centre of the chamber was a huge altar above which loomed the inevitable metal angel. This one was only twice the size of a man but somehow it seemed larger, more pregnant with life and energy and mystical meaning. This one was somehow different, more life-like. The ominous flicker of its wings hinted at small movements as if it was somehow coming to life. There were fires in its inhuman eye-sockets which seemed to study the room. In the shadow of its wings, standing behind a massive metal lectern a man led the chanting. He was garbed in red, and his head was cowled. A metallic mask glittered from beneath the cowl. It was a perfect replica of the face of every angel I had seen in the city. On his chest was a convoluted holy symbol, the badge of his office. In his hand he held a ceremonial sword which reflected the flames so well it seemed to be afire itself.

Rows and rows of chanting priests, hundreds of them, knelt in the open space around the altar, genuflecting towards their masked leader. My heart sank when I looked upon them for I remembered the havoc that but a single one had wrought on our old company. I paused, fully expecting to be burned alive in a firestorm of evil magic, but the robed mages merely kept intoning ritual words. All of their gazes were focused on the distant figure of the chief cultist. All of their voices echoed one vast evil chant.

All of these psykers were wrapped up in some dreadful ritual, one that was coming close to its conclusion. I followed their gazes towards the centre of the chamber. I knew somehow, without needing to be told, that he was the focus of all this adoration, that all of the wicked power swirling around the room was flowing towards him and that his was the guiding intelligence behind the evil magic being worked here.

Macharius obviously came to the same conclusion at the same time. He raced forwards like a champion running towards a confrontation with his ultimate foe. Drake followed him. Anna went with them, her movements a fluent dance. She shot and kicked and chopped with her bare hands and every movement was deadly. Wherever she went, men died.

Voices shouted warnings. The heretics still did not quite understand what was going on. It was the only advantage that we had but we took all we could get from it. Macharius fought like one of the Emperor's chosen. Everything that got in his way, he killed, using the chainsword with the ferocity of a daemon and the skill of a master swordsman. His pistol spoke again and again and every time it shot, a heretic went to join the damned souls in the warp.

Drake was almost as effective. From his hands, deadly blasts of cold blue light emerged. The heretics screamed and fell over dead with no mark upon them. I found that even more frightening than the spells of the psykers. The rest of us blasted, stabbed and shot our way through the enemy ranks by whatever means we could.

I put my shotgun to the head of the nearest pyromancer and pulled the trigger. His head exploded in a waterfall of brains and blood. It splattered the psyker beside him. I would have thought that would have got their attention but the chanting never even slowed down. They paid no attention to me. They just kept right on with their ritual. Behind me, I heard weapons go off and grenades explode and I realised the others were doing the same as I was. Perhaps it was not very chivalrous to kill those helpless men but they were involved in the work of daemons and I felt like we were doing the world a favour by ridding it of them.

As more grenades exploded and more psykers died, a few of them emerged from their trance. When I looked into their eyes all I saw was flames. I knew things were going to get bad then but I did not care. I was wrapped up in killing, filled with a wild, mad rage and a lust to slaughter that was every bit as daemonic as the one that possessed these evil magicians.

I shot and smashed heads with the butt of my shotgun. I kicked as well. I looked around and saw Macharius approach the High Priest of the Angel of Fire. He chopped at the man, who was clearly reeling, and not from the blow that the general had launched but from the backlash of his disrupted spell. Macharius slashed again with the chainsword. The pyromancer parried with his holy symbol and lost the head of it. He chopped back with his own weapon, knocking the pistol from the general's hands.

Drake extended his own arms and gestured and the blue light ravened out at the heretic leader. Nothing much seemed to happen. Macharius reached out for him and grabbed the glittering chain of office that dangled from his neck. He attempted to use it to hold the High Priest in place while he brought the chainsword to bear.

The arch-heretic leapt backwards, twisting away from the incoming blow, the force of his movement breaking the chain and leaving the remnants dangling from Macharius's hands. The High Priest fell over and scrambled away. More and more psykers were coming awake and aware now but there was something strange about them. They moved like automatons, as if their souls were still floating in some distant hell and only dimly connected to their bodies.

Corporal Hesse took a bullet through his chest and then a hail of them through his body but somehow he kept moving, still shooting. Ivan staggered as a shell ricocheted off his metal cheeks. Macharius looked around for his prey, failed to find him and then jammed something in the body of the metal statue with blazing wings. He dived to one side as it exploded and only then did I realise what he had done.

He had set a grenade into the gas-tubes and started a chain reaction of explosions within it. A huge gout of flame erupted, setting fire to the ceremonial hangings. The air began to fill with the stink of smoke and flame and burning flesh. Drake stood outlined by some aura that protected him and Macharius. I gestured for the others to follow me and we scrambled towards them. I have no idea why I did that.

We seemed to have run out of options.

Casualty List Hesse

Corroborative Evidence Cross-Reference 42K9-Cross-Reference J6. Under seal.

Extract from Record of Deaths, Battlegroup Sejanus, Karsk Campaign 05.07.40012

Quota Record Form 6a

Approved: Varisov, L, Colonel 7th Belial

Compiled: Parzival, K, Captain 7th Belial

Forwarded to Battlegroup HQ, Karsk

Section 124: Record of Deaths in Combat

Site: Irongrad.

Hesse, O, Corporal, Imperial Baneblade *Indomitable*.

Cause of Death: Enemy Action.

Notes: Recommended for Order of Merit, Gates of Irongrad, Approved Pending Investigation.

Flames tore through the chamber. The robes I was wearing started to smoulder. The backwash of heat made my eyes suddenly dry. The smoke made me cough. Most of the heretics were untouched by the flames. The heat and the fire did not seem to affect them. I kept moving towards Inquisitor Drake and Macharius and Anna. I felt sure that the inquisitor's shield would offer some protection but I was not certain that it would enable any of us to survive once the heretics decided to extinguish our lives.

Anton and Ivan were right behind me and the Understudy was with them. I looked around to see if I could see Corporal Hesse. I caught sight of him out of the corner of my eye and wished that I had not. He was still alive. His uniform was ablaze. He was screaming and his flesh was starting to melt and run. Large chunks had been torn off by the explosion and blackened skin stood out against white bone. I was going to turn back and help him but the crowd was already starting to close around him as more and more of the heretic bodyguards entered the great chamber.

I dived within the bubble of energy surrounding the inquisitor. I landed with one arm on Anna's shoulder and withdrew it swiftly before she could break it. It was stupid. She had already decided I was not an enemy or she would have killed me. Immediately the air felt cooler and the sound of explosion and fire and screaming was dulled as if heard through a thick armourglas window. We glared around, desperate, at once seeking escape and sure of the fact that we would not find it. Macharius looked at Drake.

'Is there anything you can do?' He did not look defeated. He was simply asking if there were any options. There was no fear written on his face. I'm sure it was inscribed on mine.

I looked around. There was no sign of the High Priest. He seemed to have disappeared into the fire and smoke. I wished we could do the same. Drake gestured for us to follow him and began to move towards the wall. I'm guessing that he had some sense other than sight to guide him, because I could see nothing through that fearful blaze.

Behind us, the kneeling heretics began to stir from their trance. Possibly the bodyguards were trying to fight their way forwards through the flames – I could not see them, so there was no way to tell. I simply tried to keep close to the inquisitor because I had no idea what would happen if I stumbled outside the sphere of protection that he currently radiated.

Ahead of us, I saw an archway. We passed through it and down a flight of stairs, moving as fast as we could, trying to put as much distance between ourselves and any pursuit as was possible. We had no idea what we were doing now, not even Macharius, I am sure. Our plan had been to disrupt the ritual and kill the High Priest if we could.

He had escaped us even though Macharius still held his chain of office clenched in his fist. I was not sure why he still had it. Perhaps he was planning on keeping it as a souvenir if ever we got out of this place.

We raced downstairs and encountered more guards coming up. We must have been quite a sight. Our robes were burned and smouldering and we were surrounded by a halo of power. We did not give them any chance to react. We did not pause to bluff. We gave no thought to the fact that there might be hundreds of them coming towards us.

We simply leapt into battle. Macharius was in the lead, chopping with the chainsword that he still held, shooting with a pistol that he had picked up somewhere. Nothing short of a Space Marine could have stood against him at that moment. He fought like a berserk ork, full of terrifying fury with no regard for his own safety.

At least, that's the way it looked. I'm sure that within his calculating brain he had already worked out the odds of survival and attacking with such passionate fury was simply what he thought to be the optimal strategy. In any case, he cut his way down to a landing, leaving a trail of dead and dismembered bodies behind him, painting the walls with blood and entrails. We raced along in his wake, shooting survivors, putting the wounded out of their misery and occasionally, when we got a clear shot, aiming over his shoulders and taking out some of the enemy ahead.

I fought almost back to back with Macharius. A screaming heretic dived towards him, aiming the butt of a lasgun at the back of the general's head. Macharius turned a fraction of a second too late to stop him. I could tell from the expression on his face that he knew the heretic was going to connect. I pulled the trigger on the shotgun. The force of the blast knocked the heretic backwards even as it sprayed Macharius with his blood. The general nodded to me in acknowledgement of what I had done and returned to killing. I saved Macharius's life there but it's certain he saved mine a dozen times simply by killing the enemy near me. Under the circumstances it seemed impolitic to keep score although I am certain, in this, as with so many things, Macharius forgot nothing. His nod was in recognition of a debt between us, one that would eventually be repaid.

When I was not there to cover his back Anna was, moving gracefully, precisely and with eye-blurring speed. She seemed as inhuman as a Space Marine as she kicked and clawed and shot. She had the same terrifying speed and grace.

I'll say one thing for the heretics – they were brave. Even in the face of Macharius's terrifying rampage they stood their ground and were killed to a man. Maybe they simply had no choice. Maybe they did not have time to realise what was happening. To me, everything seemed to be happening with the slowness of a nightmare, which is often the way things happen when you're in combat. Taken by surprise, perhaps they simply did not have time to react and what I think of as courage was simply a stunned lack of response.

Suddenly the fight was over. The heretics were all dead. We stood on a huge landing that looked out over one side of the cathedral. Beneath us an army of fire-winged angels stood poised for flight. Above us, in the central sanctuary, explosions still raged.

'At least we've disrupted the ritual,' said Drake. 'And bought ourselves some time.'

'How much?' Macharius asked.

Drake shook his head. 'Perhaps a day, if we are lucky.'

Looking around I could see the same look of disappointment on every face, except that of Macharius. After the carnage we had wrought, we had hoped for more.

'The High Priest is still alive. He is the locus of all this,' said Drake. 'The vessel of all the power. He will be able to bring the psychic backlash under control. I am sure of it.'

'It looks like we need another plan,' Macharius said, obviously not a man to let a little adversity discourage him.

'What are we going to do now, sir?' I asked.

He turned and stared out the window for a moment, looking at all of the aircars flying below us.

'We need to get out of here,' Macharius said. 'There's nothing more to be done in the city. We won't get another chance at the High Priest of the Angel of Fire. They'll be on their guard now.'

Drake shook his head wearily. He was tired and pale but you could see that a formidable will still drove him onwards. He was not going to admit to any weakness in front of us. I doubt very much that the man had admitted to any weakness even to himself. He was that sort. 'We still need to stop them. We've delayed the ritual for a while. They'll start again soon and their daemon-god will manifest himself on the surface of this world.'

'We need an army to break through,' Anton said, scratching his face with one long, claw-like hand.

'Precisely,' Macharius said. 'We need an army. Fortunately we know where to find one. And at least we have located the exact point at which we must strike.'

I was astonished by Macharius's definition of good fortune. Apparently, as far as he was concerned, all we needed to do was make contact with our forces on the surface of Karsk and the problem would be solved.

From the look on his face, you could tell that the general thought that this would prove no insuperable obstacle. Drake nodded agreement. Under the circumstances, I don't suppose there was anything else he could do. Macharius did not look mad. He looked like a man in full possession of his senses. I suppose in a way he was. He had decided that there was only one way to save the situation and that we needed to proceed accordingly, and there was nothing that I could really disagree with in that. So even if hundreds of leagues separated us from our army, we were going to have to make contact with it.

'We will have to do it soon,' Drake said. 'We've done no more than buy ourselves a little time.'

'Then we'd best get going,' Macharius said in a tone that brooked no dispute.

Macharius had already decided the best way out of the city. His brain never stopped calculating, even when the odds against him seemed insurmountable. 'We need to get to the airfield and we need to get our hands on a flyer.'

He had it all worked out in his mind you see, and he could say things like that as if we were not on our own in the middle of a hostile city. And for all the self-evident madness of his words, there was a confidence about him that made you believe it was possible. We walked through the cathedral as if we were flanked by Chapters of Space Marines, with Macharius in the lead and Drake just behind him and the five of us, the Understudy, Anton, Ivan, the New Boy and myself swaggering to the rear.

Fortunately for us everything in the cathedral was in chaos. The surviving prisoners must have put up an epic fight against the heretics and it seemed as if the sheer boldness of our attack on the High Priest had stunned them.

I could understand why. If I had been in their position I would not have believed that so small a group of men would have assaulted so strongly held a position myself.

In any case, it worked to our advantage. We raced through the chaos, just one more group of uniformed men, apparently dithering as the heretics tried to reassert control of the situation. We did our best to keep to the emptier ways of the cathedral but when we had to, we shouldered our way across packed corridors and massive naves with all the confidence that Macharius inspired.

No one questioned us and soon, by devious ways, we found ourselves on an emergency walkway, looking down over one of the massive gas pipes that fed the fires of the cathedral. We raced across it. It was as broad as a military highway. I caught a clear view of the roiling crowd below us. The vast open space around the cathedral was filled with people. They screamed and chanted the name of the Angel of Fire. Obviously, they knew that something was going on within the cathedral and it had stirred them to the edge of the abyss of fanatical madness.

As a soldier of the Emperor it is hard to imagine heretics having faith but they do. The problem is that their faith is misplaced. Zeal, which in the service of the Emperor would be truly holy, becomes something worse than wickedness. Looking down on the vast maddened crowd, lit by the fiery wings of thousands of evil Angels, I shuddered.

Those people down there had no idea what it was they were so desperately keen to protect. They had been misled or they had misled themselves and there was no time to teach them the error of their ways any more. Time had run out. Now all that was left to us was war, if we could get in touch with our army, if we could warn them what was happening, if they could get here in time to stop the manifestation of a greater daemon or something worse.

I could see that I was not the only one affected by the sight. Drake had paused, looking down over the protective barrier on the edge of the great gas pipe. There was a look of horror on his face and something more, something I would not have expected to see there: sympathy. I dismissed the thought as an illusion created by my own fevered mind. Who ever heard of an inquisitor feeling sympathy for anyone?

Looking down at that seething sea of heretics, I felt only a sort of numbness. All of them seemed lost. Of all of us, only Macharius seemed certain. In some ways, the more terrible the situation became, the more certain he became. The more indecisive we looked, the more decisive he looked. Perhaps that was simply the effect of my own confusion. In any case, I know that at that time Macharius was the rock upon which all our faith settled. He, at least, seemed to have no doubts that he was worthy of such devotion.

We raced along the top of the gas pipe heading towards a vast arched entrance between two towering hab-blocks. As we got closer, I felt the heat of the fire-winged angels once more. They gazed down at us and in that moment they seemed alive and hostile and I wanted very much to be in a place where I never had to look upon them again.

We clambered down the exit ladder from the pipe and landed on the huge pile of trash propped up against the walls of an alleyway. Even here, oceans of rubbish had gathered and scavengers made their way through it seeking whatever pitiful remains would keep them alive, whether it was food or some half-functional thing that they could sell. They gazed at us with blank, uncomprehending eyes. At least their gaze did not hold any fanaticism, only hunger and a nasty expression that made me glad I was armed. These were men who would do anything to keep themselves alive. I realised then that most of them were beggars who normally would have sought alms in the great square surrounding the cathedral and had been forced out of their normal pitches by the surging crowds and the violence of the uprising. We raced down the narrow alleys between the tumbled mountains of trash. Rats as large as dogs scuttled away from our racing feet. Cockroaches as long as a bayonet dived into the rubbish like soldiers seeking cover in a trench. The stink of decomposing food, of mould and rot mingled with the gassy taint in the air.

My heart pounded. My breath came in gasps. Sweat ran down my face. My eyes felt dry and yet, for all the horrors that I had seen, I was starting to feel strangely optimistic. Despite my worst fears, I was still alive and I was free, although the Emperor alone knew how long that was likely to last. Somehow, we had escaped from that vast horde of heretics, and had not yet been burned alive to feed the terrible god that the heretics were hell bent on summoning. Perhaps the Emperor was watching over us, or at least over Macharius. Until almost the very end he always had that thing that all great commanders need: luck.

It was obvious that we had stirred up a huge hornets' nest. Sirens bellowed out across the city. In the distance I could hear the roar of the crowd surrounding the cathedral. Where we were, all was eerily quiet. It was as if the vast majority of the citizens were huddled in their homes waiting to see what would happen.

At that moment in time, I felt a long way from the certainties of Imperial law. Strangely enough, having been given something to compare it with, I had never been more certain that the Imperium was worthy to rule this place. I even felt a certain nostalgia for the Imperial Guard and its crude, slow-moving, bureaucratic processes. I would have welcomed marching into camp and being surrounded by my comrades more than anything else in the universe just then.

We sloped on through the gathering darkness, not quite

certain of what we were going to do except that we were going to follow Macharius to the bitter end.

We huddled down in the shadow of a cave accidentally created in the giant mound of trash. It must have been some primitive instinct that made us do that, to crawl out of sight, for there was no other real reason. The only people around us were the hordes of scavengers and they paid no more attention to us than anyone else around them. If we had looked weaker or less well armed they would have seen as us as prey but as it was we were untouchable. Overhead aircars quartered the sky. Searchlight beams probed into the darkness. I could not avoid the suspicion they were looking for us.

'We need to get to the airfield,' Macharius said. 'We need to find a vehicle that can get us out of this place.'

He said it as reasonably as a man discussing walking down to the canteen to get lunch. He spoke in that calm, powerful voice and all of us just nodded our heads as if what he was saying was sane.

I will say this about Macharius, he never let the fact that he was planning something completely unreasonable stop him from contemplating the possibility of it. In his mind, to come up with something was to do it. For him, there was no difference between visualising a thing and executing it. He had no doubts in his own competence and somehow he projected the idea that he had no doubts of yours. Drake just nodded as if he saw the sense of this as well, then returned to making inscriptions on his data-slate.

'We won't find an aircar in this part of the city,' Anna said.

'You are right,' said Macharius. 'We'll need a place where they are more common.'

Wearily, we picked ourselves up and began to move again, looking for a way out of this vast maze of rubbish and scavengers and a way back into the wealthier parts of the city where such things as flying vehicles were available to be stolen.

The first thing we grabbed was a groundcar. It was easy. Anton jimmied open the window with his bayonet. Anna invoked the engine spirits aided by a piece of sanctified wire. There was not much room for all of us inside the car, big as it was, but we crawled in and took to the highway between levels.

Macharius knew where the nearest airfield was. Drake found a route on his slate. He had ingested all the information from the datacores into it before the rising. I drove. It seemed like my duty. I even felt a certain nostalgia to be behind the controls of a vehicle again although it was nothing compared to a Baneblade.

Everywhere we passed signs of warfare. There were burned-out vehicles at numerous crossroads. Some of them bore the marking of our regiment, an ominous omen. Gangs had risen across the city, taking advantage of the general chaos to go on a looting spree. I saw nobles and outcasts fighting in the streets, for the pure unadulterated joy of combat, as far as I could tell. One side certainly did not need the loot. Or maybe they were all skanked on blaze.

In other sections, the Sons of the Flame were already out in force. They moved through the streets with companies of bodyguards, flaming halos surrounding their heads.

Here they rounded up opposition for burning. There they preached a sermon to a fast-gathering crowd. I watched them all scroll by through the armourglass of the groundcar window. I listened to Drake's directions and kept the vehicle on course. In the back, most of them slept. Macharius sat wide-eyed, planning. The Understudy's eyes were sinister black pits. He said nothing, did not move. I wondered what was going on in his head. Anna studied the crowds with her usual calm.

Over everything there still brooded the terrifying sense of presence. I was not surprised by the hysteria in the city. Everyone must have felt it as much as I did. They were reacting in their own way and I suspect the thing the priests worshipped was feeding on it and drawing strength. When I caught sight of the faces of Ivan and Anton and the New Boy I knew they felt as I did, possibly worse, that reaction to what we had done was setting in. We had done our best and we had failed and time was running out.

The road twisted and turned through the hive, climbing levels and then swooping lower, curving back in on itself like the spiral staircases of the cathedral. The Angels watched over every junction, perched on every building. Crowds were visible in every square. There seemed to be a lot of burning going on. Drake followed my gaze.

'They are making sacrifices. It is all part of the great ritual now.' He looked sick, but returned to making inscriptions in incomprehensible Inquisitorial runes.

Document under seal. Extract From the Decrypted Personal Files of Inquisitor Hyronimus Drake.

  Possible evidence of duplicity on the part of former High Inquisitor Drake.

  Cross-reference to Exhibit 107D-21H (Report to High Inquisitor Toll).

I dread what is happening here. The evil of what is being done hangs over us like a vast cloud of doom. I sense terrible flows of power here and a portal being opened into the deepest pits from which the hell-spawn of Chaos crawl. It is difficult to remember that not far from here the mightiest force assembled in recent Imperial history stands waiting. Yet, for all its power, it will be useless unless it moves into action. When the Angel of Fire bestrides this planet once more, not all our army's strength will avail it.

The High Priest of the Angel is still alive and while that is the case all that seething energy has a focus and all of it is tied to the thing he wishes to summon. Our reprieve, if reprieve it is, is but temporary.

Perhaps the most disturbing aspect of this business is the thought that we have provoked this manifestation of cosmic evil. If we had not come here, perhaps the pyromancers would never have summoned up the will or courage to begin their summoning. Perhaps we have driven them to it as the only recourse in the face of our overwhelming might.

I must scourge myself for letting such thoughts skitter into my mind. We cannot take responsibility for the evil heretics do. We can only take responsibility for any failure on our part to stand against it. It is our duty to prevent the Angel of Fire becoming manifest if we can. This is the deed the Emperor asks from us.

Looking at my companions, it would be easy to believe the task is hopeless. We are so few and the enemy are so many. Still, in the history of the Imperium the faithful few have often overcome the heretical multitudes. Think of Saint Leone facing the Hordes of the Mithralists, or the Sage Paladine's band of monks bringing the word to the Cabal of Jewelmakers. No, there are many examples in Testament and Scripture to stiffen our spines and harden our resolve in the face of seemingly overwhelming odds. Ah, but how easy it is to be inspired when reading such things in the comfort of a distant reflectorium. How difficult it is to keep the faith in the face of such overwhelming evil.

Nonetheless, we must persevere, and we must, in the name of the Emperor, triumph. If we do not, the consequences will be dreadful for this world and the Imperium.

We passed through a massive arch and emerged onto a concrete plain with a view out over the great lava deserts and the vast array of industrial structures that surrounded the great hive of Irongrad.

I could see pipes running away into the distance and gigantic refineries and huge hangars containing who knows what. It was not that which held my attention though – it was the airfield itself. A number of flying vehicles were arriving and departing. There was a good deal of military traffic, doubtless part of the local air force fighting against the Imperial Guard armies to the south. There were several tethered airships of enormous size, used for interhive transport during times of peace and which had now been requisitioned as troop carriers. Even as we watched, we could see monstrous lines of infantrymen queuing up to board them from massive docking towers.

This looked to be as close as we were going to get so we piled out of the groundcar and made ourselves ready. At the edge of the huge airstrip we could see a number of small flying vehicles. It was then that Anton mentioned something that I was sure was on all of our minds. 'Can anybody here fly one of those things?' Anton said. 'Or is this the time that I begin my improvised pilot training?'

'Both the inquisitor and I can do so,' said Macharius.

'I can too, sir,' said Anna.

That ended all argument. It was now simply a case of moving downslope, passing the perimeter defences of the airfield and getting aboard one of those flyers. Easy, I told myself sarcastically.

'We going through the wire,' Macharius said. He brandished the chainsword that he had carried all the way from the cathedral just so that there was no doubt about how he intended to do that. 'There are guard towers down there and there will be divination engines set to spot intruders.'

'I can take the towers and override the systems, sir,' said Anna. She seemed completely confident in her ability to be able to overcome whoever was guarding those engines, justifiably so, I suppose.

'It would take too much time,' said Macharius. 'We need to go now,'

'As you wish, sir.'

'Can you shield us, high inquisitor?' Macharius asked.

Inquisitor Drake nodded. Obviously, they trained inquisitors in more things than theology wherever he had studied. He said, 'Stay very close to me, all of you. If you get beyond a few arms' length, you will be out of the range of my protection.'

We stayed close to the inquisitor like we knew what he was talking about. None of us liked relying on psyker powers for our protection even if those powers were wielded by an inquisitor.

We began to move down the side of the hive, cautiously, looking for divination engines and minefields and all of the other things that you might expect to encounter around a military airfield in time of war.

If there were minefields, no one had marked them and I found myself becoming more and more tense with every step I took. Macharius led us to a spot between the guard towers. His keen gaze scanned backwards and forwards and I knew that he was looking for sentries patrolling the open space between those towers. I could not see any, but that did not mean they were not there. Perhaps they were standing, smoking, behind one of the pillars that supported the wire. Perhaps they had already spotted us and were lying in wait, weapons ready to open fire as soon as we got within range. It's astonishing the things that your mind comes up with in situations like this.

We reached the edge of the wire and took up positions to cover Macharius in case anyone closed with us while he was cutting. He slashed through the wire with one sweep of the chainsword and then paused for a moment, listening.

If any alarm had been given it was not audible to us, but that did not mean anything. Somewhere, in some distant control bunker perhaps, a red light was flashing and alarms had started to sound.

Macharius gestured for Anton to go through. Anton did so and then the rest of us followed until only Macharius and I were left on the far side of the wire. I gestured for him to go ahead like some polite gentleman at the door of his club in the upper reaches of the hive. Macharius grinned and went through and I took a last look around to make sure that no one was creeping up on us from this side of the fence and then I followed him myself.

We began to move across the plascrete plain, moving closer to the flyers that Macharius had already picked out. They were small local transport models of a variant I was not familiar with. They were armoured though and they had turrets, which might well prove useful, providing no one was already in them and ready to shoot us down. It all seemed to be going too well. I thought for a moment that the luck of Macharius or the Blessing of the Emperor shielded us still. It was Ivan, as usual, who had to spoil things by pointing out that this was not in fact the case.

'Watch out,' he said, indicating off towards the control bunkers of the airstrip with the barrel of his lasgun. I immediately saw what he meant. From out of the central bunker, a number of wheeled vehicles had emerged and were moving in our direction as fast as they could be driven. Either the alarm had been given or someone had spotted us and mustered the guards. It looked like we were going to have a fight on our hands and it was not a fight that we could win.

'Run,' said Macharius, moving towards the nearest of the flyers.

I don't think I have ever covered ground as quickly as I did then and I suspect that the same was the case for the others. Ground crew surrounded the flyer. They had been running checks on the systems and preparing the vehicle for flight.

One of them looked at us and shouted something. Anton did not wait to see what would happen next. He pulled the trigger on his lasgun and burned the man down.

I heard the roar of machine engines close behind us and turning I saw the enemy vehicles were almost upon us. I aimed my shotgun at one of the buggies. The huge balloon tyre exploded and the vehicle skidded into another buggy with a crash of metal on metal.

Men screamed as they were crushed between the two. The others opened fire on us. We kept moving towards the flyer, shooting at the ground crew, even though they were not armed. None of us wanted one of them to get inside and disable the vehicle or even attempt a take-off before we got there. Sirens were sounding in the distance now and I could see the lights of more buggies coming closer.

We were within the shadow of the flyer when the rest of buggies rolled to a stop and disgorged their cargo of armed men. I counted at least twenty of them, all of them in the uniforms of the local defence forces. One of them was a priest of the Angel of Fire. I suspected that they were in every important, strategic location, overseeing the local warriors in exactly the same way as our commissars oversaw us. At the sight of that red-robed heretic, my heart sank.

The alarm had very definitely been given and if we did not manage to get away in this flyer, it was obvious that we were never going to manage to get away at all.

Macharius had already leapt on board along with the inquisitor, and the others were following them up the loading ramp. Only the Understudy and myself were on the ground now. I pumped the shotgun and aimed at the priest and pulled the trigger. He saw what I was going to do and raised his arms in a gesture that I am sure had some cryptic, mystical significance. He never got to complete it before something took his head off. I looked around and saw Anna standing there with that huge gun in her hand.

Whatever protected those heretic psykers from las-bolts clearly had no effect whatsoever against those high-calibre, sanctified slugs.

The guards kept coming closer. I kept shooting and backing away up the ramp on the back of the flyer. Metal flexed under my feet even as las-fire melted the metal of the walkway. The smell reminded me of the factorum workshops of my youth with their casting forges and sacrosanct welding engines.

The flyer began to move, taking off even with the loading bay open. I tumbled forwards and I felt the shotgun slip out of my grasp. I clutched it tight and then a claw-like hand grabbed my shoulder and pulled me backwards with such a jerk that I almost fell over. The Understudy had caught me and was dragging me inside.

As ever, he ignored the shots of our enemies as if he simply could not see them. This time one of them hit him and I smelled burning cloth and burning flesh. He grunted but he did not scream and he kept pulling and I kept scrambling and then the loading bay ramp began to fold itself into flight position and the movement of its hydraulic systems tumbled us into the body of the aircraft.

I heard strange sounds as the flyer's systems creaked under the strain of the take-off: the sizzling sounds of melting paint and metal where las-fire impacted on the hull. Worse than that was the thunder of metal on metal as some sort of heavy weapon was brought to bear. The hull gave way as if an ogryn were hitting it with a sledgehammer. Dents appeared and the flyer began to wobble in the air as if the force of the shooting was driving us off course.

I lay on the floor gasping and trying to calm my nerves. I have never minded being in a tank when it was under fire but there was something about being in an aircraft in similar circumstances that made me want to void myself with fear.

I forced myself to stand upright despite the lurching of the aircraft. A loud scream echoed within the hull and I looked around quickly to see what had caused the panic. It was only Anton shrieking with pure pleasure, as if this was some sort of joyride and he was some sort of child. I fought down the urge to punch him and instead turned to face the Understudy.

I wanted to take a look at his wound but he had already stripped away his officer's jerkin and was inspecting the scorched skin beneath. It looked nasty. There was a huge blister that had burst and peeled away revealing the moist, sticky flesh beneath. I began to rummage through the emergency medical kit near the rear loading-bay door. Within a few moments I found what was needed and was spraying the damaged skin with synthi-flesh. It closed over the wound, filled with air bubbles and resembled nothing more than a large wart but it would protect the damaged flesh until it could heal. The Understudy nodded as if to thank me and then sat down and strapped himself in.

I looked forwards and I could see that Macharius and Inquisitor Drake were within the cockpit, wrestling with controls. They seemed to be moving them at random and the flyer jumped all around the sky.

Had they gone mad, I wondered?

I looked at the porthole and realised that there was some semblance of sanity in what they were doing. Heavy bolter fire tracked our flight and sometimes impacted on the armoured hull. I could also see that there were other flyers coming in pursuit. I looked at Anton and Ivan and I said, 'Can you two lazy bastards do something? Doesn't this flying heap of junk have some turrets that you could be inside?'

They looked at me as if I was speaking another language. If it had been a tank and if it had been on the ground they would have taken up position at once but outside the environment that they were familiar with, the idea had never occurred to them.

'Why don't you go bloody fly the thing?' Anton asked.

'I would but we already have two people doing that,' I replied.

'Well maybe you should take your own advice then!' Rather than arguing with the idiot I decided to do just that. I found a ladder that led up to the topside turret and in a few seconds I was strapping myself in and chanting litanies that I hoped would activate the weapon.

I ran through the invocation drills with my hands, pushing down the sacred spheres that I hoped would perform the same function as they did on a ground vehicle. I grabbed the handles of the weapon in exactly the same way as I would have grabbed the handles of a similar one in a tank. And then I leaned forwards and looked through the sight and got my first view of our surroundings and the things that pursued us.

The exterior of the hive skimmed by below. Enormous towers rose like tall, narrow fungi from the side of a mossy hill. Industrial effluent ran down the terraces like lava down the side of a volcano. I could see the multi-coloured lights of the jewelled windows of the hab-blocks and vehicles going about their journeys below us. In the distance, a couple of similar flyers to the one that we were in pursued us. They were already shooting with heavy bolters.

I put in a comm-net ear bead and listened but all I could hear was Macharius talking into the local system. 'We need to take those down now,' he said calmly. 'If we don't we'll have other airborne swarming all over us in a few minutes.'

I suspected that that was going to be the case anyway but now did not seem like the time to argue about it. Instead I concentrated on shooting and sent a stream of heavy bolter fire towards one of the oncoming flyers.

It swerved to one side, an angry insect trying to avoid being swatted by a drunken man. I kept shooting and tracking it but it moved too fast for me and I had no skill with this weapon.

It was luck more than anything else that destroyed my target flyer. As the pilot swerved to avoid my shot, one of his flyer's stubby wings struck the side of a nearby building. Immediately, the flyer swerved out of control, tumbling end over end and wing over wing. The damage would not have destroyed it if the pilot had been able to regain control but he simply did not have time and his tumbling vehicle smashed into the side of another hab-block and exploded. Splinters of broken metal smashed the nearby windows. A gas jet within the building ignited, causing blowback. A trail of flame shot out of the side of the hab and I was very glad that I was not alongside when it happened.

The other enemy flyer had gained altitude and was somewhere above us. I could tell by the bolter fire contrails coming down in the sky. Looking up I saw the vehicle's running lights. I sat as far back in the seat as I could and the guns tilted upwards but they couldn't elevate enough to get our pursuer into my sights. There was nothing I could do from the present angle. I spoke into the comm-net and said, 'Take us up and I can get a second shot at the bastard.' As an afterthought I added, 'Sir.'

I heard Macharius chuckle and we began to swing upwards. At the same time other turrets on our own craft opened fire and I guessed that Ivan and Anton had finally decided to join the party. All three of us managed to target the flyer but it was just as armoured as our own vehicle and it withstood the impact.

The enemy weapons had found the range now and they kept shooting at us as we kept shooting at them. It was simply a case of which flyer's armour gave out first or which of us found a weak spot in the other's hull. I began to play my turret's fire over the enemy flyer. The impact points sparked. Nothing gave way.

We gained altitude and then suddenly, sickeningly, we flipped over and looped down behind the enemy. I dangled upside down in the turret, trying to stay focused. The other pilot panicked. He veered to one side. We kept shooting, hammering the vehicle with our fire. Macharius dived suddenly and brought us alongside. We kept firing, our bolter shots impacting all along the side. Macharius nudged the other flyer with the stubby wing of our vehicle, forcing it into a nearby wall. It smashed hard, hull breaking apart. Our fire finally took effect, hitting some vital internal part. The explosion turned the enemy flyer into a fireball.

We cheered and flew on, racing over the hive exterior like a runaway rocket, staying low and dodging at speed between the buildings. I rotated my turret so I could look behind us to scan the sky for pursuit. I saw the running lights of hundreds of vehicles but nothing that looked as if it was coming for us.

I offered up a prayer of thanks to the Emperor as I watched Irongrad recede into the distance. It loomed behind us like an impossibly vast mountain, covered in glittering contrails of light and lava. At its peak, the monstrous figure of the Angel of Fire loomed, fiery wings spread wide and illuminating the swirling multi-coloured clouds above it. I had a sense of an ominous terrifying presence growing where it stood.

'What the hell is going on down there?' I heard Anton ask.

It took me long moments to see what he meant. On the vast industrial perimeter of the hive, it looked as if rivers of fire were boiling up from underground springs. The earth was cracking, buildings had tumbled. Pipes were broken. In a dozen places they vented flames. Ahead of us the wastelands were split by great fiery chasms. Lava bubbled forth, forming rivers and lakes. The flyer carried us closer. The sight was awesome. I was reminded of our original landing site. It looked as if a new lava sea was being born in front of us.

'I don't know,' I said, 'but I do not like it one little bit.'

Once the city was well behind us, Macharius set the flyer down in the desert. He did not give any explanations. He merely picked a flat-topped mesa and landed. All of us climbed out and began to inspect the flyer and I understood why he had done so. The aircraft was enormously beaten up. In places the hull looked as if it was just about to fall apart. Somehow the general had nursed the flyer this far but I doubt that it would have gone much further.

'Never an adept around when you want one,' said Anton with his usual attempt at humour.

'There are other things to worry about even if we can fly much further,' said Macharius.

'Sir?' I asked.

'If we get too close to our army we risk being shot down by our own air-cover. This is a heretic vehicle with heretic beacons and I doubt anyone will believe us if we tell them who we are.'

'Bad security, anyway,' Drake said. 'If any enemy aircraft are in the area and intercept the call, they can kill you with one strike.'

I looked out into the distance. A massive dust storm was moving across the desert, a monstrous, moving cloud that obscured everything in its way. It took me a second to realise it was no dust storm.

'I think the point has just become moot,' I said.

Inside all those clouds of dust was a huge army. I could see the enormous shadowy shapes of Baneblades and Shadowswords, each a mobile fortress of plasteel and ceramite, each giving a sense of total invulnerability. All around them were thousands of Leman Russ battle tanks and even more Chimera armoured personnel carriers. Valkyries swarmed the air above them like a cloud of angry hornets. It looked like the Imperial Guard had decided to return to Irongrad in force. Macharius must have seen this from the cockpit. It was obviously why he had chosen this spot.

'I think we have some trouble,' said Anton. I immediately understood what he meant. Some of those Valkyries were descending towards us. Eagle-eyed pilots had spotted us and were coming to investigate. I prayed to the Emperor that they would ask questions first and shoot later. I was not entirely sure that I would do that under the circumstances but I hoped that the pilots might prove to be somewhat less aggressive.

Macharius had already thought of that. An emergency flare arced skywards, set by the hands of the Lord High Commander himself. I immediately understood his thinking. If we were scouts and spies we would not draw attention to ourselves like that, not unless we were very stupid, which is a possibility you can never rule out when dealing with some. I hoped the pilots would have more respect for our intelligence than that. I knew it would not be long before we found out.

Soon a Valkyrie hovered in the air above us, weapons trained on us. We kept our hands in the air as a second airship descended and soldiers spilled out covering us with their lasguns.

'Keep your hands in the air, and don't make any sudden moves,' said an officer.

'Captain Argus, is that you?' Macharius said. I was suddenly very glad of his talent for being able to remember people's names. The officer's jaw dropped. He looked like a man who had just encountered a ghost, which is exactly what he thought he was seeing.

'Lord High Commander Macharius?' he said. He looked astonished, as if he could not quite believe what he was seeing.

'In the flesh,' Macharius said. 'We talked when I decorated you after the Battle of Khalion.'

As with so much that Macharius did, it was perfect. It let Captain Argus know that he was exactly who he said he was. No spy could have known a little detail like that. You could see the captain standing a little bit straighter as he came under the general's eye. All of the other soldiers suddenly looked as if they were at attention. I am somewhat proud to report that they did not stop covering us with their weapons though.

'And I must see General Sejanus at once,' said Macharius. 'There is much that needs to be done and very little time to do it in. This world is in the gravest danger and we are the only people that can save it.'

It should have sounded utterly fantastic, completely implausible. But when Macharius said things like that, men jumped to obey. He strode forwards and no one pulled the trigger of a lasgun. They might have done if it was me or Anton or Ivan but they would not do it to him. Drake followed him and Anna then the Understudy. To my surprise, Macharius beckoned the rest of us forwards as well. 'You've been my bodyguard this long,' he said. 'You can manage it for a bit longer.'

It was spoken with just the right amount of weariness and humour. We stepped into the Valkyrie filled with pride and a desire to do our duty.

Within seconds we were aloft and heading into the middle of the great dust cloud raised by the army.

As we flew, the pilot must have made a report, for entire squadrons of Valkyries dropped into place around us and formed an honour guard for our protection. I looked at Macharius again as he stood there, calm and implacable, and I began to feel as if I was standing at the centre of the world and that it was moving around me to wherever Macharius went. I began to understand some of his confidence and some of his self-belief. He was one of those men that the world really did rotate around, the focus of all attention.

Some of it spilled over onto us. I could see some of the soldiers were looking at us and wondering who we were. We were with Macharius so we must be important. It was a heady feeling and I suppose in some ways it was true.

We had come out of the inferno of Irongrad along with the Lord High Commander. We had guarded him as he had guarded us. We were in some sense his comrades-in-arms. I wondered if he would remember that after today. I knew I was always going to.

The Valkyrie set us down beside an enormous headquarters tent, a vast self-erecting pavilion of flexi-metal capable of being set up within minutes and taken down just as fast. It was big enough to hold a dozen Baneblades. Arcane science let it blend in with its surroundings like those desert-dwelling, colour-changing lizards. We emerged from the aircraft to be greeted by cheering crowds who had obviously braved the settling dust storm to catch a glimpse of the returned Macharius. Somewhere in the midst of the confusion, Anna simply disappeared. One second she was there, the next she had vanished. I looked around but did not see her. I doubted that anything could have happened to her so it must have been of her own free will.

Such was their joy that you would have thought that Mecharius had risen from the dead, which I suppose in their minds he had. They had thought he was lost in the fall of Irongrad and now, beyond all hope, he had emerged from the desert to lead them once more. I began to understand how stories of miracles can cluster around a mortal man. Some of the stories you hear about Macharius today make it sound as if he was superhuman but he was not, not really; he was just a man capable of extraordinary things in a time when such deeds were necessary.

General Sejanus strode forwards to greet Macharius. His

face was alight with joy. They embraced like father greeting son and I understood the friendship that existed between them when I saw that. In any other world than the one that had Macharius in it, Sejanus would have dominated the scene. He was a powerfully impressive man, somewhat shorter than Macharius and swarthy, with great bristling moustaches and eyes that glittered with suppressed fury. In the presence of Macharius though he was just another soldier, greeting a hero returned from the wars.

The two of them spoke but I could not overhear what they said and then they turned and walked beneath the huge awning outstretched beside the command vehicle. In its shadows they sat and exchanged words and Macharius beckoned us over and Sejanus spoke.

'It seems that the Imperium owes you men a debt of gratitude that can never be repaid,' Sejanus said. We just looked at him. None of us were going to contradict him. It was the sort of thing that every soldier wants to hear and very seldom does. Believe me, in the Imperial Guard, it is not often that you are found worthy of praise by your superiors. When it happens, you luxuriate in it.

'When it is time, I will see that they are suitably rewarded,' Macharius said. 'But right now there is much to be done and very little time to do it in if we are to save this world from the powers of darkness.'

The two generals began to plan. Orders were barked to servitors, holo-map grids invoked, orderlies came and went. We stood there apparently forgotten. No one had dismissed us so we stayed.

* * *

I was on the edge of dozing off when the earth shook. A commotion erupted around the table. I noticed everybody gazing at the map. It crawled and changed even as I watched. In the centre was still the huge angel-topped hive of Irongrad. Around it were still the snaking cables of the great pipelines. There was something else, something new, something that reminded me of what I had seen on my way through Irongrad. The earth was splitting all around the hive. Lines of fire appeared.

'What is going on?' Sejanus asked. Macharius looked at Drake.

'The ritual is nearing its climax. The tectonic plates of the world itself are shifting. The power of the Angel of Fire is manifesting.'

The wastelands were split by great fiery chasms. Lava bubbled forth, forming rivers and lakes. It looked as if a new lava sea was being born in front of us.

'It's a moat,' said Sejanus. 'It won't keep us out for long.'

'It doesn't have to,' said Drake. 'Just long enough for them to finish their ritual and summon the Angel of Fire.'

Macharius looked at them. 'Suggestions? Thoughts?' he asked.

Sejanus looked back at him steadily. 'We could evacuate.' He said in a tone of utmost seriousness. Macharius just stared at him and then they both laughed. It seemed like it was some sort of joke between them but for whatever reason I could not see the funny side. Evacuation seemed like a good idea to me.

'No way to get armour through that except airdrop,' said Sejanus. 'We could request our comrades in the Adeptus

Astartes drop on top of the cathedral and interrupt the ritual.'

'Without support, with the number of psykers in there?' Drake asked. 'With a daemon-god about to manifest. They might be able to do it but...'

'But we need to be certain,' Macharius said. 'I will not ask a Chapter of Space Marines to perform a suicide mission unsupported... unless I have to.'

You could see he had something else on his mind. He really did not want to send the Adeptus Astartes to a potentially fatal last stand but it was not just that.

Later, when I got to know Macharius better, I knew what it was. He did not want them getting all the glory. This campaign was his campaign. The Space Marines were not going to bail out Lord High Commander Solar Macharius. This was going to be a triumph for the Imperial Guard and for its leader or it was going to be nothing.

If that seems selfish and self-aggrandising on the part of Macharius, what can I tell you? He was an Imperial general. Even in the humblest-seeming of those there is a lust for glory. They all want to write their names in the history books and none of them wants to be put there as the fool who was saved, yet again, by the Space Marines. The least of them are like that, even the weakest, the most venal and the most incompetent. Macharius was none of those things.

'The Death Spectres are tied down on Karsk VII anyway,' said Sejanus. 'We need them there.'

Translating that from High Command speak, what he really meant was that he would see himself in hell before he would let the Adeptus Astartes get his share of the glory.

'Can we neutralise the daemon-summoners?' Macharius asked.

'I don't know,' said Drake. 'If we mass all of our sanctioned psykers and I call in all of my agents in place, maybe… We would need to get very close though.'

'We can send in a strike force mounted on Valkyries and Vultures,' said Sejanus.

Macharius said, 'They won't be able to fight their way into the heart of the Cathedral Zone unsupported and we'd lose too many to the air defences. We need to get our armour in and the bulk of our army behind it. We need to call on the people in the city who hate the priests to rise up and they need to know there is a force there that can support them. I am going to stop those damn heretics now and end their threat once and for all.'

You could tell that he meant that and I would not have given a lot for the chances of any pyromancer he personally encountered surviving. Of course that was something a lot different from breaking into the hive and seizing the cathedral.

'That's all very well, but how are you going to do it?' Drake asked. 'The earth is shifting, lava lakes are bubbling up, there's no easy way for us to get through in time.'

He was merely saying what we were all thinking. He was probably the only one there except for the Understudy who had the nerve to question Macharius. Macharius glared out through the canopy.

'We will find a way,' Macharius said.

We were not the most optimistic of groups. All of us looked at the great holo-map and contemplated the possibility of failure.

We knew we could take the hive. We had already done so once. That was not in doubt. What was in doubt was our ability to bridge the great moats of lava sliding into place around the city in time to stop the ritual. None of us wanted to contemplate what would happen if we were still on-planet when the Angel of Fire manifested. One look at Drake's sickly features was enough to convince me that it was not likely to be a pleasant experience.

There was a growing horror in the chamber. In part I suspect it was a product of the manifestation of the Angel. Even people with as much sensitivity to psychic events as a desert rock could sense that there was something wrong. There was a pressure in the air such as you get before a great storm. A cloud of gloom and despair had settled over our entire army. Macharius stared hard at the holo-map. All of his attention was focused on it. He glared at it as if he believed his hope of rebirth in the Emperor's Light depended on it. I suppose in a way it did. Concentrating, Macharius did not fidget. He merely stood there, statue-still, looking completely at rest. His gaze was fixed unwaveringly on the map, on the great hive that it was his desire to reclaim. A cold light burned in his eyes. It was as if he was staring at some hated personal enemy.

The rest of the command bustled around, bringing dispatches, discussing matters in low voices in the corner of the room. Sejanus lolled in an old padded armchair that looked like it had been brought directly from his family estate, and smoked a cheroot. Clouds of vile-smelling smoke drifted towards the ceiling of the pavilion and were sucked out into the even fouler air beyond by the extractors. The flexi-metal sides of the enormous tent bulged and rippled in response to pressure differentials. The Lion Banner of Macharius hung once more beneath the central frame of the tent. I wondered where they had dug that up from.

The Understudy looked like a machine that had shut down. His face was slack. His eyes half-closed. He was staring at the map as well and I wondered what he was seeing with those strange blue eyes.

Anton and Ivan stood in a corner like schoolboys in our old class in Ironforge Academy. They seemed to be hoping that no one would notice them and it was perfectly possible that in this august company no one would. I walked over to them.

Anton ran a bony hand across the scar on his forehead. 'Tense, isn't it?' he said and grinned his idiot grin.

'They are just waiting for you to come up with a brilliant idea and save the day,' Ivan said. 'You think they have anything to drink around here?'

His voice was gruff. Booze was on his mind. I could tell he was just as tense as Anton in his own way.

'Not many of us left now,' I said, saying what was on my mind. We had known each other so long they caught my meaning instantly. I had been thinking about Hesse. It had been the first time I really had time to do so. I felt oddly guilty about that. Hesse had been with us for a long time, had been a real link to the old days in the *Indomitable* and yet his death had completely vanished from my mind until the present. Well, I told myself, I had had plenty of other things to think about.

'Just us three now and the New Boy,' Anton said. 'I am not sure the Understudy is all there.'

'We'll raise a glass to them in time,' said Ivan. 'If we can find a bloody glass and the bloody time.'

We looked at each other. I could tell we were all thinking about Hesse and Oily and the lieutenant and all the others who had passed on in the Emperor's service. We had lost comrades and friends before but never so many so quickly. There was something about this place that felt accursed and I put that down to more than the growing influence of the ritual. Now that events had slowed down and I had time to think I felt their absence the way you feel a missing tooth in your mouth. It was uncomfortable and yet you could not stop inspecting it.

'What do you think is going to happen?' Anton asked. He sounded scared. I knew then I should be worried. If fear had managed to drill a hole through the solid rock of Anton's skull, things must be getting really bad.

'I don't know,' I said, 'but if anyone can think of something Macharius will.'

I was astounded to discover as I said the words that I really believed them. I had been mouthing them for reassurance but they came out full of faith, not doubt. I was as much surprised as anybody else. As if I had provoked him, I suddenly heard the Lord High Commander speak. 'Do you see it?'

All eyes were on him. Sejanus rose from the chair and strolled across to the holo-map. 'See what?' Drake said, voicing what we were all thinking.

'No,' Sejanus said, with what I thought was commendable honesty.

'The pattern, Sejanus, the pattern.'

'There may be one certainly, but I am damned if I see what you mean.'

'It's the same one as on the High Priest's sigil.'

'It may be so, but I never saw the damn thing.'

Macharius held something out in his hand. It glittered metallically. I realised it was the amulet he had pulled from the High Priest's neck back in the cathedral. He held it up to the light and it reflected the artificial fires visible in the holo-map. It was as if he was holding a rune made of flame in his hand.

Macharius held the symbol so that the light of the holo-globe was behind it and the shadow of part of the pattern, partially obscured by his clutching fist, fell on the map.

I looked from it to the map, and, you know, by the Emperor I could see that Macharius was right. Those shifting lines of fire were not a moat. They were flowing into the same pattern as the emblem of the Angel of Fire. I did not know whether to be relieved or filled with fear.

It seemed that we were insignificant to whatever power was manifesting itself in Irongrad. It was not creating a flaming barrier to keep us out, except perhaps by accident. It was manifesting a tribute to its own glory and might, reshaping the desert and the earth and the elements of rock and fire into a pattern that was significant only to it.

'It's very close to the sign of Tzeentch,' said Drake. 'The Changer of Ways. It's obvious now that you point it out.'

His voice was so soft it was hard to pick out the words. I think he was speaking only to himself. Nonetheless a chill passed through the room. An eerie silence fell. The inquisitor had named one of those names that it is very ill to speak, one of the greatest of all the enemies of humanity. Anton gave out a soft yelp. I understood why. Was it possible that this great daemon-god was going to manifest on the surface of Karsk? If it did, what would happen then? Even the shadow of its power was already beginning to reshape the land. Once it was fully present, what would it not be capable of?

Sejanus said, 'We can plot a path through that maze if we're quick.'

'How much time do we have now?' Macharius asked Drake.

The high inquisitor said, 'Not more than twelve hours – the power is spiking again. I can feel it even from here.'

'We had better get moving,' said Macharius, with what I thought was considerable understatement.

Once he had seen the pattern, there was no holding Macharius back. He barked out orders to all of his commanders and sub-commanders, telling them to prepare to advance. Within minutes he had sketched out a basic plan of attack with all the usual trademark details of his genius. He could see the way the lava flows were going to end up. They were not there yet but they would be by the time we were ready to attack. Our forces would sweep in to attack the hive, navigating through the labyrinth of lava. Once we were within the boundaries of the great pattern, our force would divide into three main groups, attacking all of the major southern gates of the city. Our forces were to be ready to shift the weight of the attack at any time, to follow up any breakthrough. At least half the army was held in reserve, to rush forwards when the breakthrough came. In that group would be the bulk of the psykers. They were the ones who were going to be necessary once we got within the city. Having sketched in the outline of this plan, Macharius studied the maps of Irongrad itself. Our route was clear – wherever we broke in we would need to rush down into the cathedral itself and disrupt the great ritual that was taking place.

There was nothing else for it. It was a desperate gamble, a roll of the dice; do or die. I could tell from the way he was smiling that the thought made Macharius happy.

I thought I could understand why. His destiny was once more within his own hands. He was not merely an observer standing by and waiting for the daemon-god to arrive and take possession of its new domain. He was going to do something about it. He was going to measure himself against the darkest powers in the galaxy. He might not win but he was going to die trying. And we were going to follow him. And the truth of it was, in that moment, I was perfectly happy to do so. At least, doing it his way, we had some chance. It was better than standing back and doing nothing or desperately trying to evacuate when we had no time to do so. We were going to fight and we were going to fight like men and that, in the end, was all we could really ask for.

Headquarters tent became a buzzing hive of activity. Commanders were briefed on the entire plan and rushed off to find their sub-commanders. Orders rippled out through the whole vast nervous system of the army.

Macharius, as he always did, was making sure that everybody knew what they had to do. He looked more alive than at any time since I had first seen him. I realised that this was what he lived for; this was when he was only truly alive. It's a strange thing to say about a man who always seemed so vital. There was always more life in Macharius than in two normal men even when he was at rest, but now he blazed with energy and authority, radiating calm and confidence and certainty that what he was asking could be done, and that filled those around him with a similar confidence.

I asked myself, what would happen if he was wrong? What would happen if the lava was simply flowing into some random pattern and he had simply perceived something that was not there? I realised that the truth of the matter was that it didn't matter. If Macharius was wrong, we were no worse off, and if he was right, we would soon be in a position to take the fight to the heretics.

I looked at Ivan and I looked at Anton and I could see that they were both feeling better. The dread had departed from their faces and they looked as ready for action as I had ever seen them. Even Drake had perked up; he did not look quite so sick. He walked over to a comm-board and began typing in odd combinations on the runic keyboard. I guessed he was getting in touch with his agents within the army. In the midst of all this chaos, I was surprised when Macharius walked over to us. He placed his heavy hand on my shoulder and said, 'Go outside, take a break. There will be a few hours before the preparations to advance are complete. I want you all with me when the final attack begins. You've brought me good luck this far and I'm not taking the chance of losing it before the end.'

I was at once touched and frightened. I was touched by the

fact that Macharius seemed to have some faith in us. I was frightened by the fact that even the great general seemed to believe that he was in need of all the luck he could get.

People will tell you that the great commanders make their own luck, and there is a freighter-load of truth in that statement, but even Macharius seemed to feel he had to do everything he possibly could to stack the odds in his favour. Sometimes, luck is the only difference between victory and defeat. It was strange to see that even a man as confident as Macharius felt the need of some lucky talisman. It was even stranger to look at Anton and Ivan and the Understudy and think that that was what we were to him.

We stepped outside. The dust had settled. As far as the eye could see were armoured vehicles. To the north an eerie glow lit the sky. Far, far off, the hive of Irongrad loomed, a shadowy mountain pierced by caverns of light. At its tip, a fire-winged angel stood ominously waiting. I knew it was not going to wait for long.

'Well, we're going with Macharius,' Anton said.

'I can tell you're excited,' said Ivan. He eyed the distant hive with a certain gloomy satisfaction, pulled out his hip flask and took a swig. He offered it to me.

'I bloody well am, and so are you, don't lie about it!' Anton said. He knew Ivan too well to be fooled.

I drank the fiery liquid. It tasted like Oily's coolant fluid. I fought back the wave of memories the taste brought with it.

'Well,' Ivan asked, sad eyes gazing at me out of his ruined, half-metal face. 'What do you think?'

'About what?'

'About all this. You think we have a chance?'

'What does it matter what I think? We are going in.'

'So you don't then.' His voice was flat and calm, a man discussing the chances of a dust storm coming in tomorrow morning.

'I never said that,' I said.

'You didn't have to.'

'Tell me,' said Anton. 'When we were back in the cathedral, did you think we would ever get out alive?'

I shook my head. Ivan did the same.

Anton banged his chest with his fist. 'We're still here.'

'You know,' said Ivan, 'the idiot is right.'

'Of course he is,' said Anton. His mouth shut like a trap when he realised he had just agreed he was an idiot. He paused for a moment, then pulled out a lho stick and lit it. He coughed wheezily and said, 'Maybe Macharius is lucky for us. Maybe it's not that we are lucky for him.'

'He wasn't lucky for Hesse,' I said.

'I said for *us*,' said Anton. There was an edge of desperation in his voice, as if he was looking for something to believe.

'Go read your prop-nov, Anton,' I said, not unkindly. 'It'll take your mind off things.'

The bastard took me at my word. He sat down right there in the gritty sand, pulled the book from his chest-pocket, licked his finger and began flicking through the pages until he reached his favourite part. He squinted in concentration. Strange as it may sound, just looking at him and his dumb book gave me hope. Somehow he had managed to preserve the bloody thing through all the madness.

He ran his finger along the lines, squinting with child-ish concentration, lips moving as he read the long familiar words. I was not sure I had his faith in Macharius but I had faith in him and Ivan. They would do what needed to be done.

The Understudy emerged from the tent. He walked over to where we were and we saluted him and he saluted us but we did not say anything and neither did he. He simply walked a little further and stood there, back to us, staring into the distance, seemingly unaware of the fact that he was making us uncomfortable. Obviously he just did not care. He was entirely self-sufficient, completely on his own even in the teeming swarms surrounding the headquarters. For all that though, even he had chosen to come outside and stand in the proximity of his comrades.

Perhaps there was still something human in there. Perhaps he simply needed that small crumb of comfort. Or maybe I am wrong, maybe he simply picked a random spot to stand and observe the great enemy in the distance. I am in no position to tell.

Ivan took another swig from his flask and offered it up to Anton, who shook his head, so Ivan passed it on to me. While I was drinking, Ivan produced his magnoculars and focused them in the direction the Understudy was looking. I do not know what he saw. I never asked. I just took another sip of the cooling fluid and felt it burn its way down my throat.

The Understudy stood there, still as a statue, his arms behind his back, his right hand clutching his left wrist. His head was tilted to one side as if he did not quite understand what he was seeing. Maybe he felt that way about the whole world. It had certainly changed for him. Eventually, he turned and walked back towards us.

'You better turn in then,' he said in his strange, rasping voice. 'We're going to have an early start tomorrow and the Lord High Commander wants us all to be ready.'

'We haven't been assigned quarters, sir,' said Anton.

'Then I suggest you make a billet here.' He said it as if it was the most natural thing in the world. Maybe, for him, it was. He sat down by the edge of the great flexi-metal tent and closed his eyes and went to sleep with the ease of a machine after it has been switched off. Anton shrugged, read a few more pages, then just altered his position so that he was lying down flat with his head pillowed on his arms and then he too was asleep. I looked at Ivan and handed him back the flask. He kept looking off into the distance and drinking. I'm sure he was tired but he did not seem to want to rest.

'We've come a long way from Belial,' Ivan said. He looked up at the sky, at the stars glittering coldly so far above. One of them might have been the sun around which Belial swung but I was damned if I could pick out which one. 'A bloody long way.'

I looked at his ruined face. The metal reflected the distant flames dully. I could remember times on other worlds when he had to put boot polish on it so we would not be spotted by the reflection when scouting.

'Do you regret it?' I asked. Of all of us, he had the most reason to. He had given more of his flesh and blood to the Emperor than any of us. He laughed softly and shook his head.

'No. What would we be doing now if we were still on Belial? Working in a guild factorum?'

'We'd most likely be dead,' I said. 'Those gangers wanted our hides.'

He nodded. 'Just think what it took to get us here. We pissed off the Big Man and his cronies and because of that we joined the Guard. If I hadn't got you and Anton into this, none of us would be here.'

He was right in his way. If Ivan had not tried to stop a couple of legbreakers collecting from Old Man Petrov, we would never have fallen foul of the local gangs. He looked at me. 'Sorry about that,' he said.

I shook my head. 'Nothing to be sorry about. What was there for us on Belial – long hours in the guild factorum, dying broke and broken like my old man? At least this way we can say we did something! We saw other worlds. We saw wonders. Hell, we saw Space Marines!'

He laughed softly. 'We did, didn't we? And we're bodyguards of an Imperial High Commander. We're going to be riding with Macharius. Who would ever have thought it?'

I heard the pride in his voice at that. It meant more to him even than seeing those Space Marines. I was not quite so enthusiastic but I tried to say something. What was on my mind slipped out. 'At least when we die, it might make a difference.'

Ivan cocked his head to one side and let out a low whistle as he did, sometimes, when he was curious.

'What do you mean?'

'When we walk into the Emperor's Light we will have done His will. We will have laid down our lives in His service, fighting His enemies. That's got to count for something.'

I think something of my desperation and fear showed in my tone.

'Of course it does,' he said with absolute certainty. 'There is evil in this galaxy, we've both seen it and somebody has to do something about it.'

I smiled at that. He had sounded just the same when we were boys. Beneath all the cynicism and the drinking and the anger, the same idealistic boy was present.

'I was proud of you when you beat up those legbreakers,' I said. I was too. I had been angry as well, knowing the trouble he had got us into, but now did not seem to be the time to say it. I looked over at the sleeping Anton. 'He was too.'

'I am not sure that's a compliment.' Something of his usual joshing tone returned, then he sighed. 'He's not so bad. You could ask for worse at your side when things get rough. He carried me on his back to the medicae station on Jurasik after the attack. Never left till I was patched up.'

'I remember,' I said. We had been in camp when the orks came roaring out of the jungle and smashed through the perimeter. No time to get into the *Indomitable*, just time enough to snatch up weapons and let fly. It had been touch and go then. No mistake.

He laughed softly. 'What do you think my sisters would say if they knew we were going to be bodyguards to Macharius tomorrow?'

'They would not believe it. Neither would my old man. He always told me I would swing for heresy or something else.' I thought about Anna and what she might say and I realised there was still a possibility he would be proved right.

'Macharius is a great man,' Ivan said. 'A great general, a

great leader. He will set the Imperium to rights. He'll show these heretics what for too before we are done.'

I truly wished I could share his faith in that. Ivan took a final swig at the flask and said, 'I am going to turn in now. Might be the last chance to get some sleep for a while.'

He just lay back, put his hands behind his head and nodded off. I sat there under the desert sky and studied the strange stars. A growing sense of doom was creeping over me. At some point, I left wakefulness behind but I cannot remember exactly when it was.

The blood-red sun sprang over the horizon. The heat of the day was rising, causing the air over the ash deserts to shimmer. Engines throbbed all around us. Macharius emerged into the daylight to the cheers of assembled soldiers. He raised his hands in a gesture of triumph and strode towards the waiting Baneblade. It has been decorated in his own personal colours, with the Lion seal of his family on it. There was a name too inscribed in flowing Gothic script, *The Lion of Macharius*.

I thought that showed considerable faith in his luck. If anyone knew what to look for, it would make the great tank a target. Or maybe not. Maybe anyone looking at it would suspect a trick. Or maybe I am just too devious for my own good.

Macharius looked at us and gestured for us to come with

him, so we did. I did not know what to expect but I followed him up the drop-down ladder and into the interior of the Baneblade. It had been modified more than a little. There was a mass of additional command systems and holo-maps inside the enhanced driver's chamber. It looked like the tech-priests had been very busy in this vehicle. Drake was there and a bunch of people I did not know and whose purpose I could not guess.

Macharius put on a headset trimmed with the oak-leaf clusters of a High Commander. He occupied a throne behind where the commander's normal seat would be. He gestured for the Understudy to take command of the tank, and for me to drive. Anton and Ivan had been assigned to guns. We might have been his lucky talismans but we were going to have to perform our normal duties under his eyes.

Sliding into the driver's chair was like coming home. I ran my hands over the control altars reassured by the familiar position of everything. Some things felt different. This vehicle would have a different spirit from the old *Indomitable*. I knew I was going to take some time to get used to the *Lion*'s quirks. I hoped there would be enough before we hit the lava moat around the city. I also wondered what had happened to the previous crew. Perhaps this was his reward to us. He had accelerated the process of having us re-assigned to a new Baneblade.

I listened to Macharius respond to the incoming reports from his commanders. I waited for the instruction to fire up the drive cores. It was not long in coming. The New Boy took up position beside me and waited like an apprentice. This machine was definitely different from the *Indomitable*.

It felt more alert, keener, more proud. It was not so tired. I sensed all of that as it stirred from its slumber. It did not know me but it accepted me as it had accepted a procession of new drivers throughout the long centuries of its life.

Looking out through the view-scopes I could see thousands of armoured vehicles come to life. Enormous columns began to move out in response to central command's orders. Huge plumes of dust danced skywards. We rumbled forwards towards the fires on the horizon. I felt as if we were driving to the end of the world.

If Macharius felt the same, he gave no sign. His voice was calm. His commands were clear. I paid more attention in the first few minutes to the Understudy as he rasped out his orders quietly.

It felt strange to be listening to him and not the lieutenant. It felt doubly strange to be in this cabin and in the presence of Macharius. But it felt nowhere near as strange as the idea of what we were racing towards under the desert sky of Karsk.

Drake said, 'Incoming signal from Fleet Orbital, sealed channel, highest priority, encrypted.'

'Take it,' Macharius said.

The inside of the Baneblade seemed suddenly quiet. There was something in his voice that made everybody listen. The features of an admiral appeared in the command globe, relayed down from his flagship somewhere in orbit.

'Lord High Commander,' the admiral said. 'I have read your encrypted instructions and I seek clarification. We are to begin bombardment of Hive Irongrad at eighteen hundred Imperial Standard Time if we do not receive a direct instruction from you countermanding.'

'Admiral Jensen. Those are my orders. I believe they are perfectly clear.'

'But, Lord High Commander, your force may still be engaged within the city. And the pyrite refineries. We came here for those.'

'New priorities have arisen, admiral. I have given you your orders. See that you obey them!'

'But–'

'Obey them, admiral. The security of the Imperium may depend on it. I have no time to explain further.'

The admiral nodded. He did not look happy but he looked like he would do as he was told. Macharius cut the communication channel. I shuddered when I realised what Macharius had done. If we failed to stop the ritual, the whole city would be obliterated. He had given orders that would most likely result in all our deaths, then even more chillingly I realised that if those orders were carried out we would probably already be dead.

'It still might not be enough to stop the ritual,' Drake said.

'We have done what we could,' Macharius said and returned to speaking into the comm-net as if nothing more need be said.

We swept forwards and I could see the lava flows clearly. Jets of liquid stone spurted upwards, incandescent and ruby red. The earth was cracking. Occasionally, the Baneblade shifted oddly in response to the moving ground. It felt like it might spin out of control if I was not careful. I watched all of the volt gauges and meters carefully. I kept my hands ready on the controls. I did not want to be taken off-guard by anything. We followed the paths predetermined by Macharius's discovery. It reminded me of our first approach to Irongrad. It was just as tricky and we did not have time to take things slowly and carefully.

The formation rolled on, feeling its way forwards through the shifting terrain where the sign of the daemon-god was being written on the living flesh of the world. It was slow progress and it became all the slower when the heretics realised what was happening. Not all of them were wrapped up in their ritual summoning. The great batteries on the armoured skin of the city opened fire. Swarms of flyers engaged our air-cover in battle. Within the city itself I had no doubt troops were being marshalled.

As we got closer to the city, following the channels of the infernal symbol surrounding the hive, the earth tremors became more intense and the air seemed to shimmer and pulse. Whirlpools of multi-coloured light swirled in the air. At first I thought it was some sort of heat haze. Rocks split and tanks were swallowed like men going down in jungle quicksand. That was not the worst of it.

Out of those swirling whirlpools creatures were starting to emerge. They were roughly humanoid in shape, but their outlines seemed to shimmer and shift as much as the whirlpools that spawned them. They were an odd shade of pink and they belched flame from numerous orifices that seemed to appear in their skin, like blowholes bubbling out of a mudpool. There was something awful just in their very appearance. At times they seemed as if they were not quite solid, not quite there, as insubstantial as a heat-haze or a fever dream. At other times they looked somehow more solid than a tank. They shimmered and were gone only to reappear a few strides away from where they had been. They opened mouths as wide as their entire bodies, revealing fangs the size of bayonets and roared challenges as they threw themselves at our fighting vehicles.

On hearing the panicked cries, Drake strode over to where the New Boy sat and glared through his scope. I was close enough to hear him mutter, 'The horrors of which the codexes speak. The Architect of Fate is surely behind all this.'

I did not know then what he meant but it did not sound good.

He turned to look at Macharius. 'It is worse than I feared. Lesser portals are already starting to open. This is blowback from the ritual. It will get far, far worse unless we stop it. This confirms all suspicions – the cult of the Angel of Fire is indeed a front for Tzeentch, the Changer of Ways.'

He sounded shaken. Macharius remained calm. 'The Emperor's enemies must be opposed,' was all he said.

Even their mighty fists could not do much beating against armoured hulls, but they distracted panicked drivers who swerved into the lava streams. Sometimes they clambered atop stalled vehicles and ripped off hatches, then they could reach inside and pull out terrified men, biting them in two with those enormous fanged mouths that seemed to be centred right on their stomachs. Sometimes I thought I heard them screaming, 'All is fire, all is flux, all is change.'

It was not so much their power that frightened but the sorcery they represented and I thought that if more of the creatures were waiting in the city, our infantry was going to have a tough time of it when they poured out onto the streets.

Macharius gave the command to open fire with our lighter weapons. The shimmering figures burst asunder, sometimes splitting into smaller figures, very similar but coloured an obscene shade of blue. I half-feared that they would flow back together and reform but they did not, at least not the ones I saw. Of course, such a strategy was not without its perils. Sometimes crews would open up with their heavier guns. That destroyed the daemons all right but it often would take out our own vehicles along with them. Macharius snapped out clear, concise commands to stop doing it. He insisted we use only the light guns and he was obeyed.

Other creatures began to manifest. They looked something like upturned mushrooms, ambulatory and oddly humanoid; from their limbs and maws they spewed iridescent flame. They too shimmered and sometimes seemed to wink in and out of existence as though products of some wicked fever dream. They exploded when hit though and killed what they could and I was left in no doubt as to their reality.

We rolled on towards Irongrad. Armies of shimmering, daemonic entities waited for us. We surged forwards to engage and as we did, the guns on the walls opened up on us, and Vultures swooped down to attack.

Against ordinary infantry, the daemons would have been a threat but on the open plain we simply destroyed them. I wondered what the sorcerers within the city hoped to achieve and the answer came back to me: nothing. They did not need to achieve anything. They were slowing us down, making us waste ammunition, causing a few casualties, and overrunning a few vehicles. The sheer mass of them created confusion in our ranks and the cost to the heretics was nil. The daemons were simply by-products of the ritual being enacted. They demonstrated to the people of Irongrad, and to us, the power of the Angel of Fire. They hindered us when every moment might be precious.

We made for the gates of the city, crushing our inhuman opponents beneath our treads. Occasionally the Baneblade rocked as one of the massive wall-guns came close to scoring a direct hit. Our own weapons pounded away at the fortifications now. One by one, a few of the guns were silenced. Many of our own Leman Russ had been destroyed and the fiery daemons hunted their crews. I cursed but there was nothing else I could do. Macharius kept up a steady calm stream of orders, talking into the comm-net, responding to new developments, holding the whole vast scheme of the battle in his mind as a chess-player can hold the positions of play on a board.

Somewhere in the distance our own Basilisks had opened fire, aiming at positions marked on maps or called in by field commanders. Great mushrooms of smoke and fire blossomed on the walls of Irongrad. We bounced through a crater filled with pink-skinned daemons, turning them to smoking sludge beneath our treads, bursting them like balloons filled with ectoplasmic pus. Some of our troops had already reached the main gates. Siege engineers deployed their demolition charges and lock overrides. Our tanks kept firing. Vultures strafed the walls while Valkyries deployed storm troopers to take critical positions then soared away, sending their twin-tailed shadows racing over the ground below. For once, things went with precision. I attribute it to the close presence of Macharius. In minutes we were within the walls of the city, driving down the core roads, heading for the cathedral. It was there the resistance really began.

The heretics had barricaded the streets. In places they had left lines of industrial haulers and shattered vehicles. Our heavy tanks pressed on, smashing through the wrecks and overrunning the infantry crouched behind them, reducing them to bloody smears on the plascrete paving. Our anti-personnel weapons strafed them. They stood their ground and died. I offered up a prayer to the Emperor and the tutelary spirit of the Baneblade in which we rode, and kept my eyes on the highway we broke beneath the treads of our vehicle.

In a monstrous armoured column we rode down the streets into the centre of the hive. As we progressed the feeling of imminence, of something dreadful being about to happen, became more intense. The nearer hab-blocks had an abandoned look, as if those who had dwelled within had fled, taking what they could carry with them. Here and there, the great trash-piles seemed to be spontaneously combusting. Sprinkler systems in the ceiling sent great storms of water raining down but it did not seem to help, only turned to mist. Some of the hab-blocks blazed. It was as if the whole hive were starting to catch fire.

There were more heretics but it seemed as if they were falling back before us, torn between a desire to slow our advance and to be close to the place where their unholy god was going to manifest. Perhaps the deluded fools believed the Angel of Fire would save them, that somehow, when the Angel of Fire manifested itself they were all going to be transformed in its supernatural light. Hell, maybe they would be, what did I know?

I heard Drake grunt behind me. I avoided turning to look at him, but I could not ignore his muttering voice. 'The power is spiking. What new horror is this?'

Looking out through the drive periscope I saw at once what he meant. The statues were coming to life. It sounds absurd when I say it now, but that is exactly what was happening. All of those fire-winged metal angels were starting to stretch and flex, like men waking from long sleep. I knew then that something truly unnatural was really happening in Irongrad. When statues come to life, stretch out clawed fingers and take to the air on wings of plasma fire, you know that natural law has been suspended. They soared above the burning buildings and seemed to draw strength from the blaze.

Judging from the screams echoing through the streets around me, I was not alone in my realisation. It looked like the citizens of Irongrad were starting to wake up to the truth of what the materialisation of their deity might bring. It was a miracle of sorts but it was a dark and unholy one. Statues should not come to life. They should remain decently posed and immobile. They should not twist and gesture. Most of all they should not sing. From all of the angels came a full-throated hymn of triumph, at once joyous and evil, strangely thrilling and terribly ominous. The sound did not seem loud within the hull of the Baneblade but the fact that it could be heard at all was troubling. We were supposed to be warded from the siren song of Chaos.

The living statues swooped over us, stretching out their hands and sending bolts of flame arcing down. They splattered off the side of the Baneblade. A strange aroma of brimstone and something else, not unpleasant but haunting and odd was detectable even within the tank. I assumed this must be an actual smell, working through the filters, not something supernatural.

'We must hurry,' said Drake. 'The daemon-god is almost through. Its power is starting to manifest and reality is starting to warp under the force of its power.'

'How long?' Macharius asked.

'Less than an hour.'

Macharius kept speaking into the comm-net, giving calm, clipped, clear instructions. Barrages of fire hit the daemonic angels, bursting them asunder, revealing the terrible spirits of the warp that had animated them. These looked even less human than the horrors we had seen outside, more like those vast flatfish that swim in the seas of Jurasik, although these did not swim but fly. As they were revealed, hideous screeching screams mingled with the singing of that evil choir.

We kept moving towards the cathedral, knowing that something dreadful was waiting for us.

Ahead of us, I got a clear view of the street. A huge force of Imperial troops was engaged with a horde of the heretics. Tanks crushed groundcars beneath their treads as they advanced. Heavy bolter fire shredded hastily thrown-together barricades. Lascannon chopped through formations of defenders. Buildings burned, metal angels filled the sky. Ray-like screamers dived on our troops, seized them in their maws and lifted them skywards to drop them on the ground hundreds of metres below.

Macharius ordered me to the left and directed more troops into the fray with a series of swift commands.

We drove on through the city, crushing the resistance we found. It should have made me more confident but it did not. The fighting raged through the streets. Macharius commanded it all, ordering flanking actions through side streets, sending troops via overpass and viaduct to attack the enemy from the rear. Somehow he kept the whole vast picture of the battle in his head. He had no difficulty visualising the three-dimensional topography of a hive and using it to his advantage. He dispatched reinforcements where they were needed, directed feints and strikes at enemy positions, and kept the whole Imperial army moving towards its goal in the centre of the city. All the while the clock ticked down. If he felt any pressure knowing of impending doom, no sign showed on his face or in his voice.

A gigantic explosion erupted off to our right. It was potent enough to make the Baneblade shiver and the mighty structures of the hab-blocks rock. I heard Macharius say something about a gas-refinery going up. He sounded confident. I had no idea whether this was part of his plan, something he had expected, something that he could use or whether he was merely living out the maxim that command must always seem calm and in charge. If that was the case, I have to say that no man ever did it better than he.

The streets blurred by. Explosions wracked the city. Buildings blazed, and the streets were filled with smoke and screaming people. In some places hab-towers had collapsed, partially blocking the road. In other places where there had been hab-blocks, there were merely blackened ruins. I guided the Baneblade around the rubble, kept us moving in the direction of the cathedral. All around was war and fire. It felt like the end of the world.

Massive pipes were evident everywhere. I remembered our escape from the cathedral and knew we were getting close. I could have told that from the increase in resistance. There were more heretics and more vehicles. A cohort of hastily repainted Leman Russ blocked our way. I just kept moving towards them. Our guns blazed, reducing them to so much slag, and the Baneblade pushed through the wreckage like a mastodon pushing through a herd of antelope.

We entered the great cleared area around the cathedral. The mighty structure towered over us, rising into a polluted sky kilometres above. I felt certain that somewhere up there, high atop the unholy site, that gigantic starscraper-sized statue was slowly coming to life, stretching its limbs like a giant waking from sleep, and surveying the entire world with burning, hungry eyes.

The whole vast space was filled with heretics. They lurked behind hastily improvised fortifications, blasting away at us with their weapons. Our formation deployed around us, forming up and advancing, a monstrous armoured column that could not be resisted by any human force. Overhead fire-winged metal angels swooped and dived, sending bolts of magical fire down upon us. Fire from our tanks scythed through them and split their metal bodies and revealed the screaming daemons within. Among the heretics more of those pink-fleshed horrors shimmered and bellowed. Oddly fungal flamers hopped over the battlefield, spraying our forces with daemonic fire. Through every entrance into the great open space which surrounded the cathedral, Imperial armour poured. It was astonishingly well-coordinated. Battle tanks crushed anything made of flesh that got in their way. Great lascannon beams scythed across the plaza. Tens of thousands of infantrymen began to disembark from Chimeras. The combat became close and deadly. Banners of a dozen regiments fluttered proudly above the fray. The grey tower on a white background showed the Legions of Asterion were there along with the Red Sword of the Ninth Traskian Hussars.

We moved forwards, grinding resistance beneath our tracks, surging up the enormous marble stairs of the cathedral until we confronted the cyclopean brass doors.

Pulping flesh as we went, we stormed closer. A concentrated barrage of fire buckled the doors, our Baneblade smashed through them like a battering ram and we were within, moving through the enormous vestibule, confronting heretics and steel angels. We drove onwards crushing the resistance until we had gone as far as we could go. Our tanks could move no further; not even a Baneblade could smash the enormous stone and ceramite walls and columns.

Macharius barked another order. A blaze of anti-personnel fire cleared the area around us. We were surrounded by broken bodies and ruined, religious finery. Smouldering banners covered the walls. The temple drapes provided shrouds for corpses.

'Everybody out,' Macharius ordered. 'We go on foot from here.'

It sounded insane but we had no other choice. If we were going to confront the evil at the heart of this we were going to have to do it on foot.

Document under seal. Extract From the Decrypted Personal Files of Inquisitor Hyronimus Drake.

Possible evidence of duplicity on the part of former High Inquisitor Drake.

Cross-reference to Exhibit 107D-21H (Report to High Inquisitor Toll).

It is far, far worse even than I had thought it was going to be. The forces of the Architect of Fate have manifested themselves on the surface of this world. The thin skin of mortal reality has broken and that which lurks beneath has become visible. I am making these notes in what may prove to be the final moments of my life in the hope that they may be found and benefit the Imperial force that comes after us.

Across the city, our forces are engaged with the forces of the heretics. I can see it play out on the huge battlemap that Macharius studies. In my mind's eye I can picture the proud defenders of humanity surging into battle with hordes of heretics and swarms of manifest daemons, all the hungry horrors that serve the Changer of Ways. On a thousand streets, hundreds of thousands of men are locked in combat with the forces of evil. Thousands of Leman Russes and Chimeras and Manticores roar along roadways and across bridges, seizing the main transport arteries and pushing on deeper into the city. From what I overhear on the comm-net, tens of thousands are dying and far, far more are already dead.

Our greatest advantage is that our enemies appear to be confused and fighting piecemeal. They are everywhere across the city but their leaders are more concerned with their ritual than fighting a war. Macharius commands clearly and calmly and will win against the lesser forces, but that will avail us nothing unless we get to the cathedral and prevent the manifestation of what I fear will be an avatar of one of humanity's greatest foes.

The awful truth is that we are not really being opposed. It is an illusion. All we are seeing is a side-effect of the Angel of Fire entering this world, and the token resistance of those worshippers who are in our way. It is not organised. Those who could have done that are busy elsewhere, masterminding the appearance of a daemon-god, abasing themselves before something dark and strange that they believe is coming to aid them, but which in reality is merely using them for its own purposes.

The skies swirl with daemons but that is nothing to what only a psyker can perceive. The sky above the hive is splitting. A great fissure in reality is opening. Something dark and terrible and majestic is moving through. I pray that we are in time.

We piled out of the hatches and swarmed down the sides of the Baneblade. Even that enormous, ancient presence seemed dwarfed by the cathedral.

The air smelled of brimstone and incense and a scent I remembered well from the factorum-foundries of my youth: molten metal. A strange light glowed around everything. Our surroundings looked too bright, but sometimes shadows that should not have been there rippled across walls, as if cast by something huge moving against a light which had no source in our world. It was eerie, unnatural and disturbing. Sometimes the shadow of the horrors was visible as if they were just about to manifest.

Over everything was an oppressive sense of the imminence of something supernatural. I felt like I was in the presence of something greater than human, much greater.

I was reminded of the moment when I had confronted the Titan in the rubble of the factorum but this was a thousand times worse. The ancient warmachine had been a being compared to which I was an insect. To the thing manifesting itself now, I was a microbe.

For a brief moment, I understood why the heretics were doing this and why they were so filled with worshipful awe. How many men can say they have been in the presence of a living god? Blasphemous as it sounds, the only comparable situation I can imagine is to stand before the Tomb Throne of the Emperor on galaxy-distant Terra and gaze upon the immortal being within.

For better or worse, I can say I have stood in the presence of the divine. It was evil but it was wonderful and terrible too; the sort of experience a man might only be vouchsafed once in a lifetime and then only after a long and arduous pilgrimage.

It did not take the heretics long to recover. They came at us from many of the arched entrances to the great vestibule. Macharius ordered us to hold the line. More and more of our own troops flooded in through the broken gates and soon the hall was filled with a vast swirling conflict. We had the advantage in that we had our vehicles for cover and their anti-personnel weapons cut down the incoming heretics. Of course, sometimes it went wrong and our own men were scythed into death as well. In the Imperial Guard such things are inevitable and accepted.

Ivan and Anton crouched down beside me. 'What are we waiting for?' Anton asked. 'I thought every second was vital.'

'Ask them, not me,' I said pointing to Macharius and

Drake. The general was surrounded by his personal body-guard of elite troops. More men and women in the robes of the Inquisition came to join Drake. I was surprised to see other people as well. The high inquisitor talked to them as if they were more than common soldiers. Some of them were garbed as privates, some as officers and some wore the clothes of local civilians. Anna was with them, garbed in some sort of greyish battle-armour that fitted her like a second skin.

I understood what was happening now. These were Drake's agents concealed within the body of our army and the local population. If I had needed any proof of how desperate things were, this would have been it. All of these agents were hidden in place, spies among the people of the planet and our own army, reporting directly to Drake.

'Who are they?' Anton asked.

'They are spies, Drake's agents,' I told him.

'Psykers?' he asked.

'I guess.'

'There's a bloody lot of them,' he said and shuddered and I knew then what he was thinking. They had been there all the time, walking among us, unknown and undetected, agents of the Inquisition, armed with supernatural powers. It was not a reassuring thought, even if they were, at a time like this, on our side. More and more warriors and psykers assembled around us.

Drake was surrounded by his own bodyguard now. They seemed to appear out of nowhere but obviously had arrived with the main body of our troops. They were hard, com-petent-looking men in heavy carapace armour I associated with shock troops and storm troopers. They did not have the insignia of any regiment I knew though which was ominous enough. They were armed with lasguns bigger and heavier than ours. They glanced warily about, looking for threats. Somehow they managed to interpose themselves between Drake and his surroundings without ever appearing to. One of them saw me looking and glared at me hard. I smiled at him just to be annoying. Beyond him I could see Anna talking with Drake. The inquisitor looked distracted. She looked as calm as she ever did.

Macharius clambered onto the side of our Baneblade, and looking at him I remembered the speech he had given what seemed like so long ago when we had first arrived on Karsk and thought about how much had changed since then. There was a light about him now it seemed. It might have just been a trick of the light or some eddy current of the strange sorceries that were being woven around us, but he looked like something greater than human.

This time there was no technical engine of the Adeptus Mechanicus to amplify his voice and form. This time there was just him. He stood there, chainsword raised in his fist, and he addressed us. He had that trick of being able to speak as powerfully as a great actor filling an amphitheatre even with his own voice.

'This is the hour,' he said. 'The forces of evil and heresy threaten to engulf this world. We will not let them!

'We will show these daemon worshippers how men can fight and if need be how men can die!'

His voice had a rasping metallic ring to it now. Every man there strained to hear.

'Above us, false men seek to summon a false god! They have been deluded by their own evil and their own lies. If they succeed, they will bring only darkness and inevitable retribution and death to all who dwell here. We shall not let them succeed. We shall climb into the very heavens if need be and tear down their false idol and overthrow the dark thing they worship and we shall bring the light of the Emperor's Truth to this benighted world.'

He believed every word of it and in that moment so did we. We felt the righteousness of our cause and the necessity of our victory.

'Onwards, men! For the Emperor. Smite the heretic! Follow me. To victory!'

There was nothing else for it but to follow him into the depths of the cathedral. We would have followed him then if he was leading us towards the depths of hell. It was just as well really, for that was exactly where we were going.

Step by weary step we fought our way upwards. Rivers of blood flowed down the stairs, turning them into crimson waterfalls. Burned meat and ruined flesh formed barricades built of corpses.

The heretics opposed our every footfall. They died in their thousands, throwing themselves in our way, being burned down by las-fire or blown asunder by frag grenades. They took their toll on our men, killing almost as many as they lost. More and more of our lads flooded in behind us. I could only pray that enough of them had made it to the city to keep the flow of reinforcements coming.

The air shimmered and one of those rainbow whirlpools

appeared. Out of it erupted a horde of the pink-skinned horrors we had encountered earlier, blasting flame out of their enormous fanged mouths, tearing men asunder with long, clawed fingers. The psykers around Drake responded with a surge of power and the vortex swirled shut. The daemons became marginally less stable-looking, one or two of them seemed to turn sideways on and vanish. The rest we swarmed into, shooting and stabbing. The storm troopers around Drake blasted with those heavy guns of theirs. A Horror bounded right up to me and opened its mouth to incinerate me. I stuck the shotgun in and pulled the trigger. Its rubbery flesh seemed to resist the shot. It expanded like a balloon for a moment under the force of the shot and only once it had become almost half again the size it had been did it burst. I half-expected it to explode but it did not. It mostly vanished leaving only traces of slime and a foul smell and a hail of shotgun pellets falling suddenly to earth.

Macharius swept past me along with Anton and Ivan and a group of square-jawed troopers. I raced to catch up and dived once more into the maelstrom of battle.

I was glad that there were no priests facing us. Then I thought about where they must be and what they were doing and my gladness gave way to fear.

The temperature was rising. My throat felt parched. My skin felt as if it might crack. It was a by-product of the evil magic swirling around us.

One of the psykers blasted a swathe of heretics aside with some sort of mystical bolt. Drake shouted, 'Save your strength! We shall have better use of it soon!'

The psyker nodded abashed. It was the last help of that

sort we saw. It was all down to the main strength of the Imperial Guard now.

Macharius led us, speaking calmly, exhorting us to greater efforts, blasting with his bolt pistol and slashing any enemy who got within reach with his chainsword. He was worth a company of men alone just for his physical prowess. The inspiration the sight of him brought was worth much more.

Striding towards a manifesting daemon, he looked certain of his righteousness and utterly confident of victory. He moved through the combat as if nothing could touch him, and nothing did. I have often wondered if Drake wove some sort of spell around him that day to prevent heretic fire from harming him. It seems like the only explanation to me. I have never seen any man walk as boldly across a battlefield. Macharius marched as if he believed he was invincible and we followed him as if he was.

Under his Lion banner and the banners of our regiments we fought and died. Metre by bloody metre, step by bloody step we made our way up the inlaid marble steps into the heart of the cathedral and the horror waiting for us there.

Ahead of us I could hear what sounded like a choir of possessed angels. The hymn was beautiful, haunting and terrifying. The words echoed inside my skull, singing the praises of the Angel of Fire, telling of his glories and the way he would reward his worshippers and punish those who opposed him. It should have sounded like an evil parody of Imperial liturgy but it did not. It sounded as if the singers believed utterly in the truth of the words, which I suppose they did.

It was all in dire contrast to the bloody work we were doing as we fought our way into the inner sanctum. It was in a space so packed with bodies that we were reduced to hand-to-hand fighting. The heretics fought with all the fanaticism of zealots defending sacred soil. We smashed them down in the name of Macharius and the Emperor.

The Sons of the Flame fought us every metre of the way. I clubbed one down with the butt of my shotgun, cleared another few packed metres of space by pulling the trigger and sending some more heretics to hell. Macharius chopped down more with his chainsword.

And then we were within the sanctum itself. It had been repaired from our previous visitation but not completely. Scorch marks covered the walls and floors. The lectern was still there though, as was that massive statue of the Angel in all its glory but it was no longer the focus of attention.

Ahead of us were massed ranks of priests chanting and singing their awful hymn. In front of them stood their High Priest, the focus of the whole devilish ritual. It was not he who commanded our sight though. It was the Angel. It had already manifested under the vast vaulted roof. The hanging banners already smoked and burned in contact with its burning wings. Around it everything seemed to shimmer.

It towered above us, seemingly a hundred times the height of a man. It looked bigger, as if something infinite were compressing itself into the tiny space available in our world. It came from somewhere else where its size had no limit or meaning. In my mind I imagined it larger than a planet, able to hold a whole world in its beautiful clawed hand. Its skin was the colour of bronze. Its robe was shimmering white. Its face was beautiful. Its eyes were filled with fire. Its wings billowed from its back in a cloud of gaseous plasma. It seemed immense but not yet solid. All of the flames in the temple twisted towards it, dancing worshippers genuflecting to their god.

It looked down on us and it smiled.

I felt as if it was looking directly at me. I am sure every man there did. It is a discomforting thing to come under the gaze of a great daemon. It was looking into my soul, seeing my darkest secrets, measuring every particle of sin. It knew me in a moment better than I knew myself. It knew all the dark and hateful things I wanted to keep hidden even from myself. It recognised me as one of its own. It made a beckoning gesture with its hand. There was an awful invitation in the movement. It called upon me to step forwards, to join it, to be purged by its cleansing flame and renewed.

There was a promise of immortality in that gesture and the fulfilment of all my dreams. I could walk forwards and join the ranks of its followers and become one with the immortals. I could welcome the presence of this tremendous cosmic being into my life and become part of its legion of worshippers and leave this place and conquer worlds in its name.

Visions of an eternity of splendour danced before me. I would be ruler of a world, many worlds. My enemies would fear me. Women would adore me. I would be greater than any king. I watched transfixed. I think it was curiosity that saved my soul, strange as that may sound.

For some reason I looked at Macharius, perhaps even then seeking to follow his lead. He stood transfixed. His eyes were locked on the daemonic Angel. There seemed to be some sort of direct communication going on between them. I wondered what he was seeing, what temptations were being placed before him. I was being presented to myself as a conqueror of worlds. He was already all of that and more.

What could it offer him?

I can only guess. It does not take a great deal of imagination to think of what devil's bargain it offered. There is only one thing great enough for a man like Macharius to imagine seizing, only one throne worth taking possession of. I think the magnitude of the daemon's offer was immense; the throne of all the worlds located on distant Terra.

It was possible I suppose. Imperial armies have been corrupted in the past. Imperial generals, aye and beings greater than Imperial generals, have fallen to the temptations of Chaos. Backed by the power of the daemon-gods, they have conquered huge swathes of the galaxy, temporarily it is true, but nonetheless they have conquered.

I think this is what was offered to Macharius. And if you want the truth, I think he considered it. What man would not? Offered the galaxy, anyone might pause and think. Though I might be purged by the Inquisition as a heretic for saying it, I know I would have.

Macharius looked grim. He frowned. His eyes narrowed. I looked at the heretics. If anything supports my theory of the temptation of Macharius, it is that they did not attack us. By all rights they should have. They should have struck us down as we looked in awe on their daemon-god. They did not.

I think the Angel sent them some subtle message that they should wait. It must have felt there was a real chance of winning Macharius and the rest of us to its side. That would have been a prize for it, a great Imperial commander and all his armies. It must have deemed it worth the risk.

I wondered then, as I still do now, at this temptation of Macharius. Was it possible that this entire conflict, the destiny of this entire world was merely one small link in a chain of circumstance that would bring Macharius to this spot, to open him up to this temptation?

Could a daemon really have such subtlety and foresight?

Or was this simply an aberration of chance, a moment when the destiny of two great beings became intertwined because of an accident? I do not know the answer. The only beings who truly do are not telling.

We stood enthralled, awaiting the outcome, while the Angel of Fire watched us with burning eyes.

Document under seal. Extract From the Decrypted Personal Files of Inquisitor Hyronimus Drake.

   Possible evidence of duplicity on the part of former High Inquisitor Drake.

   Cross-reference to Exhibit 107D-21H (Report to High Inquisitor Toll).

And so it came to pass that I found myself within the sanctum of the most unholy Angel of Fire. Surrounded as I was by storm troopers sworn to protect me, standing at the heart of an army of the Imperial Guard, I knew there was no safety. I sensed the vast web of incalculable power being spun out of the netherspaces of the warp, all focused on the massive apparition that loomed in front of me. I was given a sense of quite how small I was and quite how great evil can be.

It was a titanic dazzling thing, feeding on the deaths of its worshippers, drawing strength from the rituals being performed all across the city. The cathedral itself was a focal point for these, and I understood, for the first time, that all of those cages had been placed according to a very precise pattern, aligned in such a way that they would channel energy to this place at this time. In my mind's eye, I seemed to be looking down on the city, my spirit soaring clear and able to comprehend the sheer awesome scale of the massive ritual. For some reason, the attention of the daemonic entity was focused on Macharius. I sensed that perhaps it wished to recruit him, to make him its servant. If truly he was the one for whom we wait, he would make a true and terrible vessel for it. I knew that this could not be allowed. There could be no more terrible threat to the Imperium than such a one as Macharius possessed by such a thing as this.

I was at the centre of a smaller pattern, made up of the brave men and women, psykers all, who had been assembled in a final valiant attempt to forestall the ritual. I felt every last one of them through the link we shared, all of the sanctioned psykers of all of the Guard regiments, all of my agents who had been dispersed throughout the massive army. Only a few of them were present with me. Others were scattered through the cathedral, part of the fighting regiments within. All of them, at that moment, stood frozen, all of them lent me their strength.

I looked at the focus of that hellish ritual and I drew on what strength I could. We did not have even a fraction of the power that was needed to overcome that vast ingathering of cosmic filth. Such was not my intention. I needed to disrupt that lattice of force and the whole thing would spin out of control, like a mechanical engine when sand has been thrown into its workings.

It was the only chance I had. I summoned all my strength and threw a bolt of titanic psychic energy at the focal point of the ritual.

Macharius looked upon the daemon. The daemon gazed back. My glance flickered from one to the other. Drake moved up beside Macharius. Sweat rolled down his brow. Tears of blood dripped from his eyes. He seemed caught up in some invisible spiritual struggle beyond my understanding. All around people were screaming and vomiting and tearing at their own eyes with their nails as if trying to gouge them from their sockets. There was no pattern to it, save that they all seemed to be people who had come with him. Among the Guard I saw men in the uniforms of sanctioned psykers doing the same.

Even the inquisitor's mighty will was not up to breaking the daemon's spell. Macharius stood silently, seeing whatever vision the daemon had put in his mind, wrestling with whatever gigantic temptations it offered him.

All of our men were rapt in a mystical trance, just as much as the heretics who had summoned the daemon. Men knelt weeping, some caught fire and turned to ash and fell leaving only outlines of dust on the ground. Some howled the praises of the Angel and abased themselves grovelling. Blood streamed from the nostrils of the righteous and unrighteous alike. It was not just our men who were falling and burning. The same thing was happening among the Sons of the Flame.

I knew that I stood at the centre of some great swirl of events, that the consequences of what happened here would ripple out through the sector and eventually the galaxy, that worlds would live and worlds would burn in consequence of it.

Macharius looked up at the daemon. 'I refuse you!' he said.

As if taking strength from that, Drake spoke the words of a great prayer, invoking the name of the Emperor. There was a ripping, tearing sensation inside my head, as if the wave of power he had unleashed was so strong that even I could sense it. As suddenly as it had come over us the daemonic spell was lifted. We were purged of the influence of the unclean.

I raised my shotgun to my shoulder, took careful aim and fired at the High Priest. The sound of the shot was shockingly loud in the ominous silence. The chief heretic's head exploded in a cloud of blood and brains. In that moment, all hell broke loose.

The swirling essence of the daemon descended upon the corpse of the High Priest. The body slowly rose, one eye dangling from an optic nerve torn from its exposed skull. The other was filled with fire. Great flaming wings emerged from his back, a sword of fire appeared in his hands. His ruined corpse had become the vessel of the Angel. Some of the sense of terrible presence was gone.

'It has not fully manifested,' Drake shouted. 'It cannot draw on its full power. We can still overcome it.'

I was not sure I believed him.

The corpse advanced towards us. The flesh of the right cheek had been ripped away to expose grinning teeth. It looked evil and terrible and filled with awful wrath. Macharius raced to meet it, chainsword screaming in his hand. The daemon parried the blow with its weapon. It seemed impossible something so insubstantial could parry a weapon as solid as a chainsword but it did. It struck back, blade flickering forwards impossibly fast, a line of fire searing Macharius's cheek.

Drake and his psykers started to chant then. A glow surrounded Macharius, of the sort you see depicted in religious paintings of the Emperor and his primarchs. It was the first time I had ever seen it in reality. I swear a halo of light had appeared around Macharius's head. He looked like a saint made flesh, which was in its way reassuring; to survive this we were going to need the assistance of a saint and more even than that.

Macharius fought with the Angel of Fire. I thought I heard something over the roar of battle and the chant of plainsong. I realised it was Drake. He was shouting: 'Kill the priests!'

We waded in among the heretics, stabbing and

bludgeoning and shooting. I have never considered it honourable to murder unarmed men but in this case I was prepared to make an exception. The priests screamed and died. The air where the Angel had been swirled; looking up I saw what appeared to be a hole in the fabric of our reality, a gateway to somewhere else, to whatever distant, Chaotic realm the Angel had come from.

All I seemed to see were swirling colours, flames dancing in all manner of strange patterns and bearing a resemblance to whatever real-world objects my mind projected on to them. They took on shape, like those castles you sometimes see when staring into a fire. I saw molten landscapes over which rose citadels sculpted from flame and around which fluttered hosts of fire-winged angels. They were assembling themselves into disciplined regiments and preparing to jump the gap to our world.

I tore my gaze away from that portal into an alternative reality and I saw that Macharius was still engaged in hand-to-hand combat with the avatar of the Angel of Fire. As ever, he moved with blazing quickness. His motion was a blur, too fast to be followed easily with the human eye. It did not appear as if the daemon had any trouble doing so.

The Angel parried Macharius's blade with its sword of fire. If anything, its attacks were even faster than the general's. I was surprised that anything could live when faced by the full fury of its onslaught. Every time that fiery blade licked out it seemed to impact upon the general's armour. And yet, Macharius did not burn. It took me some time to realise why. He was being protected by the power of our own psykers.

As ever, Macharius had a very sound grasp of the situation. Of course, in all likelihood, he knew no more about how to deal with it than I did. On the other hand, he knew that there was someone present who did.

'Close that infernal portal before it is too late.' Drake heard and obeyed.

Lines of light began to emerge from all of the Imperial psykers and converge upon the stalwart figure of the inquisitor. He did something with all that power, channelling it into a mesh of potent energy that swirled outwards from his hands and surrounded the glowing gate. He began to pull the net tight. The opening started to close but not without resistance.

Men screamed and I wondered what was happening because there was a note in the screams that I had never heard before. The psykers around Drake started to fall, their mouths open, their faces pale, blood gushing from mouths and nostrils and eye-sockets. It was not the same sound as the heretics made as they were slaughtered, it was something else, the sound of men who were losing their very souls, having them drawn from their bodies and offered up as a sacrifice to something greater.

Beams of light emerged from Drake's hand and surged around the gateway, forming a lattice around it. His whole body was lit by the energies he wielded. His eyes blazed with the Emperor's Light. Every one of the people who still communed with Drake stood frozen. Their eyes were wide, their mouths stretched in ghastly rictuses as if screams were being torn from their very souls. One by one, they toppled and died as if their life force was being wrenched from them and used to power whatever exorcism Drake performed.

The daemon began to oppose the inquisitor's efforts and tried to get past Macharius in order to cut him down with its fiery blade. Macharius kept himself interposed. He stood between it and Drake. Seeing the Lord High Commander at risk, more and more of our soldiers pressed forwards. The Angel chopped down but it could not find a way through that wall of flesh that opposed it. What human courage and human muscle could achieve our soldiers did. They wanted to protect Macharius even at the cost of their own lives. They threw themselves forwards, again and again forming a rampart of blood and gristle. I saw Anton and Ivan struggle to get forwards. They were almost within striking distance of the Angel when I lost sight of them in the press.

I sensed the change in the atmosphere around us. Where once there was a wind of power blowing outwards into our world, now it felt as if the current was flowing in a different direction. All of the fire and energy seemed to be being sucked out of the air around us and returned to the place from which it had come, and as it did so I could see that the Angel of Fire was being drawn back into its own fiery realm. It fought every step of the way but, at last, it passed through the portal and that eerie gateway swirled shut.

And then suddenly, it was silent. The Angel of Fire was gone. The portal was closed, leaving only a strange shimmering in the air that vanished even as we watched. Drake stood surrounded by bodies. In the ultimate crisis his bodyguard of psykers had laid down their lives and more to protect him and to close the way through which the daemon had come. The high inquisitor looked wearier than any man I had ever seen. His shoulders slumped, his eyes were half-closed, he had aged a couple of decades in as many minutes. Macharius walked over to him and said something, I have no idea what.

I looked around to see what had become of my friends. Ivan lay on the ground clutching at his arm. Half his face seemed to have melted and I could tell from the set of his eyes that he was in pain. Anton knelt beside him, offering him liquor from a flask. The New Boy stood guard over them both, his lasgun held tight in his white-knuckled hands. The Understudy was beside him. His expression was as blank as ever. The titanic events we had just witnessed did not seem to have left a mark on his psyche.

My eyes kept tracking round looking for danger. There did not seem to be any. Few heretics remained and those that did seemed to have lost all will to fight. More and more of our troops entered the sanctum. Their faces wore a relieved expression as if they understood the fate we had so narrowly avoided.

I strode over to Anton and Ivan. 'How is it going?'

'We're alive,' Anton said.

Ivan just gurgled in pain. He looked up at me as if he desperately wanted to say something. I leaned in to hear what it was he had to say.

'What is it?' I said.

'Tell that bastard Anton that if he does not stop standing on my hand, I will cut his nadgers off!'

Looking down I could see that one of Anton's heavy boots was indeed on Ivan's fleshly hand. I pushed him off. At this point the Guardsmen present started chanting Macharius's name. It started slowly and softly at first, but it grew louder and it was taken up by all of the Guard present, the word rolling like thunder down the stairwell and echoing through the cathedral. It seemed as if the chant was taken up by the entire army. The stones themselves vibrated to the name and it seemed as if the word would echo out from the world of Karsk and across the galaxy.

I suppose it did. The High Commander's name became a battle-cry that would ring out down the years and across thousands of worlds. He would change the destiny of our sector and the Imperium and I suppose it all started there. If I close my eyes, I can still picture the scene so clearly, and hear the word echo through my bones like a prophecy of triumph and doom: 'Macharius. Macharius! MACHARIUS!'

Document under seal. Extract From the Decrypted Personal Files of Inquisitor Hyronimus Drake.

Possible evidence of duplicity on the part of former High Inquisitor Drake.

Cross-reference to Exhibit 107D-21H (Report to High Inquisitor Toll).

On the day after his confrontation with the Angel of Fire I stood with Macharius on the platform in the great crematorium in the southern sector of Irongrad. He looked down on the huge conveyor belt. Tens of thousands of bodies lay on it, all of them in the uniform of the Imperial Guard. The motivating engines were silent. The belts were not moving. Macharius looked down on those endless ranks of the dead as if trying to memorise them. I asked him why he had summoned me. He thanked me for my aid against the Angel of Fire and asked me what I was going to say in my report to my superiors.

I could tell what was on his mind. We had stood in the presence of a great cosmic evil. Men have been killed for less. Entire armies and worlds have, for fear that they might be tainted and turned against the Imperium. Macharius was wondering what I was going to say, whether his armies would be destroyed and he would be assassinated in his sleep or put to death by some other arm of the Imperium.

What could I tell him? He had been tested and he had not been found wanting. Perhaps he was the one we had been waiting for, for so long. Perhaps that is why the Angel wanted him as well. He would have made just as terrifying a tool of the powers of darkness as he was a champion of the Imperium.

We looked at each other. He had his hand on his weapon. I knew then that he was considering killing me if I gave him the wrong answer. I smiled and told him that killing me would not make any difference. The Imperium has other agents. I am merely one among legion. I told him I meant him no harm, that I would report that I had encountered a manifestation of Chaos and dealt with it. He asked me why.

I lied, of course. I could not tell him the real reason a faction of the Inquisition wanted him alive, just as several factions wished him dead. I told him it was because the Imperium needed him, that it must be reunited, that gigantic challenges awaited us in the new millennium and that the realm of mankind needed to be strong to face them. It played to his vanity. I could tell that at least part of him believed while the deeper and more subtle part of his mind sought the truth. There was nothing else to tell him so I asked him why he was here in the crematorium, what he hoped to achieve.

He told me of some ancient kings of Terra. They had a tradition that after a battle they would ride across the battlefield and look upon the faces of the dead who were there because of their will. In this way they understood the cost of their statecraft and what obedience to their orders truly meant. He told me that every one of those men down there on those conveyor belts was there because he had been following his orders, then he pulled the great lever that started the engines. The great gates of the crematorium furnaces opened in a blast of heat and the long lines of bodies rolled into the flames.

Macharius was still watching them when I departed hours later. I heard he remained there for a day and a night and still the bodies burned.

ABOUT THE AUTHOR

William King is the author of the Tyrion & Teclis trilogy and the Macharian Crusade, as well as the much-loved Gotrek & Felix series and the Space Wolf novels. His short stories have appeared in many magazines and compilations, including *White Dwarf* and *Inferno*. Bill was born in Stranraer, Scotland, in 1959 and currently lives in Prague.

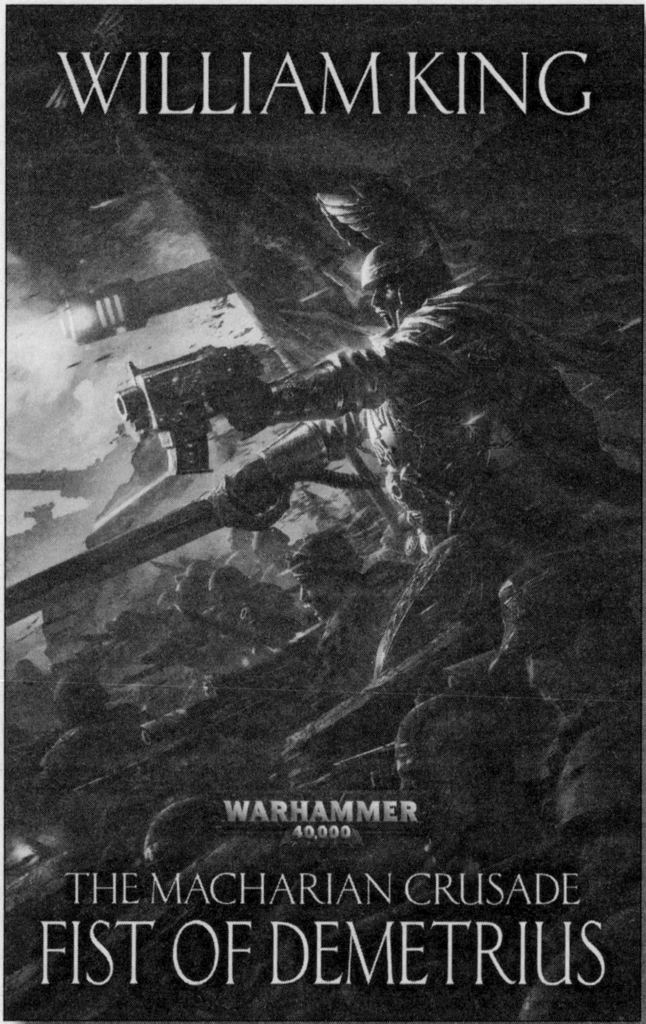

UK: 978-1-94970-401-4   US: 978-1-84970-402-1

An extract from The Macharian Crusade: Fist of Demetrius
by William King

On sale now

A scribe approached and spoke to Macharius with the mixture of precision, formality and reverence that the Lord Solar inspired in those around him. He was doing his best to ignore the shuddering of the ship – and the possibility of instant death – as he brought news of another victory. It seemed that the worlds of the Proteus system had surrendered, bringing another three planets, ten hive cities and nineteen billion people back into the Imperial fold. Macharius nodded an acknowledgement, turned and said something to another clerk, recommending the general in charge of the campaign for some honour or other, and walked on.

Two more uniformed clerks approached and saluted. Before they could even open their mouths to speak, Macharius rattled off orders to commanders who were five star systems away, instructing them as to which cities to besiege, which worlds to offer alliances to and which governors to bribe. He seemed to have no difficulty dredging up any of this knowledge. It was all there in his head, all of the details of an infinitely vast campaign, the like of which had probably not been fought since the Emperor walked among men. He ordered that more reinforcements be sent to aid them and kept on walking towards the furthest tables.

Sometimes he looked up and gazed upon the surface of the burning planet with a look of longing in his eyes. I felt a certain sympathy for him then – Macharius was a warrior, born to fight. He commanded this great force, but I suspect that he missed the thrill of physical conflict, the feeling of danger, of taking his own life in his hands. His thoughts were drifting to those final battles taking place on the world beneath us. His thoughts were drifting to the ancient artefact he had coveted for so long.

I could tell that he wanted to be there. I could also tell that he had something else on his mind, something to do with his current obsession with prophecies and divinations and ancient relics that he shared with Drake. It seemed like a bond that drew the two of them together, although the inquisitor has never struck me as a superstitious man. Quite the opposite, in fact.

Here on the galaxy's farthest rim, superstitions were common. These worlds had been far from the Emperor's light for a hundred generations and all manner of strange, deviant and heretical faiths had sprung up. All manner of weird beliefs had infected the populations, and some had even taken root among our own soldiers, although you would have thought them immune to such corruption. Clusters of prophecies had begun to gather around Macharius himself. That was easy enough to understand. The Lord High Commander seemed invincible, gifted with near-supernatural powers of foresight.

There were some who claimed he was blessed by the Emperor. There were others who thought he was a supernatural being. Reports had started to arrive of shrines being set up to Macharius on dozens of worlds, and not just by those unbelievers whose temples to false prophets had been overthrown.

The ship shook. We looked at each other for a moment before we went back to pretending that nothing had happened. An officer in Naval uniform walked over.

'A glancing strike to the void shields, Lord High Commander,' he volunteered. 'Nothing to worry about.'

'I am not worried,' Macharius replied.

'I doubt they could possibly know this was the Imperial command vessel,' said the officer. He was clearly more disturbed than Macharius as this possibility occurred to him.

Macharius nodded and the officer pulled himself together, clicked his heels and saluted. As the Lord Solar strode by, his mere presence seemed to reassure people. Worried frowns disappeared from the faces of scribes and star-sailors. Commanders must always look confident and that was something that Macharius managed supremely well.

We made our way towards one of the great command tables with utter casualness. Indeed, so relaxed was our approach that I knew that we were approaching the spot in which Macharius had the greatest interest. I had learned to read the subtle signals of his moods by then. Or perhaps I delude myself. Few men ever truly knew what the great general was thinking.

Ahead of us was the command sphere for the current conquest. On its flowing surface was a representation of the continent we could see through the dome above us. Instead of being lit by the fires of burning forests, the sphere showed representations of armies as glowing patterns – ours were green and the enemy forces were red. Various runes indicated the composition of the units. Ours glowed steadily to show that we were certain of their composition. The enemy forces pulsed with varying speed to indicate the degree of certainty as to their position and strength.

Around the table stood a variety of ranking commanders, and Drake. He was, in theory, an observer but stood with the air of a man who was actually in charge, at least until Macharius arrived. The high inquisitor was tall and slim, with a pale cold face and dark hair which now had a tinge of grey in it. Obviously the juvenat treatments had not taken so well with him, or perhaps he was simply much older than he had appeared when we first met and the drugs' effects had started to weaken.

I did not know much of the inquisitor's personal history and he never volunteered anything to anyone in my hearing, even Macharius. He was a man much more used to asking questions than answering them. Uneasiness seemed to radiate to those around him in the same way that confidence emanated like solar rays from Macharius.

The high inquisitor looked up in recognition as Macharius approached. I suspect that Macharius was as close to a friend as Drake ever had, if 'friend' is a word you can ever use in the context of an inquisitor. I had seen too much of his business over the past ten years to believe that he looked at the world with much humanity.

Macharius nodded a greeting and went over to stand beside the inquisitor. The two men were of similar height, but otherwise were as different as two people could be. Macharius was physically powerful. Drake was slender, ascetic and deceptively frail looking. Macharius wore the elaborately braided uniform of the highest ranking Imperial Guard officer. Drake wore a plain black tunic and a scarlet cloak with a cowl. Around him, a group of storm trooper bodyguards lounged like attack dogs. They eyed us as warily as we eyed them.

Drake nodded to me, which was not something calculated to make me feel any easier in my skin. He had taken an interest in me since Karsk, as he took an interest in all those close to Macharius. I had often been summoned into his presence to answer questions about the general's moods and health. I had reported these conversations to Macharius, of course, and he had told me to answer truthfully. He clearly believed that I had no secrets about him to reveal to the inquisition that they did not already know, and I suspect he was right.

Macharius turned to the adept who stood by the command altar. 'Give me a view of sector Alpha Twelve,' he said. 'Close magnification.'

'In the Emperor's name, Lord Macharius,' the adept responded. He intoned a litany and moved his hands in some ritual gestures over the altar. We looked now at a three-dimensional map of a strange city. All around it was a clear, flat zone, where the cold forest had been burned early to provide a fire-break. The buildings were ziggurats, sheathed in metal, glittering in the light of twin suns. They looked as much like fortresses as temples. They bristled with turrets, blister-bunkers and other fortifications.

War raged. Men in the uniform of the Imperial Guard fought with fanatics in the green and purple robes of the local temple wardens. Blood flowed in the streets. The natives fought stubbornly, with the courage of zealots prepared to die for their misguided faith.

They were going to. That much was obvious. Inexorably, Imperial Chimera, Basilisks and Leman Russ tanks pushed through the streets surrounding the step-pyramids, moving in the direction of the gigantic central temple. Macharius looked at the colonel who had been liaising with the ground forces.

'My orders have been conveyed,' he said. There was a question in his voice, which was not like him. Normally Macharius gave a command in the full expectation of it being obeyed and then moved on. He did not check on subordinates unless something had gone wrong, in which case he moved swiftly and ruthlessly to correct the errors.

'The ground commanders have been specifically instructed not to bombard the central temple. The soldiers know there is to be no plundering – on pain of death – and that demolition charges and heavy weapons are not to be used within the precincts of the Great Temple, Lord High Commander. I made your orders very clear on those points.'

'Good,' Macharius said, and the man seemed to swell with his praise. Like everyone else on the command barge, he knew Macharius would not forget his efficiency, or forgive his failures. He had gained credit in the eyes of the most important man in the Crusade Force and rewards would eventually and be disbursed.

The ship shook again, more violently this time. It seemed like there had been another glancing strike from a planetary defence battery. It made me uneasy. I did not like to feel that any moment I might be vaporised and that there was nothing I could do about it. This was a battle fought with weapons so gigantic that ships with the populations of small cities could be destroyed in an instant and an individual warrior could have no influence on his fate. Give me a ground battle, or even trench warfare, any time. At least there you could take cover, and take a few enemies with you when you met your end.

The glow-globes flickered. A smell of ozone filled the air. Somewhere in the distance someone screamed. Another voice barked an order. I suspect the screamer was being clapped in irons or assigned to a punishment detail.

'It seems like the enemy might be finding their range,' said Macharius. He chuckled and everybody else around him did the same. It was not that what he said was particularly funny, but when a general makes a joke, no matter how feeble, his subordinates laugh. It did dispel the tension.

Drake had ignored the near miss. He had been staring at the battle-map with total concentration, as if he could achieve a spiritual revelation if only he looked hard enough.

'We must have the Fist,' he said in a voice so low that only Macharius and those of us standing close to him could have heard it.

'Do not worry, my friend,' said Macharius. 'We shall get it.'

'We *must*,' said Drake. 'It may be one of the Imperium's most sacred artefacts – a relic from the time when the Emperor walked among us, a thing perhaps borne by one of his most trusted primarchs. A worthy gift for potent allies.'

Macharius smiled. He seemed to be considering something for a moment, which was unusual. Normally, for him to think was to act, and to act with a decision and correctness that most ordinary men could not achieve with hours or days of contemplation.

'In that case, I believe I shall go and collect it myself.'

Drake shook his head like a man hearing something he had feared, but which he had hoped not to have to deal with.

'Is that wise?' he said. It was phrased like a question but it was really a statement. Drake was one of the few men who would have dared to question Macharius. It was a thing that was happening more and more in those days, as if a rift were slowly opening between him and the Lord High Commander, as if he, so seemingly secure in his faith, was starting to have doubts in Macharius. In this case, I was with him, for I could tell from the rare and slightly unsettling grin spreading across the general's face that Macharius was serious. He really had decided to go planetside and lead the assault on the temple.

I suppose Drake knew as well as I did that once Macharius had made up his mind there was no possibility of deflecting him from his purpose, but the high inquisitor was not a man to easily admit defeat.

'You should not put yourself at risk, Lord High Commander,' said Drake. I suppose he was thinking that he would be in trouble with his superiors if anything happened to Macharius. After all, he seemed to have taken on some responsibility for the general's safety after the events on Karsk.

'I have no intention of doing so,' said Macharius. He was already striding towards the exit of the command centre, and all we could do was follow in his wake, like tiny satellites of a gas giant or a cometary halo whirling around a sun.

Anton shot me a look that I knew well. A grin that was considerably more crazed than Macharius's flickered across his face and was gone before anyone but me could have seen it.

Drake shrugged and began to stride along beside Macharius. His storm troopers moved in his wake, some of them even surging ahead as if they suspected that danger might lurk in every corridor of the command vessel.

'I shall accompany you then,' said the high inquisitor. 'You may need my services down there.'

'As ever, I welcome your company,' said Macharius. 'But admit it, you are just as keen as I to get your hands on the work of the ancients.'

A cold smile appeared on Drake's face, one of the few I had ever seen. He was a forbidding man in a position of fearful power, and I doubt anyone ever mocked him the way that Macharius did. Perhaps he enjoyed the basic human contact. It must have been rare in his life. 'I am certainly keen to know whether it is the thing we seek.'

The battle-barge rocked again under the impact of another planet-based weapon. I was suddenly glad that we were on the move, heading towards the shuttle bay. It would be good to feel ground beneath my feet again and air in my lungs that had not been recycled through a ship's fallible systems a thousand thousand times.

It struck me then that, for all his courage, perhaps Macharius felt the same way. Even for a man as brave as he undoubtedly was, waiting on a ship under attack, when any moment its walls might explode and you might be cast into the chill vacuum of space, must have been a nerve-wracking experience. I asked myself if it was possible that he was as anxious as I and just hid it better.

I dismissed the idea as ludicrous.

Order the novel or download the eBook
from *blacklibrary.com*
Also available from

and all good bookstores